I
Miss
Your
Purple
Hair

a novel by
Robert R. Chandler

I Miss Your Purple Hair

Acknowledgments

Written by Robert R. Chandler
Edited by Elizabeth Anne Chandler
Cover art by Christopher Lee Donovan

Everlasting Gratitude to:
Elizabeth, *for encouragement throughout this journey*
Nathan, *for demonstrating toughness and perseverance*

Very Special Thanks to:
Alyssa Coco, *for her original song, "Never Let Me Fall"*
Christopher Lee Donovan, *for his beautiful cover images*
Kaetii Dudek (model), *for her portrayal of "Veronica"*
The National Aviary, *for technical support*
Our Lady Peace, *for their inspiring music*
San Diego Zoo
Sony/ATV Music Publishing

Vital Consultants:
Elizabeth A. Chandler; Susan M. Roethel; Timothy K. Wikander

Editing Support:
Theresa Fischette of White Light Communications
(www.ToTheWhiteLight.com)

Manuscript Critique:
Mike Anastasia; Marie Beschen; Julia Lisuzzo; Amber McGary

Inspirations:
Deepak Chopra
James Redfield
Nancy Ann Tappe
Eckhart Tolle

This story is a love letter to my children.
"Come home safe."

Prologue

*"The human race may be compared to a writer. At the outset, a writer has often only
a vague, general notion of the plan of his work and of the thought he intends to elaborate.
As he proceeds, penetrating his material, laboring to express himself fitly, he lays a firmer
grasp on his thought; he finds himself. So the human race is writing its story, finding itself,
discovering its own underlying purpose, revising, recasting
a tale pathetic often, yet none the less sublime."*
~ Felix Adler

I receive visions. They appear unexpectedly, in the form of detailed images. These messages only come to me while awake. When the first manifested itself in 2007, I considered the experience mildly intriguing. Upon the vision becoming reality, I assumed it was merely coincidental. Once subsequent visions arrived with increasing frequency, I was compelled to embark upon research of the term, "coincidence." That led to my first exposure to synchronicity as a concept. I had previously been vaguely aware of the term, but never really put much stock in the notion. While the visions continued, I began to consider the possibility that there could be more to coincidences than I had previously believed.

Synchronistic events illustrate an underlying pattern, a conceptual framework encompassing, but greater than any systems displaying the synchronicity. The concept of a larger framework is essential to satisfy the definition of synchronicity as originally developed by Swiss Psychologist, Carl Gustav Jung.

I now possess such an acute awareness of synchronicity that the commonly held notion all coincidences are meaningless is offensive to me. However, I also reject the contention of a minority, which assigns hidden messages to all coincidences. Many insignificant, coincidental events are simply attributable to mathematical probability. Regardless, it is my firm belief that the concept of synchronicity is very real, and a reflection of the connectivity of all energy within the Universe.

The energy of all human beings, plants, animals, earth, and heavenly bodies is connected and alive. This energy is constantly evolving, moving, growing, expanding, contracting, and communicating. Two components vital to communication are transmitting and receiving. If you are not open to the transmissions, you are unable to receive. The signals are bombarding you, but you are simply unaware of the messages. Since early childhood, I have been more naturally adept than most in receiving and transmitting messages. I believe it has much to do with faith. My personal beliefs are rooted in a self-image as a powerful, independent component of the universe's connective energy.

In his book, *The Spontaneous Fulfillment of Desire,* renowned Physician, Author, and Philosopher Deepak Chopra uses the term "synchrodestiny," to describe "a state in which it becomes possible to achieve the spontaneous fulfillment of our every desire." I personally believe we all have the capacity to achieve such a state by learning to recognize and accept the endless flow of synchronous messages. This is not difficult to do. It merely requires the courage to suspend learned tendencies to become as much a receptor as you are transmitter. When you learn to cease putting up barriers, you will begin to recognize messages with increasing frequency.

We have within us the power to glimpse this "enhanced reality," but must make a conscious effort to attain the proper mind set. We can remain myopic in our comfortable state of delusion, or we can choose to see the more elusive truths within the unifying fabric of the Universe. We possess the ability to explore what lies beyond our familiar physical world to know additional layers of reality. First, we must cast aside the prejudices drilled into our minds since birth. We can then work at receiving the messages to gain a broader awareness. Once permanently attuned, we begin to receive such messages with greater frequency and clarity.

A pervasive network of energy contains the life force of all organisms. When our frail corporeal vessels have ceased to function, our unique energy survives as an immortal thread in the infinite tapestry of the Collective Soul. I consider this eternally evolving energy to be God. Divine intervention played a significant role in the creation of this book, as many of the coincidences depicted within actually happened to me. This story came together effortlessly, as if it wrote itself, and I frequently felt as though I had little to do with creating its characters or plot. In fact, I actually encountered several of the characters depicted in the story... after I had written their detailed profiles. Nearly all of the synchronicities in the book actually happened to me.

I Miss Your Purple Hair reflects my own spiritual awakening. The story celebrates unconditional love, the power of leadership, and the glorious fact that all of our souls are stitched into the fabric of the Universe. The fact that you have chosen to read this story means your mind is open and you intend to keep learning and evolving as you continue your unique journey. It is my sincere hope you live the rest of your days as a curious and caring receptor/transmitter. May such a self-image lead you to find that what you once considered fantastic can be part of your daily reality. I hope your newfound awareness will lead you to a greater understanding of your unique life mission, which in turn will bring enlightenment and inspiration.

By working together and involving all who share the dream, we will expedite the construction of the New Earth. I wish this for all of us, for the sake of humanity and in the spirit of love and hope.

△ △ △

I
Miss
Your
Purple
Hair

a novel by
Robert R. Chandler

Contents

I Miss Your Purple Hair

I Miss Your Purple Hair

"Somewhere Out There"

by Our Lady Peace (Maida/Taggart/Coutts)

Last time I talked to you
You were lonely and out of place
You were looking down on me
Lost out in space
We laid underneath the stars
Strung out and feeling brave
I watched the red orange glow
I watched you float away
Down here in the atmosphere
Garbage and city lights
You've gone to save your tired soul
You've gone to save our lives
I turned on the radio
to find you on satellite
I'm waiting for this sky to fall
I'm waiting for a sign

All we are
Is all so far

You're falling back to me
You're a star that I can see
I know you're out there
Somewhere out there
You're falling out of reach
Defying gravity
I know you're out there
Somewhere out there

Hope you remember me
When you're homesick
And need a change
I miss your purple hair
I miss the way you taste
I know you'll come back someday
On a bed of nails I'll wait

I'm praying that you don't burn out
Or fade away

All we are
Is all so far

You're falling back to me
You're a star that I can see
I know you're out there
Somewhere out there
You're falling out of reach
Defying gravity
I know you're out there
Somewhere out there
You're falling back to me
You're a star that I can see
I know you're out there
You're falling out of reach
Defying gravity
I know you're out there
Somewhere out there
You're falling back to me
You're a star that I can see
I know you're out there
Somewhere out there
You're falling out of reach
Defying gravity
I know you're out there
Somewhere out there
You're falling back to me
I know
I know
You're falling out of reach
I know

△ △ △

I Miss Your Purple Hair

CHAPTER ONE

We Laid Underneath the Stars

"We are at the very beginning of time for the human race.
It is not unreasonable that we grapple with problems. But there are tens of
thousands of years in the future. Our responsibility is to do what we can, learn
what we can, improve the solutions, and pass them on."
~ Richard Feynman; US educator & physicist

*T*he lush grass of San Diego's Martin Luther King Memorial Park provided a comfortable resting place for the physically exhausted man and his only child. They laid side-by-side, watching the sky transition from cobalt blue to deep sapphire. Raven-haired Mateo Lima and 14-year-old Veronica had spent much of the warm afternoon playing volleyball, competing in three-legged races and dancing uninhibitedly to music pumping from a portable stereo. It was a clear, late summer day and the pair had genuinely enjoyed their second corporate gathering since the hiring of Mateo the previous year. The family-style picnic was a time-honored company tradition, and this year close to a hundred members of the staff and their guests had participated.

The Stevie Wonder classic, "Higher Ground", blared from a red 2003 Corvette from the near end of the parking lot. The day had featured plenty of food and drink, and an absence of mishaps. One lighthearted moment spilled into another and the pleasant day flew by swiftly. Mateo and "Violet," as he typically addressed Veronica, had spent the carefree afternoon immersed in the celebratory atmosphere. As evening arrived, many guests had already departed or were heading to their vehicles.

It was getting late, but neither of them wanted the day to end. Their stomachs comfortably full and their legs slightly weary from dancing, they deposited themselves in the thick grass at the base of a towering palm tree. The warm air carried floral fragrances blended with hickory smoke still lingering from the barbecue.

Mateo truly appreciated the fact that Violet had clearly enjoyed the event and had so comfortably interacted with other attendees. After a few months of uneasy transition, she had begun to make new friends and embrace having relocated to San Diego, near the ocean and beaches she so enjoyed. For a teenager abruptly abandoned by her mother, she was surprisingly well adjusted, largely attributable to her secure and trusting relationship with her father.

A native of Costa Rica, Mateo was deeply sensitive and peace loving. He had so desperately wanted to keep his family intact that he temporarily sacrificed his own identity trying to placate his partner. Since their separation, he had gradually recaptured his true spirit. The uniquely powerful bond he and Violet enjoyed was entirely genuine and no external influence could ever diminish it. Mateo was encouraged by Violet's unusual maturity and often marveled at how much he was able to learn from her. She was a voracious reader who enjoyed exploring an array of themes, especially books dealing with science, nature, and philosophy.

Inspired by his daughter's infectious curiosity, Mateo recently began reading more books than ever before. He developed a fascination with the subject of quantum physics and an appetite for books on psychology. Intrigued by the work of Carl Jung and his disciples, he also grew to appreciate the work of many New Age philosophers. Throughout his life, he had always been highly intuitive, but also frustrated by many nagging questions. Occasionally, he had been able to see fragmented glimpses of the future and would often chuckle at his knack for knowing what someone was going to say or do before it happened.

Since reading several books written by Spiritual Teacher, Eckhart Tolle, Mateo began to experience clear "visions." Never before had such vivid imagery popped into his mind, but since reading Tolle's *A New Earth*, something had dramatically changed. Earlier in the year, while in the process of absorbing the book's philosophical content, he began to experience visually detailed imagery during waking hours.

One breezy May morning, Mateo enjoyed a routine run through the park, hours before Violet would wake up. Very unexpectedly, he received the image of a 'red-orange ladybug' in his imagination. He snickered at the oddness of the imagery and thought, 'Humph... a ladybug... how profound.' Although initially unimpressed, he had to think twice an hour later, when he was sitting on their front porch and a ladybug of red-orange hue landed squarely in the middle of his chest. He paused during the process of removing his running shoes, to exclaim, "Oh... so there you are!" Mateo admired the tiny visitor as it crawled along his right index finger before it fluttered its curious little wings and flew away.

The incident was the first of a series of visions leading him to carry a small journal. Although the experiences were initially disarming, Mateo felt there was nothing unnatural about them. In fact, he had begun to feel as though he was finally becoming the person he was destined to be, and was convinced the books he had been reading simply unlocked some dormant sensibility. He eventually recorded dozens of his "random thoughts" within his pocket-sized diary. The ultimate realizations of nearly all his prophetic visions defied explanation, and were too remarkable to label meaningless.

A week before the picnic, Mateo shared the journal's contents with Violet and described the circumstances surrounding each vision. Naturally intrigued by her father's descriptive accounts, she asked him to teach her how to have similar experiences. Mateo explained that the only thing he was confident of was the critical relationship between his emotional state and the remarkable incidents. He had received visions only when in a peaceful frame of mind, and explained that he sometimes intentionally achieved the desired state by meditating... and entering what he called "The Zone."

Violet was disappointed that she seemed unable to achieve the state of mind that would allow visions to appear. However, she remained fascinated and continued to practice meditation techniques. Because the two of them shared so many innate traits, Mateo assured Violet she would one day enjoy similar experiences. In response to her expressed frustration, he advised, "Sometimes the only thing we have to practice is patience... and be ready when the wind shifts."

Reclining on the crest of a gentle hill overlooking San Diego's Pittsburgh Avenue, Violet pointed to a spot in the starlit sky and asked, "See that thing, Papa?"

Mateo squinted and lifted his head ever so slightly, replying in his light Costa Rican accent, "Not really, hon', what are we looking at?" Violet grabbed his hand and made his index finger point to the spot upon which her gaze remained fixed. A very bright star, visible in the southeast quadrant of the sky, intermittently flashed hues of red and orange. The intriguing object's colors and luminosity were remarkably different from any of the white lights surrounding it.

Violet asked, "Is that a planet or something?" Mateo pondered for a moment and squinted again, fascinated by the celestial body's pulsating colors. It appeared to be something other than a typical star, but he was unsure how to categorize it. All he knew was that he was pleased his precocious daughter was at peace and enjoying their time together.

I Miss Your Purple Hair

"I'm not sure. It might be Venus, although the colors look different... kind of weird. Maybe pollution is making the colors look strange." Despite her youth, Mateo frequently solicited Violet's opinion on serious matters. "Vi, what do you think all this means; these visions and strange feelings I keep getting?" He knew she understood most of what they had been discussing and, aware of her impressive objectivity, hoped she might help him understand. She sprinkled a handful of torn-out grass across his chest and giggled in trademark fashion before responding.

"God, I don't know," Violet said with a hint of gravity. "It must mean something. I mean, not many people get to have that sort of thing happen even once, and it *keeps* happening to you! I don't think it's just coincidence; otherwise, the same type of things would be happening to me and everyone else. Maybe you're changing somehow, since you started reading all those books."

Mateo stroked his trimmed goatee and looked into his daughter's eyes. "You never cease to amaze me," he said softly. "You're probably right. Maybe I've stopped ignoring some of my 'crazy' notions and that's allowed me to recognize the signals. It could be that being exposed to a new way of thinking has awakened something that's just been dormant."

He looked at the pulsating red-orange object suspended in the black cosmic soup and thought about the tiny red heart he recently found. In preparation for Violet's upcoming birthday, Mateo had purchased a red crystal heart suspended from a delicate gold chain. She had expressed her desire for one, and the tasteful necklace he bought seemed perfect.

While walking through a colorful outdoor bazaar in early July, he spotted the necklace on display in one of the tiny vendor booths crowded next to one another. When he caressed it with his fingertips, the young Mexican woman behind the counter humbly informed him that her late father had crafted the elegant fitting for the one-of-a-kind trinket. Mateo was convinced the unique necklace would make the perfect gift for Violet, who he felt was destined to become a one-of-a-kind woman. The demure artisan carefully placed the pretty trinket in a simple black box, which she then slid into a generic brown paper bag.

Mateo hid the box under his mattress that evening and looked forward to presenting it to Violet on her birthday. The simple necklace was exactly what she had described, and he was certain she would love it... yet he found himself inexplicably obsessed with finding another red crystal heart. As much as he recognized the irrationality, he could not resist the compulsion to keep looking.

Only a few days after buying the necklace at the bazaar, he was walking through the parking lot of the Office Park where he worked. Due to a malfunctioning computer program, a trio of irrigation sprinklers suddenly popped up and started spraying. To avoid getting drenched, he took a shortcut toward his car by stepping over one of the concrete medians.

No sooner had he stepped off the curb than he found himself frozen in disbelief. Resting upon the surface of the parking lot, a solitary object glinted in the waning sunlight. He instinctively knew what it was. When he finally approached to pick it up, he was nevertheless stunned. Atop a sea of recently poured asphalt, he had inexplicably found the red crystal heart he felt compelled to find.

Mateo thoroughly examined his treasure and found it unscathed. It was indeed a red, heart-shaped glass ornament, in pristine condition. The glass charm had been lying on the asphalt on its flat backside, its rounded front exposed to the elements. It was impossible to discern how long it had been there.

Had someone lost their cherished gem when a broken clasp betrayed them? Did a jilted lover throw it to the ground in anger? Mateo carefully wiped away insignificant traces of dirt and slid the heart into the front pocket of his black dress slacks. Amazed at the discovery, he wondered if the experience contained some mysterious message he was supposed to recognize.

In typical fashion, Violet unconsciously twirled strands of her long brown hair with her index finger. Rather than comment on the story her father had just recounted, she asked, "Do you still love Mama?"

The incongruous question caused Mateo to stop breathing for a microsecond. He swallowed hard before answering, forced to search his soul for his true feelings. He asked himself, "Do I still love her? Do I?" He did so, not because he had not recently examined his feelings for Belinda, but because he wanted to answer Violet honestly; such was the foundation of their trusting relationship.

He thought awhile more before responding, "I have to be honest, and say I still care about her. I miss her a lot, sometimes. I know she must miss us too... especially you."

Violet wanted to say something spiteful, but allowed her father his moment of melancholy reflection. She suspected he sometimes wept over her in private moments. Although she had never shed any tears herself, she felt she would probably get around to that someday. For the time being, she resented that her mother had abandoned them and was furious she had so deeply hurt her father.

Mateo interjected, "Do *you* miss your Mama?"

Violet blinked her eyes a few times, fighting the urge to cry. She bit her bottom lip before answering, "I guess so... sometimes. But I'm dealing with it."

Somewhat skeptical of her nonchalant attitude, Mateo dropped the subject and instead gently patted the back of her hand. He then thoughtfully offered, "Each of us has one life and we should be true to what is in our hearts. You will find your path one day and must have the courage to follow it. If you stay true to yourself, I know you will find the answers you seek. I have faith in you." He paused before adding, "I promise... you and I will always be together, one way or another... and I will never let you fall. Do you understand what I mean?"

The pretty girl with the dancing lights in her eyes gazed at the curious star and smiled. "I understand, Papa... I really do." She sprinkled another handful of grass atop his head, and implored, "Can we get smoothies on the way home?"

△ △ △

CHAPTER TWO

Praying That You Don't Burn Out

*"Synchronicity hints at the unified world
behind the illusory veil of the material universe."*
~ Roger S. Jones, Time and Time Again, The American Theosophist

*S*cientists and mathematicians had long warned of the probability of major seismic events in various regions of the globe, but almost universally underestimated their scope and power. Future historians may one day confirm that the clairvoyants and seers were the only ones who got it right. One such individual, who resided in San Diego, made an eerily accurate prediction just a day prior to the catastrophic events of December 27th.

Jason Connor-Sable was a Sculptor, Painter, and Adjunct Professor living a few miles south of San Diego State University, where the relatively inexperienced young man taught foundation classes in three-dimensional art. A recent graduate of Rhode Island School of Design, sensitive, green-eyed Jason was the only child of two successful corporate attorneys. His parents had offered him financial support, but at 25, his pride would not allow him to accept. Instead, he struggled to cover living expenses by teaching part-time and occasionally tending bar at *lovin' cup*, a popular downtown bistro.

During his final year of college in Rhode Island, he experienced several dreams so vivid they jolted him from his uneasy slumber. He would find himself laying in a cold sweat, reeling from the unsettling sensation of crying himself awake. Although he tried to dismiss those incidents, less than a year after graduating and moving back to San Diego a profoundly disturbing nightmare forced him to take his visions more seriously. On an unusually warm December night, he experienced a startling dream.

He found himself transmuted into the mind of an elderly man, experiencing every movement and sensation from behind the eyes of an unfamiliar character. In the midst of the dream, Jason's subconscious mind desperately tried to ascertain the identity of the dream's protagonist.

'Is this someone I know?' he wondered.

I Miss Your Purple Hair

Jason had always felt uneasy in the presence of firearms, and therefore became agitated when the man in the dream picked up a high-powered automatic rifle. The old man, white-haired and hunched over, ambled across a wind-swept bridge on an exposed section of highway. Lugging the rifle in his left hand, he headed toward a sparsely lit area further up the road.

The thin veneer of ice crunched beneath the man's weathered boots. Jason felt the sting of extreme cold on his unprotected forehead and fingertips just as he felt anger and bitterness slowly transform into desperate rage within the old man's mind. From behind the stranger's eyes, Jason finally identified his intended destination: a suburban housing tract lined with well-kept houses. Their blended souls trudged onward, while the mixture of snow and sleet assaulted the elderly man's time-ravaged face. Jason could hear his labored breaths as he covered the last hundred yards leading to the first house.

The white-haired old man lumbered toward the first house – a dark brown ranch, nestled among a cluster of towering pines. He paused only briefly, and quickly continued toward the next house, then the next… and then another. At the mouth of a long driveway, he finally stopped to catch his breath and leaned on the rifle as if it were a cane. As he inhaled frigid air and exhaled stench-ridden steamy breath, he blinked his blood-gorged eyes and peered up the driveway.

Jason felt every bit as if he were standing in the man's frozen tracks on a bitter moonlit winter night on some nameless street. He could smell the pungent smoke from the home's fireplace as it billowed out against the backdrop of the coal-black sky.

The setting was reminiscent of a classic Currier & Ives painting: the two-story, white-sided Colonial with its picturesque, landscaped yard; sparkling, all-white holiday lights adorning the lamppost, bushes and windows. The heartwarming scent of fireplace smoke blended subtly with the deep aroma of pine. The ice crystals coating the snow-covered yard twinkled in the moonlight like a sea of diamond shards. The elderly man seemed impervious to the burning sensation in his frostbitten appendages as he carved a trail up the driveway. When he finally arrived at his intended destination, he faced the large picture window that looked out on the front yard. Nestled between snow-covered hedges stood an elegant marble sculpture of The Virgin Mary, her delicate hands clasped in prayer.

The old man held his breath for a moment as he detected strains of music from inside the house. A chorus of voices was enthusiastically singing "Rudolph the Red-Nosed Reindeer."

Jason's anxiety mushroomed as he tried to guess the man's motives for approaching this particular home. He desperately longed to wake up and for a brief moment was successful. Upon regaining consciousness, he was able to look around his humble bedroom through the tiny slits of his weary, aching eyes. He desperately clung to wakefulness, but soon found himself dragged back into the dream...

Once more, Jason found himself fused into the old man's mind and body, walking up the driveway and taking everything in. He heard the same joyful group of voices singing Christmas carols as he drew closer to the house.

The fragile silence was rudely shattered when a voice cut through the silent night air from behind. "Hey! What's going on there?!" the deep male voice demanded. The frozen old man turned like a well-trained Buckingham Palace guard; no discernible change in mood; no panic. He pivoted smartly on frozen toes, readied the rifle, and fired a succession of rounds. The bullets all found their marks, ripping through flesh, cartilage, bone, and arteries. Travis Szymanski was dead before his body hit the ground. The next-door neighbor wearing the overcoat over his pajamas never had a chance – no time to run, no time to pray... and no time to warn the others.

The innocent victim was merely sticking to his schedule for taking out the trash when he spotted the bizarre character trudging through the snow toward his neighbors' house. He had instinctively called out; not realizing it would be the last action he would ever take. He had been suspicious of the stranger's behavior, but never spotted the gun pinned against the opposite side of his body. The old man's heart rate never fluctuated. Jason had melded with his emotions so thoroughly he could sense every nuance of his physiology. His pulse rate was no different after squeezing the trigger than immediately before.

As the echoes of the gunshots began to fade into the night, lights switched on in almost every home on the street. Unaffected, the old man calmly turned, raised the frozen barrel of his weapon, and trained it on the beautiful picture window. His timing seemed diabolically coordinated as pair of adult-sized silhouettes suddenly presented themselves behind the glass.

Without hesitation, he fired another deafening hail of bullets. In robotic manner, the old man tucked the death-bringer under his right arm and walked back down the driveway, toward the street. He wiped the mucous dripping from his nose with his bare left hand, never missing a step as his filthy boots violated the virginal blanket of snow.

I Miss Your Purple Hair

Jason's mind was ablaze, yet he was unable to wake himself.

The old man released the contents of his bladder as he trudged back toward the lonely, ice-coated bridge arching over the meandering stream. The pungent urine saturated his tattered briefs and worn denim jeans. In what seemed like a choreographed sequence, the jaundiced, urine-soaked, inebriated murderer stopped on the double yellow lines splitting the highway. He gazed up at the crescent Moon, splendidly luminous in its lonely corner of the pitch-black sky. Thick cataracts impaired his vision, but he could see the Moon well enough.

The grizzled psychopath thought to himself, 'What happened to the stars? Where's that Goddamn Big Dipper?' He shuffled his frozen feet in a 360-degree search for his favorite star pattern. On this night, though, there were no stars, save for an exceptionally bright one in the southeast.

"Hmmph", he grunted through cracked, frozen lips. He then picked up the frigid rifle with both hands and pressed the business end against his right temple. While supporting the tip of the barrel with his left hand he used his other hand to support all of the gun's weight.

Through a frozen scowl, in a tired, raspy voice he exclaimed to the sky, "Merry Christmas, all you bastards," and squeezed the trigger with his crooked, arthritic finger.

At that moment, the nightmare released its grip and Jason woke. Emotionally drained, his heart rate had become greatly elevated. His eyes opened to a barely-lit room, comforted by the familiar surroundings of his San Diego loft. He had never before experienced such a horrifying nightmare. The memories haunted him, but once the holiday break arrived, he was grateful for the distractions of the season.

Jason had planned to spend Christmas Day at his parents' home – their family tradition. His girlfriend, Elizabeth, was spending the holiday at her grandparents' place in Tucson. Although he would have preferred to have her with him in San Diego, he looked forward to reacquainting with his cousins and the rest of his family.

While shaving on Christmas morning, he salivated in anticipation of a robust breakfast. Once showered and dressed, he raced in his silver Honda Accord to his nearby family homestead. When Jason entered the spacious, well-appointed home, his parents were in the large kitchen, near the beautiful bay window that overlooked the back yard. Sunlight streamed in, and the rich aroma of freshly brewed coffee beckoned.

In anticipation of family arriving later in the day, his mother was busily preparing ingredients for the holiday feast. After dispensing a quick hug to his mom and a pat on the shoulder to his dad, Jason poured himself a large mug of coffee and announced his craving for a sausage omelet. His father, Glenn, generally did most of the cooking on weekends, and had previously offered to prepare "breakfast-to-order."

Jason had pretty much decided to put down roots in San Diego, and the morning's glorious weather reminded him of one major reason he so loved the area. He enjoyed his meal and listened as his parents filled him in on recent happenings with work and with members of the extended family.

His father remarked that the Chargers football team appeared primed to make a strong Super Bowl run. Finished with the sports section of the local paper, Glenn slid it across the table to Jason. He set it next to the dish upon which his mother had just lovingly placed a warm cinnamon roll. The tantalizing aroma of the sweet spice filled the room and Jason felt good again, happy in the company of his parents.

While Jason skimmed the *NFL Previews*, his dad interrupted. "Hey Jay... check out this story. This place is only a few miles from your old campus in Rhode Island, isn't it?"

His father slid the folded front section of the paper over to him and a disturbing photo jumped off the page as he picked it up. The scene was dominated by an ambulance and a swarm of cops in front of a two-story white house. A light dusting of snow coated everything, including the black body bags being loaded into the vehicle.

The article recounted the story of an elderly man who approached the house on foot late on Christmas Eve, apparently intent on shooting the homeowner. The story stated, "The alleged gunman, who took his own life prior to the arrival of law enforcement, was reportedly closely affiliated with a former employee of one of the deceased victims. Officials refused to comment on possible motives for his fatal assault upon the three adult victims, citing that their investigation is ongoing."

An icy sensation wriggled down Jason's spine as he experienced a flashback to images from his recent nightmare. The details described in the article all seemed eerily familiar. As bizarre as it seemed, he was certain his dream had somehow become reality. In his heart, he knew that this was the same house, the same street, and the same cast of characters he had already experienced through the eyes of the killer. He found himself at a loss for words after finishing the article.

I Miss Your Purple Hair

When his father asked what was troubling him and whether he recognized the area mentioned in the story, Jason replied, "Uh, yeah...it isn't very far from the college, just a few miles to the east."

His mother piped in while loading the dishwashing machine, "Isn't that just horrible, such a senseless crime ... and on Christmas Eve? What kind of world are we living in?"

Confused and suddenly sick to his stomach, Jason excused himself to go outside for a walk. The morning air was pleasantly cool and the perfume of nearby flowers greeted him. He slowly walked down the quiet residential street, trying to comprehend the unbelievable coincidence of his dream and the tragic incident it apparently foreshadowed. It all seemed so surreal, especially considering the murders occurred in such close proximity to his former campus. Nothing about it made sense. He vigorously shook his head and took some deep breaths in an effort to get the images out of his mind. He walked around the block twice before returning to the house, feeling a bit less agitated. Jason reminded himself it was Christmas Day and that guests would soon be arriving.

The holiday came and went, but Jason still felt on edge. Grisly details eventually emerged regarding the murders, revealing that Honor Roll Incorporated – a manufacturer and distributor of school rings and other jewelry – had recently terminated the gunman's son. A delivery truck driver, the 43-year-old had been dismissed for insubordination and "unacceptable conduct." Records revealed that the former Marine had been diagnosed with Post-Traumatic Stress Disorder, after returning from a tour of duty in Afghanistan. He had been undergoing therapy since rejoining his family at the conclusion of the war.

In a warehouse scuffle over political ideologies, he injured a male coworker when he violently pushed him to the floor. Following an internal review, he was fired from his job. Despondent, he made suicidal threats in the presence of his elderly, adoptive parents. His alcoholic father, beset by mental illness never properly diagnosed or treated, reacted irrationally to what he considered the unwarranted dismissal of his son. Angry, drunk, and delusional, he had somehow acquired an illegal automatic weapon and a supply of ammunition.

On Christmas Eve, he announced to his wife and son he was going to the grocery store to get some eggnog. Instead, he drove to a quiet residential community and abandoned his car in the parking lot of an empty warehouse before extracting the weapon from the trunk. He proceeded to walk the remaining two miles in the lightly falling snow to the home of the owner/CEO of Honor Roll Incorporated, a 42 year-old man named Sandesh Dhatri.

One online news report read: "When neighbor Travis Szymanski, 55, startled the 73-year-old trespasser he was shot five times in the chest and killed instantly. The gunman, identified as Vernon Isaac Olette of East Providence, Rhode Island, then trained his weapon on the front picture window of the home of his intended victim and fired nearly thirty rounds through the glass, fatally wounding Dhatri and his wife, Elisabeth Moore Dhatri, 43. The couple's two children (names and ages withheld) were unharmed despite standing only several feet behind their parents."

Jason did not know what to make of the freakish correlation between his recent nightmare and the actual tragedy. He had always experienced vivid dreams and considered himself highly intuitive, but this was something altogether different... and unnerving. He chose not to discuss it with his family, but instead invited a childhood friend to dinner on the night of December 26th. His high school girlfriend, Marla Cerro, eagerly agreed to meet at a favorite bar and grill.

Over margaritas and Mexican food, Jason described the details of his dream and the eerily similar real-life event. Engrossed by his story, Marla never doubted his sincerity, but was concerned by his demeanor. Visibly distraught as he recounted the details, his lips trembled and his hands shook noticeably. She encouraged him to take a few sips of his cocktail while she covered his hands with hers, and recalled a previous incident similar to his recent revelation.

"Jay," Marla softly said, "when we were dating you told me about a dream you had that also came true, remember? This isn't the first time something like this has happened. Maybe you should talk to someone who specializes in this type of thing."

He recalled the dream to which she referred; it involved a young girl who emerged from the depths of a mysterious dark shadow, into an expanse of emerald green. A month later, news broke about a kidnapped seven-year-old Arkansas girl who had been missing for nearly three months. Remarkably, she materialized early one morning on a public golf course in Little Rock; a solitary figure who walked out of a wooded thicket, onto one of the fairways.

Though uninjured and seemingly in good health, the young girl was strangely unable to provide any useful information to investigators. Her abductors and their motives remained mysteries, but her sudden return was nothing less than miraculous. Jason had tried to put the details of that dream out of his mind over the ensuing years. He had never considered the possibility that he was able to glimpse the future, but the most recent event gave him reason to wonder.

After parting with Marla and turning in for the night, Jason experienced another disturbing dream that would ultimately change the course of his life. In the nightmare, an enormous black cloud appeared in the slate-grey sky and swelled to such enormous proportions it eventually blocked out the Sun. The gigantic cloud formation generated an impressive display of lightning and thunder amid prodigious levels of rain and wind. He saw visions of scorched, ravaged soil torn asunder by earthquakes and radically transformed by enormous tidal waves. Within the midst of the tempest, the vague silhouette of a man emerged unscathed. The unidentifiable man confidently walked through the elemental chaos and then...

... just like that, he was gone.

There was no indication as to the significance of the faceless man. Suddenly, the scene of destruction shimmered and evaporated. In its place appeared flashes of unrelated images: the iridescent colors of a peacock feather; a frightened, sobbing brown-skinned child; an enormous wall of water; and a young girl addressing a huge crowd from behind a glass podium. He witnessed a scene depicting a white dog standing solemnly amidst lush foliage, while a yellow butterfly fluttered nearby.

Finally, he was presented an image of a fair-haired woman apparently trapped beneath a pile of debris. He was surprised that he recognized specific details amidst the wreckage, and when he woke, he understood the action he needed to take. He knew he had to go to the San Diego Zoo.

Early the following morning, he called the police, newspapers, and the local office of the Coast Guard. No one took him seriously, as he described the ominous signs he had witnessed in his dream. He insisted that a major weather-related disaster loomed, and that the zoo would bear its brunt.

In multiple images that flashed within the dream, he had identified colorings and graphic markings on one of the larger pieces of broken metal beneath which the woman was pinned. From several recent visits to the zoo in recent years, he recognized the paint scheme of the gondola from the *Skyfari®* tram ride.

By early afternoon, he finally stopped making fruitless pleas to the authorities. None of them respected his assertion that a major natural catastrophe was brewing. Frustrated and anxious, Jason threw his old yellow raincoat onto the passenger seat and headed to the zoo. He used his cell phone to call ahead as he raced through driving rain and howling wind, but only heard a recorded greeting.

In his haste, Jason never saw the traffic light change from yellow to red. He was too busy gawking at the enormous, jagged bolt of electricity that struck the Earth just a quarter-mile in front of him. His car was moving well over the 35 MPH speed limit when he plowed into the back of a yellow Mustang stopped at the intersection. Shattered glass exploded in all directions as Jason's forehead bounced off the air bag that immediately inflated.

The other driver was unharmed, but extremely agitated when he burst from his car. The enormous and intimidating young man seemed primed for a fight as he made his way over to Jason, who had just kicked open his crumpled driver's side door. As soon as he departed his vehicle, the victim of his carelessness confronted him. The 260-pound 19-year-old flailed his arms wildly as he screamed in Jason's face. Amidst the steadily falling raindrops, Jason could clearly identify the unmistakable smell of marijuana that saturated the wrinkled fabric of his blue, floral-patterned shirt.

"Dude, what the fuck is your problem?!" the long-haired young man screamed. The ruddy-cheeked goliath appeared pale, shaken by the unexpected jolt.

Jason could only apologize profusely, offering up, "Totally my fault" and "I... I... I'm really sorry."

Aware that the zoo was less than a mile away, he surprised his adversary when he abruptly shoved a copy of his insurance card into the young man's meaty hand and sprinted away.

△ △ △

I Miss Your Purple Hair

CHAPTER THREE

I Miss Your Purple Hair

"There are only two lasting bequests we can hope to give our children.
One is roots; the other, wings."
~ Hodding Carter

Mateo Lima was thoroughly enjoying a typically beautiful San Diego Sunday morning at his favorite sidewalk café. He savored a spicy sip of Vanilla Chai while he lazily leafed through the December 27th edition of USA Today. The crystal-clear day began on a very positive note. Mateo generally felt most at peace and in tune with the energy of the universe in the early morning hours, especially on just such a carefree day. A pleasant floral aroma supplemented the scent of his flavored tea, and the blended fragrances triggered a string of memories...

Mateo had grown up in the beautiful Costa Rican paradise of Dominical, where his father, Manuel, worked the western coastline as a Fisherman and Tour Guide. Teresa Chavarra Lima had married Manuel when she was only 16 and he had just turned 30. Her natural beauty and charismatic personality opened many doors, and although she easily secured server positions in cafés and restaurants, the talented singer and guitarist secretly dreamed of becoming a professional entertainer.

Within Costa Rica's burgeoning tourist industry, opportunities were abundant for someone with Teresa's musical talent and charisma. Her large, almond-shaped brown eyes and lustrous mane of coal-black hair helped her make an instantaneous impression everywhere she went. A faithful and doting husband, Manuel was well aware others often lusted after Teresa, but trusted her and rarely felt threatened by her popularity. Theirs was a secure and loving relationship throughout 21 years of marriage.

Their first child, Pilar, was born prematurely with Spina Bifida and died the following day. Deeply saddened by the loss, Teresa initially vowed never to have another child; but before long, she reconsidered and became determined to give Manuel a son. Every day, she visited their church to ask the priest to pray she would produce a healthy boy. Ultimately, Mateo was the answer to those prayers, and to Teresa's great relief he was carried full-term.

I Miss Your Purple Hair

The couple's joy turned to terror when, for reasons never identified, the baby's heart stopped beating just minutes after delivery. While a nurse was gently washing him, Mateo's tiny body inexplicably went rigid and his skin turned blue. Momentary panic ensued while the nurses and doctor rushed to tend to the child. Then, just as quickly as it had stopped, his heart started beating again. Although mother and child remained in the hospital for two additional nights, soon the incident was all but forgotten.

Black-haired Mateo's expressive eyes were remarkably mesmerizing from birth. His large, dark brown irises were embellished with tiny flecks of gold. Beyond his striking physical traits, some members of his extended family noted his unusual crystalline aura. Teresa secretly wondered if she had given birth to a divine child, but quickly put such thoughts out of her head as she felt it was a sin to consider such a possibility. As a child, Mateo was a happy and mischievous spirit. Though his bond was strong with both parents, he was always emotionally closer to his mother. They were sometimes able to converse without speaking a word. Mateo never knew any different way and simply assumed other children communicated telepathically with their mothers.

When Mateo was 15, his father, Manuel suddenly died of a massive stroke. In the wake of his death, Mateo lavished attention on his mother. She grieved for more than a year before taking a job as Entertainment Coordinator at a local resort. Teresa quickly immersed herself in the day-to-day operation, and eventually became their Mistress of Ceremonies.

Mateo first encountered Belinda at a small club in Fortuna, where she was working as a server. Just 17 at the time, she had been hoping to meet a wealthy American tourist, but found it impossible to resist the charms of the handsome young man whose eyes spoke to her soul. They quickly initiated a torrid love affair, and declared their love for one another only weeks after their introduction. Winsome young Belinda was naïve and innocent, filled with dreams of becoming a star. Mateo encouraged her lofty ambitions of becoming a professional singer or actress and they discussed moving to America to pursue the vast opportunities in entertainment.

Shortly after Belinda unexpectedly became pregnant, Mateo's cousin offered him the Webmaster position at his Miami-based marketing and advertising company. Having worked as a freelance web designer in Dominical since he was a teenager, Mateo was perfectly qualified for the role. The attractive position, coupled with Belinda's desire to seek opportunities in the entertainment field, made it an easy decision. Convincing his mother to join them was simple enough, with the impending birth of her first grandchild proving an irresistible lure. At age 26, Mateo succumbed to his cousin's prodding and moved with Belinda and his mother to Miami. It was there that he would welcome his only child into the world.

Having raced through thick traffic to reach the hospital, Mateo arrived just in time to witness the birth of his daughter. He and Belinda had lived in the States for only three months when Veronica chose them as her parents. She turned out to be a rare child in many ways. Born prematurely, she had to fight for survival. Nearly pronounced dead, the tiny infant suddenly started to breathe again just as the doctor uttered the words, "She's gone."

Blessed with thick, dark hair – a family trademark – Veronica also possessed large, cocoa-brown eyes. Her paternal grandmother nicknamed her "Violet" less than an hour after her birth, in reaction to the "glorious indigo aura" she observed.

After defying her parents' impassioned protests regarding moving away from home, Belinda declared she wanted nothing to do with her family. She was stubbornly determined to explore the myriad opportunities in the States. Self-taught and merely adequate on guitar and keyboards, she possessed a beautiful singing voice, but stubbornly refused though to take lessons and was rather delusional about her limited potential. She picked up a few gigs in out-of-the-way bars, but soon became frustrated with the stiff competition and repeated rejection.

Naive and psychologically unprepared for the resistance she encountered, Belinda became increasingly depressed. She soon turned to alcohol and narcotics, abundantly available in Miami. Though they never married, Mateo remained hopeful about their future. He desperately wanted the three of them to grow together as a family. Despite the obvious lack of effort on Belinda's part, he continued to hope she would outgrow her reckless lifestyle and kick her addictions, for Veronica's sake if not her own. Unable or unwilling to combat her self-destructive ways, Belinda continued to bring disharmony to the home.

Mateo zipped down the winding brick-covered street in his black Mazda RX-8, excited to pick up his daughter. Veronica's 15th birthday had occurred the previous week, on December 20th, and it was her wish to spend a day at the zoo. Despite storm warnings for later in the day, Mateo was looking forward to their excursion.

As he left a generous tip for the server, he reminisced about a previous visit to the zoo two years ago. On that day, he had driven down the very same roads to pick up his daughter, eager to spend the day with her at one of her favorite places. A favorite memory from that day popped into his mind...

Their quaint hilltop neighborhood was a congested cluster of multi-family dwellings and apartment complexes. The pristine area was generally quiet and peaceful, mostly populated by young families and single professionals. Their unassuming condominium looked like so many others on the same block; covered in white vinyl, its small balcony protected by black wrought iron railings. The only distinguishing details were distinctive awnings of various colors adorning those same balconies.

As he approached their driveway, Mateo's iPod®, which had been set on "shuffle"; pumped music through his car's speakers. A smile came to his face when one of his all-time favorite songs, "Somewhere Out There" by Our Lady Peace, began to play. The song held special meaning for him ever since Belinda disappeared. Even though it conjured bittersweet memories, he still loved it. As he made his way closer to his new home, an unusual sight along the sidewalk demanded his attention.

As lead singer Raine Maida sang the lyrics, "...Hope you remember me, when you're homesick and need a change. I miss your purple hair..." Mateo blurted out the words, "Wow... purple hair!" in reaction to what he saw. In his rear-view mirror, he re-examined what prompted his audible outburst.

A teenaged girl sporting bright purple hair had just walked past on the passenger side. He laughed aloud as he realized the incredible coincidence he had just experienced. In precise synchronization with the lyrics of one of his favorite songs, he had involuntarily uttered the words "purple hair" in reaction to a purple-haired girl walking toward his moving vehicle. What were the odds of these things happening simultaneously? He pondered the improbability for a moment, while he pulled over to park in front of their building. Suddenly, he was startled by insistent rapping on the passenger-side window.

He was completely surprised to learn it was Violet. "Papa!" she exclaimed. "Open up, will ya?" Mateo never suspected the purple-crested teen was his daughter, and his mouth was still hanging open when she plopped into the passenger seat. "Somewhere Out There" was winding down as he leaned over to plant a kiss on Violet's cheek.

"I drove right by because I had no idea it was you!" he apologetically explained. He then added a sincere, "Happy birthday, baby," before asking the obvious question, "Purple hair... really?" Violet giggled and then shook her

head wildly as if to celebrate her colorful gesture of rebellion. Mateo pressed the issue and asked, "What on Earth possessed you to dye your hair purple?"

The radiant teenager giggled and replied, "Why wouldn't I? I like purple... and they make purple hair dye. What other reason do I need?"

Reflecting on the words in the song perfectly synchronizing with his exclamation, Mateo realized it was just the latest in a long history of coincidences. He was aware they had been occurring with increasing frequency in recent months.

Mateo recalled that day at the zoo as a joyous experience for both father and daughter. He and Violet had always enjoyed a naturally satisfying bond, so compatible were their personalities. Violet was somewhat more impulsive, but both were blessed with a great passion for life. They seemed to know what the other was thinking, often finishing each other's sentences. Their similar senses of humor sometimes generated bouts of unbridled silliness, a trait that occasionally infuriated Violet's mother.

Sadly, Belinda was never able to find peace of mind. She had always battled self-esteem issues that stemmed from her strained relationships with her own parents. In her teenage years, depression eventually led to chronic substance abuse. Her father had always been a drunken womanizer and she grew to despise him for the dreadful father and husband he was. Although she had found a kind and caring partner in Mateo, she struggled to escape the clutches of her own demons. Sober during the early phase of their relationship, her self-destructive tendencies resurfaced shortly after Violet was born.

Mateo made every attempt to help her understand and process the unresolved anger from her childhood, but Belinda could never purge the pain. A few good years were followed by tough times, and before long, Mateo became convinced that Belinda would never change her ways. The tension at home took an emotional toll on young Violet, who began to struggle in school. Aware that Belinda's endless cycle of substance abuse and depression was having a detrimental effect on their child, Mateo gave her an ultimatum.

One morning, Mateo and Violet realized Belinda was missing, with no note left behind. Later that day, Mateo notified the police when he learned she had cleaned out their joint checking account. She had obviously decided to flee rather than make an honest commitment to sobriety. Confused and lost in the turmoil caused by Belinda's drug and alcohol abuse, Violet blamed herself for her mother's behavior. She went through a rough patch marked by plummeting grades and self-imposed isolation. Once her mother finally disappeared, Violet felt a sense of relief and was able to begin the process of recovery. With Mateo's support, she eventually recaptured her true spirit and became one of her school's top students.

On this lovely late-December morning, Mateo eagerly anticipated spending the day with Violet at the zoo. It had been her specific request, in part because she so loved the animals, and in part to try to duplicate the innocent fun they experienced on their last visit. As he approached their block, he could hardly believe his eyes. A bright purple blur flashed alongside the car as he slowed to a stop in front of their building.

To his surprise, Violet suddenly popped open the car door, exclaiming, "Let's rock n' roll! Those monkeys aren't gettin' any younger!"

Mateo asked incredulously, "Violet... not again with the purple hair! When did you...?" The little bundle of kinetic energy whipped off the bright purple wig and laughed as she tossed it over her shoulder onto the back seat.

"You fell for it!" she teased. "Purple hair is *soooo* two years ago!" With that, they sped off, as ominous grey clouds gathered to the west.

Local meteorologists had forecast thunderstorms for the afternoon, and although Mateo had briefly contemplated postponing their visit, he was relieved the sky looked less menacing than expected. Violet gleefully sang along to the music playing through the car stereo. She loved to sing, and had learned to play guitar from one of her closest friends. Demonstrating potential as a musician, she had already written a couple of songs over the summer. In addition to her affinity for music, she excelled at creative writing, and employed her fertile imagination to author some impressive short stories.

Mateo affectionately looked at his only child and grinned. She was wearing the red crystal heart necklace he had presented to her on her birthday the previous week. He thought to himself that she looked hauntingly like Belinda, with her expressive brown eyes and full lips. While she and her mother shared those physical attributes, Violet had more substantive traits in common with her father. Both were fiercely independent and displayed indomitable willpower. Also blessed with palpable charisma, Violet's expressive face and bubbly personality combined to make her irresistibly charming.

Mateo could only imagine how she might evolve as she grew into womanhood. He sometimes worried she might be tempted to misuse her powers of persuasion, but was determined to mentor her to the best of his ability. Quick-witted and highly imaginative, Violet would often effortlessly narrate "little stories", weaving complex fables on the fly. Mateo sometimes prodded her by providing a simple theme to get her started. Her eyes would sparkle intensely and her energy would surge – as words became sentences, then paragraphs, and finally chapters of original content.

Whenever Violet hit full stride with her storytelling, Mateo would light up; nourished by the energy pouring from his seemingly possessed child. Any time she became immersed in her "Zone", they would form what could best be described as a psychic merger, producing inspired magic for their mutual entertainment. As they continued toward their destination, Mateo prompted Violet by suggesting, "Okay…. umm…tell me about the… uh… dragon who lived way up in the sky."

Without missing a beat, Violet responded, "Oh, you wanna know about her, huh? Okay, Pops… let's see..." Undaunted by the challenge of creating a tale based on a random subject, she launched into her story as Mateo listened intently. Violet squirmed to get comfortable in her leather bucket seat and then pointed toward the cluster of puffy clouds in the distance.

"See? She was born right there," she began the fable.

"The Silver Sea was very well-hidden among the Clouds of Destiny. It wasn't a sea of water, but actually a realm of air currents and gigantic cloud formations. The denizens were in turmoil, because the youngest dragon child had gone missing overnight. While the Dragon Elders slept, a tremendous Windforce rocked their home among the clouds. It had been the hugest storm in more than a thousand years… times ten!

In the confusion following the storm, the Elders couldn't find tiny Cerulea – the smallest and youngest of their race. Nowhere to be found, they feared she was lost forever. The Great Dragon Mother called to her youngest child, using the Summoner's Horn, which made a sound that traveled forever. Hours passed and still there was no sign. Too much time had passed and the Elders decided they had to take action if there was any chance of finding the missing child. Cerulea had never been out of their domain and they were concerned that she would be vulnerable to the unknown dangers of the outside world.

The Elders formed a tight circle and wrapped their enormous wings around one another. They entered a deep meditative state and attempted to conjure an image that might help them find Cerulea. While they were all in a trance, an image suddenly appeared. They saw their lost dragon-child, trapped within a watery, blue sphere. The Elders continued to call out to Cerulea, and for what seemed like a long time, there was no response. All hope seemed lost, but then they finally received a response. It was Cerulea answering them psychically, speaking in a clear voice.

'I hear you, Elders', she thought. 'You needn't be concerned, for I am alive and well… and genuinely happy.'

'From where do you call out?' they all projected.

'I am beneath the surface of The Crystal Waters,' she responded, 'and wish to remain here.' The Ancient Ones were incredibly concerned. They had never had anything like this happen before – a Sky Dragon child intentionally defecting from the Clouds of Destiny.

They asked, 'How can this be? What has brought about this madness?'

The dragon child surprisingly answered, 'I answer to no one but myself. My life is my adventure and my life and I have chosen to make my home beneath the waves.'

The Elders were completely dumbfounded. 'How can you live beneath the water? You are not equipped to live under the waves for you cannot breathe the liquid sky!'

Cerulea answered calmly with her mind-voice, 'You don't understand. I have adapted and evolved while you cling to your comfortable past. I, however, have been observing the fish and the sea mammals and have learned to be like them. They taught me new things because I was willing to learn. I have evolved because I never doubted I could. Now, I am enjoying my new home and my new form, and have new horizons to explore – new experiences to savor. I feel free and powerful and am content to remain here until my next transformation.'

'What is that you say?' the Elders' voice projected. 'You mean you still yearn for more change?'

'Yes,' the young one insisted with confidence. 'I intend to keep evolving and changing, to stay in rhythm with the Universe. It is always changing, yet you stay in the past. You can evolve just as I have, but only if you choose to do so. Until your attitudes change, you have but one choice: to remain where you are… just as you are. I made a different choice despite my youth, which you consider a hindrance. I chose to believe in a different fate and never doubted it was within my grasp. So here I am, living proof of my prophecy. I am not disloyal, but must follow my destiny. I hope that you will all understand one day… and should you have a change of heart, you are always welcome to join me.'

The Elders had to ponder this very strange development. The event shocked them and they struggled to understand Cerulea's words. The actions of their youngest daughter temporarily silenced the Elders. Cerulea felt she was only following her destiny. There were risks, but she believed in herself and followed her instincts, regardless of how illogical it seemed. She was afraid when she first dove into the cool water. The Elders had always warned every young one against diving into the forbidden liquid world, promising certain death. They claimed any dragon who fell from their haven in the clouds would perish. Most accepted what they were told without question, but it was Cerulea's way to challenge old notions.

She was willing to risk all for the sake of discovery. The confident young dragon had decided this was her personal destiny, so she went forward... fearlessly. To her relief and to the shock of the Elders, she was able to breathe the water just as she had breathed air since the day she was hatched. The water felt foreign against her scaly outer armor, but it only took a minute or two for her body to adjust. Cerulea had evolved to be able to breathe either element, and if she hadn't risked everything by jumping in, she and the Elders would never have discovered the truth.

Cerulea used her wings and tail to propel herself in figure eights just beneath the water's shimmering surface. As if reborn, she excitedly explored her new world. The Elders struggled to understand what motivated Cerulea and gawked at the sight of her swimming happily in the water below. The bewildered Elders asked how she felt, and she simply replied, *'marvelous.'*

Dracus, one of Cerulea's closest friends, unexpectedly shocked everyone by flying high into the sky before plummeting Earthward. The massive splash created by his entry into the swirling Crystal Waters was a majestic sight. The shock of his decision made a profound impression in the hearts and minds of the Sky Dragons.

'Dracus!' they exclaimed. *'Have you lost your mind? You will surely perish!'*

Dracus struggled to inhale the foreign element of the liquid sea. His body writhed in reaction to the foreign element in his lungs. Initially, his natural instincts rejected any thought of inhaling the water. Cerulea and the Elders all felt he was doomed. But suddenly, he took a small amount of water into his lungs... and then took a much deeper breath. To his surprise and to the relief of all, he stopped resisting and began to swim again. He breached the surface and did a back flip in the air before splashing back into the water.

The Elders all gasped and then Cerulea did a similar flip in the air before rejoining her friend. The old ones couldn't quite grasp what had just happened to two of their own... and to their outdated way of thinking. The two youngest Sky Dragons had taken an incredibly unexpected leap of faith. Out of resentment, and motivated by fear, The Elders soon journeyed to a new home high above the Earth in a far off sanctuary. They turned their backs on the two exiled children and never spoke of them again."

Mateo reluctantly interrupted after Violet was silent for a few seconds. "Well, what happened to the two young dragons? Did they stay in the Crystal Waters forever… or did they change their minds and return to the others?"

"Papa," Violet said matter-of-factly, "They had evolved. Once you evolve, it's impossible to go back. The spirit just won't allow it." She hurried to finish her story as they drew close to the zoo.

"At first they were unhappy to be exiled, and the transition was hard because there was so much to learn and unlearn. Over time though, they not only survived in the Crystal Waters, but they thrived and evolved even further… and so did their many children. Being Sky Dragons, Cerulea and Dracus lived hundreds of years and raised an entirely new generation of Sea Dragons, perfectly content to swim toward a brilliant new future.

The Elders ultimately died off and Cerulea and Dracus eventually passed away as well. But the new race of Sea Dragons flourished and became the fastest evolving civilization the Universe had ever witnessed. And, to think it all began when a young dragon made a brave choice."

"Wow, Vi," Mateo exclaimed, "you have certainly expanded your vocabulary in recent years. What a wonderful story! I was actually confused as to what part was make-believe and what part was real."

Violet smiled and readjusted herself in her seat. "It's *all* make-believe, Papa… except the part about evolution. That part's true. At least I think it must work that way. Once the first fish learned it could walk on land, I doubt it ever wanted to be limited to the water again."

They approached the zoo, and noticed that the sky had become a strikingly beautiful mixture of blue and purple. The Sun was directly overhead as the noon hour approached, and its rays painted the tops of the palm trees lining the road with liquid gold. Mateo and Violet pulled into the expansive parking lot near the main entrance and eagerly anticipated the colorful sights and sounds they were sure to experience.

△△△

CHAPTER FOUR
Down Here in the Atmosphere

"All things are connected.
Whatever befalls the Earth befalls the children of the Earth."
~ Chief Seattle, Suqwamish and Duwamish tribes

Violet grabbed her father's arm above the elbow and dragged him through the turnstiles of the popular Southern California landmark. The aromas of exotic flowering plants welcomed the excited pair. Anticipation and wonder filled their hearts as a kaleidoscope of vibrant colors and sounds welcomed them to the lush, tropical setting. Violet knew exactly what she wanted to see first, and continued to drag her father by the hand.

Mateo asked, "Baby, where are we going? And what's the big hurry?"

The precocious teenager replied through a luminous smile, "We have to hurry! Before the storm gets here... I want to make sure we have time to find it!"

"Find what?" Mateo inquired.

"You'll see," was all Violet offered.

The swell of energy relentlessly surged eastward along the ocean floor. Originating hundreds of miles off the coast of Los Angeles, it was destined to evolve, from a barely detectable underwater tremor to an irresistible force. None of the scientists or their dedicated instruments could have predicted the impending chain reaction. Before state-of-the-art equipment registered trace readings from the offshore tremors, the second phase of the unfolding tragedy had already commenced.

"Bad luck" would qualify as a ludicrous understatement for what transpired. It would be more appropriate to say that unidentifiable celestial forces had drawn up a blueprint for supreme destruction.

Violet had a very specific destination in mind, despite her sketchy familiarity with the zoo's layout. She had pulled away to scamper past countless zoo visitors toward some mysterious goal, making it difficult for Mateo to keep up. He understood his enlightened and intuitive child better than any other living soul, and appreciated that she was merely following her powerful instincts.

I Miss Your Purple Hair

Growing up, Violet had sometimes struggled to understand the impulsive thoughts and voices invading her mind, but gradually learned to accept them. Because Mateo had worked at understanding and appreciating his own psychic abilities, he was well equipped to help his uniquely gifted daughter. To the contrary, her unenlightened mother was not equipped to comprehend her exceptional gifts and instead, often criticized her sometimes unpredictable behavior.

Each negative reaction only pushed Violet closer to her far more supportive father. She had to subdue her special talents in an attempt to pacify her mother, but fighting her natural inclinations proved unhealthy. For several years, she shut down emotionally while the strained relationship with her mother eroded her morale and self-esteem.

Violet experienced her mother's resentment over her unwavering closeness with her father – as profound physical pain. So sensitive was she as a young girl that significant emotional stress often manifested as intense headaches. On occasion, she suffered visible swelling and irritation to her skin, usually along the front of her neck and along her forearms. The blotchy markings would sometimes appear so suddenly she would not have time to attempt to hide them. Such incidents led to self-doubt and a sense of isolation.

Violet's grades and morale eventually suffered to the point that the school's Guidance Counselor recommended she repeat the sixth grade. Mateo advocated for her with school authorities and routinely worked closely with her on school assignments. Her public school in Miami was one of the state's most progressive, yet was unprepared to effectively deal with super-evolved children. Mateo tried to persuade Belinda to send Violet to a private school the following year, but she would not hear of it. She was much more interested in getting her next "fix" than spending money on her daughter's education, and her selfish opposition led to months of arguments with Mateo.

Mateo was sincerely concerned about his only child, who had grown increasingly withdrawn. He was worried she might eventually seek solace in the same destructive behavior to which her mother was drawn. Belinda's precarious rapport with her daughter continued to deteriorate and Violet felt the tension between them just as one feels humidity in the air. In a private conversation one night, while working on a Math assignment with her father, she blurted out, "I want to try to help her, but I wouldn't be upset if Mama left us one day. You need to know that."

Mateo was stunned. "But she's your mother, honey. I know she has her faults, but she loves you and would never do anything of the kind. Let's try to think of ways we can help her."

Violet looked up at her father, wearing a sympathetic expression. "Papa, it's like she's not my true mother. I feel almost nothing inside when I'm around her. She's selfish and lazy, and I... I'm ashamed of her!"

Mateo swallowed hard and rested his chin on his hands, hunched over at the dining room table. Emotionally pained by his child's declaration, he had to work to regain his composure. He tried to reassure Violet that her mother truly did love her, but the exceptionally astute 12-year-old only became visibly resentful.

"Please don't ever say that again, Papa," she firmly requested. Violet's impassioned outburst nearly brought Mateo to tears. She let it all out in a stream-of-consciousness diatribe, "She'll never change. She'll always love her drugs and her booze more than anything or anybody else. She can never be a real mother because she needs to grow up herself before that could ever happen. All she'll ever do... is ruin any happiness we have."

Mateo subconsciously realized that Violet's contentions were probably accurate, but was not quite ready to admit it to himself. It was true that Belinda had struggled with the responsibilities of parenthood. She had never aspired to marriage or harbored any desire to settle down. In fact, she had secretly viewed her unplanned pregnancy as nothing less than a curse. To make matters worse, Mateo knew in his heart that she resented Veronica from the moment she was born. Many times, he tried to discuss it, but she always insisted he was overreacting. Woefully unprepared to raise a child – especially one so challenging – Belinda always retreated to her addictions.

As he reached across the table to put his hands atop his daughter's, Mateo finally realized that the woman with whom he had produced this remarkable child had become detrimental to her well-being. It was a tragic realization for someone so idealistic. He gently patted Violet's hands and said, "We'll be alright... as long as we stick together and try to be honest with each other. And I promise I will... never let you fall."

"I know, Papa," was Violet's sincere reply. She wiped a tear from her cheek and walked over to give her father a hug. She whispered in his ear, "I'm sorry if I'm being a brat."

Mateo gave her a light squeeze around the shoulders and said, "There's no need to apologize. If we can't be honest with each other..."

She knew precisely what he meant.

I Miss Your Purple Hair

Only two months later, Belinda abruptly drained their joint checking account, stole the family car, and vanished into the steamy Miami night. Mateo fruitlessly called her cell phone throughout the following day, before finally reporting her disappearance to the police. He contacted Belinda's parents and close relatives in Costa Rica, but received only half-hearted cooperation. Mateo found their obvious lack of sincere concern very typical. Her parents claimed she had not contacted them, which he was inclined to believe, as their relationship had withered ever since they moved to the States.

Belinda left a scattered trail of nothing more than vague clues as to her intentions and possible destination. She made off with $7,500, which virtually cleaned out their account, leaving Mateo and Violet to scrape for rent and grocery money. Initially, Violet was very angry over her mother's sudden disappearance but blamed her disappearance on the antagonistic relationship that had developed between them. Mateo did his best to help her cope with the pain of abandonment, but Violet struggled to forgive herself or her mother.

As months passed, Mateo's relentless efforts failed to turn up any definitive clues as to Belinda's whereabouts. Over time, Violet and Mateo eventually felt relief that they would no longer have to deal with the perpetual tension Belinda contributed. In place of stress and paranoia, trust and harmony gradually flourished. With Belinda out of the picture, there was room for enhanced connectivity between father and daughter.

Mateo had never given Violet reason to doubt his devotion and she appreciated the security he provided. To compensate for her mother's absence, Mateo doubled his efforts to understand and assist Violet in navigating her formative years. After reading several books and online articles about Indigo Children, Mateo was convinced the list of telltale personality traits described Violet accurately. She had always been a very sensitive, confident, and insightful child, although she was at one point misdiagnosed with Attention Deficit Disorder. Mateo questioned that assessment and was critical of the generic treatment the doctors prescribed: traditional medication along with some behavioral modification exercises. He made the decision to take her off the prescription meds after only a few weeks.

As she grew, Violet continued to impress teachers and classmates with her innovative solutions and unique approach to problem solving. She often challenged authority figures to justify their demands. In school, she gained a much-deserved reputation for being "a handful" and for keeping teachers on their toes. She was not belligerent so much as she was merely asking intelligent questions and challenging others to consider their vantage point before blindly barking orders.

After a year had passed without any indication of Belinda's whereabouts, Mateo decided that relocating would be the best course of action. It was time for a change of scenery... again. He discovered an opening for the position of Director of Innovation with a San Diego public relations and marketing firm. Conveniently, the company held interviews in several cities, including Miami, and they offered the position to Mateo immediately following his interview. The timing was ideal, since school was about to let out for summer. Mateo had been working contract jobs in construction for several months, and the resulting financial peaks and valleys produced a great deal of stress.

Not long after moving into their San Diego condominium, Violet felt rejuvenated. She made a handful of new friends in the neighborhood and began to emerge from her funk. Mateo bought her a new acoustic guitar and they both signed up for lessons. Possessing only marginal musical ability himself, Mateo's primary motivation was to share in one of his daughter's newest interests. Conversely, Violet displayed significant talent and often practiced late into the night.

As she became more comfortable in their new environment, Violet discovered she not only possessed a beautiful voice but truly felt at peace when she sang. She also was drawing and painting more than ever since they relocated, and was generally more cheerful – as if a veil of bitterness had been lifted. With Belinda out of their lives, both Mateo and Violet began to reclaim their former selves and were happier than ever before. Once the new school year began, she pestered teachers to recommend material related to the latest subject of her newest fascination, Marine Biology.

Early in the school year, Violet's class spent an entire day at Sea World San Diego. She took over a hundred digital photographs and filled many pages of her sketchbook with drawings of her favorite Sea World residents. Mesmerized by the dolphins, Violet lingered as long as possible at their exhibit. During their visit, the students learned that a special exhibition tank for the two youngest dolphins had recently been constructed near the sea lion theater in the San Diego Zoo.

Apparently, the dolphins were exhibiting erratic behavior and Sea World officials decided a change of scenery might relieve whatever irritation they were experiencing while creatively marketing both facilities. For weeks, Violet had pleaded with her father to take her to see the newly relocated dolphins... and for a second reason she neglected to share with him.

I Miss Your Purple Hair

"Come on, Pops!" she yelled. "You're lagging behind again. Gettin' too old to keep up?" she teased, as she continued to run toward a destination only she knew.

Mateo smiled. When it came to his daughter's passionate ways, all he could ever do was smile and follow her lead. He felt endless fascination for her imagination and zest for life. They were moving swiftly, brushing by families with strollers, elderly people in electric wheelchairs, zoo employees, and vendors. They zipped past many displays and habitats at which they normally would have lingered. Wispy branches and small, multicolored flowers brushed past their faces but they never slowed as they moved deeper into the park.

Mateo beckoned, "Where are you dragging me? I need a breather!"

At that precise moment, Violet abruptly froze in place. Mateo was bowed at the waist, hands on his knees, desperately trying to catch his breath while observing the unfolding of a peculiar scene. When he raised his head, he saw they had arrived at the Panda Discovery Center. Violet was very deliberately stalking a bird that was approaching a cluster of small trees. The beautiful peacock appeared unconcerned with the teenager in stealthy pursuit.

The distant rumble of thunder went unnoticed by many, as far from the coast as it originated. At the same time, a growing pressure deep below the ocean floor about two hundred miles west of Los Angeles was building, in bizarre harmony with the tension woven into the mushrooming clouds. Thunderstorm warnings began scrolling across the bottom of television screens.

The Weather Channel® interjected a severe thunderstorm warning for a broad region extending from Anaheim to the Baja Peninsula. Simultaneously, preliminary readings from a series of undersea tremors began registering at early warning sites sprinkled along the California coast. Minor quake activity was detected due west of Los Angeles. Seismic tremors beneath the waves of the Pacific were not unprecedented or even uncommon; and historically, they often caused no significant damage. Tragically, the readings only told part of the story, for the undersea tremors had originated at an exceedingly fragile location.

Unbeknownst to the seismologists who monitored the region, there had been a sudden buildup of volcanic pressure beneath the floor of the Pacific Ocean, several hundred miles from the coast. A new undersea volcano quickly and unexpectedly formed and its internal pressure built to dangerous levels at a highly accelerated pace. Some of the most advanced equipment on the planet recorded the first readings at an Early Warning Center located in San

Francisco, with initial readings assessed as "unremarkable", relative to the common occurrence of such minor seismic events.

Richter scale readings of between 2.5 and 2.9 were recorded late in the morning of December 27th. These were not even as high as readings from the previous two weeks, during which time a sequence of over 100 undersea quakes were recorded and tracked. The string of quakes was nothing new for the area and the insignificant levels recorded did not hint at what was to happen next.

Violet slowly trained her candy-apple-red digital camera on the adult peacock. The bird had turned its beautiful sapphire and emerald head to examine the cause of the shadow spilling over its body. She quickly took a pair of snapshots then hung her camera back over her head. "Rats!" she muttered. "That's not the one."

Mateo had finally pulled even with her and wore a puzzled expression as he placed his hand on her shoulder. "What exactly are you doing?" he asked. Violet proceeded to divulge her underlying motivation for wanting to come to the zoo so badly.

She explained that she had stumbled upon an item on an obscure Internet site about a man in Pennsylvania who discovered a very rare (he referred to it as "divine" and "miraculous") peacock in the National Aviary in Pittsburgh. According to the report, a docent at the facility had made the discovery; at least he claimed as much. The original blog post by the young man stated he had been taking photos of one of the Aviary's peacocks and detected some highly unusual coloring on one of the bird's many splendid tail feathers. The male peafowl, otherwise sporting typical iridescent blue-green plumage, was described as approximately three months of age.

The man discovered the unique aspect of this particular bird while editing his collection of images on his laptop computer. A student at Carnegie-Mellon University, he was collecting images of peacocks as a birthday gift for his fiancé. He intended to create and self-publish a small book of high-resolution photos of peacocks. His girlfriend had always loved peacocks and other exotic birds and had a stylized tattoo of a single peacock feather on her upper right arm.

A truly remarkable feature of this particular peacock existed on one of its tail feathers. The blog included a photograph of the entire bird and a blurry close-up of the unusual feather. As Violet pored over the lengthy post and accompanying photos, she was intrigued by the author's suggestion that there was something incredible about the unique tail feather. Asserting he was an expert on peafowl, he suggested the possibility that the purple coloration within the eye had never before been documented. Deeper into his post, he claimed there were "intricate symbols in gold above the eye." As the self-proclaimed aficionado continued, he described iridescent gold shapes woven into the background "resembling a Sun, a triangle and a five-pointed star."

He insisted he first noticed them upon photographing the bird, but had failed to capture a sharp image. After planning another visit to document the anomaly, he was frustrated to learn that the aviary had donated the peacock, along with three additional peafowl, to the San Diego Zoo. Apparently, their healthy surplus allowed them to comfortably donate several of their stock to the zoo, which was looking to replace some birds recently lost to a lethal viral infection. Upon reading this, Violet felt compelled to locate the peacock in question. The blog post had been dated December 15th, so she hoped the timing would be ideal to find the mysterious peacock.

Running his hand through his hair, Mateo felt fortunate to have such a confident and adventurous daughter. He had long ago recognized that he and Violet shared many traits: highly developed senses of intuition and precognition; endless curiosity; unwavering self-confidence; and a broad sense of humor. They both tended to be naturally sympathetic and in complete harmony with their spirituality, as well.

Curious and determined, Violet conducted a hasty visual examination of the bird she had cornered, and just as efficiently determined it was not the one she sought. Depicted in the visual reference she possessed, the body of the bird she sought sported similar rich emerald green and cobalt blue feathers, but was smaller than the one currently at her feet. After calmly declaring, "This isn't the one ether," she finally explained everything to her patient father.

He knew his daughter well enough to know that it would be pointless to try to talk her out of continuing the adventure. Mateo raised his trusty Canon camera and took a shot of Violet kneeling next to the beautiful object of her waning attention. She automatically looked up and smiled as she had done a thousand times before, and announced, "Cool, now let's find the real one."

Mateo laughed and grabbed her hand, and they continued their quest. Along the way, Mateo happily absorbed all of the sights and sounds within the vibrant microcosm. He would have preferred to pause and take more photos, but accepted the fact that his headstrong daughter would not be denied. They continued along the path in a southwestward direction, past the potbellied pigs and into the entrance of the lush Ituri Forest region. The dense canopy of lush, green trees created a sudden shift in atmosphere marked by noticeably cooler temperatures and a tangibly peaceful energy.

As they followed the clearly defined path that wound through the shrouded region, Mateo and Violet noticed a crimson-haired young woman taking photographs. Of average height and slender build, she was clad in khaki shorts and a hunter green tank top. Atop her head of long flowing red hair she wore a white visor. Sand-colored hiking boots completed her ensemble. When she turned her head to the side, Mateo could not help but appreciate her natural beauty. From a distance, he noted that her beautiful eyes were almost the same green as the midriff-exposing top snugly glued to her well-toned torso. Those same eyes, alert and clear, quickly darted about, seeking the next target for her camera. She quickly documented images of plants, flowers, birds and anything else that caught her attention.

Violet gently nudged her father and pantomimed someone whipping their camera around in frenzied fashion, taking photos in lightning-quick succession. She quickly snapped to attention and ended her mimicry when it appeared the photographer spotted her little act. Mateo enjoyed that his daughter was still just a typical kid, despite her sometimes startling maturity. He squeezed her shoulder to indicate he loved her just the way she was.

The mystery woman turned and continued ahead along the trail, disappearing when a bend in the path took her out of view. Violet took a moment to savor the breathtakingly beautiful environment. She had developed a penchant for closing her eyes, extending her slender arms out to the side, and breathing in deeply. She often would employ this routine when in the presence of natural beauty or an especially memorable moment. She dramatically proclaimed, "Ahhh... gotta take it all in!"

Mateo had learned to join her in these special moments, so he extended his long, tanned arms while inhaling the enchanting fragrances of the forest. In unison with Violet, he inhaled the intoxicating aroma and held it in his lungs for as long as he could. Eyes closed, his mind treated him to a virtual slide show of his daughter's life. He relived the moment of her birth, so vivid because he had been the first person to hold her. He enjoyed the image of her first day of school, when she boarded the yellow bus with her red lunch box in one hand and a flower for the teacher in the other. She displayed no trepidation on that day – only excitement. He recalled her first soccer practice, when she was only six years old. He could both see and hear her playing her first guitar and singing one of her ad-libbed songs at age eight. Finally, he savored an image of her amidst a lush forest, eyes closed and arms outstretched, smiling as she drank in the energy of the indigenous life forms. He smiled and finally exhaled. Upon opening his eyes, he saw Violet a few yards ahead of him, distracted by something in the trees.

"What is it?" he asked.

On tiptoes, Violet strained to see something high overhead. She faced him and said, "Papa, we better hurry and find that peacock. That storm is coming fast and we might run out of time. See how dark the sky's getting?"

Without saying another word, they hustled along the path until they exited the Ituri Forest into the zoo proper, emerging near the hippopotamus enclosure. Violet pulled her father along by his upper arm, clearly not remotely interested in the hippos.

"There's another one!" she whispered, before rushing toward a peacock walking alongside the path. Anticipating the rain, Mateo pulled his tattered black baseball cap from his back pocket and stuck it on his head.

Violet had already rushed over to the bird to examine it. She scrunched up her nose and announced, "Awww... I thought this was the one for sure, but its colors are wrong."

Mateo suggested they head toward the exit because of the impending storm, but Violet pretended she failed to hear him. Instead, she stood perfectly still and closed her eyes. Mateo knew what she was up to, having grown accustomed to her mannerisms. With her camera hanging from her neck, she set her denim backpack at her feet and placed her hands on her hips. After a few deep breaths, she stood locked in a peaceful trance for a few seconds.

Mateo had learned from Violet how to purge his conscious mind of the distractions his senses had accumulated. He had refined the simple process of focusing and breathing in an effort to connect to the energies swirling around him. Over the past several years, he had become adept at achieving this state instinctively, just as Violet had always done.

The wind shifted, and Mateo sensed a significant change in the air.

△ △ △

CHAPTER FIVE
I Know You're Out There

*"The intellect has little to do on the road to discovery.
There comes a leap in consciousness, call it Intuition or what you will,
the solution comes to you and you don't know how or why."
~ Albert Einstein*

For a moment, the Sun seemed incredibly bright as it filtered through the lush canopy of leaves and swaying branches bordering the trail to the south. A steady, warm breeze began to pick up while the father-daughter team made their way through the forest. The smoldering clouds they had noted earlier seemed to be clearing. Violet looked to the sky and flashed a Cheshire Cat grin before forging ahead toward the tiger exhibit. As they proceeded, blissfully immersed in the thick scent of pine emanating from the trees lining the path, Violet made it clear she did not intend to slow down.

Mateo implored, "Sweetheart, don't you want to take a few photos of the tigers? Look how beautiful they are!"

She gently protested, "Let's come back to them in a bit. I really want to see if we can find that peacock before it rains."

Mateo took a quick snapshot of the female Siberian tiger without breaking stride, determined to capture images of the magnificent creatures while keeping pace with his determined daughter. The beautiful animal appeared agitated, repeatedly jumping against the door leading to the sanctuary of its sleeping quarters. He locked eyes with the tiger for a fleeting moment, and sensed fear – perhaps an element of panic. Glancing back at the fur-coated wonder, Mateo sensed an inexplicable foreboding. Trying to shrug it off, he sped up to draw within a few steps of Violet, who had knelt down to remove a bottle of water from her backpack.

"Want some?" she asked through a precocious smile.

"Sure, honey," he answered, before taking a great gulp from her scuffed, purple water bottle. Looking beyond Violet, Mateo noticed a flash of blonde hair moving amidst a cluster of people near a bend in the walkway. He watched as the young mother swatted the backside of her tantrum-throwing little towhead son. A diminutive silver-haired couple strolled along the same path, impervious to the commotion, content to savor the sights, sounds, and smells of the uniquely beautiful realm.

Mateo literally tasted the swirling, undulating energy surrounding him and sensed the combined power of the disparate life forces. Caught up in wonderment and awe, he enjoyed the unique backdrop of rich colors and sounds. One moment, he savored the tantalizing aroma of fresh-popped popcorn a ruddy-faced young man offered his date. In the next instant, he was awash in a cacophony of human voices, animal growls and birdcalls. The breeze demonstrated its intent to influence the clouds as well as the coiffures of the paying public.

Carried on the wind and deposited atop his black sneakers, a woman's wide-brimmed straw hat suddenly appeared. Mateo instinctively bent down to retrieve it before the breeze decided to play games again. When he stood back up he found himself immersed in the beautiful, aquamarine eyes of Mia Nordstrom. The soft sunlight anointed her creamy porcelain skin in a buttery glow as she slowly extended an elegant hand to reacquire her property. She blushed ever so slightly, obviously attracted to the chivalrous stranger who kindly returned what the wind had so rudely stolen. She meekly thanked him, then turned and walked back in the same direction Violet and Mateo were heading.

Violet could not resist teasing her father. "Whoa, Pops... you'd better close your mouth before you swallow a bug!" she squealed, followed by her trademark giggle. "And, no wedding ring? Hmmm..." she teased. Mateo chuckled and playfully pinched her upper arm before they continued along the paved path.

A few paces ahead of them, Mia's cell phone annoyingly vibrated in the front pocket of her sandy-brown cargo shorts. A freelance writer, the San Diego Chamber of Commerce had commissioned her to create a web site feature on the new dolphin exhibit. She was satisfied with her research after thoroughly investigating the exhibit and interviewing the appropriate zoo personnel. Her brother anxiously awaited her return near the Entrance, while the darkening sky compelled her to make haste. Walking at a quickening pace, Mia struggled to extract the razor-thin silver phone from her pocket while maneuvering through the crowd. She followed the winding trail toward the area just west of the entrance and answered her phone, aware that Kyle was on the other end.

"Yeah, Kyle, I know you have a plane to catch. I'm on my way back to you now and will be there in less than five minutes. Did you buy that gift for Emmi, like I asked?"

Kyle replied sarcastically, "No... I forgot... even after you reminded me six times over the past two hours. Of course, I got it – the stuffed tiger. The kid's only turning one year old and you'd think it was her 'Sweet Sixteen' party. How many things have you already bought her?"

Older brother to Mia and youngest sister Anna, Kyle Nordstrom was not a bad person; just a bit impatient and slightly narcissistic. Mia got along well with him, but after nearly a week together, she was more than ready for him to return home to Pittsburgh. While he brushed a few unruly strands of his sandy brown hair away from his sunglass-covered eyes, he slumped a little deeper into the iron bench he had commandeered. On the surface, Kyle sometimes gave off a cocky vibe that was easy to misinterpret, and although he tended to look like a rock star at times, that was purely unintentional.

Like his two strikingly beautiful sisters, he was blessed with classic, chiseled features. The siblings all possessed expressive eyes that conveyed alertness and intelligence. Kyle's were a deep sapphire blue. Anna, working to complete her Master's in Sociology at San Diego State, had eyes of rich hazel and green. Most remarkable of Mia's many enviable features were her stunning aquamarine eyes. Her closest friends liked to call her "Sparkle" in reference to their unusual highlights.

A successful child psychologist, Kyle was sincerely devoted to his young clients in the Western Pennsylvania area. He specialized in working with children with traits traditionally attributed to Indigo Children, or as he called them, his "Quantum Qids." His clients generally ranged between the ages of six and eighteen, with the majority toward the younger side. These children typically struggled to focus their attention in school and bristled at some of the limitations and rules imposed by society. Kyle felt sympathy for all children in trouble, but built his practice around the unique needs of these highly intuitive kids, in part because he had struggled with similar challenges as a child.

Most of Kyle's Quantum Qids were unusually intelligent and perceptive. A high percentage frequently spoke about "connecting with other kids" via what they referred to as "The Web," referring to something different from the Internet. Many of them described ongoing psychic connections to other similarly gifted children across the world. Some of Kyle's older patients described, in detail, incidents during which they received messages across vast distances. They often raged against authority, which made them disruptive elements in the classroom and at home.

I Miss Your Purple Hair

Parents often unintentionally exacerbated their child's problems by trying to force them to conform, resulting in emotional pain and feelings of intense frustration. Many of the children expressed that they felt like "misfits", no matter what conventional treatments they had been subjected to. Quite a few of them had been previously diagnosed with Attention Deficit Hyperactivity Disorder (ADHD) and Kyle and his staff physicians often reduced their dosage or eliminated medication altogether. He worked diligently to establish new methods of treatment for the majority of his clients, which included weaning them off drugs and redirecting them to customized behavioral modification training.

Kyle's Quantums were not so much hyperactive as they were hyper-intuitive. They were also hypersensitive, hyper-intelligent, hyper-inventive, and quite frequently hyper-humorous. Fiercely independent, they were often sincerely content to spend extended periods of time alone. They could also suddenly flip a switch in their active, inquisitive minds and be the most congenial, charming companions when it suited them. Kyle had been very effective in treating the vast majority of his clients and his creative approach to working with the child's parents or guardians was bringing him much deserved notoriety in recent months.

Kyle's recently published book, *Quantum Qids: Nurturing the Hope of the Future*, was gaining popularity and he basked in the satisfaction of truly making a positive impact in the field he loved. He was genuinely committed to helping the families with whom he worked, but also admittedly enjoyed the accompanying adulation. Kyle was single, successful, and gaining new perspective from working with his clients. He had immersed himself in a great deal of existing research on the so-called Indigo Children, but his book detailed his own revolutionary techniques. Kyle drew upon years of consultations with clients and their families to arrive at the cutting edge of addressing the needs of a new generation.

Though Mia was genuinely proud of her charming brother, she was also fond of pointing out faults... like his trademark clumsiness. She approached at a brisk pace, and as he stood up from his comfortable perch, his trendy new sunglasses flew off his lap and skittered across the pavement. She scooped them up nonchalantly, smirking at the man she used to call "skunk breath."

"Your shades, sir?" she sarcastically inquired.

Embarrassed, Kyle accepted the cast-off accoutrement and bowed to his suddenly distracted sister. "What is it?" he asked.

"Uh, nothing, really… it's just that those clouds look fairly menacing. We've got to get you to the airport, so let's get moving, okay?"

Kyle grinned and put his sunglasses on top of his head before replying, "Gotta make a quick pit stop before we go, okay?"

Mia grabbed the plush tiger out of his hand and told him to meet her by the front gate. A strong wind gust tried to rip the hat off her head again as Kyle headed to the nearest rest room. She looked to the sky and noticed unusual splashes of vibrant colors. Transparent ribbons of red and orange decorated the atmosphere overhead, while the cobalt blue-and-grey mass of clouds steadily moved in from the west. Mia tucked the beautifully detailed toy tiger into her tote bag and clutched it to her chest as she perused the scene around her.

A human swarm migrated toward the exits, several of them muttering something about "a major storm" and "dangerous conditions" as they brushed past. She was finding it difficult to recall where she had parked her midnight blue BMW Z4. She knew Kyle had spoken its location into his smartphone, but was perturbed her memory was not as sharp as it had once been. The thought, *'Too much data to process,'* breezed through her mind.

Crossing directly in front of the handsome man asking for directions to the nearest bathroom, Mateo and Violet headed toward the Main Entrance. The duo cut across the busy area and headed west. As they passed Kyle, an announcement blared from overhead speakers. The Public Address announcement declared, "Due to severe thunderstorm warnings combined with reports of seismic activity to the northwest, all visitors are required to evacuate the facility immediately." Zoo staff issued rain checks at the exits and urged all visitors to leave in an orderly fashion. Given 30 minutes in which to depart, the facility would then officially close for the day.

Mateo suggested to Violet that they skip the dolphin exhibit and head directly home. She begged for "just a measly ten minutes," and he agreed, but sternly insisted that they would have to leave at that time. At 2:13 p.m., they hastily made their way toward the Wegeforth Bowl against a counter-current of humanity bound for the exits. A strange image popped into Mateo's mind. He clearly envisioned a large white dog with a full tail, standing at attention as if alerted to a trespasser. The dog appeared to be a Siberian Husky or similar breed. Its eyes were a striking shade of light blue. Mateo failed to understand what prompted the vision, but was more concerned about the details of the warning broadcast over the Public Address system.

The two adventurous souls finally reached their destination beyond the recently renovated and expanded Reptile House, now totally devoid of visitors. In collaboration with Sea World, the zoo had erected a state of the art domain for the two young bottlenose dolphins. Partially submerged into the rocky soil, the beautiful glass-front habitat stood in close proximity to the amphitheater known as The Wegeforth Bowl – home to the popular sea lion shows. The enormous tank had supplanted the hummingbird aviary, which had been relocated within the Flamingo Plaza area, not far from the entrance gates.

A beautiful backdrop of enormous rocks and lush gardens helped frame the new dolphin exhibit and the semicircle of bleachers tastefully blended with the surroundings. The plan was to keep the dolphins for no more than two or three years before reintroducing them to their original pod in Sea World. In the interim, authorities would make the decision to either dismantle the exhibit or expand the Sea World presence in the zoo. The potential benefits of cross marketing appealed to both entities and the assessment was underway.

Violet pulled away from her father and sprinted toward the dolphin tank. She scampered to the empty aluminum bleachers and stood on the lowest bench. After whipping out her camera, she immediately started photographing the saltwater sanctuary and its two residents, squealing with delight all the while. "Papa, this is awesome! I had no idea the zoo built such a cool home for these guys! It's really cool!"

Before he could catch up to her, Violet was already urging, "Take my picture with the dolphins in the background! Please?" Ever obliging, Mateo grabbed her digital camera and walked up to the top row of bleachers to get a better angle. He instructed Violet where to stand and carefully framed the effusive girl and the displaced dolphins, snapping shots in quick succession. The bright-eyed teen struck a series of comical poses, smiling and mugging for the camera in typical fashion.

A distant rumble of thunder interjected an unwelcome dose of reality to the carefree moment. Mateo glanced at his watch, noting the time as 2:22 p.m., before being distracted by movement in the background. In a shrouded garden separating the dolphin tank from the sea lion exhibit, a rustling sound stole his attention from his daughter. "What's going on over there?" he asked his wide-eyed child.

Violet strained on tiptoes and put her hand over her eyes as if it would improve her long-range vision. "Let's check it out!" was her predictable response, and the two of them bounded off their aluminum perch. They heard rustling and a thud as they pushed the overhanging vegetation out of the way and approached the little cul-de-sac nestled between the two exhibit areas.

The red-haired woman they had seen taking photos in the Ituri Forest was on one knee, feverishly typing into some hand-held device. Mateo, once again overcome by pure animal attraction, instinctively fantasized about her. In an instant, an image of him holding her about the shoulders and gently pressing his lips to hers materialized in his mind. He imagined slowly and deliberately sliding his hands over her green tank top, progressing from her waist up along her ribs.

Mateo's fantasy immediately triggered a rather obnoxious sneeze. His unusual Pavlovian reaction had occurred in similar situations in the past, leaving him feeling exposed and embarrassed. He first noticed this physiological manifestation when he was a teenage schoolboy lusting over a classmate. He initially ruled out any correlation between the psychological and physiological, assuming it was a completely preposterous notion. But as years went by, it happened with enough predictability he came to accept the phenomenon. In his lifetime, two things seemed to make him sneeze: eating chocolate... and erotic fantasies, for which the reaction still existed.

"Bless You!" Violet instinctively blurted. The scarlet-tressed woman failed to react, completely focused on the task at hand. She frantically input text into her electronic device, kneeling next to a large blue tarpaulin secured in place by three large rocks. When she finally finished her thumb-straining data entry, she peered up at them over her stylish green-tinted sunglasses. For the first time, they heard her speak.

A sarcastic, "Do you two *need* something?" were the first words uttered by the freckle-faced beauty. Violet was immediately put off by the icy greeting and shifted her attention to the nearby dolphin tank.

Mateo looked the woman over more carefully, eliciting the reaction, "Look, mister... I'm a little pressed for time here, and you should be heading out, too. Didn't you hear the warning over the speakers? Look at that sky. In a few minutes that storm will be on us... and I don't plan on sticking around for the fireworks."

Mateo was puzzled at her unwarranted arrogance, but more curious about what she was doing. A professional-quality digital camera hung from a strap around her neck, and her knee rested upon a thick notebook.

She suggested, "If I were you, I'd cut the safari short and get to my car before the shit hits the fan."

Mateo could not help but smile at her comment and shook his head affirmatively as he glanced over at Violet. She was pointing at something just beyond the long-legged woman kneeling in front of them. Mateo directed his gaze to the lump beneath the tarp and noticed something moving beneath it.

Violet began to lift the dusty shroud by one corner, eliciting a quick reaction from the redhead. "Wait! Don't touch that!" she commanded, and Violet immediately let go.

"Hey, what's the problem?" Mateo asked, perturbed at the woman's tone.

"Look, this is none of your business," she replied. "I'm doing some research here and would appreciate it if you'd just leave me alone. You don't seem to get it, but we're about to get slammed by Mother Nature and there's no time for any bullshit. The last thing I need is a couple of tourists screwing up my plans."

Mateo realized she was right in reminding them they had better start heading to their car. At the same time, he was curious about her so-called "research" and why she was so compelled to delay her own evacuation to finish what she was doing. He motioned to Violet that they should head back up the hill toward the exit, and she nodded in comprehension.

"Sorry, miss. We didn't mean to intrude," was the best he could offer as he took his daughter's hand to lead her away.

In a mild gesture of defiance, Violet snapped a rushed photograph of the woman, who appeared to be sketching something into her chunky wire-bound notebook. Just then, an unexpected rustling behind them forced Mateo to turn to the area behind the ill-tempered woman. The creature, entrapped beneath the thick plastic covering, managed to free itself from its dark prison. A large peacock suddenly burst forth and frantically scurried away. Violet instinctively knew it was the one she sought.

"Damn it!" exclaimed the self-proclaimed "researcher."

Violet ran in pursuit of the frightened creature, which had quickly dashed up the path before stopping in front of the dolphin habitat. Hunkered down amidst a cluster of flowering plants bordering the exhibit, the flustered bird attempted to catch its breath. The woman stood up, but stayed planted where she was, entering more notes. It seemed odd to Mateo that she no longer appeared interested in the peacock she had obviously ensnared.

Mateo jogged toward Violet and was impressed at the gentle manner in which she approached the peacock; instinctively silent and non-threatening in her movements. Her peaceful demeanor and genuine respect for all living things served her well whenever it came to interactions with animals.

Violet knelt a few feet from the trembling creature and spoke in hushed tones while examining it more closely. To her delight, she had finally found the bird she read about online. Brilliant flecks of iridescent gold on the tip of one of its tail feathers provided the only clue she needed.

Violet leaned in close to take a few snapshots as the Sun briefly emerged from behind the thickening cloud cover, as if on cue. When she cautiously reached down to stroke the bird's back, she was pleasantly surprised at its tolerance. Once she felt the bird was sufficiently relaxed, she carefully lifted the end of the unique tail feather to examine it more closely.

Delicate gold trails were intertwined in a strikingly unnatural design and the eye's rich purple was a color she had never before seen in Nature. The iridescence of the feather was in keeping with the typical coloring found on peacocks, but the bizarre pattern and gold filaments were nothing short of miraculous. As beams of sunlight danced across the area, Violet gingerly turned the long, fragile plume over with her left hand. What she saw caused her heart to skip a half-measure. Just as the article had described, the amazing creature possessed features even more unimaginable.

Upon close inspection, delicate threads of brilliant gold composed a complex interwoven pattern. The base color of copper gradually transitioned into violet around the edges. By tilting the feather just right, the Sun revealed the most remarkable details. It was just as the blog post described. The tip of the feather bore discernible shapes in gold – a solid disk, a tapered triangle, and a shape that resembled a five-pointed star.

Violet gently stroked and separated the tiny feathers with her thumb while her four fingers supported the tip of the plume. She was in awe of its spectacular beauty. With her mouth still hanging open in amazement, she attempted to take some close-up photographs.

It was then that the first bolt of lightning struck.

△△△

I Miss Your Purple Hair

CHAPTER SIX

Last Time I Talked to You

"All things appear and disappear because of the concurrence of causes and conditions.
Nothing ever exists entirely alone; everything is in relation to everything else."
~ Buddha

The deafening crack of thunder and enormous bolt of lightning occurred in unison. Delivered with diabolical intent, the javelin of supercharged energy struck a large transformer in the zoo's northeastern quadrant with terrific force. The impact tore the metal-encased unit from its mounting brackets and sent it hurtling fifty yards through the air. The projectile struck the stone wall in front of the African Lion enclosure, obliterating a huge chunk and spraying debris skyward.

Only a handful of zoo visitors remained, and the bolt's impact motivated those exiting the park to scurry even more quickly to their vehicles. A large tour bus had just finished loading its last passenger, an elderly Mexican woman, when the bolt annihilated the transformer. After a tour guide helped secure her in her seat, she peered uneasily out the rain-spotted window, relieved to be out of harm's way. The strike resulted in loss of electrical power on that side of the zoo, and the few straggling visitors in the area frantically ran for the exits.

Violet, Mateo, and their as-yet unnamed adversary all froze in their tracks when the bolt struck. The peacock flew from Violet's side in a panic, and she gave chase without hesitation, leaving her camera on the pavement. Mateo hurried over and picked it up, shaking his head at his daughter's impetuousness. He was poised to pursue her when another distraction commanded his attention.

The red-haired woman called out in a surprisingly agitated tone. "Hey mister! Can you give me a hand here?" she pleaded.

Although he hardly knew her, he sized her up as a rather crusty character who would only ask for assistance as a last resort. Reluctantly, Mateo ignored his initial instinct to chase after Violet and turned to approach the woman instead. Her face was frozen in an expression of genuine fear, leading Mateo to ask, "What is it?" as his pulse quickened. At first she failed to respond, her eyes fixed on a thick patch of ornamental shrubbery adjacent to the tarpaulin recently used to ensnare the peacock.

He asked again, "What is it? What's wrong?" Cold drops of rain began to dot his exposed flesh as he strained to see the cause of the concern reflected on her freckled face.

She finally whispered, "Did you hear it?"

"Hear what?" he asked incredulously, but received no response. Violet came to mind, and he decided he would leave immediately unless the woman provided an adequate answer. "All I hear is wind blowing through the trees and the falling rain. Is there something else?" Sensing his impatience, the woman shifted her attention from the bushes to Mateo.

"We have to move... now. No more screwing around. Take this!" She thrust her canvas bag toward him while wrestling with reattaching her camera's lens cap. He reluctantly grabbed the object to appease her, but his attention was elsewhere. Without another word, she brushed past him and hustled toward the top of the hill and the bleachers. "Keep your voice down," she insisted as she increased her pace, with Mateo in close pursuit.

He noticed that she repeatedly looked over her shoulder without slowing one iota. When they arrived at the clearing atop the hill, they stepped into an area devoid of people. The Public Address warning calmly, but loudly urged all visitors to leave the facility. While the ongoing lightning and mounting rainfall helped hasten the mass evacuation, Mateo suspected stragglers were still making their way toward the exits.

But... where was Violet?

He looked over at the dolphin exhibit and then toward the path to the north, but she was nowhere in sight. He called her name, but there was no reply. It had been very warm, but as the rain picked up in intensity, the temperature dropped precipitously. A very anxious Mateo felt increasingly compelled to collect his daughter and return to their safe, dry home.

"Violet!" he yelled loudly, but still there was no response. He quickly speed-dialed her cell number but heard only an annoying hiss. Concerned, Mateo speculated as to his daughter's whereabouts. He thought, *'She must have followed that damn peacock somewhere.'*

The woman accompanying him joined Mateo in calling out Violet's name while they followed the branching path, gradually getting closer to the zoo's Entrance/Exit. "Look, miss... " he said, "You head for the gates and if you see my daughter along the way, tell her to stand underneath the shelter at the first exit gate, alright? I'll head up the other trail to see if she followed the bird in that direction."

The lithe woman dryly responded, "My name's Rebecca, but I go by 'Sinnamon.' If I come across her, I'll tell her to stick where you said, but don't you have cell phones?" Mateo realized he should have thought to do that immediately and he speed-dialed Violet as the rain-soaked redhead jogged away.

No answer.

As worrisome thoughts swirled within his mind, another incredibly loud explosion of thunder shook the ground in unison with a flash of blinding light. The deafening clap caused Mateo to assume the bolt must have struck close by and he instantly worried for Violet. He pulled his damp baseball cap down over his eyes a bit further and forced himself to move in the direction of the Reptile House. Along the way, he kept calling out to Violet and hitting his phone's redial button.

The wind intensified by the minute, and now the storm was upon them in full force. Still no answer on the cell phone. The thunder rolled in, while lightning flashed repeatedly across the darkened sky. The clouds had become so thick, much of the light had been appreciably blocked out, making it seem much later than it actually was. Time held little relevance for Mateo as his concern grew. "Damn it!" he shouted. "Where are you?"

Violet pursued the peacock up the trail, past the Reptile House, and just beyond the next habitat – the Galapagos Tortoise exhibit. The frightened bird had flown over the fence and taken shelter inside a simple wooden structure provided for the tortoises. Satisfied her quarry had found effective protection from the storm; she turned to head back to reunite with her father.

At that very moment, the first major tremors struck out at sea.

A magnitude 9.6 earthquake is an epic anomaly, virtually incomprehensible to most. A chain reaction of moderate-strength undersea tremors combined to create an expansive fissure. The cavernous wound in the ocean's floor then released an unbridled surge of magma-heated energy that instigated the birth of a gargantuan tsunami. As if orchestrated by Mephistopheles himself, the towering wall of water compromised the stability of critical seismic plates along the coast of Southern California, long ago made vulnerable to just such an event. The resulting cataclysm was destined to become a destructive force of Biblical proportions. At this point, the sequential events were just beginning to develop hundreds of miles from the coast; all while a worried father focused on nothing but locating his daughter.

I Miss Your Purple Hair

As Mateo approached the Reptile House, he detected a child's voice calling out from within. Although difficult to make out the words, he could tell someone was in distress. His feet seemed to lead him toward the sounds coming from inside, although he was wholeheartedly intent on reuniting with his daughter. The sturdy concrete building was being bombarded by thickening raindrops falling through the towering trees.

A young voice pleaded, "Can someone help me? Is anyone out there?"

Upon pushing one of the two heavy doors open, Mateo discovered a teenage girl sitting on the floor, curled up in the far corner. Wearing light-blue denim shorts and an orange T-shirt, she clutched her bent left knee. She had obviously been crying. "What happened?" Mateo gently asked.

The teary-eyed girl replied, "I slipped because my sneakers are wet... and hurt my knee when I fell. It really hurts and I'm not sure I can walk." She was clearly no more than thirteen years old with light-brown skin and light brown-blonde hair. She looked to be part African-American, but her somewhat unique appearance led Mateo to surmise she was of biracial origin. Most striking of her exotic features were her haunting, honey-colored eyes.

Mateo knelt next to her and conducted a cursory exam of her knee as she wiped tears from her eyes. "Looks like a bad bruise, is all," he offered sympathetically.

She looked up at him and nodded, adding, "My sister went to find our grandfather. Did you see her?"

Mateo replied, "Well, I'm not sure. What does she look like?"

Beginning to compose herself, the teenager said, "She looks almost exactly like me and probably ran right past you when you came into the building. I don't know where my grandpa is, but we were heading to meet him when the alarms went off. I hope she found him right away, so we can go home."

Mateo was impressed with the girl's maturity. She had quickly transformed from a weeping, frightened child to a resolute, confident young woman as she used his extended hand to pull herself to her feet. She calmly stated, "My name's Leanna," as Mateo noted how young and fragile she actually was. "My sister's name is Hanna. Can you help me find her? We have to make sure our grandfather's alright... and get away from here before it's too late."

Surprised by her ominous tone, Mateo felt heightened urgency to locate Violet and get out of the zoo before the storm came through full-force. He brushed a tiny bit of dust off the back of her denim jacket and offered his left elbow. She shook her head to indicate she felt capable of walking without assistance. "It's hardly even sore anymore," she declared, as she limped ever so slightly through the glass and metal doors.

Following closely behind, Mateo assessed her at about 5' 4" tall and perhaps just slightly over 110 pounds. She carried herself somewhat larger, and conveyed a maturity greater than that of a typical teenager. The resoluteness in her eyes was strikingly reminiscent of the look his daughter often displayed. He knew better than to get in the way and instead followed dutifully behind, looking ahead over her shoulder to take stock of the situation.

The Reptile House, recently renovated and solidly constructed, had shielded them from the sights and sounds outside. They emerged to find that the storm had rapidly intensified, its driving rain now coming down with more ferocity. Trees arched their trunks in reaction to the barrage of wind and water. With visibility diminished, it was difficult to see through the chaotic swirl of water and debris. They huddled for a moment beneath a nearby palm tree and Mateo pulled some wadded up plastic from the pocket of his denim jacket. He opened up a clear plastic raincoat he had stuffed inside the pocket that morning, upon hearing the forecast for afternoon rain showers. He handed it to Leanna and she quickly draped the poncho-style covering over her head.

"I know where she is," the young girl then stated with conviction.

"Your sister?" Mateo yelled over the storm.

"No... your daughter!" she shouted back.

Although he had not recalled mentioning his daughter, Mateo decided he must have forgotten. Mateo wanted to locate Violet and make sure the two of them got to their car ahead of what was shaping up to be a nasty storm. He asked, "Where? Where is she?"

Leanna observed the raindrops violently impacting the steaming asphalt walkway before shifting her attention to him once more. "I have an idea. She's with my sister... but they're headed in the wrong direction. It's as if they're chasing someone. If we go after them now, we can catch up, but we shouldn't wait."

Mateo was confused, yet recognized the conviction in her voice. He felt she must have been relying upon intuition and her intimate connection with her sister to identify their general whereabouts. How she knew Violet had joined her sister was what had him perplexed, but there was no time to speculate. He remembered what Leanna had said about the sisters trying to locate their grandfather. Mateo touched her wet shoulder and yelled over the storm, "What about your grandfather? Do you have any idea where he is?"

I Miss Your Purple Hair

Concern and confusion reflected in Leanna's amber eyes as she responded. "Grandpa's worried… but he's safe. He said we should hurry to meet him at the entrance, but didn't know we would be separated. We have to find Hanna first, before we go to him!"

Mateo felt a ripple of energy emanating from the unusual girl – so startling that he abruptly removed his hand from her shoulder – as though it were electrified. He sensed she was somehow able to actually "know" the locations of her family members; that she was employing some sort of remote viewing ability, so definitive were her contentions.

He felt it was time to take action, and the questions brewing in his mind would have to wait. He pointed to the inclined path to the west and told his companion that's where they would find Violet and Hanna. Leanna concurred, and as they began walking, they were impressed by the quantity of debris strewn across the asphalt. Leaves of all types and sizes littered the walkway, carried by the intensifying wind gusts. The warning siren wailed and security lights automatically switched on, triggered by the alarm system.

Mateo was impressed by how efficiently this section of the zoo had been evacuated. One teenage boy, wearing a fearful expression, sprinted past them at full speed as he headed for the exit. Soaking wet, his red hooded sweatshirt flapped wildly as he ran – so fast, he appeared airborne. They pressed on, jogging stride for stride despite Leanna's considerably shorter legs. She wore an expression of determination as she scanned the area ahead of them. When she abruptly stopped, Mateo followed suit and then looked to her for an explanation.

"She's *that* way," she yelled out, and pointed down a branching path that led toward the westernmost corner of that region. Without so much as another word, they took off, winding their way along the black metal fence protecting the Galapagos Tortoise habitat. They had to step over a large tree limb that had fallen across the path and come to rest on a section of fence. A female zoo employee struggled to remove the obstruction.

Their unexpected arrival startled the young woman clad in a dark blue raincoat and official zoo employee cap. She sternly yelled, "People, you have to leave… now! The zoo is closing and this area isn't safe!" They stopped long enough for Mateo to explain they were going to fetch the two girls and then immediately depart.

Satisfied with his explanation and determined to finish her task, she went back to removing the obstruction and exclaimed, "You have to move fast! This storm is worse than predicted and you absolutely must vacate. If you see any others, please urge them to leave immediately!"

Mateo and Leanna ran along the fence, heading west toward the far side of the tortoise exhibit. As they shielded their eyes from the driving rain, they detected loud conversation just beyond their position. Mateo was relieved to identify Violet's voice over the noise of the storm. Leanna ran ahead, calling out to her sister. She yelled, "Hanna! Hanna!", as she stumbled past the end of the fence before ducking into a secluded recess just beyond the exhibit.

Mateo was not completely sure where she had vanished, but then spotted her orange shirt and saw her run to embrace her sister. Violet crouched behind the two sisters, attending to something that had captured her attention. As Mateo ran up to the three teenage girls, he could feel the energy they exuded. There seemed to be a very palpable power emanating from the group, almost as if their very proximity to one another created a tangible "happy energy." Hanna and Leanna stood next to one another, and Mateo witnessed how eerily identical they looked, right down to the way they held their hands on their hips.

Hanna was slightly heavier than her slender sister – a bit thicker about the waist. He could tell that her amber-blonde hair, though wet from the rain, was not quite as straight as Leanna's. The strands were more tightly wound and she wore it up, while Leanna's hung at shoulder length. The sisters possessed identical coloring of skin, hair, and eyes. Their facial features were so eerily similar; it was understandable that many mistook them for twins. They stood side by side and watched Violet fuss with something on the pavement.

Mateo moved closer to find Violet holding down a large, overturned black plastic tub. "Honey...what's going on? We've got to get out of here... now!" he forcefully stated to his rain-drenched daughter.

At first, Violet did not respond or even look up. She was completely focused on the large plastic basin, holding it down under the weight of her body. She finally replied. "Papa, that woman with the red hair tried to hurt the peacock! I had to get a security guard to chase her out of here."

Mateo asked, "What happened? What did she do?"

Violet had to fight through tears to inform him, "She cut off his tail feather with her scissors! It was too late when I finally caught up to her. She was already doing it! She had him trapped in a net and just cut off the feather. I yelled loud enough to get the guard to come over, and she went running back the way we came." Mateo was concerned at how upset she seemed, but was also painfully aware of the storm's growing intensity.

I Miss Your Purple Hair

Kyle Nordstrom had just finished hastily washing his hands in the bathroom when the power in the building went out. He was temporarily frozen in place, stunned by the sudden darkness. Once he blinked a few times to adjust his eyes, he was able to make out some vague shapes and locate his leather case near the sinks. No sooner had he grabbed the handle of his leather laptop bag than he heard a panicked voice from the darkest recesses of the room. It obviously belonged to a child, sobbing and calling out at the same time.

"Momma! Momma!" the panicked young voice cried out.

Kyle cleared his throat and responded, "Don't be afraid. I'll help you – just give me a minute." Thinking quickly, he reached into his pants' pocket, took out his blue iPod®, and tapped the control wheel to bring it to life. As dark as it was, the illuminated screen made a dramatic impact. Using the device as a makeshift flashlight, he cautiously made his way back to the last stall to find a little boy, apparently no more than seven or eight years old, holding onto the open door and crying. "It's okay," he gently offered, "I can help you get outside and we'll find your mother. Is she waiting for you nearby?"

At first, the child seemed unable to stop weeping and shaking, but finally muttered, "I don't like the dark... and I hate thunder even more!" Kyle felt a twinge of sympathy as he grabbed the child's hand. Mildly resistant at first, the boy was instinctively reluctant to trust a stranger. However, his fear of darkness trumped his uneasiness and he willingly allowed Kyle to lead him toward the exit, where they were greeted by the sounds of howling wind and driving rain.

The child, a somewhat chubby Indian boy with unkempt black hair, still had a trickle of tears running down his cheeks as Kyle helped pull the hood of his dark blue windbreaker over his head. Kyle asked, "Do you know where your parents are? I can help you catch up with them if you have some idea where they are."

The boy hesitated before stuttering, "Th... th... they left me here."

"What do you mean? Who left you?" the young psychologist inquired, slightly perturbed. "You must have family or friends here with you! Where are they now?"

The child mumbled, "I came on a long bus with the whole class from the church. I ran here when the thunder started..."

Kyle sympathized, having been deathly afraid of thunder and lightning himself as a young child. "I know how you feel, but we have to go out there now and find the rest of your group. Do you know where they might be?" Just then, a horrendously loud explosion of thunder jolted the area, forcing both boy and man to wince and instinctively duck their heads.

Kyle still hated thunder and despite his best efforts to reason with himself, felt nearly as afraid as he had during his childhood in Massachusetts. Some things are impossible to purge from one's psyche, regardless of time and training. The little boy covered his ears with his hands and stood frozen in place. The way the rain peppered the roof of the building, Kyle realized the storm was not going to let up soon, and his sense of urgency propelled him to action.

He rather forcefully announced, "We're getting out of here... now! I promise to protect you and help find your group. Just try to be brave and we'll find them in no time, okay?" The child failed to respond; he just stood there covering his ears and sobbing quietly. Kyle tucked his iPod® back into his shirt pocket, grabbed the boy by the arm, and sidestepped along the interior wall until they reached the doorway.

As dark as the sky had become, the subdued light was still a welcome relief. They could finally see again, but were presented with an unsavory scene. More tree limbs had been downed by the storm, leaving the once-pristine walkways littered with organic debris. Trash cans and litter were strewn everywhere. The place looked nothing like the spotless tourist attraction they had enjoyed mere minutes earlier.

Dark grey clouds swiftly moved in from the west with menacing purpose. The sounds of the wind, rain and swaying trees were nearly deafening. Kyle briskly escorted his young charge across the pavement, back toward the Zoo Entrance. The two thunder-loathing companions were drenched before they had even covered twenty yards. Kyle said a silent prayer as they sprinted toward what he felt would surely be a safe, dry sanctuary back at the entrance. There was no way he could know what was happening out at sea, just a few hundred miles from their location.

The chartered fishing vessel, *Nordic Knight*, had changed course an hour earlier, desperately chugging eastward toward its home port of Long Beach. The white-haired captain, Jon Hilgenberg, had ignored the protests of his wife, Amanda. Despite her concerns about the impending storm, he stubbornly insisted upon baptizing his pride and joy's newly repaired hull. He had calculated there was adequate time to make one circuit of his standard route. His radio had been broadcasting regular updates all afternoon, and he finally decided he was pressing his luck. Once the sky went black, he reluctantly turned the vessel and headed back to port.

Jon's long-time business partner, Rex Highsmith, had come along despite his concerns about the forecast. A slightly-built 65-year-old grandfather, Rex was Jon's elder by six years. Jon, the considerably larger man, was at the helm, while Rex clutched the rail at the opposite end of the small cabin. Rex had experienced dozens of momentous storms as a commercial fisherman in the Puget Sound region. He had survived combat during the Vietnam War, a gruesome motorcycle accident in which he shattered both legs, and a tiger shark attack while surfing in Australia. Nothing much rattled him. As Jon once commented, "How ya gonna scare a man who's spit in The Reaper's face?"

On this day, however, Rex Highsmith would become formally reacquainted with fear. The choppy waves had steadily intensified during the past 45 minutes or so and the onboard radar indicated that many other vessels had long since returned to their respective bases along the coast. The two old friends were desperate to reach safe harbor, feeling isolated and vulnerable in their storm-tossed sanctuary. The anguished sea arched its frigid back and ferociously gouged its saltwater claws into the hull of the *Nordic Knight*.

Rex looked out the skylight and grimaced, rasping in awe, "Lord Almighty... 'never seen a sky like that, Jon... never. It's gone black... blacker'n pitch. Take a look now, you gotta see what I'm seein'!"

Captain Jon turned ghostly white in reaction to the panic in his trusted friend's voice. He steadied the wheel and turned his gaze skyward to see what had so impressed his partner. Indeed, the thick clouds had assembled with alarming swiftness, now totally blocking any hint of sunlight. The time of day was 2:33 p.m., but it might as well have been midnight.

The radio had strangely gone silent while the ship was violently rocked by the gale force winds. Jon said a silent prayer while his eyes remained fixed on the black sky. A violent blast of wind slammed the boat with tremendous force, spinning it sideways to render it precariously vulnerable to the savagery of the sea. The brutal force knocked both men to the deck where they scrambled to regain their bearings. The situation had transformed quickly. Only a half hour earlier, the Sun was playfully peeking through gaps in the wisp like cloud formations while the old friends savored thick roast beef sandwiches and ice-cold beers.

Jon Hilgenberg had sailed far too long to fail to recognize what was happening deep below his precious craft in the frigid depths of the Pacific.

He struggled to his feet after extracting two more beer cans from the cooler against which his head had just crashed. After tossing one to Rex, he popped his open and solemnly remarked, "Here's to our loved ones. May God spare 'em all."

Moments later, a saltwater sledgehammer split the *Nordic Knight* in two, and the boiling tempest claimed its first two souls.

A tsunami is a phenomenon of nature, diabolical and awe-inspiring in its power and purposefulness. The magnitude of the underwater earthquake triggering this particular event surpassed all predictions, but no one could have known the worst conceivable chain of events had been set in motion. The earlier undersea tremors were not particularly destructive in and of themselves, but their timing and location produced tragic consequences.

The first series of tremors were not responsible for creating the tsunami. It was spawned by the much greater undersea quake they instigated. The ripe conditions were born of a previously undetected fissure in a large seismic plate under that region of the Pacific. When the seemingly "minor" tremors rolled together in a rapid-fire succession, they triggered a degradation that produced an enormous crack in the plate.

The Tectonic plate had become critically vulnerable to the pressures from above and below, and it shattered like porcelain. As if following a plan of evil design, there had been a steady build-up of magma in that same critical location, in the Earth's crust just beneath the plates. Immense pressure had been building for years in that location and when the opportunity presented itself, Nature discovered a convenient place to seek relief.

On the mainland, disturbing news poured in from numerous sources across the globe. As all of this was unfolding along the West Coast of the U.S., similar events were transpiring across the world. In Asia, a magnitude 9.8 earthquake was about to disfigure the landscape and forever alter the lives of billions. The epicenter originated beneath Dushanbe, the capital city of Tajikistan, and was situated in the most unfortunate location imaginable. The devastating shock waves ultimately triggered a web-like pattern of seismic events across the Asian continent... and beyond.

△ △ △

I Miss Your Purple Hair

CHAPTER SEVEN
Waiting for This Sky to Fall

*"New pictures are gradually emerging of a reality which might be synchronous,
or a constantly shifting holographic mosaic. The phenomenal world could be
more like a vast thought field, which changes depending on how we look at it.
Reality has been elevated from that of a fixed and static noun to a fluid, living verb."*
~ Yatri, Unknown Man

Violet was aware of her father's concern and tried to reassure him she had regained her composure. The rain, violently ricocheting off the black plastic basin, stung the delicate skin on the back of her slender neck. Her concern for the peacock had been so consuming she had not noticed how the storm had worsened. "Papa, you're soaking wet!" she blurted out, finally reacquainted with reality. "I guess we have to let the bird go. We can't leave him trapped in here."

Mateo agreed and helped her lift one end of the makeshift trap to release the peacock. The frightened bird bolted for the shelter of the nearby forest. In an instant, it had disappeared from sight. Mateo helped Violet to her feet and they jogged back toward the exit.

Directly behind them, Leanna and Hanna kept pace with the father-daughter tandem. The growing ferocity of the storm meant there was precious little time to waste. Mateo searched his memory to try to recall where he had parked. He longed for the sanctuary of his car's warm, dry interior. There was no way he could know the vehicle he had only recently bought was about to be obliterated.

The foursome ran toward the exit and spotted a shadowy figure heading in the same general direction about thirty feet ahead of them. They could discern the shape of an adult male, wearing a dark-colored jacket. It was nearly impossible to differentiate colors in the monochromatic gloom created by the windstorm.

Running ahead of them was zoo security officer, Dante Macchiaroli, better known as "D-Mac" to close friends and family. He had just finished helping his colleague remove broken timber from the walkway when he reacted to a disturbance heard over the raging winds. His fellow security guard, Marisol Gutierrez, had already run off to scour the northeast quadrant for stragglers. Indiscernible gibberish crackled from her walkie-talkie as she

I Miss Your Purple Hair

jogged away from Dante. No sooner had she disappeared into the maelstrom than he heard a startling explosion from the southeast. Another bolt of lightning had apparently struck something within the zoo grounds, and the ensuing crashing sounds demanded Dante's full attention.

Mia Nordstrom had been nervously pacing beneath the protective overhang at the Zoo Entrance, gazing out at the rain and hoping her brother would arrive at any moment. She clutched her canvas tote bag to her chest and muttered, "Come on, come on…. where the hell are you?" She used to tease her brother mercilessly, growing up in a middle-class neighborhood on the outskirts of Boston. In recent years, however, their relationship had matured into one of mutual respect and sincere affection.

Fortunately, zoo personnel had already evacuated all passengers aboard the *Skyfari®* aerial tram well before the supercharged energy made its direct hit. The massive bolt struck a pair of the green metal gondolas, ripping them free from the shredded twisted-steel cable from which they had dangled. One gondola crashed directly inside the zoo's main entrance gates, partially demolishing a substantial portion of its protective overhang.

Complicating matters, the thick cables which had suspended it snapped, and like a steel bullwhip, sliced completely through the wood frame of a nearby souvenir booth. Kyle arrived just in time to witness the second of the two heavy gondolas crash onto the roof directly above Mia. His eyes nearly burst from his head in horror as he watched the large metal cab slam Earthward, crushing the section of roof.

The uniquely horrifying sounds of metal twisting and collapsing punctuated the din of steady rain and howling wind. Just a handful of yards behind Kyle, an enormous palm tree shook the very foundation under his feet as it crashed to the pavement. Shocked by the sudden sequence of events, he dropped to one knee in reaction to the resounding impact, but then quickly turned his attention to his sister's perilous situation. He dropped his briefcase to the ground and sprinted over to the site of the cable car crash.

A torrent of electrical sparks spewed from shredded overhead power wires still connected to the cable car's mangled support mechanism. The panic-stricken psychologist frantically pulled debris away from the area where he last saw his sister. Ignoring the fact that he lacerated the heel of his right hand on a sharp metal edge, he desperately tried to free Mia from the cluttered mass. "Mia! Mia! Are you alright? Where are you?!" he yelled through the surging rainstorm.

The faint sound of her voice ignited his adrenaline, and he tore through the heap of twisted metal and wood with renewed vigor. Finally, he knelt in the pooling water and craned his neck to glimpse his sister's arm, which she frantically waved to draw his attention. Trapped beneath a canopy of broken steel and aluminum, she was apparently alert and aware of her predicament.

"Whatever you do, don't touch this thing!" Mia insisted, demonstratively patting the narrow surface of a sturdy-looking steel beam fortuitously wedged in position directly in front of her. Kyle froze in place for a moment, afraid to disturb anything. It appeared Mia had miraculously avoided being crushed by the collapsing rooftop, but was trapped in a confining gap within the tangled debris. Her voice sounded strong and calm, which provided an iota of relief as Kyle strained to examine the dark recess.

Before he could ask, Mia made a declaration. "I'm alright," she stated in a raspy but confident voice, "but it looks like I'll have to crawl out the side. This whole thing's about to collapse but I might be able to squeeze through a small opening behind me, if I can do it without disturbing the support. Just don't touch anything, okay?"

Kyle assured her he would not move until she gave the word, but was incredibly frustrated, unaccustomed to feeling so helpless. The rain continued, while nearby thunder shook the ground with increasing frequency. Time stood still as Kyle rose to survey the severity of the swelling storm. The zoo had been successfully evacuated, as far as he could discern, yet he worried that some stray individuals might have been buried with Mia beneath the demolished building. He glanced at the thick forest to the north, impressed by the strength of the gusting winds as evidenced by the dramatic swaying of the trees. As bold flashes of lightning appeared across all quadrants of the sky, the nightmares of his youth came flooding back.

Kyle recalled being eight years old and cowering in the musty basement of his grandmother's drafty old house in Boston. Since birth, he had a fear of lightning and thunder, and whenever a significant storm came to fruition, he would panic and run to the basement, regardless of where he was. This specific memory involved a game of hide-and-seek with his siblings and cousins on a steamy summer evening...

Kyle discovered what he felt was a perfect hiding place in the musty old basement of the 100 year-old home, and curled up in a dark corner of the small room where his grandparents stored canned goods. When he initially found the little niche beneath the lowest wooden shelf, he had been giddy with excitement. His hiding place was in close proximity to the double doors that opened out into the back yard. They were the old-fashioned wooden cellar doors mounted parallel to the ground. The rain pelted those doors and when the first crack of thunder sounded, Kyle clutched his knees and contracted his body into a tighter little ball on the concrete floor.

Kyle's reaction to thunderstorms had always been to cover his ears and shut his eyes. Feeling afraid and anxious when the storm erupted, being alone in the dark confines only exacerbated his emotional meltdown. He began to sob and rocked back and forth where he sat. Strangely, despite his fears he never considered getting up and running from the cocoon of the tiny room. He felt protected in the claustrophobic nook, even though the tears rolling down his cheeks belied that. Time passed, the storm gradually waned and the boy wiped his runny nose with his dirty hand, smearing the dust of years past all over his reddened face.

After Kyle settled down emotionally, he remained locked in the same uncomfortable, curled-up position for what seemed like hours. Even after the obnoxious thunder subsided, there he remained, wondering why no one had yet found him. He had always been a bit quirky – highly intelligent and creative in many ways. At the root of his inventiveness was the double-edged sword of unbridled imagination.

Gloating over his self-proclaimed brilliant choice of hiding places, he criticized his cousins and siblings for being 'too stupid and unimaginative' to find him. He felt they had missed one of the most obvious places to search, in that it was such a perfect hiding place – dark, out of the way and nearly soundproof. He thought to himself, 'Maybe they're worried about me – they should be by now – but if they're that stupid, they deserve to be worried. I'm staying put as long as it takes them to wise up and look down here.'

The glaring flaw in Kyle's thinking was that the adults in the house were not any more imaginative than the kids. For whatever reason, they never searched the basement, even after they began to panic over his disappearance. The children felt they had exhausted every possible hiding place and came running into the first floor of the creaky three-story house, squawking in unison that Kyle had "disappeared!"

The adults frantically quizzed the breathless children and concluded Kyle was indeed missing. They actually began to speculate he might have been kidnapped or had wandered off and gotten lost in the storm. Together, they searched all three floors of the house and then went outside, half of them to the front yard while the others went out back.

From his dark and dusty little alcove, Kyle heard them repeatedly calling out his name from outdoors. "Ky-le, Ky-le!" they called out into the darkness. He heard them, yet refused to reveal himself. Instead, in his childish arrogance he thought, 'Why are they so stupid? They never even opened the doors to the cellar. How dumb are they?'

In his condemnation, mind you, he was referring to the people he loved. In his arrogance, he could not get beyond marveling at their incompetence, unable to accept they might have innocently forgotten to search the basement. For a moment, he wondered if they might have ruled it out, figuring he would have never had the courage to descend those cobweb-laden cement steps to reach the creepy fruit cellar.

'Well, they shouldn't think that,' was what went through his young mind. 'They ought to know I would hide anywhere... to win the game.'

The voices became louder and more panicky, but the collection of adults and children never did open the cellar doors. 'How stupid,' Kyle thought. 'If they're really worried, you'd think they would search everywhere!' He held his ground as long as he could, until he realized he could really find himself in deep trouble if his family went so far as to call the police. By the tone of their voices, he felt the concern had escalated enough.

He finally uncurled himself, brushed a pile of dust and bugs out of his unkempt hair, and stood up in the middle of the tiny, dark room. Following a couple of sneezes, he wiped his nose again, before mustering the courage to reveal himself to the throng of panicked family members.

For reasons he was too young to understand, Kyle was more angry than contrite. As he pushed the heavy cellar door open, he took a quick look around the back yard and saw no one there. Muffled voices seeped from the kitchen, and he could make out silhouettes on the yellowed window shades. When Kyle nonchalantly entered through the side door, everyone just froze. He immediately noticed his tall, bald-headed father, standing at the head of the kitchen table, frantically dialing the phone. His worried mother stood at his side, wringing her hands. Kyle's assembled sisters and cousins, all under the age of twelve, were huddled in the next room, no one making a sound.

Kyle stood in the doorway; like a dingy little statue, his mouth hung open and liquid dripping from his nose. The first to spot him was his father, who immediately dropped the handset back into its cradle. His expression was one of both relief and amazement. "Kyle!" he blurted out. "What... where on Earth have you been?"

I Miss Your Purple Hair

His slight, blonde-haired mother ran to him, dropped to her knees and squeezed all the air out of his lungs. He protested by trying to push her arms away, but she refused to release her vice-like grasp. The other kids finally came running over, most of them looking relieved and curious at the same time. No one said anything at first. Finally, his father made his way across the white-and-black tile floor to wedge himself between Kyle and his mother. In his most authoritative voice, he asked, "What the hell happened to you? Do you have any idea how worried we were?"

Kyle remained motionless and suppressed the urge to reply, "Not worried enough to search the basement." Instead, he kept silent as long as possible before responding. Feeling vastly outnumbered, he offered the politically astute answer, saying, "I didn't know you were so worried. I was just hiding in the basement, waiting to be found. That's all."

His mother knelt down and started wiping his runny nose and washing his filthy face with a damp dishcloth, as Kyle writhed in protest. The other kids stood nearby, still dumbfounded. After a few stern admonishments from his dad, Kyle was excused and told to join the other kids in the front porch for dessert. As the cadre of children shuffled through the living room, Mia elbowed her stubborn brother, whispering so only he could hear, "You're such a jerk. You're just lucky you didn't get your little butt spanked!" Kyle simply brushed his shaggy blonde hair away from his blue eyes and smirked – smugly satisfied he was smarter than everyone else. Mia found her brother very hard to understand at times, but at the same time, found his unconventional attitude entertaining.

The adult version of that arrogant little boy currently faced the most frightening situation he had ever encountered. Desperately worried for his sister, he had no choice but to wait. He finally remembered he had the young nameless boy in tow when they arrived at the site of the disaster. Scouring the area, he spotted the child huddling inside a nearby souvenir stand, temporarily sheltered from the relentless rain. He waved and the frightened boy meekly responded in kind. Reassured that the child was safe, he returned his attention to his sister.

"Mia!" Kyle called out. "Mia! What's happening? Can you see any way out of there? What can I do?"

He was relieved to hear her answer, albeit a somewhat agitated "Chill out, big brother! I'm fine. Just give me a minute, alright?" He actually managed a chuckle and shook his head, dispelling water like a dog. After what seemed an eternity, Mia emerged at the far end of the rubble. She hoisted herself atop a pile of debris and then gingerly walked toward him, arms outstretched to maintain balance. He laughed as much out of admiration for her inimitable pluck, as from profound relief.

Extending a rain-drenched hand to assist her over the last obstacle of twisted metal, he then asked, "Hey, what happened to your hair? Are you hurt?" Mia had initially been trapped beneath hundreds of pounds of debris, her hair pinched between the heavy cable car and an unrecognizable metal object. Ever resourceful, she somehow managed to produce a pair of cuticle scissors from the bottom of her purse and cut off a swath of her hair to gain her freedom.

Although Mia's new hairstyle was decidedly lopsided, she had only suffered minimal bruises and cuts; in particular, one long, shallow slice along her right thigh. Ripped clothes and a radical new haircut were acceptable alternatives to what might have been. While the rain continued to drench the disheveled siblings, they briefly embraced before ducking into the tiny shelter with the young boy.

Mia quickly concluded her wounds were all relatively minor, and she and Kyle focused their attention on the young boy. Despite the surprisingly warm temperature, the child's teeth were chattering as he clung to the wooden frame inside the shelter. Eyes shut tight, he seemed to be fraught with panic over the unfolding events. After Kyle quickly clued Mia in, regarding his interaction with the boy, she knelt and placed her hands on his shoulders.

Mia reassured him he was not alone, despite the unknown whereabouts of his group. In her calmest possible voice, she said, "It's going to be fine. We won't leave your side until we get you back to your friends, okay?" Kyle stood in the open doorway, to shield Mia and the scared child from the driving rain. He admired the fact that, just moments after enduring her harrowing accident, Mia was unselfishly tending to the needs of a complete stranger. Bleeding from lacerations on her forehead and the long cut on her left thigh, she disregarded her discomfort to tend to the child cowering before her.

"Can you tell me your name?" she inquired. The shivering, brown-skinned boy could only blink his eyes a few times before reaching out to grab Mia's arm. She asked for his name again then attempted a few other questions. She asked where his group was supposed to meet, who was with him when he entered the zoo, and what form of transportation they used. No reply. He only clutched her wrist more tightly while staring into her eyes, unable to speak. Mia solicited her brother's informed opinion. Peppered by the relentless rain just inside the doorway, Kyle surmised the boy was understandably disoriented and in a mild state of shock.

Kyle firmly stated, "We have to reunite him with his group as soon as possible and we've got to get out of here too. Let's gather our stuff and take him to the parking lot with us. We're bound to find his people somewhere out there."

Sparks of electricity suddenly erupted from the exposed wires protruding from the nearby rubble. As Mia and Kyle surveyed the surroundings, they realized the situation was worsening. The rain had been coming down in such massive volumes that pools were forming in the lower areas nearby. A stream of rust-colored mud was flowing toward them from the higher elevations, and the once pristine walkway was filled with organic debris and trash from nearby vendor stations.

At one point, Mia clutched the base of her neck with a muddy hand, cast a concerned look at Kyle, and asked, "Can this day get any worse?"
He set his jaw, picked up the rest of his belongings, and said, "We just have to stay calm and get this boy to safety. Everything will be fine as long as we just stay calm and get the hell out of here."

Just then, a woman's scream pierced the steady din of the storm. The siblings' heads snapped around toward the source of the noise – the base of the paved trail to the west. The nameless boy's eyes flew open wide as he and his adult companions watched a man, a woman, and a boy run toward them, along the path. Arms flailing and belongings scattering, the trio ran by, splashing through puddles of muddy water. They finally stopped at the smoldering wreckage of the demolished cable car. None of them even seemed to notice the two fair-haired adults or the dark-complexioned child under the waterlogged San Diego Padres cap.

Instead, their collective gaze focused squarely on the path behind them, as if they anticipated the arrival of some ominous pursuer. That sense was conveyed by their body language and fearful facial expressions. Tense moments passed while six sets of eyes remained fixed on the same spot to the west. The wind drove thick sheets of rain across the mouth of the path, while the dense grove of trees on either side swayed violently. There were, however, no visible signs of anyone or anything that might have pursued the newcomers.

Kyle finally broke the pregnant silence by shouting out, "What is it? What were you running from?" Mia took stock of the obviously terrified group, clearly a family which had been slow to evacuate: a man, approximately 6' 7" in height; a tall, athletic-looking woman; and a boy no more than nine or ten years old. The three dark-skinned people appeared wet and disheveled, but uninjured. Uncomfortable in their soaked and soiled clothing, they huddled in a tight cluster, still apparently anticipating something coming down the inclined path. Kyle tried to get their attention once again, but before he could call out to them, the unmistakable crack of a gunshot rang out.

A solitary dark figure clad in rain gear staggered down the path toward the waterlogged congregation. With his gun held at shoulder level, aiming skyward, the stranger stumbled closer while repeatedly looking over his shoulder. Once he arrived in front of them, he pivoted, dropped to one knee, and trained his pistol in the direction from which he had arrived. Huge raindrops splashed off the barrel of his .38 caliber revolver, but he held it steady in anticipation of some unknown threat.

The six bystanders stood locked in stunned silence, trying to comprehend what was happening. The air temperature had dipped somewhat, but it was still oddly warm for a late December day in San Diego. The blustery wind continued to whip with increasing velocity, depositing leafy branches at their feet. "Everyone... stay calm!" the zoo employee loudly barked. "No reason to panic; I have this under control. Please move toward the exit!"

Dante Macchiaroli had never before drawn his weapon during three years with zoo security. On this momentous day, however, he had just fired a live round at someone or something, an action he did not take lightly. His steady hands, both of which supported the pistol, belied his racing heart. As rainwater splashed into his eyes, he took a deep breath and prepared his mind for the inevitable. His inner voice calmly repeated, *'Stay cool. You've been trained for this and you know the procedure. Stay cool... and be ready.'*

The tall man hovering close to his wife and son broke the tension, asking, "Wasn't it behind us? Do you see it coming this way?"

Dante responded quickly by yelling out, "Don't worry! We're probably safe now, but let's not take any chances! Start making your way to the exit... please!"

Those words barely spoken, a mysterious figure appeared at the far end of the trail from which Dante had emerged. A man of average build stumbled headlong in fear-induced panic. In his desperation, he dropped his brown briefcase into a puddle and never even considered going back to retrieve it. Dante lowered his weapon to his side as soon as he recognized it was just another straggler making a mad dash for sanctuary.

He stood to engage the winded newcomer, very anxiously asking, "Did it follow you? Where is it?"

The sandy-haired, stocky fellow doubled over and struggled to catch his breath after his arduous sprint. He slid a few strands of wet hair away from his rain-spattered round-rimmed eyeglasses and gasped, "I'm not sure! You shot it, right? I thought you shot it!"

The tightly wound security guard, his steely eyes still trained on that same path, furrowed his brow and answered, "No. I fired one over its head to frighten it, but it took off and I didn't see where it went next! Where did *you* come from? I never saw you back there. I hope you didn't think I was shooting at you!" The rather tense middle-aged man, sporting a powder-blue necktie, grey dress shirt, and black slacks, peered over his blue-tinted prescription sunglasses and glared angrily into Dante's eyes. His pasty white skin was as much reddened from the strain of running down the path as by his angry reaction.

"You should have killed it when you had the chance! You only succeeded in chasing it into the forest, and now that thing is still on the loose. It could be anywhere now. There are still more people out here and it's your job to protect them. Maybe you ought to give *me* the gun!"

The irritated man's gravelly voice became increasingly strained. "What the hell happened to the other security guards, anyway? Other than you, I only saw *one* since those damn warning sirens started going off. Why don't you radio them and tell them about your blunder so they can hunt that thing down?"

Mia could no longer hold her tongue, frustrated by the accident she had narrowly survived, the relentless storm and now the presumptuous stump of a man berating one of the zoo's security guards. "Hey!" she yelled sternly, "Take it easy, mister! This isn't the time for pettiness. In case you hadn't noticed, the damn sky has opened up and if we don't move our asses now, we'd better start building ourselves an ark!" Turning to Dante, she asked, "So, what was it that made you fire your gun?"

The chestnut-haired security officer glanced over at the young boy standing with his parents and then shot a quick look over to the frightened child cowering in the nearby building before replying. "Uh... it appeared to be a large wolf – one of our mature males – no more than ten yards from these people when I spotted it. I had to do *something*, so I fired a warning shot to scare it off." Then, gesturing with his head toward the man in the necktie he added, "I swear I never saw any sign of this guy up there! Everything's just happening too damn fast right now!"

The tall, dark-skinned man pulled himself away from his family and eased over toward the two men locked in a stare-down. Not only was he nearly a foot taller than either of the other two, he was striking looking with his trimmed beard, clean-shaven head and dark brown eyes. With a sense of gravity, he asked, "You sayin' we've got wild animals runnin' loose around here, on top of havin' to deal with this storm?"

An enormous bolt of jagged lightning suddenly flashed to the northwest, causing all eight of them to flinch. The very ground beneath their feet shuddered as the terrific crash of thunder punctuated the moment. "There might be more people in that area," Dante announced matter-of-factly to no one in particular, "and I've gotta go get them."

He pulled a blue walkie-talkie from the holster on his hip and spoke very loudly into it. "Rover Three to Rover One... Rover Three to Rover One... please respond! Over." At first, there was no discernible response. He shook the handset vigorously, to shed a surprising amount of water. Before he could utter another word, a female voice crackled through the receiver.

"Rover One to Rover Three, I read you. Hands full here at the moment... evacuation in progress... Over." Dante could barely hear her voice over the rain, the flowing tributary of muddy water and the wind whipping through trees. He shook accumulated water from the handset once again and attempted to communicate with his colleague. "Rover One, what is your current location? Over."

The reply was scrambled, most likely due to the intense electrical activity in the area. "This is Rover One... black bears... require medical kit... repeat, require first aid... (garbled words)... Rover Six en route to my location... (interference) ... will update status..."

"Arghh!" Dante grumbled, "This is not happening! None of the other channels are working. How can we be expected ...""

His rant was cut short by the agitated voice of the well-dressed man with the sandy-brown hair. "Aw, what are we doing, standing here like damn fools? If you want to go back looking for people who may or may not still be there, go right ahead. As for the rest of us, it's obvious we've got to get out of this place immediately!"

Unprecedented in scale, the sheer magnitude of the earthquake born that very moment cannot easily be put into proper historical perspective. The very term "earthquake" is somehow woefully inadequate. The series of undersea seismic eruptions triggered the towering tsunamis, which bore down upon much of the California coast. The quake's preliminary build-up was caused by violent ripples of energy deep below the surface of the land, a series of devastating tremors that dislodged critical Tectonic Plates.

Wave after destructive wave shook the sea floor and fractured what lay beneath the surface, creating a whip-like destructive force. The first tsunamis erased enormous segments of coastline in mere minutes. In a synchronous, worst-case cataclysm, the waves triggered a chain of tremors that ultimately generated the most destructive earthquake in recorded history. In many locations spanning the world, the seas churned violently, creating enormous whirlpools.

A minor fissure that had existed for centuries along the sea bottom just west of San Diego was transformed into a major undersea chasm. In turn, it transformed into a gargantuan divide that drew in water at a rate of millions of gallons per second. Resulting from these associated events, hundreds of earthquakes began transfiguring every continent.

The planet came undone as if peeled like an orange, leaving doubt the fractured Earth would ultimately survive.

△ △ △

CHAPTER EIGHT

You're Falling Out of Reach

"If the Earth does grow inhospitable toward human presence, it is primarily
because we have lost our sense of courtesy toward the Earth and its inhabitants."
~ Thomas Berry

Her trademark crimson hair was soaked to the roots. Rebecca "Sinnamon" Sinclair splashed her way through a minefield of puddles as she backtracked through the dense Ituri Forest. Along the way, she was forced to dodge falling leaves and branches. Only several minutes earlier, she had passed through the turnstiles and nearly reached her car in the main parking lot when she agonizingly realized she had dropped her small black leather case at some point prior to locating the peacock. Inside the case were three memory cards filled with precious images. A freelance photographer and part-time *paparazza*, she supplemented her income by scouring the Internet for leads on potentially profitable subjects.

In the past year, she had more than tripled her income by peddling some of her remarkable photos. The most valuable included celebrities, some of whom she had befriended to betray. She had acquired most of the other images via less reprehensible means. Sinnamon was adept at acquiring hard-to-get images of rare objects, unusual animals, or natural phenomena, often taken from unique or high-risk vantage points. In an effort to obscure her identity, she insisted on being credited only as ©*I Am Not Here Photography*.

Independent of one another, Violet and Sinnamon had learned of the peacock acquired from The National Aviary by stumbling upon the same online article on the same day. Both had felt compelled to find the bird as quickly as possible. One, a young girl with genuine passion for all creatures, great and small, wanted only to satiate her curiosity. The other, a jaded 27-year-old, felt no remorse whatsoever when she used the small surgical scissors hidden in her pocket to cut off the peacock's miraculous tail feather. Her only motive was financial profit, and the memory cards inside her missing case contained potentially valuable images of the bird, taken prior to the impromptu surgery.

Heavy raindrops assaulted Sinnamon as she nimbly navigated the dense forest. She had already retraced her steps and decided the bag must have been left where she crouched to take close-ups of some unusual plant life ringing the base of one of the trees. Sinnamon had reentered the forest just moments before the lightning bolt hit the *Skyfari®*. The bolt struck in close proximity and with such concussive force that she temporarily lost much of her hearing. Once recovered, she spotted her case resting against the gnarled trunk of a mature banana tree. Shielded by thick foliage, the case was barely damp despite the volume of water unleashed by the clouds. The opportunistic woman quickly snatched up her property and arched her back to stretch out tense muscles.

A shrill chorus from the treetops drew her attention to an agitated cluster of small monkeys. They were frantically migrating in a southbound direction, screeching as they leapt from branch to branch. As the racket built to an unnerving crescendo, she deftly readied her camera to document the manic display. The troublesome raindrops dotting her lens added another element of reality to the images. She assumed that the cacophonous gang of irritated guenons and swamp monkeys were following their primal instinct to seek refuge from the burgeoning storm.

Sinnamon put the camera away and turned back, anxious to return to the shelter of her cozy apartment. Though wet and exhausted, she had acquired what she came for: the peacock's tail feather and a collection of images to sell. The feather she had stashed inside a clear plastic bag intrigued her, but she had not yet had time to inspect it. As she backtracked to the Entrance, she figured there would be plenty of time for that once she was home.

Approaching the area just east of the tiger habitat, she was surprised to encounter a stocky man in a yellow raincoat. She thought it peculiar that he was walking toward her rather than evacuating. It was apparent he was not a member of the zoo's staff and she braced for a confrontation when he intercepted her.

"Hey!" he yelled out, "Are there any other people up that way?"

Sinnamon tugged at the brim of her visor before answering dryly, "No. I was just up at the far end of the trail and didn't see anyone else. But that doesn't mean there aren't some people *beyond* the forest."

Jason Connor-Sable quickly surmised she was one of the stragglers for whom he was concerned. He advised her to make haste in departing, but stated his intention to continue searching. She scrunched up her freckled nose and commented, "Why the hell are you doing this? Security is sweeping the place right now. I saw two of them heading north and I'm sure there are others clearing people out. Who *are* you, anyway?"

As raindrops splattered against his raincoat, the sandy-haired artist quickly shot back, "I'm just trying to help out... that's all. I had a feeling there were some people left behind and my instincts brought me this way. I'm gonna make one full circuit and then get out of here as fast as possible. I assume you're heading out immediately, right?"

Sinnamon adjusted the thick strap of her shoulder bag as she winked at the stranger. "Have a nice day," were her sarcastic parting words as she brushed past him. Jason was less than enthralled by her acerbic attitude, but with his mind on his mission, he shrugged it off and headed in the opposite direction. Meanwhile, in another section of the park, Mateo Lima was ushering a contingent of three teenage girls toward the promise of shelter.

At the time the lightning annihilated two of the aerial tram's gondolas, the girls had been following closely behind Mateo in single file like a trio of ducklings. Violet, Leanna and Hanna were anxious to take shelter from the storm. When the two metal gondolas came crashing down, the horrific clamor prompted Mateo to lead them under the expansive partial roof of the Wegeforth Bowl. Immediately after the lightning bolt struck, an image of The Wegeforth Bowl's protective overhang popped into Mateo's mind. With little hesitation, he led the nervous, rain-soaked teenagers to the site where many animal shows were held. As it turned out, his decision to assemble beneath the Bowl's roof turned out to be remarkably fortuitous.

Huddled beneath the protective covering, Mateo began to sense the gravity of the situation, and his instinct to protect his daughter and the other girls dictated his actions. Sirens blared and the pre-recorded Public Address warning looped repeatedly, instructing all to "immediately evacuate the premises." He asked Violet to check the door at the far end of the wall behind the stage and all three teenagers hurried to investigate. Disappointed to find the door locked, they looked back with disappointment in their eyes.

Their hopes for shelter were immediately dashed. They had witnessed members of the security team locking the doors to many of the enclosures and buildings, leaving little choice but to run for the exit or try to wait the storm out where they stood. Leanna and Hanna were supposed to meet their grandfather near the exit, yet he was nowhere to be seen. Mateo considered sprinting for it and hoping their grandfather would be waiting there, but the storm had become so ferocious it was nearly impossible to see one's own feet.

Mateo felt solely responsible for the safety of the children in his care and wanted only to ensure their safety. He made his way to the back of the stage and put his arm around Violet. As he squeezed her close to him, they stood awestruck, gazing out at the fury of the storm. He closed his eyes and tried to calm himself in an attempt to achieve some clarity. In a matter of seconds, he successfully lowered his pulse rate and controlled his breathing, something he had taught himself in recent years. The routine was his way of meditating, enabling him to enter a state of calm whenever he felt the need. The practice sometimes led to the manifestation of visions, and once again, they infiltrated his sub conscience.

He received a clear image of green trees and driving rain, punctuated by intermittent flashes of light. He then saw an impenetrable monolith, apparently constructed entirely of stone. A faint golden aura enveloped the object, indicating potential significance; at least that was his interpretation of the fleeting images. Following that brief moment of clarity, he suddenly opened his eyes and addressed his daughter and the two siblings.

"Girls, please," he calmly pleaded, "we've got to stay here a little while longer. Let's all stand against the wall until the rain lets up just a bit. We'll be safe and dry for the time being, and as soon as the storm eases, we can make a run for the gates. If we wait it out here, maybe a security patrol will drive by in one of their vehicles and we can get a ride to the exit. How does that sound?" The girls, relieved to be out of the wind and rain, all nodded affirmatively. Mateo smiled reassuringly and then joined them as they all planted their heels against the base of the imposing back wall. The rain was driven so forcefully by the wind; it was still splattering them despite the roof. They were, however, significantly more comfortable for the moment. Unfortunately, their relief would be extremely short-lived.

At 3:28 p.m., the first inland tremor arrived. Produced by the tsunamis, the first minor shock waves jolted the greater San Diego area at the height of the storm. At first, Mateo and the girls believed it was more thunder rolling inland. They all huddled together and pressed their backs against the wall. Mere minutes later, the next tremor left no doubt as to what was actually happening.

The second wave shook the structure's very foundation, knocking both Violet and Hanna to the floor of the main stage. Mateo was staggered too, but instinctively grabbed Leanna by the arm to prevent her from falling over.

In the confusion, Mateo had not initially realized that Violet's head had struck the floor's unforgiving surface. His eyes were fixed to the north, where the trees were moving in an unholy manner. The Earth ruptured directly beneath the forest floor, undulating and then bursting outward, creating a horrific scene. The entire forest appeared to bend and shift laterally, as if set upon some enormous conveyor belt. The sight was both mesmerizing and terrifying as enormous, mature trees snapped in half or were sent crashing

Earthward. Lightning flashed across the sky and the rain continued its assault.

Mateo turned away from the nightmarish scene to check on the girls, only to discover his precious daughter lying unconscious on the cracked cement. "Violet!" he shouted. He made a first step toward her limp body, but was dropped to his knees by yet another, more powerful seismic wave. Leanna latched onto her sister's shoulder, but the two of them were tossed to the floor like rag dolls, landing near Violet's motionless body. Initially knocked on their backsides, the siblings propped themselves up on trembling arms and gazed into Mateo's eyes. He struggled to slide himself along the floor over to Violet. It was at that precise moment that the earthquake heralded by the previous tremors unleashed its full fury.

Historians would mark the time of the transformative event as commencing at 3:33 p.m. on December 27th. The Earth, wounded and angry, declared unequivocally that it would always have the last word in determining humanity's fate.

The earlier tremors were mere whispers compared to the deafening roar delivered by the planet at the historic moment. The pressure created by the chained events at sea finally manifested as massively destructive eruptions from beneath the planet's surface. The sheer magnitude and scale of the earthquakes marked a watershed moment in the world's chaotic history.

Molten lava stored in underground reservoirs was unleashed in the form of spewing geysers. Where the Earth's fractured surface was violently forced upward, massive segments of land were reshaped in an instant. As the process unfolded over a remarkably short time frame, huge sink holes indiscriminately pulled dirt, rock and all manner of life forms to abysmal depths. The sky had become as black as coal and gale force winds drove the heavy rain sideways.

Unbeknownst to the few innocent souls remaining at the zoo, colossal changes were altering the landscape of the entire planet. This was no isolated event, but rather a global disaster – a series of improbable coincidental events that chained together to profoundly reshape the planet's geography. Billions of lives were impacted, in virtually every corner of the planet. The Asian continent was struck hardest, with a massive 9.9 quake immediately followed by one so powerful it could not be accurately measured. The earlier quakes, none of which would have resulted in notable destruction of life or land, were critical contributing factors to the massive shift of Tectonic plates across the world. This synchronous confluence of energy produced a subterranean "perfect storm."

I Miss Your Purple Hair

Nothing would ever be the same for those left to deal with the aftermath. The survivors would have to recreate virtually everything, from basic infrastructure to maps to delineate new local, regional and national features. The Great Lakes on the North American continent underwent enormous transformation, merging into two from five separate entities. The associated flooding destroyed countless communities while claiming millions of lives in the process. Japan was all but obliterated, nearly completely submerged. The European continent was rendered unrecognizable, with virtually half of the land either buried beneath the seas or set ablaze by volcanic eruptions.

Within the microcosm of the San Diego Zoo, many buildings and platforms collapsed or were annihilated. The succession of brutal quakes created jagged fissures and cavernous pits, some percolating with molten lava and others filled with endless nothingness. Tremors continued throughout the night, with the Earth's fragile outer shell still shifting and buckling from the intense subterranean pressures.

Though the evacuation had been effective, those who had departed earlier were no safer than the few left behind. Many perished or were fatally injured trying to make their way home as roadways, bridges, and entire city blocks were demolished. Capsizing highways devoured thousands of vehicles while disintegrating bridges tossed others through the air as if they were toys. Massive explosions and fires sprung from damaged oil reserves and gasoline stations.

The destruction of vast stretches of coastline resulted in a drastic reconfiguration of the United States' West Coast. The land was violently reshaped in a multitude of locations, with enormous sinkholes and mountain ranges suddenly appearing where none formerly existed. Aftershocks rumbled across the planet and rendered great segments of the geography unrecognizable.

Countless individuals fought for their very survival, and the lives of the young, the infirmed, and the elderly were indiscriminately erased. Randomly ending the existence of the wealthy and the impoverished, the educated and the ignorant, Death conducted its rampage across the planet. The faithless and the pious suffered the same fate. Either directly or indirectly, all of the natural world and its living souls were affected in some terrible manner. The day humanity never dared envision had come to pass: a catastrophe so magnificent in scale, no contingency plan could have made the slightest difference.

△△△

CHAPTER NINE
I Know You'll Come Back Someday

"Death is a stripping away of all that is not you.
The secret of life is to 'die before you die'- and find that there is no death."
~ Eckhart Tolle

ateo Lima was considered an exceptionally "good" man by most who knew him. Regarded as humble, sincere, and good-natured, he was known for his sympathetic and generous manner. As is often the way of the truly humble, he never thought to give himself much credit, figuring he would live his life as well as he could and then trust God to pass judgment when all was said and done. Battered and bruised from being tossed like a rag doll, Mateo wound up on his back in a shallow puddle filled with lukewarm muddy water. For this kind-hearted soul, "all was said and done" on the morning of December 28th.

At precisely 1:53:33 a.m. on the darkest morning humankind had ever witnessed, Mateo Lima's heart ceased beating. The gentle father of one, and devoted friend to many, had stopped breathing. Finally, there was peace for his tired soul. The moment had finally arrived for him; the moment he had occasionally dreaded; the moment he had not anticipated until many years later. He had presumed the moment would wait until after the graduations, the wedding, the baptisms, the birthdays, and the recognition ceremonies surely ahead for his daughter. He had imagined those joyous days awaited him; that there would be too many celebrations and accomplishments to count. While he had experienced a subtle sense of foreboding in recent months, he never anticipated this day of suffering and finality.

A deep laceration beneath Mateo's left eye oozed rivulets of bright red that meandered across his prominent cheekbone. Tiny scarlet drops rhythmically broke the surface of the water in which his body rested. Rain continued to fall, diluting the blood on his face ever so slightly when a random drop would find its mark. Darkness had descended upon the rubble of what was formerly a meticulously landscaped, pastoral region of the zoo. In the strange pitch-blackness behind his closed eyes, nothing existed – other than a latent longing for eternal peace and true enlightenment. A day that had begun with such promise, saturated in the soothing embrace of a radiant Sun, had suddenly turned into the nightmare of all nightmares – the end of days… for billions, including Mateo Lima.

The glorious mechanisms within his now-motionless physical shell ceased to function at a breath away from 1:00 a.m. – and yet, the soul of this good man rejoiced. Finally free of the restricting tethers and rules of the corporeal world, the splendid energy comprising his true essence sang out in utter ecstasy. His life energy happily departed the fleshy confines that no longer could sustain it. His conscience intact, he gradually rejoined the ethereal realm and, in a surreal moment, gazed down upon his own lifeless form.

Mateo's spirit observed the unfamiliar backdrop of grotesquely mangled land masses and demolished structures. He felt detached from anything physical – impervious to pain, climate or emotions. Relieved of the relentless demands of gravity and no longer bound by the familiar, he felt confused, yet strangely at peace. The scarred and scorched sky sported an unfamiliar appearance, featuring an oddly tinted Moon partially obscured behind tattered strips of grey. He was unsure what had happened to him and to the world, but was somehow aware that the momentous event had drastically altered the future.

His soul, or perhaps merely his point of view, had somehow taken a position high above the scene. Mateo gazed upon his own motionless body, lying face-up in a depression filled with muddy water. It was a curious sight, impossible to fully comprehend or accept. The smoldering lava-filled fissures and craters presented an image reminiscent of a Hollywood depiction of prehistoric times. Nothing about the imagery made sense. He tried to accept what he was seeing as reality but his thoughts insisted it was nothing more than a bad dream – an epic nightmare. Just as he had subconsciously done within his own nightmares in the past, he asked himself if he was witnessing reality or if the distasteful images were merely products of his imagination.

Once his attention shifted to the unsavory image of his daughter's lifeless form being supported and cared for by the nearly identical Armstrong sisters, he realized what was happening was all too real. He was surprisingly aware of his life force waning as it yearned for release from the bounds of the physical realm. He agonized between accepting his demise and acting on his compulsion to aid his injured daughter. At some instinctive level, he very deeply wanted to relinquish all control and willingly pass into the next phase of existence.

On another level, he felt something commanding his soul back to the realm of the living, a powerful force infusing him with the determination to start breathing again. Temporarily stuck in limbo, he was tempted by the Siren's call of an existence devoid of pain and worry; one filled with answers and infinite discovery. At the same time, however, Mateo desperately longed to rejoin his daughter and take action to ensure her survival. In the end, an external force ultimately cast the deciding vote.

By the early morning of December 28th, not much remained of the Wegeforth Bowl. The quakes had thoroughly decimated the land surrounding the home of the popular sea lion show. Mateo's decision to encourage the girls to stand beneath the building's expansive roof had been critical to their survival. While much of the building had been reduced to unrecognizable rubble, the sturdy wall against which they stood miraculously survived. Although the lives of the three girls had been spared due to that fortuitous decision, Violet had been rendered unconscious. Approaching 2:13 a.m. on the morning after, the petite 15-year-old remained still.

Leanna, who had blacked out after being tossed to the ground, had regained enough composure to crawl across the fractured floor of the stage to kneel next to Violet. While she held the unconscious girl's left hand, she rocked back and forth and chanted something under her breath. Hanna, partially covered in a cloak of red dirt, was barely recognizable but physically intact. By a stroke of luck, she had slid across the stage floor on her backside, until she finally splashed into the long, curved tank in which the sea lions usually frolicked. It had become partially filled with mud and debris during the massive upheaval, and she fortunately landed atop a generous mound of wet grass. She had only suffered a slightly twisted lower back and minor bruises across her neck and face, but was otherwise unscathed. Still in shock, she groped through the darkness, trying to follow the sound of her sister's voice.

Rain continued to fall, but its intensity had mercifully diminished. The grounds in the immediate vicinity had been rendered virtually unrecognizable. Illuminated by the pale light of the full Moon now eerily tinged in a red-orange wash, Hanna observed a monstrous wall of *something*. Still stunned and disoriented, she narrowed her eyes and tried to comprehend what had happened to the environment. The partly obscured constellations indicated that the land had been raised to incredible heights all around them. It appeared they were trapped within an enormous crater. Hanna rested upon sore and scraped knees – wet and bewildered, staring in disbelief at the gigantic wall menacingly cloaking her in shadow.

I Miss Your Purple Hair

The sturdy structure of The Wegeforth Bowl had ultimately spared their lives, at least for the moment. However, much of it and its pool had been demolished, and the expansive stage torn asunder by an underground battering ram. The concrete pool's foundation was cracked in the middle and an enormous quantity of water had already escaped. One broken section of the curved, elongated moat was now overflowing with thick mud. Hanna became aware of a disturbingly unfamiliar odor as spiraling plumes of steam carried toxic gases released from underground reservoirs.

Lost within a nightmare, 13-year-old Hanna was confused and very afraid. Turning her attention toward her older sister once again, she recognized they had temporarily lost their vital connection with each other during the height of the quake. It was as though the tumultuous event had severed their powerful psychic bond. Slowly, she could feel that invisible connection returning as she observed Leanna tenderly caring for Violet. Hanna, younger by less than a year, had finally rejoined her sister and the unconscious teenager they had only recently met. She listened intently to her sister's whispered prayers and observed as she wiped specks of mud from Violet's face with the dampened corner of her orange T-shirt.

Hanna closed her eyes and psychically melded with her sister. She felt her own hands assist Leanna in the slow, careful process of wiping away the traces of clay and dirt from Violet's cheeks and forehead. She telepathically communicated the simple prayer she and Leanna had memorized, delivering the healing words in harmony amidst the rhythmic hiss of the rain falling around them. Their prayer was intended for both the unconscious girl and for her similarly disabled father, flat on his back in a muddy pool a few yards away. They had recited the prayer on previous occasions and had it committed to memory. Now, they softly repeated its words in unison:

"Collective Soul, allow me to fulfill my intention to heal. Transfer my energy to those in need. Collective Soul, allow me to fulfill my intention to heal. Transfer my energy to those in need..."

The soft, blended voices of the highly evolved pair conveyed energy into the bodies of both Violet and Mateo. Their repetitive chant, though not set to any melody, sounded very much like a lilting song. Hanna continued to clutch Violet's hand while their voices wove a fabric of genuine caring and faith between the millions of cascading raindrops.

Hanna was completely focused upon her sister and joined forces with her in a powerful psychic bond that shielded them from external distractions. This method had become instinctual for the girls, who developed other similar procedures over the years. No one had to teach them any of it; they "knew" to collaborate in order to maximize their innate abilities and invigorate their evolution. They had connected with Violet's mind, and desperately tried to impart enough healing energy to rejuvenate her, yet she remained motionless.

Mateo suddenly was no longer able to view the scene from a lofty perspective, having returned to the world of the living. He was eminently aware he had returned to his familiar physical vessel. His eyelids fluttered for a few moments, casting particles of dirt and water into the heavy, humid night air. Mired in focused concentration on the needs of the daughter, the Armstrong sisters initially failed to hear the faint rustlings of the father. Mateo had slowly begun to regain consciousness. He found himself in a bizarre predicament: flat on his back in a shallow puddle of mud, gazing up at the strange-colored Moon, clueless about all that had transpired.

The rain finally relented but the clouds still appeared ominously heavy. Mateo painfully parted his dry, cracked lips to utter a raspy "...Violet...," before repeating her name a bit more emphatically. There was no response. Though nearly 3:00 a.m., the warm night air was uncomfortably thick with humidity and laced with the pungent, foreboding odor of sulfur and smoke. Mateo noted that the ferocity of the winds had diminished and the night air had become almost still. Muscles aching, he mustered the strength to drag himself from his muddy tomb, and rolled onto his stomach. Finally on dry ground, he tried to catch his breath and compose himself, coughing from irritation to the lining of his throat. His ribs ached with every agonizing hack, and his reddened eyes burned from the toxic fumes emanating from the Earth.

Everything looked terribly wrong to Mateo as he surveyed his strange new surroundings. Where once stood an impressive, modern structure was nothing but a shattered remnant. In the murky darkness behind the enormous pile of debris, a gargantuan wall loomed. Overcome by a strange sense of entrapment and suffocation, he was not yet fully aware how prophetic those feelings were. Thunder still threateningly flexed its deep baritone in the distance while the hiss of mist-like rain provided the background music. All the while, another foreign sound – the sound of voices locked in unison – softly repeated some indiscernible chorus.

In a different section of the park, Jason was all too immersed in reality. From where he sat, leaning his bruised back against the base of a thick tree, the world was a tangled pattern of green, brown, and red. Amidst a sliver of forest that had somehow been spared, all he could see was a mass of leaves, a cascading river of mud and a stream of water tainted with his own blood. He had been following Rebecca "Sinnamon" Sinclair out of the Ituri Forest when the massive quake struck. The earth beneath their feet suddenly transformed, with little warning whatsoever.

A long swath of the forest's once-stable terrain split apart in one violent moment while massive walls of dirt and rock suddenly pushed skyward. Insurmountable barriers of rock denied passage to the north or west of their position. To their east and south, a gigantic chasm formed when an expanse of land collapsed more than 40 feet. The rain, falling steadily for so many hours prior to the quake's arrival, produced massive mudslides that uprooted smaller trees and deposited them into the newly formed ravine.

Amidst nature's turbulent display, Jason had received scrapes and cuts along the left side of his neck and face, and had bruised his right shoulder. His raincoat had been shredded when he was forced through broken branches and thorn-covered brambles. Long surface gashes covered a portion of the left side of his torso. The blood seeped through his cotton shirt and soaked into the muddy soil upon which he sat. Though light-headed from blood loss and from being unceremoniously thrashed around, Jason had composed himself enough to assess his situation. Confused as to where he was and what had happened, he made a thorough visual scan of the environment and began to understand just how desperate his situation was.

Wedged between the broken trunks of several enormous trees, he surmised he must have been thrown backwards. Directly behind him stood an imposing wall of rock, timber, and dirt towering over 30 feet high. The absence of light made it impossible to make out many details, but he observed what appeared to be another towering obstruction blocking out the sky directly west of where he sat. The air had become thick with moisture from all the rain, prompting him to shed his tattered raincoat and hang it on the stub of a broken branch. In the distance, he could see broken trees, snapped in two and draped over what remained of the trail through the forest.

The scene's nightmarish quality was enhanced by the eerie silence, which sharply contrasted the deafening roar of the quakes. Despite the soreness in his neck muscles, he cocked his head to look directly overhead. A strange indigo veil coated the heavens and only a handful of insignificant stars were visible. Though the rain had all but ceased, a fine glaze coated every element of the emerald realm. He tried to clear his mind and called upon a breathing technique he had practiced as an athlete in his high school glory days.

I Know You'll Come Back Someday

A former soccer player, Jason had also studied psychology as fervently as he worked on physical conditioning. He had developed a meditation technique to cleanse his mind before competitions, a practice that in time became automatic as he approached any significant challenge. Considering the unknown prospects of his immediate future, he realized it was imperative to purge fear from his mind.

Enduring the piercing pain down the left side of his torso, he adjusted his position to allow unrestricted airflow into his lungs. With his right leg bent beneath his body and left leg outstretched along the ground, he felt he could properly begin his process for achieving inner peace. Jason closed his eyes and began a pattern of inhaling and exhaling very deeply and deliberately. He felt himself beginning to calm and could tell that his pulse rate was slowing little by little. Clarity and a genuine sense of peace gradually returned to his soul. He began to breathe easier, feeling more relaxed and somewhat less afraid. In his dark corner of the forest, alone and unsure, he had still found a means of tapping into the tranquility he had always cherished. The techniques he had mastered as an athlete were accessible when he needed them most. He succeeded in achieving a state of relative serenity and, with his eyes still closed, tried to envision what had happened to everyone and everything in the vicinity.

Jason recalled the lightning storm and the local strikes that sent waves of electricity through his hair, teeth, and spinal cord. He remembered the shock associated with the initial tremors and the feeling of dread that immediately swelled within his chest. For a brief moment, he relived that profound fear and was subsequently returned to the precise moment he realized what was happening below ground. As he became conscious of the emotional tension reanimated by those memories, Jason used his inner voice to compensate...

'Relax... relax... relax. This is just another challenge. Everything is fine as long as I can breathe and think. Just breathe and think, breathe and think. I can handle this. I am powerful. I can only win. I can only win...'

All of his self-help books and audiotapes had been well worth the investment. Jason felt rejuvenated, calm and clear headed... and ready to do what was necessary to survive.

Sinnamon Sinclair was not particularly thoughtful or sympathetic. She went through life consuming, maneuvering, anticipating opportunities and preying upon the weaknesses of others. Not particularly evil-minded, she was primarily focused on her own comfort, and rarely on the needs of those around her. She simply never gave much thought to other people, except when she needed emotional support, sustenance, security, or shelter. At 4:01 a.m. on December 28th, she needed all of those comforts and more. Unaware of her location, she only realized that she was flat on her back atop a jagged rock formation, immersed in a network of intertwined tree branches and foliage.

The fabric of the cosmos appeared precariously close beyond the dense network of plant life scraping against the tanned skin of her face. It was impossible to fathom how she had been deposited atop a towering mound of stone and dirt. That was, however, the predicament she was in. She propped her bruised and battered body up on one elbow and clung to a still-anchored tree root with her free hand. Peering over the edge, she strained to see if she could make out anything familiar in the pitch-blackness. In utter amazement, she realized she had somehow been elevated along with tons of dirt, stone and vegetation, to an alarmingly high altitude. She found herself at the same level as the treetops around her – that is, those that remained set in their original, pre-quake locations.

Sinnamon kept closing and reopening her eyes, hoping the exercise might magically compensate for the absence of light. As her vision gradually began to adjust to the conditions, she realized she was in trouble but was unsure just how worried she should be. She took inventory of her physical status in her typically methodical manner. She felt no obvious pain, but systematically tested all of her extremities one by one; to make sure nothing was broken or otherwise damaged. Her sinewy legs checked out perfectly and as she brought them up to her chest one by one, she was relieved to find no sign of injury.

She slowly lifted her arms, reached to the sky with each hand, flexed her fingers, and formed a fist with each one. Once again, she detected no discomfort or limitation of movement in her extremities. She drew in several deep breaths, testing her lungs and rib cage for any signs of damage. Realizing she had struck her skull fairly hard against her pillow of leaves and twigs, she ran her hand over the back of her head. Once again, there was no apparent damage – other than a pair of bumps. As if subliminally reminded, she decided to examine her breasts while lying in the dark new world into which she had been dropped.

While systematically feeling each side for telltale pain or discomfort she wryly muttered aloud, "Perfect as always." Sinnamon wore delicate silver rings through both nipples and was relieved to find they had not caused damage to her tender skin. She then moved on to physically examine her abdomen, pelvis, and lower back. Finally, she cautiously rolled over until she was laying face down, supporting her head and upper torso with her folded arms.

Glancing down at her left forearm, Sinnamon wiped away mud and grime from the favorite of her nine tattoos – an elegant black-cloaked sorceress with a crow perched upon her raised arm and a staff of light in the other. She had suffered an ugly scrape, extending from elbow to wrist, along the outside of her right forearm. The only other injuries she identified were bruises to her right thigh and hip; and a slightly bruised left heel.

An experienced runner, Sinnamon was in excellent physical condition and accustomed to minor injuries. Regardless, she felt tremendously relieved to have escaped such a calamitous event without suffering permanent damage. Still, she found herself stranded atop an imposing formation of Nature, and ran through her options while peering down at Jason. As her eyes grew more accustomed to the limited light, she was able to make out more details. The area looked nothing like it had just before the enormous quakes. The once-beautiful forest of healthy, thriving foliage had been transformed into an otherworldly landscape of broken timber, smoldering ash, and gaping fissures.

The mountain of rock upon which Sinnamon stood towered high above the recessed section of land supporting Jason. Still populated by trees and bushes undamaged by the shifting of the earth, the triangle-shaped segment of lush grass cradled him. A bit groggy, Jason finally spotted Sinnamon's shadowy figure through the vegetation that partially obscured his line of sight. After he raised a cupped hand to his mouth and called out to her, she stood and responded, yelling, "What the hell is going on? How'd all this happen?"

Edgy and impatient, Sinnamon kicked a cluster of small rocks over the edge with her muddy hiking boots and sized up the situation. She contemplated climbing down the eastern side of the formation, but was not keen on risking a fall and possibly suffering broken bones or worse. The rain had left everything wet and slippery, making a climb very dangerous. She estimated it was at least a 15-foot drop, but knew she had to rejoin Jason. He had struggled to his feet, and made his way closer to the base of the mass atop which Sinnamon stood. He craned his neck to look at her and then assessed the nearby region. He took note of one enormous tree, which stood close to the southeastern edge of the towering rock formation. He felt it offered the best opportunity for Sinnamon to reach the ground.

Jason inquired as to Sinnamon's physical state, and she quickly assured him she was fit and relatively undamaged. He asked, "Do you feel strong enough to make that jump?" as he pointed to the towering fig tree. She uttered no reply. Instead, she unceremoniously yanked the white visor from atop her head, threw it behind her, and sprinted the dozen or so strides toward the edge before launching herself headlong at the towering tree. Jason breathlessly watched, awestruck as she soared through the air high above him. Like some red-haired feral cat, Sinnamon landed squarely upon a prominent branch, grasping it firmly with both hands. As if she had done so a hundred times before, she quickly dropped to the branch below, systematically shimmied around the trunk and descended little by little.

In awe of Sinnamon's display of courage, Jason moved to the base of the tree. As she progressed, some of the tree's accumulated rainwater came pouring down, splashing Jason. "Sorry 'bout that!" she smirked, while she continued her determined descent. Once she had reached the lowest branch, she realized she was still over eight feet above ground. Jason gestured for her to jump into his waiting arms and she smugly cocked her head and sneered.

Just then, a powerful aftershock rocked the area. The impact knocked Sinnamon off balance and flung her from the branch. She instinctively reached back and nearly succeeded at latching onto it again. Instead, her hand slipped off the wet bark. Though she managed to slow her momentum, she could not prevent plummeting to the ground. Jason had somehow maintained his balance during the tremor, as if he knew it was coming. He lunged to catch Sinnamon and saved her from serious injury when she came crashing atop him. Her momentum sent them both sprawling to the forest floor.

Straddling Jason's torso, the freckled firebrand rose up on sore knees and patted his shoulders firmly while she laughed heartily. "Nice catch!" she wisecracked through a toothy grin. Jason, who in recent years had lost some athletic tone and grown a little soft around the middle, had the wind knocked out of him. He managed a somewhat pained smile and then nodded his head to acknowledge her comment. As she tensed her muscles in an attempt to get to her feet, he noticed a tattooed ring of dark blue encircling her exposed navel.

"Are those… words?" Jason asked, straining to catch his breath. "What… does it say… there?"

Sinnamon shot back, "Read for yourself. You oughta recognize it."

Jason strained to see in the murky light, but managed to make out the script tattooed around her navel. *"If… it's the… end of days … I'm goin' out in style,"* he read aloud. "Why do I know that?"

As she rose to one knee, Sinnamon smartly replied, "Are you a real fan… or didja get that shirt at Goodwill?" She alluded to the black T-shirt he wore, bearing the official logo of the Australian rock band, *Airbourne*. Jason finally realized the words in her tattoo were from the lyrics to their song, "Too Much, Too Young, Too Fast."

"Oh... right," he grunted as she extricated her thighs from his sore rib cage. "That's one of my favorites, too."

"Yeah? That's swell," Sinnamon quipped, "... It's more or less my life story."

Sinnamon rose to her feet and brushed water droplets and dirt from her clothes while Jason struggled to stand. He was still reeling from the rapid-fire succession of events, trying to come to terms with the destruction surrounding him. He felt summoned to this place by his vision, but now regretted following that inclination. Sinnamon was in possession of what she had come for and regarded the storm and subsequent earthquake as inconveniences. She quickly surmised they had but one route available – south – back the way she had originally come. The path to the north was impassable and the scent on the wind indicated that fires had broken out to the northeast. Plumes of grey smoke were barely visible against the sky's dark canvas.

"Is this as bad as it looks?" Jason rhetorically asked his leathery companion.

Never one to mince words, Sinnamon coldly replied, "It's worse – *way fucking worse.*"

The storm and the tremors had worked together to mutilate the environment. Barely able to see in the pallid moonlight, the two silhouettes slowly made their way through a maze of broken timber, independently praying they were on the right path back to the zoo exit... and salvation.

△ △ △

I Miss Your Purple Hair

Chapter Ten
Lost Out in Space

"We are caught in an inescapable network of mutuality, tied in a single garment of destiny. This is the way our universe is structured. We aren't going to have peace on Earth until we recognize this basic fact of the interrelated structure of reality."
~ Dr. Martin Luther King Jr.

Sprawled face down in the gooey mud alongside a heap of indistinguishable metal fragments, business mogul, Aaron Kemper slowly lifted his head to assess his surroundings. In the inky darkness, it was nearly impossible to see his own stubby-fingered hand in front of his face. Desperately hoping he would stumble upon them, he blindly groped in the thick mud for his round-rimmed prescription sunglasses. The humorless middle-aged man had little experience dealing directly with challenging situations. His family's wealth had shielded him from suffering and rendered him ill equipped to cope with adversity. He was as saturated with fear as he was with rainwater when his fingertips finally brushed against his submerged glasses.

When the worst of the tremors hit, Aaron had been clinging to a sturdy steel signpost near the zoo exit. Moments before he jogged down the paved pathway, the aerial trams came crashing to the ground, sealing off any direct escape route. His decision to trust the fortitude of this particular support post had probably saved his life. The thick, tempered steel pole survived the quake although it had been crimped and bent at a 20-degree angle. When he finally awakened, he was lying on the ground just a few yards from the still-anchored post, not fully aware he was still drawing breath.

His vision limited by the utter absence of light, Aaron vigorously shook his square head and squeezed his eyelids shut. Dirt particles scattered wildly as he brushed debris from his arms and shoulders. With his mud-tinged fingertip, he pressed the button that activated his expensive wristwatch's illumination feature. Amazed it was nearly 4:00 a.m., he could not believe so much time had passed. He remembered being poised to depart the zoo at close to 3:30 p.m. the previous afternoon. How had so much time elapsed? He contemplated the possibilities and surmised he must have suffered a blow to the head during the quake; either that, or he passed out due to shock.

I Miss Your Purple Hair

Aaron had never needed to develop any coping mechanisms. Rather than negotiate, he wielded his influence like a bludgeon, hammering out convenient solutions to his problems. He had earned his reputation as an egocentric bully. Aaron had made an art of leveraging his political power and inherited wealth to open doors, close deals, and entice women to exchange their dignity for the promise of financial reward. This eldest son of a highly successful real estate developer had never really wanted for anything.

"Mother of God," he muttered under his breath, as he struggled to his feet. "What the hell happened?"

The previous afternoon, Aaron Kemper had been delivered to the zoo in a beautifully appointed limousine, piloted by his personal driver. His family had funded construction of a splendid flower garden near the center of the zoo and he was to speak at the dedication ceremony. The television news crews always enjoyed his antics at public events. Aaron almost always provided a good sound bite or controversial quote, and occasionally did something outrageous. From his lurid suggestions to young women, to spewing racist comments, he was a reporter's dream. Even if they did not end up with material they could air, they were almost always entertained by his behavior.

Members of the San Diego press were fond of saying, "If Kemper's there… cover it." On this most recent occasion, he had delivered a very dignified speech about supporting the efforts of the San Diego Zoo, a favorite destination of his late mother. Television Reporter, Andrea Kim, a bit of a bulldog in her own right, tried to get under his skin at the conclusion of the formal presentation. She had noted his lascivious glare during the dedication ceremony and could not help but feel violated. While he picked up his briefcase and bid farewell to local dignitaries, she intentionally lingered.

A lifelong bachelor, Kemper had a predilection for young women; especially pretty, petite Asians like Andrea. He had noticed her at a prior event and made inquiries with some of her camera crew. When later informed, she stuck a finger into her mouth and feigned vomiting. She waited to intercept him as he started for the exits. She stood in his way and forced him to stop directly in front of her, their toes almost touching. He smiled arrogantly and conducted yet another painstaking visual inspection of her breasts, but she stubbornly stood her ground; unsmiling, unblinking, and decidedly unimpressed.

"Is something troubling you, Miss?" he sarcastically quizzed. She remained silent and motionless, staring into the beady eyes behind the blue-tinted lenses. Her sour expression spoke volumes.

"Look, I don't have time for games, fortune cookie. You're blocking my way," he icily growled.

The principled young woman shook her well coiffed head of black hair and replied in an equally chilly tone, "You disgust me, Mr. Kemper. I just wanted to let you know what I think of you and your pathetic act."

"Is that all you have to say, little girl?" the pompous ass retorted.

"Yes. I have nothing else to say to you,'" she calmly answered. Her obvious anger and resentment made no impact on the callous twit. He just leaned in closer and sniffed her hair in an obviously aggressive manner.

"You do *smell* good... perhaps a little bitter, but still good enough to eat," he whispered menacingly into her ear. Offended by the lewd comment, she reacted by thrusting both arms into his chest. He quickly regained his balance and laughed in a derisive tone as he literally brushed her aside and arrogantly strutted away from the site of his latest hollow political speech.

As he advanced toward the exit, he shook hands and smiled exaggeratedly, in a calculated effort to get noticed every step of the way. Andrea Kim watched in silent disgust, tears welling in her eyes. She had encountered such offensive behavior before, but there was something especially disappointing about the despicable actions of this privileged oaf. The encounter triggered a flashback to another ugly incident. At age thirteen, a trusted relative sexually abused her. Like Aaron, her cousin "Sonny" felt no remorse for his actions. He had betrayed the unspoken trust she once took for granted and Andrea never fully recovered.

Aaron Kemper never spent another second thinking about his most recent victim. He maneuvered through the crowd, focused on getting to his waiting vehicle and then to dinner with a potential new sexual conquest – his new 22 year-old intern – at his exclusive country club. He had no way of knowing he would never again set foot on those manicured grounds or that the vibrant young intern would be dead within the hour.

Currently mired in surreal ugliness, Aaron was stripped of all the comfortable trappings he had taken for granted. Covered in dirt, hungry and afraid, he held a trembling right hand to his forehead and wondered what how he would ever get out of this nightmare. He looked up to the heavens and, for the first time in a long while, he begged God for help.

A close friend once referred to Victory Cooper as "a force of Nature." Tall, athletic, and confident, in many ways she was the epitome of feminine potential. Her radiant dark brown skin was one of her most envied features and her equally dark eyes reflected her intellect and inner fortitude. Known to family and friends as "Vic," she was fiercely protective of her husband, Dwayne and their only child DeAngelo. Of Dominican-Jamaican descent, she stood out in a crowd, not only for her fiery personality, but because she was nearly 5' 10" tall.

At the height of the tremors, the three members of the Cooper family had been hurrying toward the partially demolished Zoo Entrance pavilion. Only a few dozen yards from reaching the turnstiles when the earthquake rocked the region, they were violently scattered across the ravaged terrain. Disoriented and covered in debris from the shattered building, at 3:58 a.m., they were just beginning to regain their faculties. Partly buried beneath an array of splintered wood and unidentifiable vegetation, the somewhat stoic patriarch had suffered first-degree burns on both forearms and a huge bump on the back of his head.

During his abbreviated basketball career at UCLA, a severe knee injury forced him to retire from the sport. He was regarded as a top professional prospect when his right patella was shattered and two major ligaments were shredded during a practice session. Despite reconstructive surgery and a long rehabilitation, he was never able to fully recover. He reinjured that same knee when the tremor knocked him to the ground. Simultaneously, downed power lines sent a fan-like shower of sparks across the area to ignite the fire.

DeAngelo Cooper had been plenty frightened *before* the tremors arrived. The unusual intensity of the rainstorm and proximity of the lightning strikes had unnerved him terribly. When the ground buckled beneath his feet, the chubby 10-year-old fell onto his back. His head snapped back but miraculously missed striking a large, jagged rock, and he was fortunate to only suffer minor bruises and a pair of scraped elbows.

Amidst the dark, otherworldly environment a concerned mother crawled on hands and knees toward her son's familiar silhouette. Rendered speechless by fear, DeAngelo cowered amidst broken branches and upturned soil. She repeatedly called out his name but he failed to respond, still lost in the cluttered chaos of his mind and the nightmare that had suddenly shattered his once-secure reality.

The Coopers were a typical middle-class American family – hard working and financially comfortable. Often, their greatest concerns included agreeing on which movie to watch or planning their next vacation. They suffered their occasional head colds and griped about health care and gasoline prices, but more often than not their daily problems were the concerns of the privileged – not about survival, but about bringing more comfort into their already comfortable lives. DeAngelo was completely unprepared to deal with the shock of the natural disaster that had literally turned their world inside out. He rocked back and forth in a little ball while his concerned mother groped through the smoke-laced darkness to find him, guided by his quiet sobbing. In the distance, the thunder rolled and lightning flashed while a light drizzle continued.

Dwayne, still trying to sort out what had happened, grimaced over the pain in his knee. His mind replayed the moment during a routine Friday practice session in college when blind-sided by a teammate. The regrettable incident stemmed from a misunderstanding created when another teammate misrepresented Dwayne's interest in the angry player's fiancée. The third party had his facts wrong and his irresponsible gossip triggered the life-changing incident. During a routine scrimmage, the misinformed teammate intentionally stepped directly in Dwayne's path and delivered an elbow to the side of his head, sending him crashing to the unyielding court.

Unfortunately, Dwayne's legs became entangled with those of a teammate, and they fell in a twisted heap. One moment of misguided fury destroyed Dwayne Cooper's once-promising basketball career. His shredded ligaments and broken kneecap healed to some degree over time, but were never the same. Meanwhile, Dwayne was forced to come to terms with the disintegration of his childhood dream; that of playing professional basketball. He was considered a legitimate professional prospect prior to the accident. His girlfriend broke off their relationship shortly after realizing he would never play again. Her dreams had been tied to the fame and financial bounty associated with a career in professional sports. When the hope of realizing that dream evaporated, so did her dedication to Dwayne.

As is often the case, the emotional pain surpassed the physical discomfort, despite the year of rehabilitation Dwayne endured. The residual damage prevented resumption of his athletic career, but the emotional scar colored every day since the incident. The bitterness he clung to for so long dissipated somewhat over the years, but he never fully regained the will to implicitly trust.

Marriage and fatherhood had brought a large degree of satisfaction, and with the influence of his strong-willed wife, he strengthened his faith in a higher power. Raising his introspective and deeply sensitive son sometimes proved to be a great challenge. Dwayne had previously struggled with intimacy in relationships and DeAngelo required a lot of attention. If not treated with great honesty and compassion, he tended to retract and become disconsolate. DeAngelo had always displayed intelligence and wisdom beyond his years. He often asked probing questions about issues beyond the focus of most young children. Intelligent and sympathetic to the needs of others, he was a loving and thoughtful boy. While he was deeply loved by both parents, they were sometimes perplexed by his behavior.

DeAngelo had remarked that the world was "hurting" and that humanity "needs to fix things." His parents assumed he was simply echoing the views of some of his teachers and classmates regarding environmental awareness. They had encouraged him to think about ways in which their own family could do more, and made some lifestyle adjustments to satisfy him. He would drop the subject for a short time but it would inevitably resurface. One Saturday morning over breakfast in the large eat-in kitchen of their suburban San Diego ranch home, DeAngelo unexpectedly broke out in tears. Although fussed over by his mother, he could not be consoled. Amidst his tears and reassuring words from both parents, he blurted out, "I think it might be too late. There's just too much to fix."

When urged to elaborate, the distraught boy blinked his enormous brown eyes and replied, "No one ever talks about all the things people have already destroyed, or all the people and animals that have been killed for no reason. Too much bad stuff has been going on for so long. It's just too late to make it all good now."

While his parents attempted to console him, they failed to fully comprehend what was going on in their only child's mind. From his idealistic viewpoint, he simply was unable to reconcile the long history of abuse perpetrated upon the planet and its most innocent and defenseless denizens. DeAngelo felt there had been evil intentions behind what was often attributed to mere ignorance, and sensed a dangerous build-up of negative energy stored within the planet's memory.

Meanwhile, the Armstrong sisters continued to hover over Violet, silently pouring their combined energy into her unresponsive vessel. While immersed in prayer, they envisioned a plan of action. A shared image of a dolphin swimming alongside a human being of indeterminable age and gender interrupted their trance-like state. They had long ago learned to trust such imagery and fully accepted the message. The sisters rose to their feet and turned their attention to the southeast and, specifically, the site of the dolphin exhibit.

Lost Out in Space

As dark as it was, they could barely see one another, let alone a structure that may or may not have survived the quakes. Undeterred, they both "knew" the temporary facility had withstood the destructive force of the natural disaster because they sensed the presence of the two dolphins. They presumed the message they received was somehow related to Violet's condition. Before they could take action, a baritone moan broke the stillness of the night and hijacked their attention.

Several yards from them, a man had fought to return to the only existence he knew... and back to the daughter he unconditionally loved. Mateo Lima had passed into the next realm for a brief moment; by the laws of Nature, he had died. A tiny spark of life force remained, however, and he chose to return to a bleak reality. The unfinished business of ensuring his daughter's survival was foremost in his mind. The first breaths of reentry into the dimension of the living transferred painful shards of electricity through the sensitive tissue of his lungs.

Mateo managed to gather sufficient strength and moved toward the barely discernible forms huddling nearby. When he drew himself alongside the three girls, he initially struggled to recall who they were and what brought them together. His passion for life and devotion to his child bolstered his resolve and compelled him to gather his senses.

There was no need to exchange words as he knelt beside his daughter and the two strangers who tended to her. He looked into their honey-tinged eyes and fully understood that they only wanted to assist Violet. In the aftermath of his rebirth, he sensed their intention to take her to the dolphin exhibit she had been so excited to see.

Mateo got down on one knee and placed a gentle kiss on his daughter's warm forehead. She was inhaling and exhaling shallow breaths, and he put his hand over her heart for his own reassurance. He whispered her name directly into her ear, eliciting no reaction whatsoever. Weighing his few options, he considered the inherent risks in moving Violet without knowing the extent of her injuries. He examined her as best he could and did not detect any significant physical damage; no broken bones, and no bleeding other than minor scrapes on her forehead and knees. She had landed upon a folded tarpaulin that may have spared her from serious injury to her spine.

Mateo was reluctant to move her, but his instincts told him to trust Hanna and Leanna. From the time he had rejoined the three girls, the sisters had been praying quietly, sitting on their knees next to Violet. Mateo closed his eyes and prayed for guidance. He tilted his head back and opened his mind for any sign that would help him make the proper decision.

Moments later an answer arrived when he envisioned a sparkling pool of blue water. The song "Crystal Blue Persuasion" came to mind in synchronization with the peaceful imagery. Mateo recalled a verse in the lyrics: *"... Better get ready; gonna see the light; love, love is the answer and that's all right; So, don't you give up now, so easy to find; Just look to your soul and open your mind..."* He imagined lowering Violet into the welcoming embrace of the cool water of the dolphin tank and envisioned her suspended in the revitalizing liquid. He knew Violet would dehydrate and be at risk for long-term damage if she remained unconscious for too long.

The air had become warmer and its pungent stench indicated a growing toxicity, which also concerned Mateo. At the very least, he knew the water would provide temporary relief from the harshness of the transformed environment. He considered the added therapeutic benefit of the water's buoyancy on Violet's back and neck.

Hanna, unharmed but obviously frightened, meekly asked, "Mister, what happened? Was it an earthquake?" She needed to hear it from someone else before she could accept what she already knew.

Mateo tried his best to voice an appropriate response. "Yes... a very big earthquake, I'm afraid. Are either of you injured?" Despite being tossed about, Hanna reported that neither she nor her sister had suffered serious injuries, and Mateo quickly returned his attention to his motionless daughter.

Leanna gently touched the back of her sister's hand to signal Hanna to rise. Mateo's eyes had adjusted as much as they could to the unusual darkness; enough to see the sisters stand shoulder to shoulder and turn their backs to him. He was at first perplexed, but then began to understand their intention. When Hanna took Leanna's hand in hers, he anticipated what was about to transpire. The girls waited while Mateo securely cradled Violet in his arms and rose to his feet. The two sisters began chanting very quietly in unison, much as they had done when reciting their prayer of healing. Although Mateo was unable to make out their words, he could discern the soothing tones of their beautiful harmony.

He was instinctively compelled to follow their unified voices through the treacherous pitch-blackness. Whatever mysterious beacon guided the two girls through the debris-laden environment, they were inexplicably able to sidestep all obstructions. Their blended Siren's call allowed Mateo to tread slowly yet confidently behind them, carrying his daughter in his arms.

Within minutes, they emerged on the other side of a constricted passageway lined with overgrown foliage. The sound of splashing water blended with the soft voices of the Armstrong sisters, signaling Mateo that they had reached their desired destination.

A sigh of relief escaped his lips as each girl clasped one of his arms and led him to the dolphins. Their gentle guidance provided a profound sense of security, for reasons he did not fully understand. As though they had rehearsed the moment, they acted in synchronization, with peaceful resolve. He found himself being led up a small set of stairs. *'This must be the platform the dolphin trainers stand on,'* he thought. His escorts paused and made room for him on the aluminum platform.

The Moon was nearly full, and when the clouds parted, its reflected light made a welcome difference. Mateo was finally able to make out the configuration of the dolphin tank. The sturdy metal railing surrounding two sides of the raised platform were intact and offered some sense of security as he gingerly maneuvered. Violet's rhythmic breathing reassured him as he carefully sat at the edge of the platform, still cradling her.

For a moment, his mind raced wildly as he sat holding his unconscious daughter, his legs dangling in the water. "How did this come to be?" he wondered. In what seemed like the blink of an eye, a joy-filled afternoon at the zoo had turned into a fight for survival marked by his child's injury and his own near-death experience. Now, two mysterious teenagers had led him to fulfill an overpowering compulsion to place his unconscious daughter in the dolphins' watery realm. He felt he was either losing his grasp on reality... or hallucinating.

The sensation of cool water against his skin helped draw him back to reality. The subtle rising and falling of his daughter's chest was a sobering reminder the time had come to take action. The air smelled slightly less toxic around the tank and the rhythmic sounds of splashing water were soothing. There was no sign of the pool's residents, leading Mateo to wonder if they felt threatened by the intrusion. Though determined to avoid putting Violet at risk, he could not deny the profound urge to deliver her to their domain. The two sisters had so confidently led him that it all seemed preordained.

Suddenly, a large splash shook him from his ruminations and caused him to clutch Violet more firmly to his chest. Certainly, the dolphins must have signaled their objections to the invasion of their home. He then realized it had not been the tank's residents, but rather, the two girls who had been standing alongside him. Leanna and Hanna had suddenly jumped into the water, boldly abandoning the safety of the platform. Once again, Mateo was impressed by the decisiveness of the unusual teenagers. They just suddenly leaped off the deck and into the water, despite the uncertainty of its depth... or the reception they might receive.

"Girls, are you okay?" Mateo called out into the darkness. "Where are you? Do you need help?" At first, no answer came – only the sound of splashing water. "Tell me you're alright... please!" he shouted.

"We're fine," Hanna called out. "Hold on. We'll be there in a minute." Mateo nervously strained to locate them in the water, but it was still too dark to see much of anything. It was a colorless, monochromatic world with so little natural light. Just then, he remembered his phone was tucked into the front pocket of his jeans. Supporting Violet on his lap, he carefully retrieved it. One of the applications installed in the device was a simple utility that produced light. Nearly blinded by the sudden influx of light at first, Mateo quickly appreciated the enhanced visibility enabled by the bright purple glow.

He placed the phone next to him on the deck, its screen facing skyward, producing an impressive luminous canopy. In the water a few feet away, he spotted Leanna and Hanna gracefully making their way toward him with an unidentified object in tow. As they came closer to the light, he could see that they had discovered a rather sturdy looking black platform, approximately 10 feet square and a few feet in depth. Mateo surmised that the dolphin handlers must have used it for interacting and training. It provided a perfect means for getting Violet safely into the tank without leaving her vulnerable to its inhabitants.

The girls drew close and Leanna used an attached nylon rope to lash the floating platform to the metal deck. Her sister did likewise and within minutes, Mateo lowered Violet onto its surface. While he gently laid her down, the two gifted girls helped stabilize the platform from the water, where they seemed quite comfortable despite the bizarre circumstances. Mateo thanked them for their help, and then reached down to scoop a handful of the cool, salty water.

He and Violet had made frequent trips to the beach on weekends, during the years in Miami and since moving to San Diego. Belinda never cared for ocean swimming, so Mateo and Violet would often take off together on hot afternoons, from the time she was about four years old. Violet was an excellent swimmer and rather fearless in the water, having always lived in close proximity to an ocean. Mateo surfed throughout his youth, using second-hand boards acquired from friends or relatives. He never let financial limitations prevent him from enjoying the simple pleasures in life, and surfing and swimming were lifelong passions.

He gently wiped his daughter's forehead with water, careful to keep it out of her eyes. He brushed her delicate skin with the soothing liquid and lovingly caressed her scalp, feeling for any evidence of injury. Satisfied that there was no bleeding or obvious physical wounds, he concluded she had probably suffered a concussion. Determined to keep her hydrated, Mateo was deeply concerned not only for her, but for all of them. Too dark for a proper assessment, he had no way of knowing just how much damage the quakes had caused. For the time being, his focus was on Violet and the two girls in the water. He took a few slow, deep breaths and tried to gain some clarity through silent meditation...

'Inhale. Exhale. Inhale. Exhale. You have to protect these children. Be strong and provide some damn leadership.'

The thoughts helped him relax and achieve some semblance of lucidity. When Mateo asked the Armstrong sisters if they were afraid, Leanna replied, "Just worried about our grandfather... but this water feels good, actually."

Hanna chimed in, "I wonder where the dolphins are."

Mateo paused to consider that the dolphins might possibly attack the girls out of instinct. However, his concerns lessened when he looked out across the water's surface and sensed only tranquility. He had learned long ago to find a place in his soul where he could objectively assess the situation by reading the energy. While not always completely accurate in analyzing a particular situation, he was generally able to detect impending danger. He had experienced a strange uneasiness in the days leading up to the earthquakes, but had brushed those feelings aside, determined to make the most of a special outing with his daughter.

In retrospect, he regretted not paying proper heed to those signals. Had he cancelled the planned visit to the zoo, they would be safe at home now. Mateo felt a pang of guilt when he considered that he had received warnings on a subliminal level, but had chosen to ignore them. It was not the first time he made such a mistake. This time though, the consequences were enormous. He decided it was senseless to wallow in regret, so he returned his attention to the young girls.

Violet continued breathing peacefully while Mateo applied cool water to her forehead and neck. Hanna and Leanna clung to the side of the floating platform, treading water comfortably. Leanna asked in a barely audible voice, "Mister, do you think our grandfather is safe if he was waiting at the exit?"

Mateo closed his eyes and tried to read any signals that might provide some indication. Normally, if he had close contact with someone over time, it greatly enhanced his ability to tune in to their unique frequency. Having never met their grandfather, it was impossible to get any reliable read on him and he simply replied, "I pray he's fine, but we have no real way of knowing what's happening with *anything* just yet. As soon as the Sun rises, we'll start to search."

Leanna began sobbing quietly and Hanna wrapped her arm around her. Mateo was aware the two girls were extremely intuitive and most likely more adept than he was at reading the environment. He wondered what they might have sensed when they reached out psychically for their grandfather.

Suddenly, a commotion in the water disrupted their concentration. Finally, a sign of life from the tank's residents. At the far end of the rectangular structure, a small splash, quickly followed by a larger one, provided the first evidence the two inhabitants were alive and well. There was nothing aggressive in their actions, so Mateo and the girls were alerted but not alarmed. "Maybe you want to get out of there, girls," Mateo calmly suggested. Their lack of response told him they were perfectly content to remain.

"We swam with dolphins before," Hanna matter-of-factly claimed.

Leanna chirped, "Yeah, a couple of times; once in Hawaii and twice in the Bahamas… or maybe it was three times, I don't remember."

Hanna clarified, "Um, it was twice in Hawaii and then we did it twice in the Bahamas and once on that trip to Puerto Rico, remember?"

For once, they sounded like normal teenagers, Mateo thought. A weak smile crossed his face as he pictured the two sisters laughing and teasing each other during happier times. He was determined to protect them and help get them out of the situation as quickly as possible.

Just then, the dolphins emerged, swimming very cautiously to within a couple feet of the Armstrong girls. They actually giggled, rather than retract as others might have understandably done. Their prior experience was fortuitous, in that they were supremely prepared to coexist with the dolphins. Though Mateo's concerns for Violet preoccupied his thoughts, he paused to absorb the beauty of the four sentient beings communing peacefully.

As it approached 5:00 a.m. Mateo realized the Sun would soon be rising, and he planned on getting Violet to a hospital as quickly as possible. His instincts told him there was more to the disastrous event than the obvious, but he reminded himself to keep his wits. Mateo prayed his role would become clearer with the advent of morning. His temporary confusion had dissipated and he felt fiercely devoted to ensuring the safety of the three children in his care. He remained hopeful that they would all soon be able to make their way home.

The distant thunder provided evidence that the storm had not yet cleared. Several hundred yards from the dolphin tank, Sinnamon and Jason were all too aware of Nature's dominance. Though still too dark to make significant progress, the mismatched duo was inclined to take action rather than remain passive. Sinnamon had a tiny pocket flashlight attached to a ring of keys, and had cleverly entwined it in a stretchable headband to fashion a makeshift miner's helmet. The miniscule light projected by its fine beam was barely visible, but in the shrouded jungle environment, it provided a semblance of security.

The region was a quagmire of wildly varied elevations, its surface features ranging from pools of thick mud to jagged rock protrusions. The terrain's harshness and unpredictability made progress difficult, yet they inched toward what they hoped was the proper destination. After weighing their options, they had agreed to head south toward the parking lot beyond the zoo exit. They presumed their first order of business was to locate their vehicles.

Jason followed directly behind Sinnamon, at times reaching out in the darkness to grasp her arm, for reassurance as much as stability. She led the way, reaching out with both hands to brush away the many branches and low-hanging foliage that dominated their environs. A much different sound suddenly contrasted with the ambient hissing manufactured by the moisture dripping from the treetops. A menacing growl stopped the intrepid pair in their tracks.

Originating nearby, the noise affected them on a primal level. Jason instinctively reacted by squeezing Sinnamon's elbow and pulling her to him, indicating they should remain quiet and still. In any other circumstance, he would have been on the receiving end of a slap across the face, but the normally feisty redhead was feeling vulnerable. She stopped dead in her tracks, held her breath, and attempted to get a clear reading on the point of origin of the disturbing sound.

They listened intently for another growl, both still as statues and silent as shadows. No sound came. Each was concerned by the proximity of the original noise, clearly the telltale growl of a large predator. Whether it was produced by a large feline or some other animal was unknown, but there was no doubt they were in the company of a creature that could do them serious harm. The quakes had freed some of the zoo's residents, and in the dark and treacherous environment, the two vulnerable humans were at a distinct disadvantage.

Seconds passed like hours before Sinnamon finally sneered, "Stop digging your motherfucking fingernails into my arm or I'll feed you to whatever's stalking us."

Jason was too nervous to acknowledge her, and the specific words of her crude warning never actually registered with him. Nevertheless, he understood her intent and released his vice-like grip on her densely freckled upper arm. He shushed her quietly, fearing her voice had already conveyed their location to whatever it was that had likely picked up their scent. With all that had happened in such a short time, neither of them had considered that the shifting of the land could have released some of the zoo's large predators.

'Jesus,' Jason thought. 'As if we didn't already have enough to worry about...'

For all her bravado, Sinnamon was not foolish enough to tempt fate in this instance. She turned her angular frame slightly, so that she and Jason stood shoulder-to-shoulder. Slowly, but with clarity of purpose, she pulled him by his wrist to a seated position on the floor of the drenched forest. They huddled together in silence – ears pricked for any telltale noises. Never before had Rebecca Sinclair felt so vulnerable.

"The best course of action here is probably inaction, right?" Jason finally whispered into an ear adorned with seven tiny multicolored gemstones.

In a monotone voice, Sinnamon replied under her breath, "I'm down with that. Now just shut up and we'll be alright." There would be no argument and the exhausted pair eventually fell asleep, shrouded by thick foliage. They slept undisturbed in their jade cocoon, and while they napped, Jason experienced another vivid dream...

Jason walked slowly through a foggy atmosphere across an expanse of white sand. Barefoot, and naked beneath a simple white cotton tunic, he traversed the vast realm toward a shimmering multicolored light. When he drew close to the source of radiance he discovered an enormous lake, but was strangely unable to advance to the water's edge - blocked by an invisible force. He laid his hands upon the strange barrier's surface to discover a "living wall" undulating beneath his sensitive palms.

Lost Out in Space

Undaunted by the barrier's bizarre properties, he attempted to walk through it, but was deterred. He was powerfully attracted to the radiating, sparkling light, yet frustrated by the rejection. Jason dropped his hands and stared into what had become a spinning, multifaceted gem radiating soothing beams of white light filled with tiny glimmering crystals.

Jason was mesmerized by the visual splendor of the flowing movements of the sparkling elements. He tried to focus on the central source of light but was unable to discern any identifiable shapes. The myriad sparkling particles began to cluster and he was ultimately able to recognize the form of a human being. The vague form never appeared to stabilize, its flowing energy in constant transition.

Finally, the central light source rose high into the star-covered sky. Once it reached a preordained altitude, it spun wildly... until the glittering pinpricks of colored light scattered – dispersed by virtue of the host's rotation. While the crystal fragments exploded into a dazzling kaleidoscopic display and then melted into the darkness, the purity of the central light source remained.

Jason noted the absence of peripheral details, save for the sand, water and the starlit backdrop. He found he could comfortably stare directly into the core of the white light despite its stunning luminescence and purity. Rather than the discomfort he expected, he instead experienced an overwhelming calm. It was as if he was enveloped in a soothing milky armor.

Why he felt so good was a mystery, but rather than try to analyze it, he only wanted to bathe in it forever. Immersed in its soothing beauty, he detected movement in his peripheral vision. The sky suddenly spawned additional spinning gems of light. They appeared out of the mist, becoming clearer and brighter with each passing second. Suspended in air surrounding the original shape, at first they all spun in place independently; but, after only a few seconds, the newer gems were absorbed into the original form - causing it to spin even faster. It ultimately spewed out thousands more identical copies of itself in a wild display of light trails carried on waves of milky-white energy.

The newest offspring spun and sparkled as they, in turn, produced great numbers of identical spawn. The process repeated until the sky was saturated in there were so many brilliant gems the night sky had been transformed to daylight. In the wake of the transition, he could no longer see the original shape. 'Strange,' he thought, 'I still 'feel' its presence... but don't see it anywhere.'

The sky had become a watercolor backdrop of blues and purples highlighted with countless glistening specks. He stood with his toes perilously close to the water's edge and happily basked in the newly rendered sky's *unparalleled beauty. Suddenly, he felt compelled to try to move forward again. This time, there was no barrier to deny him and he moved beyond the spot where the invisible energy formerly existed. He tentatively entered the crystal blue water, noting its perfect temperature, just slightly cooler than his body. He waded out a bit further into its soothing embrace, and a wave of serenity enveloped him.*

Jason would later recall being aware of a growing presence from the moment he immersed himself in the water. Not any identifiable, singular presence, but rather a symphony of separate energies. Similar to the singular voice of a hundred-member choir, he felt the combined presence of many individual energies.

For a fleeting moment, his own spirit bonded with the others in a choreographed dance across the water's surface. They effortlessly blended and soared in a maelstrom of boundless exhilaration; twisting and turning in a display of unadulterated joy. Then, as if of a single mind, the collective energy broke the water's surface and generated a glittering waterspout surging with limitless power.

Jason felt his very essence merging with the others. Although he retained his unique identity, he also sensed he had blended with all the others to become something much more powerful and complex. A sense of peace came over him as he reveled in the dance, playing his humble role as one component in the embodiment of the strange yet benign life force. So euphoric was he in the midst of the dream, he never wanted to separate from the other energies.

Unfortunately, the dream had to end when reality came screaming once again. "Hey! Wake up or I'll leave your sorry ass here!" reintroduced him to the harsh reality of his current situation. Sinnamon had just untwined her well-toned frame from his contrastingly fleshy body and was adjusting her brown leather belt. The darkness had lifted during the few hours they slept, and the morning brought a much clearer sense of what they faced. As he struggled to his feet, Jason began to fully appreciate the extent of the devastation.

The quake rendered the Ituri Forest nearly unrecognizable. Due to the dramatic reshaping of the terrain, towering walls of dirt and rock surrounded them. During the night, Jason had envisioned a much larger area of flat land and imagined they would have little trouble walking over the debris to reach the exit to the southeast. Unfortunately, that was not the case, in that so little negotiable land remained. They were limited to no more than an acre of relatively flat land, in the shape of a pie wedge, with the broader end to the north and its point culminating in a mass of twisted vegetation to the south.

Reminiscent of an adventurer in an action film, Sinnamon pulled a large hunting knife from the sheath attached to her belt and began hacking away at the overgrowth. Organic fragments sprayed everywhere with each long, arcing slash. Her knife was nearly as effective as a machete but the thick growth made progress slow. Jason felt humbled by the impressive power that had so thoroughly transfigured their environment, and wondered how extensive the damage had been. His thoughts turned to his parents, only a few miles away in their pleasant cul-de-sac home.

Sinnamon was obviously hell-bent on finding a way out of the claustrophobic sliver of real estate, and Jason made sure to stay clear of her wildly slashing blade. Jason was the passive type, with a tendency to over-analyze and ruminate. Although still awestruck by the gravity of their plight, he was impressed by Sinnamon's aggressive, take-charge attitude. He was actually starting to feel grateful that fate had thrown them together.

'This chick's not gonna wait for anyone or anything,' he thought, as he watched the redhead slice through the dense brush.

He followed closely behind; convinced they were headed in the only direction that could conceivably lead to escape. The high-pitched screeches from the treetops provided reassuring evidence that other life had survived.

"We're not the only ones who made it, dude. Listen to that racket," Sinnamon remarked between slashes. At that very moment, behind them to the north, the din generated by the birds and monkeys was suddenly punctuated by a series of low, menacing growls.

"Christ... better keep hacking there!" Jason loudly suggested.

Without missing a beat, Sinnamon smartly assured, "I'm on it, boss."

The temperature had risen due to the suddenly radiant morning Sun. Jason looked at his watch, noted the time as 7:03 a.m., and then began using his arms and feet to break or brush away as much of the overgrowth as possible, staying out of range of his companion's blade. Side-by-side, they made slow but steady progress, trying to unveil the quickest way out. They kept working to carve out a new path toward salvation, spurred on by the realization that the predator they heard earlier was likely still in pursuit.

△△△

I Miss Your Purple Hair

CHAPTER ELEVEN

I Watched the Red~Orange Glow

"A new species is arising on the planet. It is arising now, and you are it!"
~ Eckhart Tolle

Kyle Nordstrom draped his long right arm over Mia's shoulders and pulled her a bit closer. In the early morning light, the misty silhouette of the wolf explained the long, low howl that shook them from their slumber. They had managed little more than two hours of sleep before being rudely disturbed. To the north of where the eight survivors clustered, a solitary wolf peered at them from behind a fan of fern-like foliage. It stared through crystal blue eyes, a thick collar of white fur surrounding its large head.

Assuming the quakes had freed the creature from its habitat, Mia anxiously whispered to her brother, "Shouldn't we run? What do we do?"

Kyle had no more experience with wild animals than his city-dwelling sibling, but instinctively knew to avoid hasty movements. He calmly replied, "There's nowhere to run, even if we wanted to, so let's stay calm, everyone. I don't think it means us any harm. It's probably as disoriented and afraid as we are after all that's happened."

Admiring her brother's composure, Mia agreed and quickly added, "It doesn't seem threatening, lying still there in the grass. Maybe it was injured in the quake... but just to be on the safe side, let's start moving in the other direction."

Kyle's actions demonstrated his concurrence and he slowly but deliberately led the others further away from the wolf. The morning Sun provided improved visibility, although long shadows cast by the towering walls diminished the effect. Even so, they finally got a clear picture of just how desperate their situation was. The exit had been completely blocked off, its surrounding structure virtually annihilated by the crash of the sky tram. The surrounding land mass had been greatly disfigured during the upheaval and a towering mountain of rubble and debris now stood where had previously existed a direct pathway out of the zoo.

It was as if a Goliath had employed its enormous hands to surround them with a huge ring of Earth-hewn blockades. Thirty-foot walls of dirt and rock encircled them, forming impenetrable barriers. The land upon which they stood was twisted and uneven with unnaturally placed rock formations. Only a triangular area of approximately 75 square yards remained traversable. The group slowly walked in the direction of the narrowest point of land to the southwest, away from the wolf lurking amongst the green wisps. They proceeded with great caution, as aftershocks threatened the very stability of the ground beneath them.

Victory Cooper tried her cell phone and just shook her head. Dwayne reached for the Blackberry device buried in his pocket and learned it had been damaged during the quake – its outer shell cracked and its screen shattered. "Damn it!" he yelled as he angrily threw the now-worthless object into the side of the towering mountain.

Mia had already tested her phone, only to experience the same futility. She tried tuning its built-in radio feature, but quickly learned it was a waste of time. No signals were transmitting, or perhaps the enormous stone barriers were somehow causing interference. Everyone racked their brain for ideas, but there was no way to find out the fate of their loved ones and friends, and no way to discover how much of the world had been affected.

Interrupting the temporary silence, Kyle called out to the group from atop a rocky outcropping, "I suggest you shut off any phones and put them in your pockets for now, to save battery life. If we burn up what little we have, we may regret it once we get to a clearing." Everyone recognized the wisdom of his statement and quickly followed suit. DeAngelo quietly complied, but felt extremely vulnerable, in large part due to the sighting of the white wolf.

Noticing his trembling lower lip, Kyle encouraged the child by suggesting he team up with the other young boy. The frightened child, who had barely spoken since being found, displayed signs of shock as he cowered in a dark recess of sand-colored rock. Clearly afraid of the wolf they had spotted, he had squeezed behind a comforting cluster of rocks that had burst up through the Earth's surface the night before. Partially obscured there, he had been quietly sniffling since waking. Except for him, the small group of survivors made their introductions to one another.

34-year-old Victory Cooper, a lifelong Christian who always carried her small red bible, silently prayed as she led her limping husband and frightened son through the debris-strewn area. She silently prayed for the safety of her son and husband and for the preservation of her parents and siblings. With no way of connecting with the outside world, she could only pray the destruction had not extended beyond the zoo. She noted a caustic stench in the air, unaware there were toxic fumes emanating from nearby pockets of volcanic content.

They had reached the western limits of the traversable area, and stood at the foot of a craggy incline along the base of the wall.

A Type One Diabetic, Aaron Kemper felt ill. His slightly blurred vision and shaking hands indicated his need for insulin and nourishment. Unbeknownst to the others, he also had previously been diagnosed manic-depressive; something he took great measures to hide from the media and his colleagues. His wealth afforded him many luxuries, but maintaining privacy was always difficult with all the media attention he attracted.

Unfortunately, the leather briefcase he had thrown to the ground earlier not only contained his laptop, PDA, and cell phone; but more importantly, the insulin and related supplies he desperately needed. That case and its precious contents apparently were now forever lost to the officious poseur, swallowed up by the Earth. Aaron struggled to gather his strength as he dutifully followed behind the others, uncomfortable with the forced interdependence.

Dante obviously labored on a badly injured right knee, having torn his anterior cruciate ligament when the violent tremors tossed him backwards into a six-foot deep pit. During that awkward plunge, he also received a minor concussion when his head banged against the unforgiving rocks at the base of the sinkhole. Toughened by a history of physical and mental conditioning at Temple University where he earned a reputation as a tough-nosed blocking fullback, he was better equipped than many to endure pain. During the night's turmoil, he had also suffered a deep contusion to the orbital bone of his left eye, and was sporting a bright purplish bruise there.

Dante surveyed the surroundings and the odd red-orange sky with a profound sense of concern and fear, but was determined to hide his burgeoning feeling of futility. The environs that had become so familiar to him after three years on the zoo's security force were now virtually unrecognizable. The area's only identifiable landmarks were the broken remnants of the entrance/exit shelters and the ruins of the nearby snack shop. Despite his aching head and the burning pain in his knee, 31-year-old Dante had the presence of mind to snatch up some provisions from the shop's scattered inventory. When he shuffled over to scavenge without so much as a word, the rest of the party took notice and silently followed suit, stuffing small packs of snack foods, packaged T-shirts, and bottled water into their purses, pockets, and backpacks.

Aaron gruffly complained, "What's the point? We need to head the other direction and see if there's some way we can climb that mass of overgrowth and rock. The damn parking lot isn't more than 100 or so yards to the southeast. The fires are to the east. Maybe we can climb that span to the south, and then work our way to the cars." No one responded; instead, they all continued gathering and organizing whatever they could find. The nameless boy rummaged for intact bottles of water, lining them up in neat rows along a flat segment of asphalt walkway.

The entire group, stuffed pockets and all, finally made their way toward the wall of debris to the west. Once assembled at the foot of the blockade, they stopped to discuss their options. Young DeAngelo spoke first, pointing out something he had noticed as they approached the towering stone obstacle. Pointing at a spot about twenty feet above ground, he declared, "Look... up there! I see light between the red rock and that shiny metal thing!" Victory, standing directly behind her sharp-eyed son, corroborated his discovery. Between a red-hued boulder and a displaced metal utility pole, a sliver of sunlight was just barely discernible.

"That's our best hope, right there," Dwayne chimed in.

Aaron used a souvenir T-shirt he picked up off the ground to wipe sweat from his furrowed brow before voicing his disagreement. "What the hell are you people thinking? If you seriously think there's any way we can dig through that rock with our bare hands, you've all lost your minds. We need to head to the south and get to the parking lot. That's where the rescue squads will be. Even if we did get through this wall, where would that put us... deeper into the zoo? This is ridiculous..."

An exhausted and frustrated Mia interrupted his rant, speaking sternly yet with calm resolve. "Look to the north and east," she ordered. "See all that grey smoke blowing toward us? The volume has increased over the last few minutes and the wind's blowing toward us. To the southeast, there's more smoke... and a wall that's easily 15 feet higher to negotiate. I don't see any sense in pushing our luck, and that glimpse of daylight is the only ray of hope I've seen since this nightmare started." A mass of dried blood decorated the side of her forehead, rendered more visible since she had cut off a substantial chunk of her hair.

Victory held her weary head in her hand and sighed deeply. In her Jamaican accent she asked, "They'll be sendin' help soon, right?" Nobody initially responded. Tears suddenly came to eyes already reddened by toxic components carried on the breeze. "Rescue teams have got to be comin', don't they? Maybe we should nurse our wounds here 'til we spot a helicopter or our phones start workin' again. It's probably just a temporary outage and once they restore service we can dial 911 and let them know there are people trapped in here."

I Watched the Red~Orange Glow

Dwayne eased over, gently held her face in one enormous hand, and placed a light kiss on her cheek. His deep voice had always been soothing to his wife. "Baby, take a deep breath. You might be right about waitin' it out here. We got a little food and water, and it won't be long before the cops and military come lookin'. I think maybe we oughta stay put. I bet the cell phones will be up and workin' by tonight, anyway." Gesturing with a head-tilt toward Dante, he added, "An' this dude's got a gun on him, so that wolf ain't nothin' to worry 'bout, either. If the wind blows those fires closer, they still gonna be blocked by these mounds of rock."

DeAngelo argued against his parents. "No way!" he exclaimed. "We can't stay here! We should at least try to get through that opening up there. Can't we get to one of the other parking lots that way, too? It's getting hotter since we woke up and this air is burning my throat and eyes. Let's keep going. I don't wanna stay here... please!"

Dante's knee throbbed and he was still battling the cobwebs cluttering his mind. He knew it would be difficult to attempt to scale the foreboding mountain but recognized the futility of waiting in the constricted canyon, cut off from the outside world. He suspected the earthquake's impact was far-reaching and surmised it could be a day or two before any rescue operation reached them. As isolated as they were in the shadowy chasm, he also realized how challenging it would be to make visual confirmation of their location. If the breakdown of cellular service was as widespread as he feared, it could be a very long wait before they could summon help.

As he clasped the pistol holstered on his belt, Dante's scraped and bloodied knuckles sent pain signals to his brain. He had never had to use his gun on the job until the day before and did not relish the thought of drawing it again. Dante had always been a fun-loving, easygoing guy who enjoyed sharing a few cold beers with his buddies at a favorite bar over most other pursuits. In the past year, he had rededicated himself to a workout routine and dropped some of the excess weight he had added to his stocky 5'9" frame following an abbreviated stint in the Army.

"D-Mac," as he was commonly called by friends, began to grasp the grim reality of their situation, and came to an inevitable conclusion. For a long moment, he locked his brown eyes with the haunting ice-blue irises of the wolf – which remained motionless, stretched out in its grassy nook only a short distance away. Dante felt sympathetic toward the animal rather than threatened. The solitary wolf was just as much a victim as they were, similarly displaced and trapped by powerful forces beyond its influence. The animal's calm demeanor indicated its apparent resignation to being completely powerless to escape. He had expected it to be pacing nervously or frantically probing the boundaries of their confines. He presumed that the solitary creature must have already exhausted all options, but was nonetheless impressed by its composure.

Aside from that appraisal, Dante felt an inexplicable emotional connection with the wolf. It was as if he received a sense of peaceful reassurance directly from the animal. He actually felt grateful to the dignified creature for those perceived intentions and resolved to return to rescue it, if they were eventually successful in breaching the wall to the west – the only reasonable direction to proceed, in his estimation. Finally, he addressed the rest of the bedraggled party.

"It's time to move, people," he somewhat forcefully declared. Nodding toward DeAngelo he added, "The young man's right. That bit of sunlight's enough to suggest there could be a way through to the other side, and then we should be able to backtrack to the parking lot. Of course, that's assuming a lot about the state of things on the other side of this barrier."

Kemper could no longer stifle his opinion nor disguise his arrogance, ranting, "Bullshit! Who the hell appointed you Ringleader? You think that gun automatically makes you the *de facto* shot caller? The parking lot is to the south, people. There's no way of knowing what other obstructions lie to the west beyond this wall. Even if we did make it through we could find we wasted precious time and energy only to be further away from where we need to be. I say we climb that pile of rock to the southeast, regardless of how steep it is, to get closer to where the rescue teams can pick us up. For all we know there are hundreds of other people just past the summit and we'll have all the help we need to escape this deathtrap. That's the only plan that makes sense."

Mia felt her usually cool Swedish blood begin to boil. "I'm with the security guard on this. He knows the layout far better than any of us, right? If he thinks we should head in this direction, I'm willing to believe it'll put us in a better situation than the one we're stuck in now. If we can fit inside that narrow gap, we'll know whether or not there's reason to continue. Personally, I have no intention of staying put any longer. The air's becoming fouler by the minute and my guess is that breathing it isn't healthy; and there's no way I want to wait for those fires to spread this way." Mia searched the eyes the other frightened souls and discovered her answer there.

Kyle smiled in reaction to his sister's declaration before making an effort to rally the others by commenting, "Let's saddle up then! I'll take point – been rock climbing since I was a kid anyway."

Aaron was never one to be compliant and found the proceedings unamusing to say the least. He angrily threw his empty water bottle to the fractured asphalt beneath his $500 shoes and loudly reiterated his personal intentions. "You all do what you like, but I don't intend to risk life and limb heading off in the wrong direction! Anyone serious about getting out of here now ought to think hard and come along with me to the parking lot. I'll gladly go it alone if I have to... but it'll be that much quicker if there are more people moving rocks."

Dwayne Cooper was torn between the logic behind Aaron's contention and the lure provided by the sliver of soft sunlight in the other direction. His responsibility was to his family and he wanted to do whatever he could to get them back home to Los Angeles as quickly as possible. Their first significant vacation in three years had plunged them into a nightmarish situation and it was all he could do not to put the blame on himself. DeAngelo had hoped to visit the Grand Canyon, a trip the family had discussed for years. Dwayne nevertheless lobbied with his wife and son to make San Diego their destination, after reading an online article about the new dolphin exhibit. His lifelong fascination with the creatures had been the primary motivation, but a separate, impossible-to-identify force also beckoned him to the zoo.

He had felt a powerful desire to visit during this particular holiday season, for some mysterious reason. For months, he imagined strolling along the zoo's tree-lined paths, his arm around his son and his wife's hand in his. He envisioned visiting the two displaced Sea World dolphins and savoring DeAngelo's reaction to their antics. Some unknown force compelled him to be there on this particular day and, despite honest efforts to consider other options, he could not shake the feeling that the zoo had to be their destination for a holiday getaway. Eventually, he wore down both Victory and DeAngelo and sold them on coming to San Diego. The enormous sense of guilt he now felt was wreaking havoc with his emotions.

Dwayne's overriding priority was to make the wisest possible choice, one that would guarantee the quickest resolution to the crisis at hand. The others were all but strangers who left him confused. He was tempted to follow the tantalizing lure of the light leaking through the mountain to the west. At the same time, he acknowledged the undeniable logic behind trying the more direct route toward the parking lot, regardless of the disdain he had begun to feel toward the acerbic Aaron Kemper. He looked to his wife for her thoughts and before he could ask for it, she expressed her opinion in trademark style.

"Darlin'… this one's a fool," she blurted, extending her angular chin toward Aaron. "He's just bein' pigheaded. I say we find out what's behind that sunlight. Let's not waste any more time arguin'. If this man wants to climb that other ridiculous mountain, I say good luck to him – but we should stick with the others and start climbin'."

Dwayne knew Victory made sense and more importantly, felt she was wise to be wary of Aaron's arrogant persona. He finally sided with the majority, commenting, "Okay, Vic, okay. I'll do what I can on this one good leg. Let's get started so we can make it home before the Sun goes down."

Not inclined to give up quickly, Aaron made one last ditch appeal, resorting to the only leverage he held. "Five thousand in cash to anyone who goes with me and helps clear a path to the parking lot. We'll be home by evening while the others will still be stuck in this hellhole. I'll give half now and the rest when we set foot outside. Even if we hit a dead end you'll be twenty-five hundred richer and can still rejoin the others… if it comes to that."

Kyle had already started ascending the face of the western wall and was so focused on maintaining a secure foothold he barely heard the sales pitch. Within several minutes, he made worthwhile progress and was not remotely inclined to turn back. His determined sister was close behind, spotting reliable footholds for her brother as they pressed on. She clearly heard Aaron's desperate offer and decided it was just further evidence of his egotistical attitude.

Young DeAngelo was tantalized by the notion of getting his hands on the five grand and he chirped up after pondering the prospect for a few minutes. "Hey Dad," he whispered, "Why don't we do it and at least get half of it? We could still help the others if it's too hard going up that other mountain." Dwayne had half-expected his son to jump at the promise of such a significant amount of money but had no intention of deviating from his commitment to investigate the sliver of light. One perturbed glance communicated his lack of tolerance for any arguments, and DeAngelo immediately abandoned the notion.

Without responding directly to Aaron, the three members of the Cooper family deliberately made their way to where Mia and Kyle Nordstrom were carefully negotiating the imposing mountain of rubble. Ever the opportunist, Aaron had worked to become a keen observer of people and recognized a glimmer of interest in Dante's expression. The usually gregarious "D-Mac" did not believe in bucking the odds and felt that the fires encroaching from the east could conceivably threaten their location if the winds shifted. In his gut, he was confident he and Kemper could find some way to reach the parking lot, but inherently wanted to stick with the large group even if heading west seemed somewhat illogical.

Five thousand dollars was a very tantalizing lure in light of the substantial debt he had incurred during the past year, thanks to his gambling addiction – currently in remission. He figured he could ease significant stress by erasing one particular outstanding debt with a local sports bookie. In a hurried reaction, he made up his mind to take one last gamble after no one else showed any inclination to take Kemper up on his offer.

"I'll do it," Dante stated in a deliberate monotone, locking the rest of the survivors in momentary disbelief.

Most everyone understood the need to stick together and had presumed Dante's knowledge of the region would be critical to their survival and ultimate escape. With no way of knowing what wildlife might be lurking on the other side of the wall, they also understood that his handgun was an equally precious commodity. Before anyone else could chime in, Dante informed Aaron, "But I want it all up front... and that's non-negotiable. If I'm gonna put my life on the line I want the iron clad guarantee of having that five grand in hand. If you're the kind of man I think you are, you get where I'm coming from. Besides, I'm the only one willing to go along for the ride and I happen to know every square inch of this place like the back of my..."

Frustrated, Victory interrupted the negotiations by emphatically injecting some sense into what she felt was a ridiculous debate. "Like the back of *what*? That was before Mother Nature tore this place up, mister! It's not the same place you knew yesterday. Don't you understand? We have no idea what's goin' on with our families an' the world outside this place. We don't even know if there's any chance we can climb out of this hole we're in. If you're thinkin' money makes a bit of difference right now, you're nothin' but a fool. We need to stick together an' find a way out of this before those fires choke the life out of each an' every one of us."

Precariously perched fifteen feet overhead, Mia echoed Victory's sentiments. Her foremost thought was to quickly resolve the dissension and get everyone mobilized in order to maximize the limited light they had. "Boys, this is ridiculous. We need your expertise to make sure we can get out of here, Dante. You can't seriously be considering gambling everything to go along with his bad idea, for just a few thousand dollars."

Ironically, Mia had used the term "gambling" as an intended negative, with the wrong man. In a twisted way it was the gamble of going against what he knew was most logical and sane that appealed to Dante, a manifestation of the darkest side of his lifelong weakness. Dante wrestled with his decision but when Aaron sternly beckoned and agreed to pay him everything in advance, he began limping in the direction of the smug bureaucrat, outstretched hand aching to be filled. Aaron produced the cash from the money belt hidden beneath his tailored white shirt, and dramatically slapped the bills into Dante's palm. The money seemed to reinvigorate the one-time Boy Scout who, despite his banged-up body, appeared more determined than ever to escape.

Dante and Aaron headed toward the foreboding barrier to the southeast and before long were out of visual range, blocked from the others' sight by debris. Dante shoved the crisp bills into the front pocket of his pants and tried to analyze the mountain of earth as he limped ever closer to its base. He chuckled to himself that Aaron had invested five thousand dollars in someone who was not even physically sound. *'What an asshole,'* he thought to himself. *'He has no clue what we're facing. He just wants to buy his way out of it but there's no way we're gonna climb out in this direction. Just look at the size of the thing!'*

Aaron knew nothing about the severity of the ligament damage Dante had suffered. He presumed he had no more than a slight sprain and had not cared enough to consider the extent of the injury, or whether it might limit his compatriot-for-hire. Kemper was in less than ideal condition himself, sweating and laboring to breathe the increasingly toxic air. The pampered thug was far from being in adequate physical shape to navigate such an intimidating obstacle. Upon a fleeting assessment of the mountain towering before them, Aaron barked, "Just beyond this is salvation. You can thank me when we walk down the other side. Now, let's get going. We'll stay ahead of those fires and be long gone before any aftershocks come along."

Even though Dante had inadequate time to ponder the possibility, he naturally understood that aftershocks were probably inevitable. He put the thought aside and plucked a slender steel rod off the ground to use as a walking stick. When Aaron motioned for Dante to follow his lead he willingly pacified the smarmy politician. The red-hued tinge to the enormous collection of dirt and rock seemed strange, evidence of the dramatic upheaval that swapped the familiar geology with what lay hidden beneath for many years.

With every step, the pain in Dante's knee produced sharp, burning agony but he was determined to grind it out. Aaron was delusional about their prospects for escape, choosing to put his head down and take one step at a time. With each additional foot of progress, he felt he was that much closer to calling his limousine driver and being delivered to his luxurious condominium.

He anticipated a long bath followed by a full body massage before heading to his country club for a gourmet meal. He had always dealt with adversity in this manner; leaning on his wealth and privilege as a convenient crutch that protected him from having to roll up his sleeves and work toward a resolution. He never felt vulnerable because he simply did not have to.

High along the jagged face of the foreboding wall, Kyle Nordstrom flirted with disaster. He had almost reached the sunlight-leaking fissure when he lost focus for a split-second and his black shoe slipped on a cluster of loose rocks. For a moment, he and everyone watching were sure he was about to fall the entire 18 feet to ground level. Climbing several feet below him, Mia audibly gasped and reached out in futility with a scratched and singed right arm. Her left hand clung to a granite fence post embedded in the amalgam of unidentifiable debris and rock. For a split second, she allowed fear to infiltrate her thoughts and nearly abandoned any hope of escaping through the wall. She was obviously unfazed by her brother's near-disastrous misstep once it registered that he had righted himself.

"Kyle!" she called out. "Wait 'til I catch up. Just chill out there for a second and when I reach you we'll check out that crack in the rock together." She quickened her pace and arrived at her older brother's side before he had a chance to respond. Mia was naturally quite nimble and felt motivated by Kyle's misstep to advance more quickly. If there were to be more tremors and aftershocks, she was determined to get through to the other side before they arrived. Despite his gaffe, Kyle seemed to enjoy the challenge of the climb and flashed a slight grin when Mia draped a weary left arm over his shoulder.

He looked into her eyes and observed, "Life sure throws some strange stuff at you, doesn't it? Pretty damn amazing. I mean, this enormous barrier didn't exist just hours ago and now we're climbing it like a couple of mountain goats." Mia drew in a deep breath and noticed how foul the air had become, more saturated with offensive chemical odors than just a half-hour earlier.

She responded to Kyle's musings with, "I'd have to say I'm glad we're going through this together, but ...all things considered... I'd rather be in Philadelphia, pal." He laughed aloud for the first time since the sky had fallen, and felt an infusion of energy, courtesy of his fair-haired sister.

"What's it look like up there?" yelled Victory from ground level, obviously referring to the gap in the wall as well as the mountainside's general composition.

"The footing is surprisingly good, actually," snickered Kyle. "Hold on for a minute, while we check out the hotspot." He and Mia shuffled sideways with their backs against the wall's surface and their feet supported by a conveniently located six-inch wide ledge. Small rocks and particles of debris tumbled down around them as they inched closer to the spot where diffused beams of light leaked through.

Upon inspection, Mia and Kyle discovered that there indeed existed a significant break in the surface of the mountainside. Evidenced by sunlight passing through, the gap appeared to completely dissect the wall of rock as they had hoped. Albeit narrow, dark, and unpredictably shaped, it seemed conceivable that an adult of average proportions could enter and at least make it partway through. There was ample clearance to allow an individual to stand upright before shimmying sideways between the craggy interior walls.

Mia immediately volunteered to enter the gap to ascertain its limits, asking her brother for his phone, for use as a source of illumination. With only subdued sunlight seeping through, some source of artificial light would be necessary if they were to attempt exploration. "Battery's already half dead," Kyle glumly mentioned as he handed her the device.

"It'll last a good while longer," Mia confidently replied, as she returned her attention to the gloomy passageway. She had assessed the uppermost terrain and felt that the likelihood of getting everyone up and over the top would be far more treacherous and time-consuming. As she eased her slender 5'8" body into the narrow opening, she silently prayed the gap would lead to salvation.

The passageway's constricted configuration magnified the velocity of the breeze entering from the west and Mia's blonde hair danced in its playful current. At first, it perturbed her to have strands of her hair and particles of dirt further obstructing her already limited vision, but then she realized it was an encouraging sign. The fact that the wind was channeling through the void indicated that the passage indeed penetrated to the other side. Whether or not it would be navigable throughout remained to be determined, as did what awaited them on the other side.

Mia put aside fears of a collapse from below or above that could result in her entombment. The others watched Mia bravely disappear into the shadowy crevasse. Kyle followed, reaching out for her extended hand. An eerie silence followed the moment they vanished into the murky passageway. Six sets of eyes were fixed on the spot where Kyle disappeared and prayed for any sign of hope.

△△△

CHAPTER TWELVE

Lonely and Out of Place

"We frail humans are at one time capable of the greatest good and, at the same time, capable of the greatest evil. Change will only come about when each of us takes up the daily struggle ourselves to be more forgiving, compassionate, loving, and above all joyful in the knowledge that, by some miracle of grace, we can change as those around us can change too."
~ Mairead Maguire

The pain in Dante's knee steadily worsened, yet he pressed onward among the rocks. It had been more than twenty hours since he had eaten anything, so he reached into the pocket of his zoo-issued blue jacket and grabbed a candy bar plucked from the ruins of a snack shop. "Ah, good ol' Snickers..." the native Philadelphian grunted as he stripped the wrapper from the half-melted chocolate confection. "... mmmmm... always hits the spot... even in a damn earthquake!"

Having ascended nearly 15 feet, Aaron's breathing became noticeably labored. He leaned against a sandstone outcropping to take a few gulps of lukewarm water. Earlier, he had slid two of the badly dented plastic bottles into his suit coat pockets. Insulin deficiency, coupled with lack of nutrition and the mounting humidity contributed to his light-headedness and increased anxiety. The San Diego region was well-known for its relatively dry air, but the intense storms and ensuing quakes drastically affected weather conditions. The air was heavy with moisture and laced with acidic elements that irritated his sinuses and brought tears to his burning eyes.

Aaron had never maintained faith in much of anything, let alone the blind promise of what might lie beyond the mountain upon which he stood. His directed his misplaced anger and resentment toward Dante as though the catastrophe was somehow his fault. It was typical for the ultra-privileged oaf to view any inconvenience or crisis as a personal affront. He resented being forced to confront reality on such an intimate level. Aaron's decision to head in this particular direction had vastly more to do with arrogance and his propensity for being contrary than any real inkling that it represented the best chance for escape.

Beads of sweat trickled down Aaron Kemper's furrowed brow into his beady eyes, their composition of saline and sulfur delivering yet more irritation. He viewed the struggling, slow moving Dante with disdain. In his

119

estimation, the security officer was nothing more than "a punk" who was failing in his responsibility to protect every visitor to the zoo. He felt Dante should have taken the lead and scouted the perimeter of the environment before recommending options based on his superior knowledge of the Park. He grew increasingly resentful watching the "lowly" security officer savor each bite of his candy bar as though it were the last he would ever eat.

Immediately after tossing his empty water bottle away, the smug elitist sarcastically barked, "Snack break's over, Rent-a-Cop. It's time to earn that five grand." Dante already had the cash in pocket and was not particularly motivated by anything Aaron had to say. He disliked the pompous oaf from the moment they met, which had served as additional incentive for relieving him of his money.

Dante shrugged off the comment and mumbled, "Yeah, yeah… I'm about as ready as I'm gonna get."

Still almost twenty feet shy of the summit; progress had become increasingly slow and painful for both men. A light breeze promised some relief, but turned out to be far less than refreshing, infused with caustic chemicals as it was. Dante led Kemper by only a few feet and every time he looked back to check the status of the wealthy, libido-driven snob he felt the urge to abandon him. He realized it had been foolish to separate from the others to tackle the imposing barrier. He had deviously intended to go through the motions, banking on the likelihood that Aaron would inevitably decide to rejoin the others while there was still a chance to save face.

Since beginning their ascent, Dante had strained through tear-filled, swollen eyes to scan the uneven face of the gargantuan barrier for the slightest hint of a gap. Over an hour into the arduous climb, there was still no indication of any such shortcut. So jagged and foreboding was the surface at the higher elevations, it had become obvious they were highly unlikely to succeed in scaling it. Kemper cursed his decision to preside over the dedication of the new garden his firm had financed. When he heard of the impending storm, he had been tempted to assign the chore of delivering the perfunctory speech to the corporation's Director of Public Relations and Marketing. Inexplicably though, he felt compelled to personally attend.

His true feelings of regret mutated into anger and resentment directed externally, as was his natural tendency. On this historic day and in this unfortunate circumstance, Dante was the unfortunate scapegoat: a convenient victim who unwittingly put himself in the direct path of Aaron Kemper's ire. Aaron was having trouble thinking clearly after more than an hour of climbing. He was hungry, thirsty, soaked in his own viscous sweat; wanting only to escape from the unfolding nightmare.

When Dante slipped and awkwardly crashed onto the narrow outcropping of rock, his pistol abruptly ejected from its leather cradle and ultimately came to rest directly at Aaron's feet. Without so much as a speck of concern for the young security officer's well-being, the bespectacled thug behind the hundred-dollar necktie calmly bent down and picked up the weapon. Writhing in pain as a result of his undignified fall, Dante was initially confused about what had occurred. His mangled knee ligaments suffered further damage when his 175-pound frame twisted awkwardly as he tried to prevent his head from striking the unforgiving surface.

Coated in fine particles of brick-red dirt, Aaron fondled the gun's black grip. Shooting had been a hobby since he was a teenager and he had amassed a modest collection of firearms over the years. He comfortably cradled the pistol in his left hand and admired the way the smooth metal barrel reflected the diffused sunlight. He had no intention of relinquishing the tarnished firearm now that it had found its way into his possession. Dante was immersed in pain; broken and exhausted on the ground, looking up at Aaron Kemper's smug visage. As soon as it registered in his mind that his pistol had found its way into his hands, he understood how vulnerable he had suddenly become.

"Get up," was the command that slithered between the tautly drawn lips of the man in control. Aaron struck an intimidating pose over Dante's prone body, brandishing the symbol of superiority at the end of an exaggeratedly extended left arm. He snickered at the pathetic plight of the obviously concerned and weakened younger man. Though still woozy from fatigue, he was invigorated by the shift in power. "You can't seem to catch a break, can you?" he derisively mused, smiling a toothy grin while he gazed down at the unfortunate target of his disdain.

Wobbly and pale, Dante grimaced and slowly rose to his aching feet, the majority of his energy evaporated. He recognized the ludicrous nature of their surreal situation; armed with only a sketchy awareness of what had happened to their world and virtually no reason for hope beyond what blind faith they clung to. For a fleeting moment, he recalled a fond childhood memory – when he had escorted pretty classmate Madeleine Myles to the Ninth Grade Spring Fling in Philadelphia.

He recalled sweating profusely as he tentatively wrapped his right arm around her slender waist and clasped her delicate hand in his. She mirrored his awkwardness and nervous apprehension, yet ached to take home a memorable experience from her first school dance...

Dante recalled the light yet delicious aroma of her floral perfume greeting when he nervously pressed his cheek to hers. He could still feel the tingling sensation where his sweaty palm pressed against the soft fabric of her dress at the small of her back. Nervous couples huddled in individual cocoons housing varying degrees of fledgling passion. The forgettable band of pimply teenage musicians played a barely-recognizable version of the Bee Gees' "How Deep is Your Love" while cheesy multicolored lights cast kaleidoscopic patterns over the crowded dance floor. At that moment, young Dante Macchiaroli felt truly alive...

Once again, his imagination allowed him to experience the delectable scents, sounds, and physical sensations of that magical moment from more than fifteen years ago. For a moment, Dante basked in the simple joy experienced by a nervous, pimple-faced boy lost in discovering the mysterious charms of his willing female counterpart. Far too swiftly, the alluring fragrance of Madeleine's perfume melted away – replaced by the pungent, sulfur-soaked stench of reality.

It finally registered with Dante that his gun had found its way into the hands of the sweaty, bloated man standing before him, and he suddenly understood his unenviable position. The sharp pain that had been isolated to his right knee had expanded to send shock waves through his entire leg and into his lower back. His most recent tumble had not only caused additional damage to his knee but had resulted in injury to his back. In addition to his physical anguish, he was in agony over the fact that he had allowed his pistol to fall into the untrustworthy hands of the gloating miscreant.

Dante detected Aaron's increasing instability but was unsure whether the cause was the physical exertion, lack of nutrition or some extenuating circumstance. "What's wrong with you?" he sheepishly inquired.

Aaron was not about to divulge the details of his insulin dependency or any other vulnerability as he felt the need to maintain a position of perceived superiority. He smugly replied, "Me? I feel fine. You, on the other hand, look like death warmed over. Neither of us is going to last long if we waste more time flopping around on this ledge, so let's get moving again while we still have some strength left." As he spoke, he waved the gleaming pistol around as if to add unnecessary emphasis to his words.

Dante recognized the ludicrous nature of the entire scenario. The way they were heading, he knew they were never going to make it. The mountain of rock was simply too treacherous to climb. To make matters worse, the pain in his knee and back led him to doubt whether he could make it to the base even if Aaron decided to swallow his pride and rejoin the group. Although he regretted his foolish decision to follow the scent of money, he realized the futility of dwelling on the past. Reflecting upon the absolute foolish choice he had made, he realized his first and only priority should have been to help himself and the others escape the confines of the zoo.

"Look, I really hate to dampen your spirits on such a nice day; but my goddamn knee is so fucked up right now I can barely think," he sarcastically sneered at his antagonist before adding, "… and I'd appreciate it if you gave me back my gun before we do anything else." Aaron had anticipated Dante's request but had no intention of complying.

In fact, he had already rehearsed his comeback: a terse "That is not happening."

Beads of sweat covered Aaron's red, puffy face from his widow's peak to his dimpled double chin. Without his insulin or an adequate supply of water, his condition had rapidly worsened and his thoughts had become increasingly clouded and confused. His initial inclination was to give up, return to the others and wait to be rescued; however, a different inner voice told him to force Dante to press onward to find a way beyond the ridge looming above them. His frustration was about to boil over as he struggled to sort through his inner conflict.

He recalled a recent encounter with his father in the War Room of the company's pristine downtown San Diego office. Chief Executive Officer and owner of Kemper Worldwide Development, 76-year-old Helmut Kemper was widely regarded as an unwavering tyrant; as demanding and critical of his two unremarkable sons as he was ruthless and opportunistic in business. He had built his fortune in real estate development and investment over several decades and ruled an impressive empire worth close to four billion dollars.

A Type 1 Diabetic who also suffered from Parkinson's disease, his health had seriously deteriorated in recent years; yet he stubbornly bristled when any of his confidants suggested he consider retirement. His two sons had been on his payroll for many years, but he had little confidence in either of them being ready to take the helm. He viewed oldest son Gerhard as little more than a liability due to his lifelong struggles with depression and anxiety. "Gary" as he was commonly known, had seemingly spent more time on psychiatrists' couches than in his office in the opposite corner of the building from his father's enormous suite.

The mother of his only two children had been a KWD employee – the Associate Personnel Manager in fact – when they began a clandestine love affair, over forty years earlier. Helmut had only recently moved his fledgling operation from New York City to San Diego, looking to capitalize on what he correctly identified as "one of the world's juiciest markets" for real estate development.

An orphaned Austrian immigrant, Helmut Kemper's lifelong ambitions revolved around the accumulation of property and wealth. He had cut his teeth at a fast-paced real estate firm on Long Island, quickly becoming their top salesperson due to his tireless work ethic and aggressive business practices. His fellow salespeople called him, "The Austrian Bulldog," because of his unyielding and tenacious nature. Universally disliked by his peers at the company and frequently argumentative with the company's Sales Manager, one too many confrontations led to his dismissal after only five years. His arrogance and fiery determination accompanied him to Southern California where a mere month later he established his own business out of his one-bedroom apartment just north of San Diego.

Within two years, Helmut Kemper had leased the entire first floor of a modern yet modest corporate office building in the city, and had hired his first employees. Among them was a slender young woman, with flowing strawberry-blonde hair. Barbara Jean Burkhart was a quiet yet efficient office manager he had stolen away from one of his former clients. She was a soft-spoken, naive 25-year-old when he first noticed her one afternoon during one of his presentations. He was immediately attracted to her and decided he would find a way to get her to join his growing business. While he admired her intelligence and quiet efficiency, he admitted to himself his lust for the alluring young woman with the hypnotic green eyes.

Intoxicated by Helmut's meteoric success in business and steamrolled by his relentless amorous advances, she eventually succumbed and they began a long, secretive relationship that led to marriage shortly after she became pregnant with Gerhard. Aaron was born three years later. To many in the community they seemed to be the epitome of an idyllic upper-class American family. Their country club lifestyle and frequent trips to Europe and the Caribbean soon became all too familiar. Sent to private school, the boys were also afforded the finest college educations money could buy.

Over the years, Kemper Worldwide expanded and flourished, and Helmut served on numerous boards while wielding influence with high-ranking capitalists and politicians. He and his family waded knee-deep in the American Dream and became equally intimate with all of the associated payoffs and pitfalls. Along with the spoils of the privileged life came boredom and the constant yearning for the next high. Those who have all that they want inevitably seek something more. Helmut indulged his insatiable, lusty darker side by fornicating his way through a succession of mistresses while Barbara's demons introduced her to dalliances with alcohol, narcotics, and a litany of cosmetic surgeries.

By the time he turned sixty, Helmut barely knew his sons; his wife was addicted to pain killers and on was on five different prescriptions for various psychological disorders; and his own alcoholism had seriously compromised his health. His first heart attack occurred at the third tee at a celebrity golf tournament hosted by his corporation in Pebble Beach. Playing in a foursome with the former mayor of Los Angeles, a legendary Hollywood director and an up-and-coming recording star, he collapsed immediately after striking the ball. Airlifted to the nearest hospital, his life was spared that day; although a few years later a second heart attack and simultaneous stroke left the right side of his face paralyzed.

His wife of over 40 years ultimately overdosed on a smorgasbord of prescription drugs after years of living in a fog-like stupor induced by booze, pills, and stifled resentment. Helmut seemed to take his wife's death in stride, but then again, he had never been sentimental or introspective and had become comfortably numb as the years passed. Emotionally distant, he had missed out on a great deal of life's simplest joys... and the sands in his hourglass were close to running out.

The relationship between Helmut and younger son Aaron had never been very comfortable or fulfilling for either of them and in recent years the grey-haired patriarch had expressed increasing frustration over qualities he felt were missing in his two sons. He lamented their lack of leadership ability and often remarked that they were "soft" and "spoiled by their pampered lives."

Standing in front of his father's spacious teak wood desk just an hour before setting out for the dedication ceremony at the zoo, Aaron felt no affection whatsoever for the old man. Instead, he caught himself fantasizing yet again about the day when his father would finally be out of the way and the reins of Kemper Worldwide would find their way into his own greedy hands.

Older brother Gerhard had expressed his utter lack of interest in managing the company, rendering Aaron the uncontested heir.

Despite his shrewd avoidance of the subject with the media, there was no longer any doubt within the organization as to who would take over when the "Austrian Bulldog" finally relinquished control or expired. *'Why do you keep living, old man?'* were among the thoughts that went through Aaron's polluted mind while he listened to his father drone on about some details he wanted conveyed at the dedication.

A mere day removed from that moment, the undeserving son slavered over the prospect of his father's demise. Without so much as a speck of concern for any suffering his father might ultimately endure, all he could picture was standing in front of an open coffin and putting on a good show for the media, company executives, and members of the extended family. A smile came to his face despite his predicament. Regardless of the gravity of the situation and his physical discomfort, he grinned at the thought of his father's death while wiping beads of sweat from his brow. In Dante, he saw just another nameless pawn to be used or stepped over. The hobbled security guard stared back at his adversary in disbelief, finally coming to understand that he was dealing with a man who would do almost anything to get his way.

Not far from their location, a band of determined individuals was making significant progress. The serendipitous discovery of the crack in the mountainside had provided the fragment of hope that encouraged them onward. Mia had pushed aside the last few loose chunks of rock to gain access to the interior of the mountain. To her great relief, the influx of air announced the possibility of reaching another open section of the zoo on the other side. Upon further investigation of that spot in the otherwise impenetrable barrier, they learned that it did indeed continue through the immense mountain to the opposite side via a winding path of varying elevations.

By crawling under obstructions, leaping across uneven gaps, and sidestepping through tight passages, Mia and Kyle successfully emerged on the other side. Their challenging trek through the mountain was aided with illumination provided by the glowing screens of their two iPods®. Into the welcoming embrace of sunlight, they emerged, temporarily blinded by the painfully intense contrast. Though the cave exit was situated more than twenty feet above ground level, conveniently placed footholds and ledges appeared to offer a relatively safe pathway to the bottom. "Thank God," Mia gasped, before turning around to help pull Kyle through the tight opening.

They stood on the ledge and gazed west through the clutter of broken trees, fragments of metal and unrecognizable debris to find another sprawling area, still somewhat intact. In the dull morning light, they saw that the area bore an eerie resemblance to the triangular region they had just left behind: similarly surrounded on all sides by towering blockades of stone and earth. Their spirits immediately buoyed when they identified several clusters of trees still rooted in the soil.

They saw no conceivable pathway to the parking lot along the higher elevations and had no way of discerning if there was any way out at ground level. They surmised that the most sensible course of action would be to descend and explore, but before they could embark upon their quest, they needed to guide the other survivors through the claustrophobic passageway. The flaxen-haired siblings took one last look at the valley below, and then re-entered the wormhole with a renewed sense of hope.

They had no way of knowing that only a short distance below them, four weary souls huddled together to enhance their own odds of survival. A humble man and three teenage girls were engaged in the battle of their lives. Sharing the placid saltwater domain of the resident bottlenose dolphins, they had spent the first hours of the morning conserving their strength.

Violet remained motionless, her head securely cradled in her father's strong arms. Mateo continued to caress her forehead with water from the dolphin tank and kept her lips moist with the contents of a bottle of water scavenged from what little remained of a splintered refreshment stand. Her eyelids fluttered repeatedly, delivering glimmers of hope to her worried father. Mateo, Leanna, and Hanna had been praying for hours. In hushed audible tones, they transmitted their healing energy into the body of the unresponsive fifteen-year-old.

Taking a break from the intensity of the healing circle, Hanna inadvertently discovered the names of the two dolphins while swimming the perimeter of the tank. "Yuna & Tidus" was inscribed on a small acrylic plaque she found mounted to one of the posts supporting the black mesh sunscreen. Moments after Hanna shared their names with the others, it appeared as though the dolphins became more playful with the two girls. She stressed the proper pronunciation of Tidus as 'TEE-dus', a name she recognized from the popular video game, *Final Fantasy X*®. It was as though a virtual barrier had been eliminated once they were aware of the dolphins' names. Leanna and Hanna each clung to one of the dolphins and rode around the tank in tandem, the foursome effortlessly forging a physical, emotional, and psychic bond.

I Miss Your Purple Hair

Mateo smiled for the first time in a while, moved by the beautiful genesis of the harmonious bond. Still gently caressing Violet's forehead with the fingertips of his right hand, he lost himself in the peaceful scene displayed before his weary eyes. He watched contentedly as their accommodating hosts effortlessly transported the remarkable sisters in a counter-clockwise pattern. His concerns centered on Violet's well being, but he also felt a distinct connection with and obligation to the two other girls.

Throughout the course of Violet's life, Mateo had always tried to speak with her as if she were an adult, even before she entered pre-school. He learned, early on, that she fit the profile of the typical Indigo/Crystal Child – if the term "typical" actually applies. She was never satisfied with the shortcut answers some would toss out for the sake of convenience. As soon as she could speak, at about 14 months, she asked "Why?" and "How?" with sometimes-annoying regularity. Certainly a challenge to raise at times, Mateo grew to anticipate that Violet would ask questions no matter the situation, until she was satisfied. He learned to be conscientious about providing thoughtful responses, for fear of an endless loop of questions. It was accurate to say that his daughter was "training him" to better suit her needs.

Since Violet's mother had rarely interacted in such a patient and caring manner, Mateo gladly carried the burden of nurturing her voracious appetite for information and enlightenment. From a very early age, they enjoyed involved discussions at bedtime, at the breakfast table and on long walks in their favorite park. They never ran out of topics and often, Violet surprised her father with remarkably mature insights. Concern over the unavailability of Violet's mother motivated him to help her develop an independent attitude as emotional insurance. Well equipped to cope with her mother's abrupt departure years later, the training proved to be fortuitous.

The soothing sounds of water lapping against the interior walls of the tank blended with the enchanting laughter of the Armstrong sisters. Mateo closed his tired eyes for a moment and thought about family members in Costa Rica and his mother, back in Miami. He pictured her in her kitchen, where she loved to spend hours tinkering with old family recipes. He and Violet had enjoyed a chat with her via videophone on Christmas Day during which they discussed flying her out to the coast at Easter. He imagined she was baking the almond tea cookies he loved and could virtually smell their delicate aroma. In his heart, he felt she was safe, but feared for her nonetheless.

Upon reopening his eyes, Mateo saw that the Sun had burned through a portion of the dense cloud cover. Leanna was asleep in a fetal position directly behind him, while Hanna contentedly floated among the dolphins. "Shouldn't you get out of there for a while?" he muttered, despite his drowsiness and parched throat. Hanna was surprised when his voice broke the relative quiet, but then finally nodded and swam over to board their floating base of operations. She curled up with her sister and soon joined her in the arms of Morpheus.

Physically spent, they all slept through the afternoon. The dolphins were perplexed by the prolonged absence of their trainers and weakened from lack of sustenance. Even so, they seemed to respect the peaceful solace the humans obviously required to recharge their energy and consciously curtailed their usual playful activities in accommodating fashion. While Mateo and the teenage girls all slept, another band of survivors worked their way through the interior of the enormous blockade to their east.

The individual the group had been most concerned about before they entered the opening actually turned out to be very little trouble. The young boy who had remained silent since the quake struck seemed most likely to balk at the prospect of entering the dark passageway. As it turned out, he effortlessly scampered along the jagged rocks directly in front of Kyle, but when DeAngelo tried to take his hand and lead him toward the opening, he refused to budge. Everyone encouraged him to take the hand of the other child, thinking it would provide a sense of security. Instead, the chubby eight-year-old only felt safe with the one person who had already won his trust.

The skittish little brown-haired boy with the unusual blue-grey eyes suddenly brushed past DeAngelo, Mia, Victory and Dwayne and made a beeline toward Kyle. He tucked himself directly behind the sturdy young psychologist and latched onto his left elbow with his stubby-fingered, dirty right hand. His gentle, yet deliberate nudging clearly indicated that he was willing to follow the others into the unknown recesses of the mountain as long as Kyle would be his escort and protector. Without looking back, Kyle patted the child's shoulder to indicate he did not intend to disappoint him.

A few moments before they finally entered the serpentine channel, Kyle took one last glance back toward the southeast, wondering what was happening with Dante and Aaron. Hours had passed since they parted ways and he wondered if they had succeeded in finding another way out. He prayed they had successfully breached the wall to the south and were already alerting rescue personnel. In the process of scanning the territory he was leaving behind, Kyle noticed the tufted white tips of the wolf's ears peeking from behind the tall grass near the base of the eastern wall. He experienced a pang of sympathy for the displaced animal; knowing that – barring a miracle – it would likely suffer a tragic fate.

Buoyed by the reassuring leadership provided by Mia and Kyle, the six beleaguered souls warily inched their way through the heart of the mountain. They had gathered up and distributed a hodgepodge of light sources in the forms of Blackberry devices, MP3 players, cell phones, and Mia's key chain flashlight. Only partially illuminated by diffused sunlight, many areas of the winding passageway were cloaked in darkness due to its irregular formation. Without the array of electronic devices, the journey would have proved far more treacherous.

Progress was fraught with danger, as a single misstep could have resulted in injury or... a calamitous descent. The potential deterioration and collapse of the wormhole was of great concern, as there was no way to assess its structural integrity. They took each tenuous step amidst a constant shower of fine dirt particles. Along with the sounds of the human caravan's movements, the thuds of large rocks falling from above punctuated the steady hiss of tiny particles raining down.

Kyle kept close tabs on everyone, in particular the youngest member of the group, who remained attached to him like a remora to a shark. He positioned himself adjacent to a precariously obscured crevasse midway along the path and carefully helped each person across safely. His stabilizing hands were as instrumental as his reassuring words in ensuring safe passage over the dangerous gap. Mia maintained the lead position and intercepted each individual. Once they regrouped, she continued to lead them ever closer to their goal. She and her brother were perfectly suited for such duty: steadfast, confident, and gentle while maintaining constant communication. Dwayne and Victory, strong and capable in their own right, acquiesced to Mia and Kyle, appreciative of their steady guidance.

As the exhausted group approached the tunnel's final segment, Kyle struggled to squeeze through the last, narrowest gap. Of the six individuals in their contingent, Kyle had the broadest frame and experienced the greatest difficulty navigating the more constricted areas. Standing sideways, his sore feet clad in uncomfortable dress shoes, he inched his way forward while a fine powder of debris coated the top of his head and sweat-covered neck. The little Indian boy on the other side grabbed Kyle's hand and pulled with all his might to help his guardian angel through, ever closer to the promise of salvation.

Lonely and Out of Place

As Kyle finally scraped his way through to the far end of the dark, dusty gap he suddenly flinched – in reaction to a sharp noise that rang out from behind him to the east. "What the hell was that?" he asked the darkness. It sounded like a firecracker or a car's backfiring exhaust. Due to the conditions, however, it was impossible to know. The sharp 'pop!' echoed within the walls of the twisting wormhole. The constant sounds of crumbling infrastructure created a blanket of white noise that obscured any sounds from outside. Kyle thought it might have been an explosion related to the nearby fires or perhaps another volcanic eruption. The mysterious noise nagged at him as he pressed on, and he wondered if whatever had occurred might have affected Dante and Aaron.

The dust-coated, disheveled group slowly worked their way to the end of the trail, where the welcome sight of sunlight seeping through the opening in the rocky wall beckoned to them. First to breach the threshold was Mia, her golden hair obscured by a coating of dirt. A beautiful red-tailed hawk, its broad wings proudly outstretched to their enviable limit, drew lazy circles against the red-orange sky that greeted her eyes.

The aperture spilled them out onto a flat, shelf-like outcropping of rock, dirt… and metal. A broad platform of corrugated aluminum from some demolished structure jutted out ten feet over the open area beneath them. They found themselves about fifteen feet above the region below, brought closer to ground level by the unpredictable turns of the earthen tunnel. Once Kyle finally emerged, coated from head to toe in granulated dirt, the entire party stood together and absorbed the sights and sounds. A steady breeze delivered a mixture of poison and perfume as the sulfur-laced currents picked up hints of the nearby flora and fauna. Despite the unnatural blend, the wind also whispered a subtle message of hope.

It had become late afternoon and the Sun was already sinking low in the late December sky, mostly obscured by the thick blanket of red-tinged clouds. Huge walls of rock ringed a broad patch of terrain that housed the Wegeforth Bowl and The Children's Zoo. Victory peered out over the edge of the platform and asked, "Wasn't the Reptile House over here, too? It should be directly below us, yeah?"

Dwayne knelt down, despite his sore left knee, and repeatedly pounded his right fist against the strange platform under his feet. His actions produced a series of echoes laced with a decidedly metallic component. *Bang, bang, bang!* The sound echoed off the mountains. "Why are you doing that, Dad?" asked DeAngelo.

I Miss Your Purple Hair

Dwayne stood, put his hands on his hips, and replied, "I think we might actually be standing on some of what's left of the building. This is part of the roof. The ground came up through the middle of the building and just tore it in half." Sure enough, upon further investigation they all saw what appeared to be The Reptile House, still relatively intact fifteen feet below, at the base of the massive wall.

Holding onto his father's back with one hand, DeAngelo leaned over to take a closer look at what remained of the shattered structure, and a disturbing thought compelled him to ask, "Hey, that's the Reptile House, right? If it's been wrecked like that, does that mean the snakes and lizards are all crawling around loose?"

Careful not to contribute to the obviously mushrooming sense of alarm, Dwayne responded in a calm monotone, "Well, some of them probably didn't survive the quake... and the rest are probably still in their cages... or long gone by now."

Each of the survivors pondered the unnerving possibilities before the group began the challenging climb down the craggy mountainside.

△ △ △

CHAPTER THIRTEEN

Defying Gravity

"Civilization can only revive when there shall come into being in a number of individuals a new tone of mind, independent of the prevalent one among the crowds, and in opposition to it - a tone of mind which will gradually win influence over the collective one, and in the end determine its character. Only an ethical movement can rescue us from barbarism, and the ethical comes into existence only in individuals."
~ Albert Schweitzer

Given the treacherous footing and limited visibility, Jason and Sinnamon were running faster than should have been possible. Forced to vault over uneven, slippery stone formations, they splattered through pockets of thick, gooey red-tinged mud. The mist had finally stopped falling and the Sun burned a hole through the odd-colored red clouds, boosting the air temperature to over 90 degrees. In their half-blind panic, they stumbled upon a newly formed pathway carved through the Ituri Forest. The panicked pair raced south-by-southeast, in single file, over the misshapen land mass. The unidentifiable growls from behind served as compelling motivation and they were relieved to discover a narrow, but traversable pathway after they crashed through a thicket of gnarled bramble. The previous day's steady deluge had carved a serpentine rut into the bed of the forest.

"Damn it! Faster, dude! Is that really your top gear?" Sinnamon yelled from behind, hot on Jason's heels. While a much faster runner, due to her rigorous fitness regimen, there was no room for her to pass him along the twisting, overgrown route. They wound their way in a southerly direction, bringing them ever closer to where they expected to find the zoo exits. With no way of knowing the condition of the park's other regions, they could only assume they were heading toward salvation... and not toward greater danger. Brushing branches aside and accumulating a cross-hatch pattern of cuts from the network of thorny vines, the mismatched pair raced through the treacherous overgrowth, propelled by their fear of the unidentified beast in their wake.

They navigated a blurry patchwork of greens and browns, their ears filled with the sound of feet splashing through puddles. They were surrounded by the constant hissing of water falling through the trees and the frenzied chatter of monkeys overhead. By the time they finally reached a clearing at the end of the slippery trail, they were both exhausted. Jason had abruptly halted his momentum and bent over with his hands upon his knees when Sinnamon barreled into him, sending them both tumbling to the rain-soaked ground, six feet below. They wound up sprawled across the muddy swath of land; sweaty, filthy and physically spent.

Jason had the wind knocked out of him when he fell face-first to the ground. He rolled onto his side and tried to comprehend what had happened. His redheaded companion was lying nearby, in obvious pain, writhing on her back while clutching her lower-left side. "You alright?" he meekly inquired. Sinnamon grimaced and rolled her eyes before shooting an angry look at the source of her frustration.

She forced a sarcastic retort through tightly drawn lips. "Not exactly, Bud… *unhh*... I could've done without that last bit. Next time we find ourselves running in a blind panic through a damn forest... get behind me, okay!?" They both somehow managed pained laughter in reaction to her ludicrous statement while they struggled to their feet. The winding trail had led them to a small outcropping covered in wild grasses. Ringed with trees both broken and intact, they struggled to get their bearings. Fifteen yards ahead of them appeared to be a drop-off, and they cautiously approached the precipice without saying a word.

The atmosphere felt starkly different, as they were exposed to the filtered rays of the harsh Sun. The air felt significantly warmer and the pervasive humidity weighed heavy on every living thing. Jason and Sinnamon, bloodied and spent, stood motionless at the edge of the island in the sky and gazed upon the unfathomable scene below. Rebecca Sinclair was not easily impressed or intimidated, but the sight that unfolded beneath them delivered a jolt of harsh reality. Jason, frightened and struggling to breathe the caustic air, turned his head to check Sinnamon's reaction to what they were witnessing – a land of desolation and death.

The mangled world below was a scene straight out of *Dante's Inferno* – from the reshaped land to the smoldering craters spewing toxic gases. Splintered trees, ripped from long-established homes in the soil now exposed their roots to the harshness of the Sun. The destructive quakes had transfigured the carefully designed park, with all of its logically placed patterns and pathways, into a nonsensical patchwork. From where they stood, nearly 20 feet above the next level of solid ground, they spotted the corpses of several large animals partially buried in the rubble among the debris-littered rock formations.

The sobering evidence laid out before them like a scene from the worst nightmare imaginable – from the rust-colored sky to the impossible disparity between the newly formed mountains and the shadowy valleys below. Sinnamon swallowed hard and looked into Jason's worried eyes. "Things are more screwed up than I imagined," she whispered, more to herself than to her horrified companion. She rhetorically asked, "How did anything survive this? How the hell are we still standing?"

Jason felt the sting of the acidic air in his tear-filled eyes as he responded, "I don't know… but I wonder how many others might be injured... or dead out in that mess."

Sinnamon hung her head, struggling to accept the horror they were witnessing. She then inhaled deeply before declaring, "Well, we damn well can't just stay up here… and whatever's chasing us can't be far behind. Let's get down there and see what's what. We've gotta find some drinkable water soon or we won't last very long."

Jason dropped onto his belly and inched to the edge of the cliff overlooking the newly formed wasteland. "We can probably climb down over there," he exclaimed, pointing to a possible route along the rocky wall to the southwest. Although the thick mist between them and the valley floor obscured their vision, it was obvious any hope for escape required reaching ground level.

Against the backdrop of animal sounds, steady rain and wind whistling through the trees, the intrepid pair began their cautious descent. Sinnamon took the lead, determined to control her own destiny. She had always been more loner than leader, and felt little loyalty to Jason. As they began their tentative climb down the rocky cliff, her thoughts turned to her mother and older sister, who both lived just east of San Diego. She considered the unnerving possibility that the disastrous quake might have affected the lives of those she most cared for, but quickly decided to evict such thoughts from her mind.

Less than 200 yards to the southeast, Mateo was alarmed by unexpected sounds from an undetermined location. Jarred from his slumber, he thought he had been dreaming when he first heard the far-off voices. He glanced at his daughter's angelic face and then over to the curled up figures of Leanna and Hanna, asleep next to him. "Girls! Wake up!" he urgently whispered. Upon opening her eyes, Leanna immediately recognized the sound of human voices, and she quickly sprung to her bare feet and perched on tiptoes in an effort to identify the source.

I Miss Your Purple Hair

Approaching their adopted headquarters atop the dolphin exhibit was a bedraggled group of strangers led by a weary, yet composed looking blonde woman. "Oh my God," Leanna and Mia simultaneously exclaimed in stunned fashion. Initially crestfallen to see that they weren't part of a rescue team but merely victims like themselves, Mateo's spine stiffened. He felt instinctively protective of his vulnerable child and wary of the approaching group. Hanna rose to her knees to see what was happening and was surprised at the sight of the four adults and two children gingerly approaching across the uneven ground.

Mateo waved his right arm side-to-side to signal a friendly "welcome", just as Hanna and Leanna swam across the tank for a closer look. Dwayne Cooper, physically exhausted and drenched in perspiration, placed a protective hand on his son's shoulder as they approached. While the area they discovered after passing through the core of the mountain was largely traversable, it was very limited in size. Similar to the region they had just left, they found themselves in a triangular patch of land surrounded on each side by mammoth rock formations. Whether the inner foundation had sunken or the surrounding walls had risen during the earthquake was impossible to determine.

Mia's quizzical expression gradually changed to one of sincere concern. She observed the Armstrong sisters hoisting themselves out of the water and onto the tank's textured concrete ledge prior to shifting her attention to the sight of Violet's motionless body cradled in her father's arms. Mateo patiently waited for the angular blonde to draw closer so he could get a better read on her. His initial impression was that she was a woman of intelligence and courage, evident in her confident stride and willingness to take the lead. It was obvious she was the Alpha character of the rag-tag assembly, from the expressions on the faces of the others and the confidence she projected.

Before making any attempt at personal introductions, Mia blurted out the first thing that popped into her head, "Can I do anything to help?" in obvious reference to Violet's condition. Mateo was impressed by her apparently genuine concern.

He replied, "She's been unconscious since this all started, as far as I can tell. I'm not sure how long, since I was knocked out for a while too, but it's getting close to 18 hours or so now."

"Who is she?" Mia asked meekly.

"My daughter," was all Mateo could utter before his tears began to well up. He composed himself quickly and, with his gaze fixed upon Violet's fluttering eyelids, added, "She's everything to me and I have to help her. I'm sure you understand."

Moved by Mateo's obvious devotion to his daughter, Mia quietly replied, "Yes, I can see that. Maybe there's some way one of us can help." Mateo asked Mia if anyone in the group had any medical training and she immediately thought of Dante. She circled around the side of the tank and then climbed the steps to the platform. She knelt on the deck, adjacent to the floating platform that supported Mateo and Violet.

"Would you mind telling me her name?" Mia gently inquired of the broad-shouldered man. At the same time, Kyle and the others engaged Leanna and Hanna in conversation at the far end of the structure.

"Her name is Veronica, but she prefers to be called 'Violet'," he responded with obvious affection.

"Veronica's one of my favorite names," Mia softly said, before inquiring, "Why do people call her Violet?" Mateo shared an abbreviated family history with the impressive stranger while he continued to use his fingers to wet his daughter's dry lips with the last remnants of bottled spring water at his side. She admired his sincere affection for his daughter, starkly evident in the anecdotal information Mateo shared.

She also admired the way he continued to anoint his daughter's lips, forehead, and cheeks with water and the way he cradled her in his strong arms. Mia asked Mateo about the other two girls and he shared what little he knew. She remarked that there was something "unique" about them; not only their physical appearance but how they moved in unison, "like birds in a flock." He smiled weakly and took a moment to observe the Armstrong sisters, who had encouraged the two boys to join them in the water with the dolphins. DeAngelo barely hesitated, only pausing to seek permission from his mother. Coated with powdery dirt from their arduous trek through the mountain's wormhole passageway, the heat and humidity had only added to everyone's discomfort.

By the time Mia and Mateo finished becoming acquainted everyone else had climbed into the tank, eager to wash away the dirt, sweat, and traces of blood. The cool saltwater initially stung all of the scrapes and cuts of the entire party, including the nameless little boy. Tidus and Yuna were remarkably hospitable despite the invasion of their domain by more humans. The dolphins maintained a low profile for the first five minutes or so after the last of the group slipped into the water.

I Miss Your Purple Hair

Kyle had stripped out of his grimy clothing, down to his dark blue boxers and light grey T-shirt, and was enjoying the respite from the difficult trek through the mountain. He swam over to Mateo and Violet's plastic raft and introduced himself. Asking all the standard questions about concussion symptoms, Kyle was convinced Violet must have suffered just such an injury. When he asked Mateo whether he was aware of any potential path out of the zoo, his answer was disappointingly negative.

Regarding food and water resources, Mateo mentioned he might have spotted the remnants of another snack kiosk along the base of the wall to the west. Despite the indisputable urgency to find more water, his primary concern was Violet's condition, which he expressed in no certain terms.

Kyle thoughtfully suggested that he and Mateo lower Violet into the water, hoping there might be some therapeutic benefit to hydrating her parched skin. If nothing else, the water would provide temporary respite from the caustic, heavy air and keep her body temperature down. Mateo agreed and they carefully worked together to lower her into the cool water, supporting her small frame from the platform's edge.

While Mateo kept Violet's head out of the water, Kyle supported the weight of her limp body. Moments later, without saying so much as a word, Dwayne and Victory Cooper swam across the tank to join them, helping to support Violet while they made their introductions. Victory was a superb swimmer, completely at home in the water, having spent a great deal of time in the ocean throughout her early childhood in Jamaica.

Shortly thereafter, as the hazy Sun began to disappear behind the enormous earthen blockade to the west, the entire collection of survivors had gathered, surrounding Violet and helping to support her at the water's surface. The storm had moved on over the previous hour, leaving a peaceful stillness in its wake. The pair of dolphins had been conspicuously absent for 30 minutes or so, hiding in the far corner of the tank. Finally, the aquatic acrobats warily approached the pleasantly surprised bipeds treading water at the western end of the tank.

Both Kyle and Mia reassured the "nameless boy" that he had nothing to fear, yet he clung tightly to Kyle's arm so as not to float away from his de facto guardian. He nervously watched the dolphins ease close to the raft, between Dwayne and Mia. A soothing cloak of peacefulness gently draped itself over the area, and the entire human entourage was steeped in silence. The dolphins brushed up against those nearest them, as if to extend a friendly greeting and perhaps to gain a sense of their guests' intentions.

No words were spoken for a few minutes as the eclectic collection of mammals huddled around the floating platform. Leanna finally broke the silence when she began to recite another healing prayer she and her sister had created. In her softest voice, she projected sincere wishes for recuperation toward Violet.

"We thank you, Collective Soul, for blessings granted and wisdom shared. Now we ask once again for your guidance and strength as we bring together our healing energies. We humbly ask that you hear our prayer of healing..."

On cue, Hanna began the prayer in harmony with her older sibling. Together, they softly spoke the words while the others listened and observed. "Let our strength becomes our sister's strength; Let our energies combine to heal and sustain her; We are one with her ..."

As the two girls quietly repeated their healing prayer, Mateo stroked Violet's forehead and placed a kiss on her cheek. Her eyelids continued to flutter and her breathing remained shallow, yet consistent. He glanced up and noticed the reactions of each of the individuals encircling their floating base. Kyle had his eyes closed and head bowed, as did Dwayne, Victory, and Mia. DeAngelo's attention darted between his parents, the nearby dolphins, and Violet. The boy with no name clung to Kyle and was fixated on the dolphin on the opposite side of his adopted guardian. He appeared calm, yet wary of the tank's residents, who were as involved as the humans in donating healing energy to the girl at the center of everyone's attention.

Victory very quietly mouthed the words of the prayer along with the Armstrong sisters while tears slowly rolled down her prominent cheeks. Mateo realized that, without voicing their intentions, everyone had joined hands around the perimeter of the rectangular raft while they focused their attention upon Violet. Suspended in the cool saltwater, the collection of disparate souls focused upon the unconscious teenager in a collective effort to ensure her recovery. Each of them took a unique approach. Mia visualized Violet rising to her feet and approaching her father, arms outstretched and smiling. Kyle envisioned an abstract mass of glittering, white energy drawn from each of their bodies and absorbed into Violet's small frame. DeAngelo imagined an angel, complete with large, white wings and a halo, lifting Violet's body and enveloping them both in an aura of white light.

Mateo was emotionally moved by the impromptu expression of genuine concern the near-strangers demonstrated toward his daughter. He felt a profound sense of humility and peace as he observed the faces of the willing participants in the spiritual healing exercise. There was the serene face of young Leanna, decorated in tiny freckles, eyes closed and bearing an expression of utter tranquility. Kyle appeared calm, yet intently focused on his thoughts as he floated between one of the dolphins and the young Indian boy, who refused to leave his side.

Mia looked over at Mateo, tiny beads of water along her shoulders and arms sparkling in the waning light. They locked eyes and shared a fleeting moment of intimacy as everyone else silently continued to transmit their energy. All the while, Leanna and Hanna recited their healing prayer. Mateo could not help but be impressed by Mia's simple beauty and the sincere concern she projected toward Violet.

Amazing to Mateo, the dolphins' behavior was remarkably similar to that of the Armstrong sisters: apparently fixated, as indicated by their demeanor and body language, on Violet. At least that appeared to be the case, since they remained motionless, wedged snuggly between people on either side, with their noses pointed toward Violet. Mateo wondered if it was possible they were consciously sharing their energy with his daughter; if they instinctively knew to join in the attempt to transmit recuperative energy. It felt so to him and he sensed that the others involved also realized as much.

The chanting had been going on for some time, and their voices blended to create a unique harmony. Mateo closed his eyes once more and basked in the comforting generosity and sympathy that flowed all around him. Time elapsed and he entered a state of peaceful meditation while the Armstrong girls continued to pray.

The first sign that something had changed was subtle and fleeting. In his half-asleep state, Mateo thought he was dreaming. It then happened again: a subtle little twitch; the minimal movement of a slender arm snapped him to attention. She was moving! His daughter was returning to him, indicated first by the tensing of her forearm, detected by his calloused palm. His eyes snapped open and he was the first to see Violet awaken. He was unable to prevent tears from flowing as he observed her writhing and stretching her legs and arms. When her beautiful brown eyes finally opened and gazed up at him, he smiled and whispered in a raspy voice, "Welcome back, baby."

The first words out of her mouth were, "I'm so thirsty. Can we get smoothies?" Mateo hugged her tightly, aware that she would be the last to learn of the devastation surrounding them. He had spent the last 15 years diligently shielding her from physical harm and from the harshest aspects of life. Having been dropped into a worst-case scenario of epic proportions, his first concern was still for her general health and well-being, and he was hesitant to move her. The people who were clustered in the water breathed a collective sigh of relief upon hearing Violet's voice for the first time. Were their healing efforts in some way responsible for expediting her return to consciousness?

As if on cue, the two dolphins, Tidus and Yuna, dove beneath the water's surface, and then turned and vigorously swam toward the middle of the pool from the spot where they had been hovering next to the platform. Suddenly, with all of the humans in observance, they dove to the 12-foot depth of the tank and then breached the water's surface and performed one of their many aerial stunts, twisting and flipping before splashing down and dousing everyone in a torrent of saltwater. Their exuberant display caused Violet to sit upright before her father could intervene. A smile lit up her face when she realized whose home they were sharing. "How'd we wind up here?" While asking no one in particular, she added, "Did I fall asleep?"

Everyone laughed and then began to disperse in an effort to provide a semblance of privacy for Mateo and Violet. Mateo asked if she hurt anywhere, and her reply was negative. Other than a mild headache, she claimed nothing else really troubled her. She asked if she could sit up and Mateo searched her eyes for any clues as to her true condition. She seemed lucid and alert despite her lengthy disengagement from reality. Very gradually, the dancing lights returned to her eyes.

With minimal help from her father, Violet was able to sit upright at the edge of the floating platform. She dangled her legs in the calm water; and although she felt light-headed, it was primarily due to lack of food and water. Her speech seemed unaffected and her barrage of questions indicated to Mateo that her mind was undamaged, although he admonished her against taking any unnecessary risks. He patiently brought her up to date on what had happened, cautiously avoiding speculation on unsubstantiated details. He was quite sure that the quake was one of monumental proportions but had no way of guessing the true extent of the destruction. In spite of their precarious situation, Violet expressed greater concern for the fate of the outside world than for their immediate plight. Mateo had no answers to give – only questions of his own.

Over the next several hours, the group huddled around a makeshift fire next to the disintegrated remnants of the Wegeforth Bowl. Darkness had fallen and they had feasted on an assortment of snack foods scavenged from a demolished refreshment hut. Hanna, Leanna, DeAngelo, and the nameless boy had made a game of finding and retrieving as many sealed plastic bottles of water as possible and discovered twenty of them intact. Dwayne and Victory took on the task of assembling any foodstuffs into neatly organized stacks, moving them into the small shed next to the dolphin tank. They were concerned about the elements and any scavenging animals that might take what precious little supplies they had.

While the younger children rummaged through debris for anything edible, Violet and the others discussed possible plans for the next morning and expressed their concerns for the situation at hand. Kyle, who had thrown on his slacks and shirt after drying off, suggested they find shelter for the night. He offered to investigate the nearby Reptile House, half-demolished by the earthquake but at least partially intact. He acknowledged concerns regarding potentially dangerous animals which may have been freed, but offered to ascertain if it would be feasible to sleep inside the building.

Everyone else agreed it was a good idea, moments before a strange sound from the northwest suddenly hijacked their attention. Something crashed through the thick vegetation that bordered the region, quickly followed by a thud... and then another loud thud. Their small barrel fire barely illuminated a 12-foot radius, so they could only rely on their hearing for information. A very clear audible outburst sliced through the silence and put everyone on high alert.

"You idiot! Are you fucking blind?" someone angrily shouted.

Mia jumped to her feet at the same time she posed the rhetorical question, "What the hell?"

A second voice in the darkness, this one deeper in tone, muttered something indiscernible in apparent response to the derisive comment. The entire party of adults remained frozen in place while the children quickly regrouped and crouched behind them. The sounds of people approaching became increasingly loud but the darkness obscured the sources of the disruption.

Finally, two figures emerged from the misty darkness. Sinnamon and Jason collapsed to their knees in plain view, both of them gasping for air and covered from head to toe in hundreds of tiny, razor-thin lacerations. They were battered and bloodied from their panic-driven descent down the craggy face of the mountain that separated the Ituri Forest from this comparatively hospitable oasis. They had managed to drag their bruised and exhausted bodies toward the flickering glow of the campfire, like two desperate moths to a flame.

"I've... got.... one.... question," the red-crested cynic gasped. "Where...the hell... is... the rescue squad?"

Victory and Mia scrambled to their feet and brought water to the two newcomers, sizing up their bruises and cuts while handing each of them a bottle. Unaware of whom she was dealing with in Rebecca Sinclair, Mia innocently asked, "Where'd you two come from?"

The blood-and-dirt-covered mercenary sarcastically replied, "Well, me and Junior here were just playin' with the grizzly bears when this big boom kind of ruined our picnic..."

Despite struggling to catch his breath, Jason intervened in an attempt to defuse the tension Sinnamon had just sprinkled into the atmosphere. "Look, we're both frazzled and don't know which end is up just yet. Some *thing* was chasing us back there and we had no idea where we..."

His somewhat crude compatriot rudely interjected, "Yeah, yeah... they don't need a blow-by-blow. We can all read your blog later for the fascinating details. We were pretty much trapped in the forest last night and got flushed down here by some wild animal that must've been sprung from its cage. We never saw what it was but we damn sure heard it, and it was coming up fast from behind. It's likely right behind us, so if you have anything for self-defense, I suggest you get prepared. Otherwise, we'd better take shelter. We can chit-chat after we make sure we aren't on the dinner menu, okay?"

Sinnamon's matter-of-fact announcement understandably motivated the beleaguered band of survivors. They hurriedly snatched up their valuables along with any rocks, sticks, or other implements that could serve as weapons. Kyle led the way toward the ruins of the Reptile House while the other adults made sure they shepherded the children along as hastily as possible. Dwayne and Victory grabbed the hands of the nameless boy and their son, respectively, and waited for Mateo to help Violet stand up on wobbly legs. Once the two of them limped to the doorway, arm in arm, Mia did a quick head count and kept an eye on the section of the park from which Sinnamon and Jason emerged.

Because they were all sore, bruised and exhausted, it took longer than normal to shuffle over to the building. At its closed doorway, Kyle and Dwayne peered inside in an attempt to assess the viability of the structure. While the back half of the building was entombed under tons of rock and organic debris, the front was still intact and apparently secure. In the failing light, they could barely make out any details of the interior. Mia stepped forward and aimed her red flashlight through the glass doorway. Although visibility was limited, they could discern a rather spacious inner atrium flanked by what appeared to be glass displays lining the walls on either side.

Kyle noticed that the tremors had bent the door frame and cracked the thick metal lock mechanism. The twin doors were skewed and left slightly ajar, misaligned within the frame. Off in the distance, the low, protracted howl of a wolf pierced the caustic evening air and forced the entire party to freeze in their tracks just outside the doors. Motivated by the sound, Kyle grabbed the door handle and lunged into it, and the group spilled inside as one.

Just as suddenly, DeAngelo turned and burst back out through the same doorway. Victory whirled around and ran in pursuit of her son, who was sprinting back toward the fire. She yelled, "Dee! Get back here right now!", but before the words escaped her lips, he was already on his way back with two burning torches in hand. She greeted him with a swat on the rump and an angry glare. "Don't you ever do that again, young man! You can't be runnin' 'round like that, without me or your father along with you!"

The energized young boy was slightly perturbed by what he felt was an over-reaction by his mother, but was proud he had the courage to retrieve the torches he and his father had fashioned. In the group's haste, they had neglected to grab them from the fire. It was extremely dark in the power-starved building and the torches provided much-needed illumination, especially since the place could literally be crawling with all types of dangerous creatures.

Towering over everyone, Dwayne grabbed one of the torches and held it overhead, projecting a blanket of flickering light over most of the expansive inner sanctum. Although the roof had been partially torn off in one isolated section, it turned out to be a blessing as the jagged, asymmetrical hole conveniently allowed the torches' smoke to vent into the night sky. However, rainwater had also found its way in through the same opening and a puddle covered a portion of the floor.

The group was relieved they did not spot any snakes slithering across the floor, and the central atrium – almost completely undisturbed – was more spacious than it appeared from outside. Everyone agreed that their first order of business was to secure the external doors in case whatever animal responsible for the howling came scavenging. Mia and Victory had the presence of mind to bring the assorted snacks and bottled water along, but had left some of the stash behind. They were therefore concerned that hungry animals roaming the area might be attracted to the scent.

Dwayne quickly removed his thick, black leather belt, tightly wrapped it around the two metal door handles and tied it in a tight knot. "Saw this in a movie once," he wryly stated as he forcefully tugged on the two ends once more for good measure. It was obvious that an enormous mass of subterranean material had been forced skyward, destroying the back portion of the well-constructed building. As the group investigated the main room, they were confronted with a bizarre wall of rock that had severed the southern half of the building from the rest. A thick plate glass case enclosing some of the poisonous reptiles sported a jagged diagonal crack across its face, but strangely, little else within the intact portion of the building had been disturbed.

After familiarizing with the layout, everyone relaxed a bit and sorted through the rations. Thinking the sturdy edifice would serve them well as a 'home base' for the evening, they all pitched in and organized the food and water as well as all of their electronic devices and tools. Upon inspection, they determined they had sufficient water and food to survive for a couple days, if need be. Among the belongings dredged up from their purses, briefcases and pockets, they assembled a collection of light-emitting devices such cell phones, MP3 players and small flashlights. Without any means of recharging the batteries, they all agreed to limit the use of all the devices as much as possible.

While Leanna led a brigade of children on a torch-lit exploration of the building's interior, Violet and the adults sat on the floor in a large circle and discussed their state of affairs in detail. Violet reassured everyone she felt "pretty normal, aside from being hungry and craving a strawberry smoothie." The trademark sparkles had not yet fully returned to her eyes, yet she appeared sufficiently lucid, reassuring Mateo she had largely recovered from her injury.

Kyle described what had transpired in the other section of the park with Aaron and Dante, which opened up an entirely new conversation, centered mainly on Dante's deep knowledge of the zoo – and the pistol he was carrying. "That gun could really have come in handy, y'know," Victory suggested.

Dwayne leaned his shaved head back, stroked his goatee, and added, "You got to wonder whether they made it out. Neither of 'em seemed to be in good shape and they must've really worn themselves out, but if they did make, I'm sure they'll be sendin' help for us soon."

Mia took a long swig of water from one of the plastic bottles and then asked, "And if they failed?"

Dwayne glanced her way and replied, "Then they're probably doin' what we are and tryin' to rest up for another push in the morning." Everyone

145

nodded in agreement and briefly talked about Aaron Kemper and the money he offered Dante to go with him.

Victory interjected, "Somethin' evil 'bout that one. While he'd like to buy his way out of this, he's got to realize there's no way to do that. Maybe we should have tried harder to get Dante to stay with us. We could really use his knowledge of this place... and that gun of his. I wonder if any other security guards are still roamin' the park, lookin' for survivors like us."

Mateo closed his weary eyes and attempted to get a reading on the whereabouts and condition of the two men they had left behind, but found it difficult to focus. He finally contributed to the conversation by adding, "It was probably necessary that they went off their separate way. I think they needed to find out something for themselves and everyone has a right to do just that."

Kyle quickly interjected, "... and it's just possible they *will* succeed in getting out and that'll be the best thing for all of us!" Sinnamon and Jason had remained silent since entering the building. Physically exhausted, they sat side-by-side, leaning against the stone wall.

Violet took a hard look at the redhead in the hunter green tank top and khaki cargo shorts and realized she was the same woman who had clipped the peacock's tail feather just before the thunderstorm struck. She played it cool and nudged her father while subtly gesturing with her eyes. Mateo immediately understood and visually explored every aspect of the well-toned, freckled woman seated in the corner. He remembered the first time he had seen her in the lush, Eden-like setting of the Ituri Forest. That felt like such a different time and place, before any of this horror had begun. Mateo recalled the involuntary physical attraction he felt as he examined her lightly freckled, turned-up nose and alluring, bowed lips. Then suddenly, he sneezed – just as he had the other day when he unexpectedly encountered Mia for the first time.

"Bless you!" Violet blurted out, followed by a knowing chuckle. She realized that her father had been gazing longingly at Sinnamon when his sneezing reflex was triggered once again. Violet made the connection between arousal and the sneeze and recognized the irony of her father being attracted to the very person whom she regarded as a nemesis of sorts. Still angry over what she regarded as a brutal act of disfigurement perpetrated upon the peacock, she harbored resentment toward the object of her father's lust.

"Papa, did you forget what I said about closing your mouth the other time?" she teased, before laughing and rocking back and forth where she sat. Mateo just blushed after tearing his attention away from the object of his desire.

Jason had been silent, inspecting the myriad scratches covering his arms, neck, and legs. He had stripped off his white cotton shirt and was using it to daub the blood still oozing from the lacerations. His mood was sullen and he was finding it nearly impossible to fight back the tears now that he finally had a chance to contemplate the scope of their predicament. All he could picture was Nature sweeping his parents away with its terrible onslaught. Jason was uncertain whether his vivid imagination was responsible for the horrible images etched into his brain or if he was experiencing another premonition. All he knew for sure was that he felt sick with worry for the people he dearly loved.

Predictably, it was Sinnamon who felt compelled to shift the mood by diverting the group's focus, suggesting they all introduce themselves now that they had some time to kill until morning. "Just like the first day of school, right kids?" she playfully urged, winking at Violet at the same time. Violet smiled to indicate her sincere willingness to accept this new person into her life. Somewhat wary of her, Mateo smiled too; but his slightly raised eyebrow told his daughter he was reserving judgment for the time being.

They then began trading stories and in some cases, explaining what drew them to the zoo on the fateful day of December 27th. Sinnamon explained she had "picked up a gig." A wedding in the zoo was scheduled for an upcoming weekend, and she claimed she had come to take photographs for her web site. The rest of the group were impressed by her range of talents in both photography and music. They had no way of knowing she withheld the fact that she also visited the zoo in pursuit of the same peacock Violet had sought. By coincidence, Sinnamon had seen the identical blog post, and though their motivations were vastly different, their individual determination brought them to the same destination at precisely the same moment.

Violet chose to say nothing about being inspired to visit the zoo to find the unique feather, aware that it presently rested somewhere inside the canvas bag tucked discreetly behind the small of Sinnamon's back. The memory of the encounter during which she witnessed the calculated removal of the feather by the same hard-boiled woman still irritated Violet. Whether the sinewy redhead even made the connection was unclear, so Violet elected to keep her mouth shut. So much had happened in the interim between that unsavory moment and the present.

I Miss Your Purple Hair

Jason made a similar choice not to relate the details of the nightmare that prompted him to drive to the zoo. He felt confused about his recent rash of dreams, and did not feel prepared to share any of it, at least not just yet. While unable to make a direct association between what his dream revealed and their current situation, he was aware of some striking correlations.

The torches had long been exhausted by the time they concluded their cursory introductions, and as midnight approached everyone agreed to try to get some much needed sleep.

△ △ △

CHAPTER FOURTEEN
All We Are is All So Far

"In times of change, learners inherit the Earth, while the learned find themselves beautifully equipped to deal with a world that no longer exists."
~ Eric Hoffer

Around 3:05 a.m., Jason's panicked screams shattered the silence and echoed off the walls. Sinnamon, who'd been asleep propped up against a nearby display stand, jumped to her feet and stumbled backward until she struck the back of her head against the unforgiving granite wall. "Jesus!" she exclaimed as she pushed her body away from the wall with her two arms. After yelling out in his sleep, Jason was awake and very much confused.

"What is it?!" he asked frantically, eyes darting about wildly.

"It was *you*, you flippin' moron! You scared the hell out of everyone with that blood-curling scream!" Sinnamon chastised. Jason's eyes popped open wide and he laughed in reaction to her comment. "What the hell's so funny?" she asked incredulously.

Jason relaxed and leaned back against the wall before responding, "It isn't 'blood-curling.' The term is 'blood curdling'... 'curdling', okay?" Sinnamon was not amused by the ripple of laughter circulating around the room. Although she rarely exhibited insecurity, she was sometimes embarrassed by her slippery grip on proper grammar.

"What was it, Jason? What caused that outburst?" Mia calmly asked. His screams had awakened everyone, and he had to take a moment to distinguish his dream from the harsh reality they were facing. Wearing a pained expression as he rubbed the back of his neck, Jason relived his nightmare.

"It was a terrible dream," he began. "The world was being ripped apart by tidal waves and quakes. There were fires everywhere, cities in ruin... and the sky's color had permanently changed to a strange shade of orange. I don't think I should go on with this... I don't want to upset everyone. Let's just say it was the worst nightmare I've ever had. Sorry I woke you all."

Mia felt inclined to demonstrate concern while providing a calming presence for the benefit of the others, especially cognizant of the children. She thoughtfully considered the situation before responding to Jason. "No wonder you reacted like you did. A nightmare like that would be upsetting to anyone.

In light of what we've all just lived through, I'm not surprised. We probably should all prepare ourselves for such dreams, but we have to remember that they're just dreams... and not a reflection of reality. Until we get out of here and head back to our homes, we don't have a clue as to the actual extent of the damage from the quakes. As far as we know, we may be the unfortunates sitting at Ground Zero, and the worst of the destruction may be isolated to this location. We just don't have any information yet."

Dwayne piped in, "That's right. I don't believe dreams mean much of anything. Once daylight comes, we need to make our move and find a way out of this place. That's all I know." DeAngelo, who had been barely awake, slid along the floor to deposit his weary head in his father's lap and fell asleep again.

Sinnamon could not resist expressing her opinion, although she kept her voice down, rather uncharacteristically. Sitting in a dark corner, she pulled her knees up to her chin and rested her head there before speaking in measured tones. "Let's be honest, okay? This earthquake obviously did extensive damage. We have no cell phone reception whatsoever. That's clue number one. If the destruction was isolated, we'd still hear something on our phones, right? And there hasn't been one helicopter or airplane or friggin' hot air balloon in the sky since everything happened – not one."

Sinnamon glanced over toward Jason, barely able to make out his features in the nearly pitch-black environment. She was able to see his eyes, wide open and fixed upon her face, enough to know she had his undivided attention. By the silence in the room, she surmised she had everyone else hanging on her words, too, so she continued. "I'm not into spreading doom and gloom, but we have to face facts. Sure, I don't have any way of verifying jack shit either, but the signs are all there. This thing obviously took out a lot more than a few cable cars and animal cages. We can't be thinking any rescue teams are coming any time soon, because they probably aren't. We have provisions to last a couple more days... and then we'll be in dire straits. As it is, we aren't gonna stay strong eating pretzels and candy bars, so we've gotta take action as soon as it's light enough out there... like this dude just said."

Victory chimed in calmly with, "His name's Dwayne, Miss. I do agree on that last point. We can't be passive 'bout a thing. At dawn, I say we gather up the tools and every bit of food and water we can find, and then find a way out."

"What about that wild animal we heard?" the nameless boy meekly asked.

Before anyone else expressed their surprise at hearing the child speak, Sinnamon attempted to calm his concerns by offering up a response. "Kid, I have a six-inch hunting knife and plan on using it to make a spear, so don't worry about any animals that might be out there. Besides, they're gonna be way more scared than any of us."

Without missing a beat, the boy answered back in a slight Indian accent, "My name's Ravi... not 'kid'."

Kyle gave him a squeeze as if to say, "Way to go!" and Sinnamon meekly replied, "Oh, sure thing... Ravi... got it." Jason thoroughly enjoyed seeing an eight-year old stand up to the somewhat obnoxious redhead. In the dark, she could not see his smirk, but suspected it was there just the same. Kyle was pleased to see the boy emerging from his self-imposed silence and knew to allow him to determine when he was ready to offer up more information.

During the night, Mia and Violet had jockeyed for position to be as close as possible to Mateo and wound up flanking him. At some point during the few precious hours they slept propped against the wall, Mia's head found its way onto Mateo's right shoulder with Violet curled up against his left side. For a brief moment in the middle of the night, Mateo's eyes opened and he realized he was supporting them. He smiled contentedly before drifting back to sleep for another hour or so. Despite the fear and uncertainty he felt oddly at peace with this quietly confident woman on one side and his cherished daughter on the other.

Often, throughout the course of many shared experiences, Mateo would step back from the immediacy of a moment to ponder Violet's place in the world. He recognized her impressive intellect very early on, but some of her more unusual abilities were less simple to label. Mateo was a highly intuitive person, capable of knowing things in a way the average person could not. Over recent years, more than one friend or acquaintance referred to him as an "Indigo" – a term used to describe highly evolved humans.

Author and Researcher Nancy Ann Tappe first coined the term in the early 1980s after recognizing a rapidly growing percentage of the children being born possessed indigo-hued auras, something new and unusual in her experience. Through some bizarre twist of fate, Nancy Tappe was born with a highly unusual misalignment of two components within her neurological system, resulting in her enhanced natural ability to see the human aura – the field of electromagnetic energy surrounding the human form. Rare, she is equipped to see the colors generated by the frequencies of these fields, which are as unique to the individual as fingerprints.

I Miss Your Purple Hair

Mateo had grown to recognize many of his own Indigo traits, since researching the phenomenon at the urging of a former companion. Many researchers contend that a small percentage of Indigos were born into the world as early as the early 1920s. The phenomenon has steadily become more prevalent – indicative of a shift, perhaps a quantum leap, in human evolution. He considered the possibility he was one of the earlier Indigos.

From his earliest days, he felt like he simply never fit in with the vast majority of the people he knew; whether family, classmates, or business colleagues. He had always been unusually sensitive: physically, emotionally, and psychically. As Violet grew, he not only observed similar traits in her, but became convinced she was further evolved and gifted in ways he could only admire. Despite what he recognized as an evolutionary gap, their powerful bond flourished.

Mateo breathed deeply as he hovered between consciousness and sleep. His mind raced through a virtual slideshow of the last ten years with Violet. Hints of her potential were scattered throughout those vignettes. Over recent years, she had acquired an acute awareness of humanity's self-destructive tendencies. Baffled by the ongoing disrespect for the planet and the propensity for violence, she began to feel guilty for not personally doing more to make a difference.

As she entered puberty, her dreams became much more vivid, conveying to her a message of urgency about the dire state of the planet. A child who seemed to paint and write constantly, she also composed music on her electronic keyboard. Many of her paintings, drawings, and original compositions were expressions of her sincere concern about the health of the planet and the consequences for humanity. She sometimes would ask her father what she could do, and he typically urged her, "Do what your heart asks of you."

During recent years in Miami and San Diego, Violet had involved herself with causes she sincerely supported; from recycling to combating global warming, to wildlife preservation. Often, Mateo would donate time and money to the same causes. When he could, he would work alongside his determined daughter, not only to protect her but to support her emotionally. There were times when the many commitments became a bit overwhelming, but the next day they would roll up their sleeves and work that much harder.

At age 12, Violet created a blog called *Random Acts of Violet: InspirActions*. Initially, it was a site listing opportunities for community involvement with an emphasis on sustainability and animal rights. Over time, she learned much by doing the research necessary to identify the most honest and effective organizations. She began to employ her impressive writing skills to author compelling, sometimes controversial editorials that shed light on the merits of these organizations. By age 13, she had gained a healthy subscribership and was spending most of her free time writing, updating the site or doing volunteer work for a variety of organizations.

Once she and her father relocated to the West Coast, the popularity of her blog exploded and her anonymity began to evaporate. Although initially reluctant to appear on camera, she was featured on a local news show. At Mateo's gentle prodding, she finally acquiesced and participated in a panel discussion on volunteerism and environmental activism. At the time, she was barely 14 and by far, the youngest member of the panel, yet she made a lasting impression upon thousands of viewers.

Producers of a nationally televised morning talk show saw the broadcast and invited her to take part later that summer in a show themed *Blogging a Better World*. The special program centered upon a surge in "young people using their words to inspire and mobilize large numbers of citizens to change the world." Violet discussed the invitation with Mateo, and together they considered what international exposure might mean for her. After another week had passed, a member of the production team contacted Violet again, providing additional information about the program's format.

When she shared the communiqué with her father, he simply asked, "Is there really any good reason to decline?"

She paused only for a moment before responding, "I just don't know if I'm ready for that kind of attention. But, if you think it's a good idea, then I'll do it. I started this. Now I guess I have to follow through, huh?"

Mateo thoughtfully commented, "True leaders are courageous by nature. You have a gift for reaching people and awakening what they didn't realize they had within; that's powerful stuff, Violet; stuff that helps define a leader of the rarest type. Failure to share such an exceptional gift would be sinful, wouldn't it?" He could tell by the sparkle in her eyes that she had already decided to accept the invitation. Later that year, on a sunny Sunday afternoon, they flew to Los Angeles and Violet appeared on the "live" broadcast the next morning.

During the program, she spoke eloquently about the need for all people to come together and contribute to the restoration of the Earth's resources. Through anecdotes surrounding the volunteer work she had been involved with for years, she effectively communicated the simple message that, regardless of one's age or social status, people can make profound contributions to heal the Earth for the sake of future generations. The next day, her blog was flooded with so many posts she temporarily shut it down while Mateo constructed a more robust web site to house her growing content.

Her exceptional charisma inspired many viewers to examine their level of personal involvement. The network was besieged with comments and questions surrounding this eloquent, yet humble teenager and her causes. People wanted to know what organizations she represented and how they could contribute time and money. So mature and comfortable was she that many viewers were convinced Violet was older than she appeared. Some went so far as to accuse the show of lying about her age. Within a few weeks of the broadcast, Mateo constructed an automated web site portal for funneling donations to Violet's favorite charities.

In the ensuing year, Violet continued to reach an increasing number of people through her web site. She also embarked upon writing her first book of inspirational stories gathered from experiences with various organizations. The day before their visit to the zoo, Violet had received a letter of interest from a publishing house in San Francisco. It was her plan to draft a reply in the evening, after they stopped to pick up dinner on the way home.

Mateo looked at his wristwatch to learn it was only 3:40 a.m. and then savored the heartwarming image of his daughter, peacefully at rest. He listened to her gentle breathing and said a silent prayer for her full recovery. He visualized her as a young woman, signing books for her loyal readers and raising funds in support of various causes. One image depicted her as an adult addressing a large crowd of supporters in a beautiful, outdoor setting. Mateo could almost feel the gentle breeze caressing his face as he observed Violet making her way to a crystal podium to the cheers of an enthusiastic throng. For a moment, he put the current predicament out of mind and basked in the reassuring sense of hope the vision inspired.

At her insistence, Violet had Mateo explain and subsequently teach her the technique, whereby they would consciously minimize interference from visual and aural stimuli. They collaboratively developed the process when she was just 12 years old, employing a breathing pattern which slowed their pulse rates to achieve a unique state of peaceful relaxation. They learned to activate what Violet called their internal "hidden eye". With it, they scanned the target's energy field. They not only visually assessed obvious physical signals (facial tics, eye and muscle movement, and pupil dilation), but were also able to peripherally perceive auras. Eventually, Violet became more adept than her father and learned to rely upon her newfound ability as much as any of her more traditionally accepted senses.

Sleeping soundly, Violet shifted her 5′4″ body while Mia woke to the realization that her head had been resting upon Mateo's other shoulder. Slightly embarrassed, she straightened up and leaned back against the wall next to him, whispering a gossamer apology. Mateo quietly assured her there was nothing to apologize for as he admired her gentle sincerity. He turned to get a good look at her and despite the lack of light, came to the realization that she was the same woman whose straw hat he had retrieved just before the thunderstorm began. He could only vaguely make out her facial features, but her breathy voice triggered the memory. On that blustery afternoon, he was only aware of her physical beauty, but in the intimacy of the current setting he began to form a deeper impression. Mateo sensed a soul yearning for greater enlightenment. Since they first met, he had observed her intently absorbing all that was going on around her while demonstrating intelligence and sensitivity.

Sitting in silence in the dark corner of the damaged Reptile House, Mateo felt oddly at peace. Despite the gravity of their situation, he felt confident there would be an acceptable outcome. His focus remained primarily upon his daughter and himself, yet he felt genuine concern for the rest of the contingent sequestered in the damaged building. He felt sure that the catastrophic earthquake only represented a limited aspect of a greater crisis. His premonitions over the past year had suggested that a major storm or other natural calamity was imminent, yet he could never quite piece the clues together.

Despite recognizing the grim possibilities of what might be transpiring across the planet, he felt calm. Mateo was convinced that much had changed over the past few days, yet felt a sense of buoyant optimism he could not fully comprehend. He felt sure they would somehow find a way out of the confines of the zoo and was equally confident Violet would be safe and secure soon. Even though she was merely an adolescent, he felt it was her destiny to make a difference in the world. Her selfless attitude, magnetic personality and superior communication skills gave him reason to believe her future would involve inspiring others. She had already provided glimpses of that potential, reflected in the popularity of her blog and web site.

Although Violet had demonstrated startling maturity throughout her life, she was a typically carefree and playful girl the majority of the time.

However, Mateo had recently witnessed an increasingly pensive side. She understood, as did her father, that although the technological means to connect an enormous percentage of the world's populace were in place, there was a dearth of inspirational leadership. Violet recognized the critical need for that element in the world.

Many of Violet's blog subscribers praised her "inspiring leadership" and expressed gratitude for new clarity in their lives. At first, she was a bit intimidated by the weight of that responsibility but soon accepted the obligation as part of her personal mission. Mateo had been staring blankly at his daughter and, whether or not there was a connection, she began to stir.

"Papa... what time is it?" she mumbled in the darkness. He tapped the face of his wristwatch to activate its LED light and whispered that it was 4:18 a.m. Violet quietly moaned and rolled over onto her back before sitting up and sliding closer to Mateo. He patted her knee in a gesture of love and reassurance. The weary teenager fondled the tiny red crystal heart dangling from her necklace and softly said, "My new necklace will always remind me of you, Papa. Thanks for getting it for me." He smiled, and although Violet was unable to see his expression, she could feel it. He recognized that she was doing what she had always done in the face of a challenge; she was presenting a calm presence in her own best interest... and for the benefit of those around her.

Admiring her inherent courage and composure, Mateo simply replied, "Happy birthday, sweetheart."

A whisper from nearby chimed in with, "Strange place for a party, huh?" They had unintentionally awakened Mia, who then asked, "Is it really your birthday?"

Fighting off a yawn, Violet answered in hushed tones, "No, not today. My birthday was actually about a week ago... December 20th."

Mia declared, "No kidding? December 20th... that's *my* birthday, too! Isn't that a strange coincidence?"

Violet and Mateo independently wondered whether the coincidence was meaningless. They had learned that synchronicities were often linked to other synchronicities and almost always pointed to something more substantive within a short span of time. From experience, they both learned how imperative it was to maintain a state of receptiveness, in anticipation of the inevitable forthcoming clues.

Mia sat up straighter and rubbed her eyes, complaining about the sting of the acidic air. She learned that Violet had just turned 15 and informed her that she was 29 years old. Feeling the ice had been broken, Mia confessed, "You know, I've always loved the name 'Veronica', and have thought, if I ever have a daughter I would give her that name. Would you mind if I call you Veronica?"

"Sure... that's fine with me," she whispered, careful not to wake the others. Mia went on to tell Mateo and Violet that she and her brother Kyle had grown up in Salem, Massachusetts before college beckoned Kyle to Carnegie-Mellon in Pittsburgh and Mia to San Diego State, where she studied Philosophy and Communications. A freelance writing assignment from the local Chamber of Commerce brought her to the zoo on Saturday with Kyle, who was staying with her while in town to make a presentation at the Convention Center.

When Mateo inquired about the assignment, Mia responded, "I'm working on an article about the dolphins and the zoo's cross-marketing program."

Violet and Mateo immediately recognized another eerie parallel, as the dolphins were among the primary lures that brought them to the park, too. Was this just another meaningless coincidence? Mindful to resist drawing premature conclusions, they independently decided to wait – and remain observant in anticipation of additional synchronicities. Still, Mateo could not help but wonder if there was some divine influence bringing the three of them together under these incredible circumstances.

Just then, a meek little voice spoke from a dark corner. "That's my birthday, too," whispered DeAngelo, still reclining alongside his sleeping parents.

Mia, sitting closest to the origin point of the disembodied voice, asked "What's that you said?"

The young boy crawled over a bit closer so as not to wake his parents and reiterated in a forceful and deliberate whisper, "My birthday's the same day as yours – December 20th. I'm 10 now!"

"Wow, what are the odds of that?" Mia wondered aloud. "Now, if *everyone* else here has the same exact birthday, I'll really be creeped out!"

Dwayne Cooper, stirred by their voices, stretched out his right arm to encourage DeAngelo to return to his side. "We have more important things to worry about than birthdays and coincidences," he muttered to no one in particular. DeAngelo scurried along the floor and pulled himself close to his mother once again. He closed his eyes and tried to quell memories of the howling they heard the night before. Thankfully, the soothing rhythm of his mother's breathing helped calm the frightened boy and he fell asleep again.

I Miss Your Purple Hair

Little more than thirty minutes elapsed, during which time Mia dozed off while sitting up, as did Mateo. Violet was unable to sleep any more, her mind preoccupied with thoughts about the synchronicities that were accumulating. She wondered what role Mia would play in everything, and fantasized that perhaps she was destined to provide the companionship she knew her father longed for. Along with her curiosity about the roles everyone was there to fulfill, she was concerned for the dolphins, the wolf, and all the other animals throughout the zoo. With so little information as to the extent of the damage, she feared the worst for the park's most helpless residents, trapped in their enclosures.

It was still fairly dark outside when a loud bang jolted everyone from their tenuous rest. An unmistakable gunshot rang out from just outside the front doors. The shocking blast jolted everyone. Dwayne stood in front of his family, extending his arm to encourage them to stay hidden in the shadows behind him. Mia grabbed Mateo's shoulder and whispered in his ear, "Veronica should move to the back of the room with the others." He asked her to take his daughter to join the others, farther away from the doors.

Able to navigate the room by virtue of the slightest trace of light seeping in, Kyle joined Mateo and Sinnamon. They had both moved next to the doors to try to glimpse the source of the noise. Sinnamon peered over Mateo's shoulder and spotted a vague silhouette moving toward them from the direction of the dolphin tank. It was still too dark to make out many details, but then suddenly, a shadow appeared across the glass door and someone vigorously rattled its metal handle, causing everyone to jump back.

It was Dante, pleading, "Hey! Open this door! Open it now!" while banging on the glass with his closed fist. Kyle hurriedly removed the leather belt from the latch and Dante burst in and tumbled to the floor. "Shut the door... hurry!" he yelled from his ignominious position, fear etched upon his face. The sky had decided to open up again just moments before Dante, soaked and dirty, arrived on their doorstep. Mateo and Kyle worked together to pull the doors closed and lash the belt around the handles again, before they returned their attention to Dante.

"Where's Kemper?" Mateo asked anxiously, as Sinnamon and Kyle assisted Dante to his feet. For a moment, he just stared outside and failed to reply. Mateo could clearly see he was under incredible stress. Breathing heavily and his pupils dilated, his wide-eyed gaze was locked on something out in the misty darkness, beyond those surrounding him.

Victory implored, "What is it? What're you starin' at out there?"

158

"There was an animal... a large animal," Dante announced through trembling lips.

"What *type* of animal? Did you kill it?" DeAngelo asked.

"Not sure," Dante gasped. "It was too dark to see... and whatever it was, moved very fast. Maybe I got it, but I can't say for sure. It spooked me and... I guess I panicked."

"Where is Kemper?" Mateo reiterated.

Still agitated, Dante shook rainwater from his hair and stared out into the darkness when he answered rather somberly, "He wouldn't give up his insane belief we could climb that mountain of rock. It's impossible; trust me. Far too steep; we kept reaching dead ends. Finally, I had enough of that bullshit and told him I was going to catch up to you. Of course, he reminded me of the money, but I threw the cash in his face and told him he could shove it. When I turned my back on him to head down the mountain, he grabbed my pistol and trained it on me. I laughed in his face and told him to shove that too, and kept climbing. He told me I was 'as good as dead', and threw my gun down to the base of the mountain, where I found it later. He said he had his own gun and didn't need mine."

"So, he kept going? Do you think he made it on his own?" Mateo asked.

"Last I saw, he was foolishly trying to climb at a different point, but I knew it was no use. There's just no way anyone could climb that thing without the right equipment, but he wouldn't listen to reason. So, I followed the path you all took and came through the mountain the same way. It's a good thing I had my flashlight on me or I never would have made it through alive. The damn batteries died just before I reached the opening on this side."

Dante was noticeably pale and trembling from exhaustion and stress. Mia tried to calm the battered security guard, quietly reassuring him, "It's okay, it's okay. You're safe in here now. Just catch your breath and I'll get some water. We brought most of the provisions in here." She helped him over to the central room where rainwater was accumulating in one spot.

Violet, hovering between the two areas, noticed Sinnamon fidgeting with her canvas bag, having strayed off by herself again. From the moment she first encountered Rebecca Sinclair, Violet sensed a troubled soul fettered with elements of anger and hostility. At the same time, she detected undertones of sadness that appealed to the sympathetic side of her psyche. It seemed clear that the rather abrasive "loner" was reluctant to trust anyone.

I Miss Your Purple Hair

Violet had learned to resist instinctive urges to prejudge. She therefore considered the initial clues mere building blocks for her ongoing assessment of Sinnamon. Still, she recalled the incident when the redhead, her green eyes conveying a rather tempestuous spirit, clipped the peacock's tail feather. Violet could not fully understand what motivated her to perpetrate such an act, and she wanted answers.

CHAPTER FIFTEEN

Somewhere Out There

"For nothing is fixed, forever and forever and forever, it is not fixed; the Earth is always shifting, the light is always changing, the sea does not cease to grind down rock. Generations do not cease to be born, and we are responsible to them because we are the only witnesses they have. The sea rises, the light fails, lovers cling to each other, and children cling to us. The moment we cease to hold each other, the sea engulfs us and the light goes out."
~ James Baldwin

*I*t was the morning of December 29th, and Sinnamon crouched beside an expansive display case along the western wall of the building when Violet approached. In another corner, the Cooper family huddled near Dante, and Victory was cutting off the lower part of the leg of his trousers to assess his injured knee as best she could. At 5:50 a.m., traces of sunlight finally began spilling into the building. Violet stopped in her tracks when the Sinnamon snapped her head up to see who was approaching.

The polite teenager meekly stated, "Sorry if I startled you. I tend to walk quietly."

"No, you're fine," the brash woman generously offered. "Seems both of us go by nicknames, huh? I go by Sinnamon and you're... Violet, right?"

"Yeah. Well... it seems no one ever calls me by my real name anymore... except in school and stuff. My real name's Veronica, but it's okay if you call me Violet, too."

"Don't worry, Violet. We're gonna get out of this mess, y'know? Your father seems to know what he's doing and we're all lucky to be in one piece. We'll find a way out of here or someone will come for us. It's only a matter of time."

"I'm not really worried," Violet calmly stated. "It is what it is and we just have to put our heads together and figure out the best thing to do."

"Your parents really prepared you for coping with life's challenges, I see."

"Not my parents... my father."

Sinnamon shrugged off Violet's statement and kept rummaging through her utility bag.

"There you are," she muttered, as she extracted a small container of prescription medication from the clutter. "Without these I swell up like a balloon. Stupid allergies are out of control."

Violet watched as Sinnamon popped a tiny red capsule into her mouth and swallowed it dry. "Don't you want some water? I can get some ..."

"Nah," Sinnamon replied as she waved off the gesture. "I'm used to roughing it, with all the hiking and camping I do; and we ought to ration the water... just in case."

Violet took the opportunity to scrutinize the fiery young woman with the hard-boiled persona. The diffused light spilled over Sinnamon's face as she continued organizing some objects along the floor. She assessed her as very physically fit; in her late twenties; resourceful, capable and quick-witted. The word "cunning" came to mind, too. While somewhat hesitant to do anything to alienate her, Violet could no longer suppress her curiosity.

"Can I ask you something?" she sheepishly asked.

Sinnamon got to her feet, holding her freshly reorganized canvas bag by its thick strap. "You want the peacock feather, don't you?"

Taken aback, Violet was unaware she associated her with their earlier confrontation. "Well..." was the best she could muster.

"Here... take the damn thing," she stated flatly. "I don't know what you plan on doing with it, but it's probably not much use to me now, not after what's happened. Making a few bucks off some freak of nature isn't at the top of my priority list anymore. Besides... there may not be anyone left to sell it to."

Her chilling comments were delivered in her typically flippant style, but it was obvious she was worried like everyone else – worried for herself, her family and for the world beyond the walls that entrapped them. Violet eagerly seized the miraculous feather from the calloused fingers of the mercenary and then watched her turn heel and cross the room to find out what the rest of the group was discussing. In the transfer of the feather Violet finally was able to read the ornate script tattooed in black on the inside of Sinnamon's right wrist: "*Nevermind.*"

The curious girl held the feather at eye level, allowing the delicate light seeping through the gash in the roof to spill over it like honey over a warm breakfast roll. It was the first time she had been able to closely inspect what had compelled her to visit the zoo. Mateo had been keeping a watchful eye on Violet and Sinnamon from the other room, aware that his daughter was likely inquiring about the very object she was holding in her right hand. He draped his arm over her slender shoulders and together, they surveyed every minute detail of the natural wonder they had believed was lost to them forever.

"Just look at that..." Violet gushed, referring to the patterns and shapes woven into the iridescent fabric of the feather. "Do you see it the same way I do?" she wondered aloud.

"Tell me what *you* see, baby," Mateo gently requested.

Violet rotated the feather very slowly, so that the diffused light danced over its ridged surface. "How beautiful. It kind of looks artificial, but it's anything but that. This is a miracle in my hands. I never realized..."

Equally impressed, Mateo still felt the need to hear Violet interpret what they were observing. "Yes, yes," he concurred. "Describe the details to me, so I know I'm not imagining this."

"Okay," she began, consciously trying to be analytical. At a glance, the multicolored eye of the peacock feather was rather typical in appearance, bearing dazzlingly beautiful hues of blue, green, copper and indigo. Inexplicable, however, were the unusual threadlike strands of gold, which seemed to be woven into the eye of the feather. Tiny, glittering filaments were wrapped around individual ribbon-like barbules. "This gold sphere toward the tip could be interpreted as the Sun – which is what the guy wrote in his blog post."

She continued, "Look... there's another shape here... a narrow triangle – between the sphere and this tiny star. It widens slightly as it fades into the background. Do you see what I mean, Papa?"

"Yeah, I see that" her awestruck father acknowledged. "It's much more amazing in person than in the photo you printed off the web site. Up close, the three shapes are really clear. But, what are all these tiny golden threads? They're beautiful, but they don't look like anything I've ever seen in Nature before."

For a fleeting moment, Mateo experienced a distinct sense of dread. The feeling was profound, but he elected not to express it in terms that might disturb Violet. Instead, he stated what he knew in his heart to be true; that this was not an insignificant oddity in his daughter's delicate hand, like some goat with a singular horn growing out of the middle of its head. Instead, he was inclined to believe it conveyed a message, another synchronistic clue. He recognized that this very object had served as the primary catalyst for both Rebecca Sinclair and his daughter to arrive at the same place, at the same time, on the same day. That alone might be explained away as an insignificant coincidence, but that their paths had repeatedly crossed and that they found themselves among the handful of survivors was difficult to reconcile.

I Miss Your Purple Hair

Mateo asked Violet a question that suddenly popped into his mind. "Vi, I need to ask you something important. Without thinking too much, who, among these people, is the one you feel may have a message for you?"

Taken aback by his solemn tone, she stammered, "J... Jason?"

"Okay. I imagine you aren't quite sure why he came to mind first, but trust your instincts," Mateo advised. "There will be another sign that may have significance; the idea is to be patient and stay alert for it."

Violet furrowed her brow and tried to understand why she had blurted out the name of someone she barely knew, but concluded that there was nothing logical about it whatsoever. She had spoken his name almost involuntarily, merely reacting to her father's goading. She had never spoken directly with Jason, nor particularly noticed him in the midst of all the chaos. Glancing at Jason, Violet saw that he was sitting alone on the cold floor, scowling at his non-functioning cell phone once again.

She guessed he was probably in his mid-twenties and decided that he was not a bad looking guy. His curly, sandy-brown hair was disheveled after sleeping on his rolled up cotton shirt. His beefy chest was covered by his snug black crew neck T-shirt emblazoned with the silver *Airbourne* logo. Violet thought his best feature, aside from his charmingly shy demeanor, were his green eyes, which conveyed his genuinely friendly and generous spirit. His irises seemed noticeably larger than most, a physical trait Violet had recognized as increasingly prevalent in Indigos. Jason appeared very approachable, which helped Violet feel comfortable thinking he could prove to be of importance to her in some as yet unknown manner.

Returning her attention to the feather, Violet asked, "What could this all mean, Papa? Have you ever seen anything like this in your life?"

Mateo took a moment, drew in a deep breath, and exhaled slowly before answering telepathically...

'No, I never saw anything like this before. It's nothing short of miraculous. So much of what's happening here is terrible in many ways, yet miracles are occurring at the same time. The story Kyle told us last night was just one example. Although a freak lightning bolt struck the sky tram and sent it crashing directly on top of his sister, she walked away unharmed. Their group found themselves trapped in a dead-end canyon and somehow, a passageway that runs all the way through the mountain conveniently appeared. The dolphins' temporary home, which would seem more vulnerable than many of the surrounding structures, somehow survived the earthquake and suffered *no obvious damage, enabling us to commune with the group and renew our strength in the soothing water.'*

Violet responded in kind...

'Yeah, I was thinking the same thing, Papa. Isn't it weird that Jason and Sinnamon were running blindly from some unseen animal, and just happened to end up where the rest of us were camped out? I mean, they could have hit a dead end or wound up somewhere else. It just seems too perfect.'

Mateo refrained from speaking aloud, strictly using non-verbal communication...

'This may sound crazy, but I can't seem to shake the feeling that we're somehow being... protected. Of course, this is a major disaster and we still have no way of knowing how we're going to get out of here, but it still feels like everything is going according to some great plan. Maybe I'm losing my mind...'

'No, Papa. I don't think that's crazy, because I feel it too.'

Violet gently slid the peacock feather into the inside pocket of her blue nylon jacket, which she tied around her waist before adding...

'It's as though there's peace within me, in spite of being in the middle of a nightmare. I feel like I know it's going to be fine, but we still have to go through the bad dream. I can't explain it just right, but maybe you know what I'm trying to say. It's like, I feel I should be a lot more scared and upset... but I'm not and can't understand why.'

Mateo sent his heartfelt response...

'Yes, I do understand what you're saying. I was very worried while you were unconscious and I didn't know if you'd come back to me, but once you woke up, I felt alive again and filled with a peaceful sense I've never felt before. It's almost as if I feel superhuman or invincible ever since I knew you were okay. Maybe it's just my joy and relief, but it feels unlike anything I've ever experienced.'

Their intimate conversation was abruptly shattered by the sound of someone pushing the outer doors open, causing them to whip their heads around to see. The rising Sun had burned off some of the thick grey cloud cover, yet it was still raining. Dwayne and Kyle had unstrapped the belt from the handles and pushed open the twin doors at the entrance, eager to find a way back to the rest of the world.

Dante led the way, gun held at his side in anticipation of any unwelcome encounters with the resident wildlife. He limped noticeably despite the snug wrap Victory had applied, crafted from long strips of cotton made from his light-blue dress shirt. Following directly behind him, Dwayne was not faring much better due to the less severe, yet painful injury to his left knee. The previous day's soaking in the saltwater tank had cleansed the scrapes and cuts but the internal damage would require surgery to repair. Though hobbled, he was still able to keep pace with the others. Jason, Victory, Mia, and Sinnamon lingered in the area directly outside the doors. The gently falling mist welcomed them to the second morning of "Humanity 2.0."

"Hold up!" exclaimed Dwayne, freezing everyone in their tracks. He pointed in the direction of the ruins near the Wegeforth Bowl, but Violet and the others, left at the doorway of the Reptile House, could not see from their vantage point. She led the other children out into the mist, following in the footsteps of the adults. Once in the clear, they saw Dwayne and Dante kicking at something on the ground alongside a pile of broken concrete and twisted metal.

"What is it?" DeAngelo nervously yelled to his father.

"Don't worry... it's dead," he yelled back through the steadily falling veil of moisture. The morning sky was a smoky shade of grey, and the air still smelled like a strange mixture of fire and brimstone.

"*What's* dead!?" young Ravi anxiously required knowing.

"It's a pig of some sort; a wild pig. But, it's dead... nothing to worry about," Dwayne announced to everyone. He had picked up a long metal rod from the rubble and was poking at the carcass amidst the debris. He turned to Dante, who was standing uncomfortably next to him, and said under his breath, "Gunshot wound to the neck; pretty impressive shot, given the darkness and all," implying that it was the animal that spooked Dante the night before. "Looks like one of the pigs we saw in the Children's Zoo the other day. We aren't far from where that used to be, so this one must have been hiding in the weeds yesterday. It probably came out, looking for food, when it ran out at you."

Dante nodded in agreement with Dwayne's conclusions. He commented, "The good news is, we can eat this. Let's take it into the building, out of the elements. Someone here must know how to prepare it." Dwayne called Jason and Kyle over to help carry the piglet back to the Reptile House, where they set it on the floor in the very back of the large display room. Sinnamon offered up her hunting knife and Dwayne agreed to prep it. His childhood experience as the son of an avid deer hunter in Ohio would be put to good use.

Sinnamon used water from the dolphin tank to wash off a large section of plastic tarp she found rolled up on the broken stage of the Wegeforth Bowl, and they laid it out to serve as a surface for butchering the unfortunate creature. While she and Dwayne went off to tackle the unsavory task, the others began to gather wood in preparation for building a fire once the mist eased up. Leanna and her sister made a beeline for the dolphin tank to reacquaint with their new friends, closely followed by DeAngelo and his protective mother.

Ravi, unnerved by the sight of the dead pig and worried that other animals were lurking, cowered behind his emotional anchor, Kyle. "Let's go back inside," he pleaded, despite his uneasiness about seeing the animal carcass again. "We can stay inside the building and close the doors again and still see out."

Kyle knelt down and put a hand on each of the young boy's shoulders to calm him. "We're going to be fine, Ravi, I promise," he said in his most reassuring voice. "That pig never would have meant harm to anyone, but it's gone now. Why don't you and I go check on Tidus and Yuna and make sure they slept well last night. We can climb up and hang out on the deck, or even go in the water again if you'd like; and that's just as safe as the building, since we'll be high above ground and able to see everything from there. What d'ya think?"

The little boy blinked his eyes and thought hard, wiping away a tear with the back of his hand. "What about the wolf?"

Kyle had nearly forgotten about the howling they heard the night before. He tried to recall the sound's general point of origin. "Ravi, if I remember right, it sounded a long way off in the distance, beyond that very tall mountain. If whatever made that noise was nearby, then we would have heard it again or would have at least seen some sign of it. With all the noise we've been making, it probably got scared and is long gone by now. Besides, Dante has a gun."

"Oh, right," he happily sighed. "The gun; I almost forgot. Okay, let's go up on the deck with those girls." Kyle patted his Padres baseball cap and led him by the hand over to join Hanna, Leanna and the dolphin mates. The rain had become a fine mist and the red-orange Sun was rapidly warming the atmosphere.

"Ah, another lovely San Diego morning," Kyle sarcastically muttered.

"What did you say?" the little Indian boy innocently asked.

"Nothing, I was just admiring those pretty colors in the sky."

"Yeah," Ravi agreed. "It looks like the inside of one of those red grapefruits... sort of."

"Right, it looks a lot like that, Ravi." Kyle was doing all he could to help keep the boy calm, while at the same time aware of the ominous reality of a sky that appeared permanently transformed.

Everyone had readily agreed that their first priority was to get some nourishment into their starving bodies, so Mia and Mateo eagerly worked together to gather firewood and kindling from every possible source. They were fortunate to find an ample supply, including splintered two-by-fours, chunks of plywood, broken tree limbs and other remnants of a once-idyllic habitat. With help from Victory, they fashioned a makeshift fire pit, and, on either side, positioned a pair of empty steel drums that DeAngelo had spotted near the back corner of the Wegeforth Bowl stage. Five segments of rebar rods they dug out of the ground made for a functional barbecue grate when laid across the drums.

Hours went by as everyone hustled to get things organized. Sitting on a three-foot high rock formation directly in front of the newly fashioned fire pit, Mia paused to catch her breath. With little solid food in her system, she tired much faster than usual. Mateo winced nearby, fussing with a splinter embedded in the heel of his left hand. "Come over here and let me take a look at that," she urged. He sat and showed her where the half-inch shard of wood had almost completely buried itself in the base of his palm.

Mia reached into the front pocket of her beige shorts and located a tiny Swiss army knife. "Never leave home without it!" she remarked with a smile. "You never know when the next natural disaster's going to strike." She paused for a moment and choked back tears, before apologetically adding, "Not really funny, is it?"

Mateo chose not to reply, but rather preferred to relax and entrust his hand to the young woman with the aura of cobalt blue and the unusual, aquamarine eyes. She composed herself and gently took his hand in hers. He immediately sensed a source of energy that flowed directly from her, into him, the moment their flesh first contacted. He looked into her eyes but she stayed focused upon the shrapnel in his hand and squeezed a little tighter to keep him still.

He had never experienced such an impressive influx of energy from another person. It was as though he was injected with adrenaline laced with sedative. He immediately felt as though his pent-up anxiety was washed away by a soothing, yet invigorating shower. She was restoring his soul with healing energy while simultaneously tending to his physical needs.

Rejuvenated on multiple levels, Mateo partly attributed the intensity of the feeling to the fact that Mia was an exceptionally beautiful, sensual young woman he indeed felt attracted to, as his daughter had so playfully pointed out. He had very fleetingly lusted after Sinnamon along the trail in the Ituri Forest, but his reaction to Mia was something much more profound. In light of all they were dealing with, those emotions could not survive and flourish the way they might have under normal circumstances. Mateo consciously suppressed any romantic notions for the time being, well aware of the greater priorities. Still, there was no denying his sincere attraction.

"Got it!" Mia triumphantly declared, as she finally plucked the intruding object from the heel of Mateo's tender left hand. He felt immediate relief and his thoughts briefly turned to the ancient fable of Androcles and the Lion. He started to reluctantly remove his hand from the bare skin of Mia's thigh but she held it hostage by tensing her grip on his wrist, blurting out, "Wait a second. Hold on, okay?"

"Another splinter?" Mateo asked.

"Wow," she said, "I don't believe I've ever seen anything like this before."

"What's wrong?" he asked.

"No, no... there's nothing wrong. I've just never seen anyone with such clear markings," she declared as she raised his hand slightly and hunched over to examine it more closely. "I read palms as a hobby – been doing it since I was younger than Veronica – and I've done hundreds of readings. But, this is the first one like this. I almost can't believe it." Mateo remained silent, content to listen to her explanation. Mia turned to him and quizzically asked, "Who *are* you?"

Blushing a little, he did not fully understand what she was implying. She returned her attention to his calloused palm, and with her free hand pointed at a particular spot. "You've never had a full reading?" she asked, incredulously. Mateo just shook his head, pouting in playful fashion. She continued, "Wow... well, see this, right here? You never noticed this?" He shook his head again and wore a dumbstruck expression. She sighed and shook her head for different reasons. She found it somewhat surprising that a man who appeared so vastly enlightened had never explored such things at some point in his life.

"This marking here... it looks like a small star, right? Do you see it? This is your Mount of Venus, and on it is this deeply etched star. I've only rarely seen such pronounced star symbols and have *never* seen one on the Mount of Venus like this! Amazing! And your entire hand is covered in triangles; not just intersecting lines forming them, of which you have many, but you also have *independent* triangle symbols within your hand. That's freakish! I'm sorry, I mean no disrespect. I mean, it's highly unusual to see *one* well-defined triangle and yet, you have *six* – in addition to about a dozen or more that are intersected by other lines." She caught her breath and then asked once more if he had ever been aware of these traits before. He shrugged and asked what it all meant.

Mia sighed and collected herself. She brushed aside the swath of hair she had been forced to crop in order to escape the wreckage of the sky tram. "I look pretty ridiculous with this bizarre hairstyle, huh?" she timidly asked while looking deeply into his eyes.

"Not in the least," he softly answered. "I actually like it and thought it was some new 'look', until you told the story."

Mia cleared her throat and shifted her focus back to Mateo's palm. "Triangles are somewhat uncommon, and generally denote mental acuity. They're always a very positive sign. When they appear on a specific mount as an independent marking, then there is a much more profound meaning. See, in this case, this triangle sits alone on the Mount of Apollo. That indicates very powerful talent in aesthetics… art and other creative pursuits. Then, you have some other clearly defined triangles. Have these always appeared so pronounced?" Again, Mateo just shook his head, obviously clueless.

Mia continued, lost in fascination over the unusual lines etched within the hand of the 42-year-old. "Mateo, you're obviously an exceptional person. You seem to be a pillar of strength regardless of what's going on around you; and you've raised a remarkable daughter, largely on your own from what I gathered last night. I've observed you over the last couple of days and you seem to operate on a higher frequency than the rest of us... with the exception of Veronica, of course. Now, I see these remarkable indicators and it's a bit much for me to grasp."

Mateo was genuinely confused. "What is it you're so impressed with?" he asked in all sincerity. "It may be true that my daughter is very bright and unusually intuitive, but I can't take credit for that. All that came along with her when she came into this world. I don't think I'm anything special. I work hard for a living and try to be a good father and role model for my child – like many people do. The wrinkles in my hand may be interesting, but I don't know what they mean, if anything."

"Forgive me for saying so, but I see a man of great destiny every time I look at you. Perhaps you're already fulfilling it as a great father, or... maybe there's something even bigger you're supposed to do. It could be that you're destined to be famous or something. This star symbol... it's extremely rare as far as I know... extremely. What it tells me is that you have a very important life purpose... but I don't think it's materialized for you yet. The only worrisome thing is that, where it's located..."

"What? What does that mean? You sound different...," Mateo begged for clarification.

Just then, a commotion demanded their attention. Dwayne and Sinnamon noisily emerged from the Reptile House, dragging the tarp filled with the meat of the butchered pig. Just as Mateo was going to offer a helping hand to the pair of volunteer butchers, another distraction took precedence.

Victory suddenly yelled out, "No! I don't believe you!" She and Dante had been talking near the demolished remains of the still partially intact public rest room. With the water supply obliterated, they were unable to flush the toilet, but it was preferable to using the bushes and building ruins.

Dwayne came limping over to investigate, as quickly as he could with his stiff leg holding him back. "What's wrong? What happened, baby?" he asked through an expression of concern. Victory stood toe-to-toe with her protective husband and he took her hands in his. Mateo and Mia got up and joined the rest of the group, now surrounding the couple. Victory looked over to make sure the children were all preoccupied with the dolphins and out of earshot before sharing what Dante had told her.

Pointing at him as he sat a few yards away, Victory explained, "This man just told me that other, older fellow, took his own life – killed himself with that gun right there – after we left them the first day. He told me the other man stole his gun and shot himself! Now, does that make sense to any of you? It smells funny to me. I mean, wasn't he some rich man and all? Why would he just up an' kill himself like that, of all people? I'm sorry, but... I feel like this one's hiding something. It just smells wrong to me."

Kyle stepped in and attempted to defuse the tension. "Dante, what's going on? What did you tell her just now?" The beleaguered young guard seemed drained of all energy. Fixed on him, Mateo tried to get a feel for his emotional state. He looked for telltale signs in his physical mannerisms and attempted to read his aura. Dante fidgeted where he sat, accumulated beads of sweat on his brow.

"It's true," he began, "I felt I had to tell the truth, so you all know everything I know. We shouldn't have secrets. What I told you before wasn't exactly true. Kemper surprised me and pulled the gun from my holster, but when I grabbed for it, I missed and fell onto my back. When I opened my eyes, he was standing over me and pointing the gun in my face. He demanded that I help him find a way over that damn mountain. When I laughed and told him he was crazy, he squeezed off a shot that ricocheted off the rocks a few inches from my head!"

Dante nervously continued, "He totally lost it at that point. He was screaming obscenities and just about frothing at the mouth. I've never seen anything like it. The way he waved the gun around, I was sure he was going to kill me. Once he stopped ranting long enough for me to say something, I told him to calm down – that I'd try to help find a way out again if he put the gun away."

Raw anguish played out across his dirty face, as Dante related the rest of the story. "At that point, I expected him to order me to get to my feet and continue climbing. But, instead… he suddenly turned his back to me, put the gun to his head and blew himself away. Just like that! He had just given up, I guess. He told me he was a Diabetic, and lost his supplies somewhere. Maybe he was suffering from lack of insulin… or he might have had a few screws loose to begin with. I didn't want to say any of this when the kids were around, y'know?" He covered his face with his hands and wept, while Victory and Mia tried to console him. Victory apologized for doubting him earlier; feeling foolish after hearing the whole story.

Once Dante had released some of his pent-up stress, Dwayne asked, "Is he dead, for sure? I mean, what did you do with his remains?" Victory shot an angry look at her husband and gestured toward the kids, but it was obvious the sounds of the dolphins splashing about made it impossible for them to hear their conversation.

Dante sighed heavily before answering. "He was dead, for sure. I checked him out. Believe me. But there was no way I could carry his body down that steep mountain. You see how I can barely walk. We were over twenty feet high when it all happened. So, I buried him… beneath loose rocks I gathered from the mountainside. It felt wrong to leave him like that; but you have to understand, I had no choice. At least I covered him as best I could, so he's not exposed to the elements and birds. When we're rescued, we can direct people to pick him up. It was all I could do to get down in one piece on this bad leg."

Victory encouraged him to calm down and put it out of his mind, while Mia rubbed his shoulder and offered sympathy. When Dwayne informed

Sinnamon and Jason of whom they were speaking, Sinnamon sneered and walked away, adding, "I ran into him a couple years ago at a club in Hollywood. He was a total douche bag, so I don't imagine it's any great loss."

Mateo shook his head in reaction to Sinnamon's crude comment, all the while studying Dante. Mateo was not convinced he was being completely honest, although there was sincerity in much of his depiction. Something about it rang false and Mateo had witnessed an unexpected, dramatic shift in Dante's aura while he spoke. With people moving back and forth between them in front of a rather complex backdrop, aura viewing was especially difficult. He decided it was impossible to conclude much from the color shift midway through Dante's recounting of the sad tale. Still, he was left with lingering questions about what had actually transpired, and felt uneasy with the fact that Dante still had a gun in his possession.

Kyle had remained silent, trying to comprehend the story and listening for any indications of insincerity laced within Dante's speech patterns. His training as a psychologist and experience in the field had helped hone his listening skills, making him adept at picking up the most subtle auditory signals. From where he was standing, about fifteen feet from Dante, he surmised certain details were purposely left out or glossed over. He was convinced Aaron was dead, but not confident in the validity of the details.

Kyle recalled hearing what he thought was a single gunshot while the group was inside the wormhole passageway. He had been at the back of the line of survivors, and the only one to hear the noise coming from the canyon to the east. Subsequently, he decided not to mention it, figuring that Dante had fired the weapon to scare off the white wolf they had seen lurking in the vegetation to the north. Now he realized that noise marked the termination of a man's life and knew there would be many questions once they found their way back to civilization.

What Kyle did not fully realize was that the least of their worries were the circumstances surrounding Aaron's death. The civilization to which they all wanted so desperately to return barely existed anymore. The earthquakes that ripped through Southern California were among the most powerful in severity, but many of similar magnitude had struck across the globe. Unprecedented incidents of tsunamis affected every continent, producing multiple seismic chain reactions. Entire landmasses were either submerged or completely fragmented. The aftershocks continued across the planet, bringing the death toll to staggering levels.

I Miss Your Purple Hair

With worldwide communications crippled, the infrastructure collapsed and the vast majority of the world had been plunged into darkness. Wildfires and floods broke out over much of the Earth's surface, causing irreparable structural damage. The chain of events in deep recesses of the oceans triggered volcanic activity across the world. One of the hardest hit regions, the Hawaiian island chain, was all but wiped from the face of the planet.

During the two days that the survivors were trapped within what was once the San Diego Zoo, over four billion human lives had been lost. Aaron Kemper's demise was a tragedy for him and the handful of people to whom he mattered, but in the grand scheme of things, it was tantamount to a non-event. Still, these innocent survivors were like so many others, isolated in dark, lonely places no longer recognizable. Regardless of the grander situation, they still had their personal stories to play out and their individual destinies to fulfill.

Dante felt drained, yet relieved to have finally informed the others about what had transpired on the opposite side of the towering mountain of rock behind him. Mia suggested that he try to relax and drink some water and snack on the bag of salted peanuts she handed him. Spirits gradually began to lighten as the group prepared for the pig roast and everyone looked forward to an actual meal. Mia, a long-time vegetarian, could not prevent herself from salivating at the very notion of feasting on her share of the hot, barbecued pork. While Victory and Dwayne supervised the five children in the dolphin tank, Kyle ignited the kindling in the fire pit as the rest of the adults looked on.

Sinnamon restlessly fidgeted and, while as eager for the meal as anyone, visually scanned the bizarre surrounding landscape, desperately searching for signs of an escape route from their prison of rock, back to the world she knew. She feared for the safety of her best friend, Leslie, who lived only 20 miles from the zoo – more so, in fact, than she worried about her 21 year-old brother, Grayson, a U.S. Marine deployed in Afghanistan. She had no reason to believe the scope of the tragedy could possibly extend to his post, half a world away.

The intoxicating aroma of the barbecue danced on the light breeze, almost cruelly tantalizing in its promise of sensory pleasure. The deliverance lived up to the anticipation as eager mouths made short work of every last scrap of meat. With few words exchanged, everyone, including Mia, "the die-hard vegetarian," reverted to an animalistic frenzy in gorging their starving bodies. Leanna was exclusively vegetarian too, but she ate as much as any of the adults and loudly licked her fingers afterwards, so as not to miss a single bit of flavor. She instigated a hearty laugh from the group when she belched loudly and added, "I just might have to change my vegan ways."

"Let's give ourselves a little time to digest, and then we should get moving and find a passage out," Dwayne said while still finishing up a last delectable slice of pork. Everyone agreed and Victory suggested that they consolidate the water and other provisions before setting out to do any climbing. Jason and Kyle volunteered to make another circuit around the perimeter to note the best potential escape routes, and Mateo agreed to tag along. The children all helped Victory and Dwayne separate the bottled water and snack foods into individual, portable portions. While provisions were organized, Mia asked Mateo and Sinnamon to help clean up. Dante was emotionally distraught and physically barely able to walk. They all urged him to rest his leg and hang out near the fire, and make sure it was tended to.

While they lingered for a while after finishing off the last bits of meat, they finally got the chance to get to know a little more about each other. The group remained seated in various positions around the still blazing fire, when Jason, wide-eyed and seemingly naïve, suggested that they take turns sharing simple facts about themselves. DeAngelo waved his arm overhead, as though he were in a classroom, loudly volunteering by exclaiming, "Me! Me! I want to go first!" His mother scowled at first; clearly implying that he should learn to restrain himself, an ongoing sore subject in the Cooper household.

When Mateo quickly responded with, "I was hoping someone would step to the plate first!" her scowl transformed into a meek smile of appreciation.

DeAngelo stood up and announced, "I'm going to be a doctor someday."

Mateo and Kyle graciously extended a couple of supportive comments while Dwayne's reaction was, "This is the first I ever heard of it!"

DeAngelo, wanting to make a game of everything, skittishly tapped Sinnamon on her shoulder and said, "Next!" to suggest she had been tagged. She flashed a crooked close-mouthed grin and decided to play along in her inimitable way. She did not hesitate long before mumbling something under her breath while hanging her head so no one could see her eyes. Leanna was anxious for her turn so she was slightly perturbed with Sinnamon holding up the proceedings. "We couldn't hear you!" she somewhat uncharacteristically shouted.

Sinnamon cleared her throat and picked her head up, her hair spilling about her shoulders. "I have nine different tattoos and nine body piercings."

I Miss Your Purple Hair

DeAngelo immediately reacted to that revelation with a spirited "Whoa!" followed by a quick "Can we see 'em?" His father stepped in to reel in his son's exuberance, declaring "That's not polite, Dee," to which DeAngelo replied, "I'm sorry, Dad." More than a few of the tattoos were already familiar to the group: the *"Nevermind"* script on her right wrist; the elaborately rendered sorceress all dressed in black, covering much of her left arm; and the cluster of five tiny outlined stars along the left side of her long neck.

DeAngelo then got up and ran over to tag Violet, who was sitting on the ground a few feet from the fire pit. She thought for a moment before saying, "I made up 'The Anagram Game.'"

No one said anything at first and then Leanna asked the obvious question. "It's a game I mostly play with my dad. An anagram is when you scramble the letters of one or more words to make different words," Violet explained. "Whoever notices one before the other person, is the winner. It's kind of an endless game but it's fun when you discover a new one."

"You mean like, you can really scramble up the letters and make other words that make sense?" Hanna asked.

"Yeah, but you have to use all of the letters," Violet elaborated. "Papa, do you remember one of the famous ones we looked up on the Internet?"

Mateo smiled at the memory of researching anagrams with Violet about a year ago, when she came up with the idea for the game they continued to play. "Um, let me think... oh yeah... one of them is 'Clint Eastwood', which is an anagram for 'Old West Action.' Another good one is 'David Letterman'. His anagram is 'Nerd amid late TV'. Those are two of my favorites, anyway."

Violet giggled and added, "Oh! Another good one is 'Mother-In-Law', which scrambles to be 'Woman Hitler'. Ha!" The adults all enjoyed a good chuckle over that one. Mateo commented that Violet had developed an uncanny ability to spot anagrams extremely fast, sometimes within mere seconds of visualizing a word or phrase. She blushed a little, shrugged her shoulders and added, "It just comes naturally, I guess."

When Jason's turn came around, for a moment he considered sharing the fact that his dreams had recently started to become prophetic, but then he thought better of it. Instead, he mentally thumbed though some less controversial facts and said, "Every year, on my birthday, I suffer some illness or weird injury... since I was about 18, anyway."

"For example?" Mia asked.

"Well, last year, I fell out of bed in the middle of the night, and separated my shoulder when I hit the hardwood floor. Two years ago, I needed two stitches above my eye when I walked into a tree in my parent's front yard. And, the year before, I fell down the stairs at my friend's beach house and sprained my ankle so bad I was on crutches for over a week. And, I could go on and on with all the other things that've happened, but I don't want to relive them right now. Even so, I still consider three to be my lucky number for some crazy reason."

"Dude!" Sinnamon exclaimed, half laughing at his sorry tale. "Maybe you ought to just stay in bed on your birthday from now on. I mean why push your luck, right?"

"So, why is three your lucky number? What's that got to do with anything?" Dwayne asked, intrigued by Jason's odd birthday history.

Jason chuckled and replied, "Well, my birthday's October 3rd, and three has been my so-called 'lucky number' ever since I can remember. I probably shouldn't still think of it as lucky, but some things are just hard to shake."

"Hey... wait a second," Sinnamon interjected. "Your birthday... your 'day of disasters'... is October 3rd? That's my birthday, too! I don't think I was ever even sick on my birthday, though. Usually, I have a pretty damn good time on that day, if you know what I mean. I feel for ya, bud."

Violet jabbed her father in the arm with a pair of rigid fingers and muttered something to him directly. A look of confusion crossed his face and he seemed as though he might burst from holding some revelation within. "Tell 'em," she ordered emphatically.

"October 3rd ... is my birthday, too," he delivered dryly. "Pretty strange, isn't it? I also have always considered three my lucky number, but thankfully, I haven't had the same kind of ... uh... luck follow me around on that day."

"Hold on," Victory chimed in. She then tossed out the semi-rhetorical question, "Does anyone *else* here have the same birthday?" No one said a word as eyes darted back and forth around the circle. After a moment, she went on to illustrate the details she found so hard to accept. "This morning, we learned DeAngelo, Mia and Violet all share the same birthday of December 20th; and now we come to find out that three other people all have the same October 3rd birthday? Come on, that's some kind of miracle, isn't it? At least it's pretty hard to make sense of it."

Mateo agreed. "Yeah, given the strange circumstances, and being such a small number of people thrown together in this one place, the odds would be pretty steep against something like this. It makes me curious about everyone else's birthdays."

I Miss Your Purple Hair

The others took turns announcing the month and day of their day of birth, and beyond the already-established fact that three others happen to share the same birthday, there were no other matches or noteworthy patterns. A collective sigh conveyed a sense of relief that the weird coincidences did not extend even deeper. It was more than enough to consider and accept two sets of three having identical birth dates. Everyone sat there a bit stunned, trying to guess what any of it could possibly mean. No one had any answers; just questions mounting upon unresolved questions built up from the past few days.

"Okay, people," Sinnamon somewhat harshly chirped, "... let's finish organizing the supplies, split up into a couple groups and search every square inch of this place. It's only... what, nine-thirty? It's going to take time to find our way up and over one of these damn walls, so let's get going."

Dante had remained deeply lost in thought. He was experiencing physical pain from the injury to his knee and brooding over the traumatic turn of events involving Aaron Kemper. He did not utter a word, but stood up and limped over to the Reptile House, intent on doing whatever it took to get back to his family and friends.

Before entering the building, Mateo looked up at the slow-moving clouds and sensed another subtle shift in the wind. The wispy, lavender-colored clouds spun in a clockwise swirl like a dollop of thick cream in a mug of coffee. While the odd colorations were intriguingly beautiful, there was something very disconcerting about a sherbet-hued sky of orange, red, and raspberry.

△ △ △

CHAPTER SIXTEEN

You Were Looking Down on Me

"Man has been endowed with reason, with the power to create, so that he can add to
what he's been given. But up to now he hasn't been a creator, only a destroyer.
Forests keep disappearing, rivers dry up, wild life's become extinct, the climate's
ruined and the land grows poorer and uglier every day."
~ Anton Chekhov

The large tabletop display inside the Reptile House served as a convenient staging platform for Mia and Kyle to conduct the organization and consolidation of all their provisions. They compiled a small stockpile of bottled water, a few bags of chips, pretzels and peanuts, and a couple of candy bars. In hindsight, Kyle suggested they probably should have agreed to ration every bit of food and water, but none of them imagined they would remain trapped for more than a day.

Victory and Jason collected the backpacks, tote bags, and purses, and emptied their contents onto the tabletop, asking everyone to sort out anything precious or vital before they stuffed provisions into every available object of conveyance. When Victory's pocket-size red Bible went spilling out onto the table, she immediately snatched it up and clutched it to her chest, declaring, "This stays with me, no matter what." Victory rarely went anywhere without her Bible, often re-reading favorite passages whenever she found herself with a few minutes to kill.

Mateo suggested that he and Violet would be willing to lead one group to investigate the areas to the south and southwest while Dwayne and Victory volunteered to take DeAngelo and any other willing individuals, to check the north-northwest region. They understood the futility of trying to scale the mud slide to the north and had no incentive to go back through the mountain to the east again. Sinnamon elected to join the Cooper's group and slung her full backpack over her shoulders. Jason joined them and got a high-five from DeAngelo as a greeting. The remaining survivors – Mia, Kyle, Ravi, and the Armstrong sisters – predictably fell in with Mateo's party. Dante straggled behind the two groups as they filed through the doorway toward a world of uncertainty.

The two parties, equipped with their supply of water and other vital provisions, huddled for one last time before going off in separate directions.

Mateo could not help but notice how badly Dante struggled to put weight on his damaged knee and felt it would likely be impossible for him to climb, assuming they would eventually discover a reasonable path out. He asked Dante if he felt he could walk, let alone climb, and Dante broke down, depositing himself upon a mangled iron bench not far from the front of the building. Holding his head in his hands, the pent up emotions that had been swirling through his mind erupted in rivulets of tears spilling over his Sun-reddened cheeks.

"I don't think I can do it. I just can't," he reluctantly admitted through clenched teeth. "The pain's getting worse every minute, and I'm losing strength in the leg. How would I ever be able to climb? I have no choice but to sit here and wait it out... until help comes." Mateo experienced a sense of dread as he absorbed Dante's feelings of desperation. Something even more foreboding smoldered behind the eyes of the man seated before him, but the window into his soul was sealed shut. What he did fully understand was that Dante would have to be left behind.

Mateo urged him to relax and pledged they would return for him within a few hours, following a thorough assessment of the region. Rather nonchalantly, Sinnamon walked over and extended her right hand, palm open. Dante looked up from his perch on the bench, a quizzical expression on his tear-stained face. "What?" he inquired.

"Your gun," she replied. "If you aren't able to come along on our little hike, one of us ought to have it. If we encounter any beasties out here, they're bound to be afraid and starving; and I, for one, don't plan on being the 'Bitch du Jour.'"

"Wh....wh...what am I supposed to do?" he stammered. "In the shape I'm in, I'm a sitting duck if one of those 'beasties' comes this way."

Without missing a beat, Sinnamon answered, "Christ, dude... get a grip! Shut those metal doors behind you and you'll be safe," motioning toward the Reptile House. "We left some water and junk food to tide you over 'til we get back. But, without that gun, we could find ourselves in a bad way... and there's no good reason to leave it with you."

Physically and emotionally drained, Dante was unable to muster the energy to argue. He realized she made perfect sense, so he reluctantly detached the black leather holster from his belt and handed it to her, asking, "You think you can handle one of these?"

She recounted her experiences at recreational shooting ranges over recent years while he handed her the remaining supply of ammo he had stashed. "Keep the safety on unless you're prepared to use it, alright?" Sinnamon nodded and rejoined her group, electrified by the surge of adrenaline stimulated by the firearm in her hands. Dante wiped sweat from his furrowed brow and grimaced before barking, "I really hope you won't need it. Be smart out there."

Mateo had intently observed the interaction and found their individual energies dramatically different. Sinnamon seemed unflappable and resilient. When they first encountered Dante, he fit the mold of the quintessential Eagle Scout, but had been transfigured right before Mateo's eyes. He appeared to have aged dramatically and become immobilized by more than just physical injuries. While taking a long look at the weary man before him, Mateo observed a clouded, nearly monochromatic aura. Its muddied and muted colors reflected the low degree of energy within the wounded and exhausted security officer. He extended his hand to help Dante get to his feet and then escorted him to the doorway of the building.

At the threshold, Dante paused and expressed his gratitude to Mateo. Before they parted, he asked a question for which he realized no answer could be provided. "Why do you think this is happening to us?" Mateo simply bit his lip and walked away as Dante opened the heavy door and slowly disappeared into the shadowy sanctuary of the Reptile House.

To the west, Mateo noticed heavy-looking clouds moving almost imperceptibly in their direction. They were tinted purple, a pleasant, yet odd hue he had never before encountered. The light breeze of the early morning had picked up a bit, helping to freshen the stagnant air that had been draped over the region.

Mateo rejoined the others to find Violet, Leanna, and Hanna off to one side of the dolphin tank – eyes closed, holding hands and facing one another. Stopping short of their position, Mateo consciously avoided breaking their concentration. Tapping into their innate abilities as "receptors", they attempted to maximize their perception by merging energies. Although the Armstrong sisters had never met Violet before fate brought them together, a compelling bond existed between them. Violet had sometimes spoken of being "in The Web", as opposed to "going on the Web" or "surfing the Web". She described this alternate "Web" as a worldwide network of predominantly young people, most under the age of 20, who routinely communicated on a purely psychic level.

According to Violet, she had instinctively "fallen into" a method of tapping into the minds of other willing participants, around the time she entered grade school. She had described it as "consciously controlling an

I Miss Your Purple Hair

extension of (her) subconscious." She claimed it involved melding minds and thereby tapping into limitless energy offered up by millions of willing souls across the planet... and perhaps beyond.

At barely seven years of age, Violet surprisingly announced to her father, "I talked to a little girl in Africa who can see our apartment from her village." When Mateo asked if the Kenyan child was watching them on computer via satellite imagery, she shook her head and explained, "No, she doesn't have a computer... or even a television, but she really doesn't need those things. She can just see very far away, by herself. Isn't that cool?"

Understandably skeptical, Mateo asked for clarification. "But, honey, how do you know she can really 'see' us and do you really think it's even possible?" Young Violet claimed the little Kenyan girl provided specific details, such as the name of her school and the color of Mateo's car. She had provided a vivid description of the public park down the street from their house and claimed she wished to visit one day and play on the enormous Jungle Gym there.

Violet admitted she did not completely understand how the girl was able to "see" things so far away, but then surprised Mateo by excitedly saying, "She's going to teach me how to do it, too!" Over time, Mateo grew to accept that Violet had indeed begun to learn the technique. Nevertheless, he struggled to comprehend how so many could be routinely participating in such activity, with so little public awareness. On occasion, she would allude to "bad vibrations" and invariably, there would later come word of a natural disaster or other type of disturbance in the very same location. She mentioned that, in isolated instances, a percentage of individuals within *The Web* were able to forecast major events, such as natural disasters.

In many cases, some of those within this invisible network of human energy informed appropriate authorities of their predictions, yet action was rarely taken due to prejudice and skepticism. An inherent roadblock to widespread acceptance and understanding was the lack of any centralized organization. Citizens in every corner of the world, from diverse ethnic, educational, and economic backgrounds, pleaded their case to all types of agencies – in small towns and large cities alike. It was impossible to assign credibility to so many one-time messengers, with no record upon which to rely.

For a few years, Mateo and Violet discussed the need for unifying these disparate souls; some method by which they could bridge the gap between the enlightened and the vast majority, who had never been witness to such abilities. An underlying motivation for Violet's tireless work on her blog was to provide just such a forum. She and her father understood it would take years to establish credibility, but were able to envision the inevitable benefit to society.

Presently, Violet agonized over the fact that she had not properly honored warning signs regarding the natural phenomena leading to the earthquakes – a chain of clues she failed to piece together. While meditating in her bedroom the day before they visited the zoo, she felt a familiar uneasiness in the pit of her stomach. It was a telltale indicator of some unknown disturbance, but she had been so intent on visiting the zoo, she chose to ignore the warning. Despite those regrets, she accepted that she and her father, along with the collection of strangers, were playing out a necessary chapter in destiny's greater plan, and knew that there would undoubtedly be a vital role for her to play before it was over.

After some last-minute discussion, the two groups headed in separate directions, determined to thoroughly explore the surroundings and identify the best possible route out. The Coopers, with Dwayne toughing out every step on his damaged leg, led their party to the northwest, while Mia and Kyle took point and started off to the south, with Ravi glued to them. Violet and Mateo followed close behind. The two groups had synchronized watches and made plans to rendezvous at the middle of the Western wall at Noon. Everyone agreed that neither party was to take any unnecessary risks until they regrouped. Their cell phones and other wireless devices were still non-functioning, while the temperature and sickening stench in the air both had escalated as the Sun rose higher in the sky.

As her group picked their way over the fractured terrain southeast of the Wegeforth Bowl, Violet gazed at the sky and prayed for any little sound. But, there was no evidence of any rescue attempt – not the slightest hint of air traffic. Against the unsettling backdrop of the peculiar-colored sky, there were only intermittent sightings of gulls and sparrows. She resolved to remain hopeful, and reminded herself only two days had elapsed and emergency response units were undoubtedly overburdened. Violet considered the sobering possibility that the quakes could have damaged law enforcement facilities and military resources, too.

Violet began to feel a bit queasy as they approached the remnants of the Hummingbird Aviary, haphazardly strewn about the landscape. Nothing remained, other than a tremendous amount of glass fragments and other debris. In the mass of stone, metal, wood and glass, the group was stunned by the tiny carcasses of dozens of the precious birds. Their once fragile, brightly-colored forms littered the ground amidst the indistinguishable rubble. Ravi picked up a tiny emerald and sapphire corpse and held it within his open palm. "This is so sad," he stated glumly. "If only they could have flown away to someplace safe... "

Most of the ornate little bodies appeared fully intact, making the eerie sight that much more unsettling. Kyle knelt next to Ravi to inspect the lifeless little creature in the boy's trembling hand. He said a few well-considered words to calm his young charge and urged him to put the bird back down among the others. After Mia cajoled the inseparable duo to catch up with the rest of the group, they slowly moved on, tiptoeing between the multicolored, feathered creatures sprinkled over the decimated graveyard. Violet chose to follow a wide trajectory around the area, averting her eyes out of fear that the image of the rainbow death field would be permanently etched into her memory.

Mateo wondered whether the tiny birds were destroyed in the collapse of their habitat, or had succumbed to the poison in the tainted air. He caught up to Violet and whispered, "There's bound to be more like this. Prepare yourself, be strong... and don't be ashamed to turn away if we stumble across more disturbing sights."

"I'm alright, Papa," she said under her breath. "I'm just worried that this is... only the beginning. It's probably a lot worse than we first thought, isn't it?"

"Sweetheart, we don't know much for sure, yet. This is all very bad, but there's no way to be sure *how* bad until we get out of here, so let's be careful not to let our imaginations run wild. One step at a time... remember?"

"You always say that," she immediately added, although she took solace in those familiar words. She reminded herself not to make any wild assumptions, even if her intuition was telling her otherwise. "One step at a time, Papa; it'll be okay."

They moved on, with Mia striding confidently in the lead. The stainless steel walking stick she employed had been acquired from the wreckage of the snack bar. A distasteful hint of sulfur merged with the pleasant aromas of indigenous foliage to create a unique scent. It had become oddly familiar, this mixture of perfume and poison, stinging the sensitive tissue around their eyes, noses and mouths and irritating their throats. It laced the breeze that snuck in from the northwest, passed over the rocky barriers that formed the perimeter, and then swooped down across the basin they traversed.

You Were Looking Down on Me

As the group of seven approached the towering wall to the southeast, they could see the dolphin's quarters to the west; and to the east, the mountain through which they had passed the previous day. Upon inspection, they realized the enormous quakes had completely obliterated the Children's Zoo. All that remained were broken pieces of one of the small buildings at the edge of the quaint realm that had elicited squeals of delight from countless children over the years. At the edge of the Picnic Area, only a disintegrated shell remained of the charming hut that was the Children's Zoo Cupboard. The rest of the attraction's structures lay buried, crushed or reduced to rubble, lost in the quagmire of destruction.

They continued on, inspecting the imposing mountain preventing them from advancing further south. Mia faced the base of the wall, hands on hips, and craned her neck to assess the earthen monstrosity. "Kyle, what do you think; fifty, maybe fifty-five feet?" Her blue-eyed brother stood shoulder-to-shoulder with her, mirroring her stance and posture. Squinting his irritated eyes, he scanned the tower of rubble.

"This is just... incredible," Kyle stated dejectedly. "Look how the formation angles outward toward the summit. Climbing this thing would be next to impossible, even with state-of-the-art gear. There's no way we could even make it a quarter of the way to the top... and I think you're right: it's easily fifty feet high. Besides that, it's probably extremely unstable based on the way it was formed. Not good; not good at all, Sis."

Mateo and Violet stared in awe at the craggy northern face of the imposing mountain. Neither said a word, painfully aware there was no way they could ever climb it. Mateo squeezed Violet's hand to reassure her. They took one last look at the impressive product of the December 27th quake and then fell in behind the others, who had already started moving west, along its base. They had to carefully navigate jagged protrusions along the ground along the way.

There was little variance in the wall's height along the southern perimeter, and as they continued toward the area that housed the dolphin tank and the Wegeforth Bowl, they encountered spots where the surface was crumbling, forcing them to move out of range of the falling rocks. The adults instructed the children to stay behind them while they continued their deliberate exploration. As they neared the dolphin tank, it was obvious that the pair was extremely fortunate to survive the earthquake, having avoided being crushed or swallowed up by the Earth, by the narrowest of margins.

I Miss Your Purple Hair

A mere 12 feet separated the exhibit from the base of the rocky wall formation. Chunks of debris littered the area directly behind the dolphin's tank, some having missed striking the saline sanctuary by only a yard or less. Violet felt a bit sick to her stomach once she realized that the dolphins were located in a very precarious location – in the shadow of the unstable monstrosity. She deemed it nothing short of miraculous that their domain had survived the initial onslaught of the quake without so much as a scratch. Still, Violet could not help worrying about their prospects for survival. Without electricity, the dolphin's filtration system was non-functional, and she knew they would not be able to survive in stagnant, evaporating saltwater for long. She wondered how long they would last, given the rising air temperature... and the lack of food.

Violet asked, "Papa, can I search the tank to see if there's any food for the dolphins? There has to be something stored around here, don't you think?"

Mateo thought for a minute and agreed, "Good thinking, Vi. Let me ask the others if we can take a five minute break and I'll help you look. Maybe there's a built-in storage tank for the small fish they feed these guys. Why don't you start looking while I ask the others to wait."

Once he shared Violet's intentions, the others agreed to take a break to drink some water and replenish their energy. Hanna and Leanna encouraged Ravi to accompany them around the back of the tank to explore that area. When they scampered off, Violet climbed the ladder up to the tank and searched the surrounding platform. Mia, Kyle, and Mateo huddled at the northwest corner of the tank to review their situation.

Within minutes, Violet declared that she had located a recessed handle along the floor of the platform and summoned her father to help open the hinged lid. They soon unveiled a holding tank containing live fish, obviously a food supply for the dolphins during their daily shows. Assessing the limited number that remained, Mateo and Violet agreed that they should ration the silver fish in the interest of prolonging the dolphins' lives as long as possible.

After tossing four fish to each of the hungry mammals, Mateo predicted, "This supply can't sustain them for more than a couple of days." The initial excitement and relief that had accompanied the discovery swiftly dissolved. Once again, Violet felt renewed urgency, not only to save themselves, but also the stranded dolphins.

Leanna suddenly popped up behind them, trying to jump high enough off the ground to see them on the platform above. "We found something! Come down and see!"

Father and daughter quickly rejoined the rest of the group in the shadowy recess between the tank and the blockade of rock. The three youngest members of their entourage had discovered a locked door in the back of the base, partially blocked by several rock fragments that had tumbled down the face of the mountain. With Kyle's help, Mateo moved the rocks away but they were stymied by the heavy padlock securing the small door. It was obvious to everyone that breaking such a thick metal lock would be impossible. Rather than linger, they felt compelled to move ahead to search the rest of the perimeter.

They all drank a little water and started off toward the west. Violet's thoughts lingered on the locked door and whatever mysteries were stored behind its unlabeled white surface. She wondered aloud if more food for the dolphins might be stored within, while Mateo speculated there might be some useful tools inside. They agreed to give more thought to finding a way inside and planned to revisit later. For the moment, they remained focused on searching the region for a way out. Violet desperately wanted to get back to civilization and send a rescue team to save the dolphins and any other surviving animals.

The Wegeforth Bowl ruins lay ahead as the Sun rose higher, generating more heat and humidity. It was only a few minutes before 11:00 a.m., yet the temperature had reached the mid-80s. The steady breeze provided only fleeting relief. Everyone had adjusted to the air's acidic content to some degree, yet breathing it for an extended period sapped their already diminished energy. They approached the crumbling remains with a sense of gravity, recalling the height of the tremors and the trauma Mateo and Violet had experienced there.

In the diffused mid-day light, they witnessed the sobering effect of the earthquake on the once-beautiful Wegeforth Bowl. The sturdy main structure, fashioned of concrete and steel, had been knifed in two by a subterranean upheaval, and then partially buried under a deluge of debris. The semi-circular moat, where sea lions and walruses once entertained happy visitors, was now filled with thick mud, slowly drying out in the daytime heat. The stage, around which the moat wrapped, was broken and skewed at a 20-degree angle.

A crack in the surface of the land carved a ragged swath through the area – intersecting the stage, severing the mud-filled moat and splitting the concrete platform housing the expansive aluminum bleachers. Many rows of the inclined seats remained intact, but the base upon which they were mounted had been split in half, peaking in the center and sloping on opposite sides.

I Miss Your Purple Hair

The landscape featured a wildly irregular surface punctuated by bizarre protrusions that resembled gargantuan stalagmites. Other than the partially-intact sections of bleachers, there was almost nothing left. The group picked its way cautiously through the treacherous terrain, sticking close to one another and making sure to avoid any spots that looked unstable. The fragile ground sometimes cracked beneath them as they gingerly crossed its surface like water bugs skillfully navigating the viscous surface of a pond. Deep potholes generating intense heat released smoldering plumes of red-tinged steam.

While Mateo and Violet walked hand-in-hand, Kyle maintained close reins on Ravi, as they arrived at the point of convergence of the towering walls in the southwest. Off on her own a handful of yards away from the others; Mia was losing the battle to fight back tears. Although she had valiantly tried to maintain composure for the sake of the others, she was humbled by the depressing reality confronting them. She thought of her mother back in Pittsburgh, and knew how worried she must be. They always spoke by telephone on Sunday evenings, and she knew her mother must be wondering why Mia was not responding.

As he attempted to scan the scenery to the west, Mateo inadvertently locked eyes with Mia and instantly understood she was experiencing a crisis of faith. He asked Violet to join the rest of the group, investigating the shadow-cloaked southwest corner, while he spoke with Mia. His unique gentleness enabled him to approach virtually anyone, regardless of their state of mind. Mia blinked away a tear and welcomed him with an expression of complete acceptance, appreciative of any respite from the depressing search.

"It's all very sobering, isn't it, Mateo?" she asked somberly. He simply nodded, too sincere to sugarcoat the truth. His countenance conveyed an inner calm that belied his true assessment of the circumstances. Mateo's composure soothed the fair-haired palm reader like a cool mist on a hot August afternoon. Mia felt relieved just being in close proximity with him; a reaction she had already come to expect and appreciate. She took his hands in hers once again and breathed with him for a time, willingly following his rhythmic pattern in silent harmony.

Peering at her own feet, she whispered meekly, "I don't want to die here," aware that they were well out of hearing range of the others. Mateo was not surprised she was humbled by what they witnessed, but was somewhat taken aback at her expression of such a defeatist outlook. He did his best to look beyond her undeniable beauty, and to focus on the anxiety embroiled in direct conflict with her faith. "I understand what you're feeling right now, but... you must stay strong," he told her, placing her palms on his chest.

She released a prolonged sigh and responded, "Because of the children... I know. I'm really sorry; I shouldn't..."

"No, not only for the sake of the *children*, Mia," he somewhat sternly contradicted. "For *you*. This is about you right now. You have to maintain your faith and presume we'll find our way out of this mess; otherwise, all could be lost. Belief is a powerful force, and this is not the time to relinquish any of the few weapons we have in our arsenal. I promise you; you are not going to die here, not in this place. It isn't your time."

"What about you and your daughter? Aren't *you* afraid?"

"I don't intend to allow anything to happen to me... or to Violet, Mia. Let's try to only speak in positive terms from this point on, okay? As long as I have breath within me, I'm going to be hopeful about the future. It's the only way that makes sense."

Struck by his conviction, Mia recognized what it meant to have Mateo's type of unwavering faith. She felt refreshed and composed again, no longer allowing her fear to dominate her thoughts or erode her conviction. "You're an amazingly strong person," she said.

"Mia, we can *never* afford to throw away hope... or lose faith in ourselves."

Together, they greeted the others who had slowly ambled over to gather them. Mateo asked Kyle, "Did you have any luck over in that section? Did you spot any place where we could possibly get a foothold?"

The dedicated child psychiatrist stroked the stubble decorating his angular chin and shook his head. "Nothing good to report, other than finding a cool spot in the shade back there. So far, we haven't seen any section that looks even remotely manageable for climbing. These walls are ridiculously steep – much higher than the one we passed through the other day."

The realization was disappointing, yet not surprising to both Mia and Mateo. They had presumed as much, standing in the shadows of the sky scraping formations confining them. Feeling defeated, they turned their attention to the north and anticipated the planned rendezvous with the other survivors.

Meanwhile, in the region's northwest corner, Dwayne had been using a Sun-blanched tree limb DeAngelo had discovered, as a walking stick; not as a prop, but to keep some weight off his injured knee, which had stiffened further due to increased swelling. At his wife's urging, he agreed to take a much-needed break and finally set himself down on a thick formation of rock. "I'm beat," he reluctantly admitted as he stretched his painfully sore leg. The temperature had reached close to 85 degrees and the Sun had burned though much of the omnipresent cloud cover. He grimaced to think it was approaching noon, and they had yet to identify any possible escape route.

One useful discovery they stumbled upon was a portable rest room that had apparently come crashing down from the elevated region above, in much the same way that Sinnamon and Jason had. Construction work had been going on in the area overhead, and a mud slide caused by the storm had deposited the dark green, freestanding booth of nearly indestructible plastic on the basin floor.

Jason, Victory and Sinnamon all worked to unearth the object and reset it to its proper upright position. Victory remarked, "It's never even been used yet! Thank you, Lord! Miracles happen even in the darkest times." Then she quickly added, "Now... if you'll kindly excuse me," and promptly ducked inside, slammed the door and christened the newly discovered "blessing".

Jason and Sinnamon had spilled out near the same spot when they were flushed from the upper ridge the previous day, but there was now no reasonable way to climb back up the mud-coated, disintegrating face of the wall on that side. Sinnamon pointed out that they had fled in panic from the Ituri Forest region to the northwest, but explained that heading in that direction would only take them deeper into the park, potentially amongst animals that would be quite ravenous by now. Victory suggested they all rest for a few minutes, drink some of their water supply, and wait for the other group to arrive.

Jason had been crouching along the ground in the northwest corner, a dozen yards away from the others, probing the terrain with a pointed stick and kicking at something. He suddenly stood up and turned to face the others, his face noticeably ashen. Dwayne happened to look up at that moment, and noticed that the blood had seemingly drained from Jason's face. He called out to no one in particular, "What happened to *him*?" His outburst caused Victory, Sinnamon, and DeAngelo, who had been gathering up some wood to use as torches, to whip their heads around in unison, like a flock of sheep that just picked up the scent of an approaching wolf.

Jason's face wore an ominous expression. "What is it?" Sinnamon insisted. At first, he failed to respond. He turned his head to look back toward the disturbing sight, and then he turned to his companions.

"Don't let DeAngelo see this. Stay where you are," Jason admonished.

Sinnamon gestured to Victory to keep her son at her side while she walked to the spot where Jason stood, his knees knocking so audibly it made her feel sick in the pit of her stomach. "Jesus," was all she could say as she caught her first glimpse of the sight that caused Jason's reaction. Buried almost completely among the rubble was an unidentifiable human form, obviously an elderly male. Only the left arm was exposed, jutting out from the mud-caked and fractured pavement, beneath the tons of dirt and debris. Jason backed away in obvious horror at the same time Sinnamon moved in for a closer look. Even the thick-skinned mercenary swallowed hard when she realized what she was witnessing.

"We knew this was inevitable," she solemnly said, "but it kinda hits home when you're standing right on top of it." Jason staggered backwards until he arrived alongside the Cooper family, who were looking to him for some answers. They watched Sinnamon kneel down and tentatively poke at something using the stick Jason had involuntarily dropped.

"It's an elderly man, from what I can tell," the redhead suggested. "May be in his 70s… hard to say. There's a wedding band on his finger."

Sinnamon cursed and swatted at the swarm of shiny green-headed flies ecstatically darting about. She stood up and returned to the others with a look of disgust in her eyes. "Goddamnit, we've got to get the hell out of here. I can't stomach much more of this." She informed Dwayne and Victory what they had found partially buried under the tonnage of displaced rock. They speculated that the remains might belong to someone associated with one of their comrades – perhaps the Armstrong girls' grandfather – and so, they mutually agreed that one of them should intercept the other group. Victory volunteered to warn them and led DeAngelo to intercept the other party.

While Victory explained that it would be best to avoid the area of the grisly discovery, Sinnamon squatted on her haunches and picked at a cluster of grass poking out from a patch of rich, brown dirt. She tried to evict the image of the man's lifeless arm from her memory by vigorously shaking her head and rubbing her eyes with the dirt-stained palms of her hands.

In Sinnamon's imagination, she saw the man's wrinkled hand move ever so slightly, fingers twitching. She could not help but wonder if he had been buried alive. She held her head in her hands, her thick red hair pouring over her face as she tried to come to terms with the gravity of the situation. In her mind, all that had happened was a bizarre blending of her warped fantasies and dreaded nightmares, rolled into one horrible reality.

I Miss Your Purple Hair

The confident redhead had always taken pride in her independence, toughness, and guile. She used to boast that she "looked forward to the Apocalypse" because she would find a way to make it work to her benefit. She always felt she would be at an advantage over the majority "when the bad came down", as she liked to say. That was a small part of the reason she kept herself so physically fit and why she denied herself some of the creature comforts easily within her grasp. She wanted to stay hungry, to remain resourceful – for just such a time as what she was now experiencing; but, she was beginning to truly appreciate the difference between fantasy and reality.

In light of the fact that innocent people and animals were already dead or dying all around her, that she was tough and clever was irrelevant. Only a few yards away, an elderly man lay crushed beneath a collapsed wall of mud and rock. A flurry of disturbing thoughts flooded Sinnamon's mind...

'Who and what else was buried alive? How many people and animals were swallowed up when the quakes rolled through? How far does the damage extend? Could the quake have affected my sister and parents across town? Is it possible this disaster goes beyond that?'

For the first time in a long while, Rebecca Sinclair was afraid; so afraid that she bit a gash in her bottom lip without realizing it. The salty blood oozed across the tip of her tongue, startling her out of her fear-induced stupor. She realized that she had been hyperventilating and that her hands were trembling, ever so slightly. Out of nowhere, someone placed a hand upon her freckled, Sun-baked shoulder from behind. She strained her neck to see that it was Violet who had gently approached to rescue her from her maelstrom of emotions. The sensitive teen had broken away from the others when she detected intense conflict within Sinnamon's aura.

"Just try to breathe in deep and then hold it for a second," were the first words she uttered to the frightened woman. "You need to compose yourself by breathing with me to regulate your heart rate. Just follow my pattern and everything will come back into focus."

Under normal circumstances, Sinnamon might have scoffed at such a suggestion; especially coming from a teenage girl she barely knew. There was something magnificently effective though, in the way this particular teenager connected with the hardened 27 year-old. When Violet closed her eyes and urged Sinnamon to do the same, she humbly complied. She could still feel her own heart beat wildly in her chest, as if it was about to burst through her rib cage like some alien life force.

The two women, one nearly half the age of the other, faced each other and breathed in the same deliberate rhythm. After less than a minute, Sinnamon detected her heart rate had slowed and the trembling in her arms and fingertips subsided. Just minutes earlier, Violet had observed a dramatic fluctuation in Sinnamon's aura. The shifting bands of black, grey, and crimson had signified she was in crisis, and experiencing internal conflict of a potentially dangerous nature. Somewhat of a novice at aura interpretation, and with modest experience to draw from, Violet had reacted instinctively. She felt compelled to do whatever she could to defuse the anguish Sinnamon was experiencing.

After less than two minutes, Sinnamon and Violet simultaneously opened their eyes. "Did that help?" Violet asked rhetorically. She knew that the exercise had been effective in that Sinnamon's pulse rate had dropped to its normal level and her frantic breathing had slowed. The tension throughout her body had dissipated and Violet could clearly see that her aura had returned to its more typical hues of red mixed with a diffused, pulsing orange. Sinnamon wore a puzzled look but then slowly smiled, albeit rather reticently.

"Amazing... just amazing..." Sinnamon mumbled. "Who *are* you people? You and your father... Where did you learn to do that?"

Violet actually did not know how to respond to her question and all of the underlying implications. She had learned a few breathing techniques from her father, but did not consider it unusual or mysterious, as Sinnamon seemed to imply. As for her reaction to witnessing Sinnamon's emotional and spiritual distress – that was all about instinct. She read, she recognized and reacted. There was nothing other-worldly about any of that, at least not in her mind. She tried to give proper consideration to Sinnamon's perspective and wanted to provide a reaction that could at least somewhat satisfy her curiosity.

"My father and I just tend to work on learning new coping skills and stuff. It's really nothing that everyone can't do – we try to learn from each other and the people we know." She was alluding to several of her father's friends, who had over the years, shared some of their knowledge about healing and Chakra cleansing through various techniques. Some of those same friends helped Violet and her father advance their aura reading abilities too, which they continued to refine through trial and error.

"You consider these things you do 'coping skills'?" Sinnamon pointedly inquired. "I mean, I dig it and all, but you and your father – not to mention those two other girls, are operating on some entirely different level than the rest of us. At least it looks that way from my point of view. When you were breathing with me and had your hand on my shoulder, I felt a rush of soothing vibrations moving through my entire body. It felt a lot like that relief you feel when lotion is applied to sunburned skin."

Violet tried to downplay the "weirdness" factor of some practices she and her father had exposed during the past day; but Sinnamon had, in her estimation, held back from commenting for long enough. "The aura reading, for starters" she began. "I've know maybe one or two people who claim they can do it, and read an article on it years ago – but you and your father do it so effortlessly; or at least you claim to. How do I know if you actually 'see' anything or if you're just faking it?"

"Well, why would anyone fake it?"

"I don't know. Maybe you're both *nuts*," Sinnamon rather rudely suggested. "Even if you do see these so-called auras, what's the point? Don't get me wrong, kid; I appreciated it when you helped me stop hyperventilating, but this bit with the auras and the group healing is way out there for me." After a pause to catch her breath, she added, "What do you see in my aura, anyway?"

"When you're at rest?" Violet innocently asked.

"Sure... when I'm *at rest*, whatever that means," she shot back through a wry smile.

"Well," the teenager calmly replied, "You're a mixture: sort of a bright glowing orange with traces of red at the outer edges."

"And, what does *that* mean... anything?"

"I would say you're probably a very high-energy type, with tons of stamina and strength. You also have an outgoing personality and like to have adventures. You have a strong creative side and like big parties and other social functions. You also have um... uh..."

"What? What is it? Do I have some disease or something? Tell me. I can handle it."

"No, no, no," Violet assured her. "Uh, you have a very active... uh... romantic side. You know..." Violet blushed a little, embarrassed by tendencies she detected in the earthy older woman.

"Hahaha," Sinnamon knowingly laughed. "Well, no argument there! That's pretty wild. You actually nailed it on all counts as far as I can see. So, you can read all that stuff from an aura? Do you think you could teach me how to do it?"

Just then, Mateo intervened and put his arm around his daughter's shoulder. "Are you two alright?" he asked.

Sinnamon told him that she felt better, and explained that Violet had been instrumental in helping her. They discussed the discovery of the human remains and Mateo agreed that they should head back to the Reptile House to compare the findings of the two groups and plan their strategy accordingly. Everyone agreed it was the most prudent course of action and before long, the reunited gang of twelve headed back east toward their "home base".

Purposely avoiding the corner where they had discovered the human remains, they slowly began walking east along the base of the northern wall so they could all make one last assessment. Not only did they agree that it probably would be ludicrous to head in a northerly direction, its facade was obviously highly unstable, following the torrential downpour that transformed it into a muddy behemoth. They had barely made any progress when Jason startled everyone from the rear of the group, exclaiming, "Look! Up there!" The group turned to see him pointing back to the west with his fully outstretched right arm.

Atop the high western ridge stood a large white wolf. Proud and alert, the adult male stood at the edge of the grass-covered perch overlooking the valley. He appeared identical to the wolf they had spotted in the valley to the east the previous day. They were able to examine this specimen much more thoroughly, as he stood motionless in the hazy sunshine. His crystal-blue eyes were unusual for what appeared to be an adult male, and his gaze seemed fixed upon the huddled group of survivors.

Ravi's reaction was one of fear and he spun around to locate Kyle and tucked himself behind his newfound protector. Kyle patted him once on his mop of jet-black hair and said, "It's okay, it's okay... he's way up there, and there's no way to get down. It looks like he's just curious, anyway. See how relaxed he is? You can tell their mood by the tail, and his is at ease."

Dwayne suggested that it was the same wolf from the other day, but Victory quickly contradicted him. "There's no way that's the same animal. It might have been able to come through or over that mountain we passed through, maybe during the night, but there's no way it could've climbed up there. We just checked every bit of this area, and there's just no way up, not even for an animal like that. No, that has to be a different one."

Mateo looked into Violet's eyes and conveyed an expression only she might understand. Without saying a word, they communicated on a very intimate level. Violet spoke to the entire group, as if she were merely thinking aloud, "We can ask Dante about the wolves. He should be able to answer some questions."

I Miss Your Purple Hair

"Yeah," Mia stated in support of her young companion. "Let's head back to the building, regroup and talk to Dante. He might have some new thoughts about climbing out of here, since he's had the morning to consider all the options." Everyone happily agreed; none more enthusiastically than Ravi, who was not very keen on standing in plain view of the 150-pound animal. Its haunting blue eyes remained fixed upon the disheveled cluster of humanity, as they limped across the ugly, broken landscape toward the lone hospitable shelter.

△ △ △

CHAPTER SEVENTEEN

When You're Homesick and Need a Change

"All things appear and disappear because of the concurrence of causes and conditions.
Nothing ever exists entirely alone; everything is in relation to everything else."
~ Buddha

As the group approached their makeshift camp, they discovered Dante sitting atop an enormous boulder, just to the west of the half-demolished Reptile House. He propped open the doors by wedging pieces of wood beneath them, in an effort to air out the lingering stench left behind after butchering the pig. Dante had cleaned up the residual blood and tissue with a cloth he had soaked in water extracted from the dolphin exhibit. The children were given approval to rejoin the dolphins. Mateo asked Violet and the Armstrong sisters to assure him they would act as lifeguards and supervise the younger boys.

As the children ran off to reconnect with their newfound friends, Dante ominously grumbled, "They're not gonna have a lot of time to cool down."

"Why do you say that?" Mateo asked. "We all need a little break to regain strength and review what we..."

"I know, I know. But you're being followed," Dante coldly interjected.

Everyone's heads whipped around nervously, expecting to see the white wolf loping toward them. "What're you saying?" Mia implored.

There was no discernible sign of anything chasing after them, so they all looked back at Dante with puzzled expressions. "Look," he said, turning his attention from the pocketknife in his hands to the western sky. "Another storm, brewing in the west... it'll be on us within the hour." Mateo, Mia and the others scrutinized the burgeoning swell of purple-tinted clouds. It was clear to all he was correct. They had been so focused on the geography none of them noticed the looming threat. The blazing Sun, perched directly overhead in the red-orange sky, had disintegrated the cloud cover and boosted the temperature another ten degrees in the last hour.

"Well, let's allow the kids to cool off in the water until it gets here," Mateo suggested. "Kyle, can you help me patch that hole in the roof, while we have the chance?"

"Sure, good idea," the amicable 31-year-old replied. "We should be able to climb that rock formation and step right onto the roof – no sweat. But we've got to find something suitable to patch the hole with."

"We can cut a small section of that plastic tarp and secure it with rocks," Mateo offered. With that simple plan in mind, they set about executing it as efficiently as possible. Victory urged Dwayne, who was in significant pain, to sit on the bench near the building entrance. He opted, however, to limp over to help keep an eye on the children, who were already swimming alongside the dolphins in the now lukewarm saltwater. She hugged him and whispered something in his ear, and then offered to gather rocks and pass them to the volunteer roofers.

While the two men cut an appropriately sized section from one end of the blue tarp, the now-familiar campsite became abuzz with activity. The youngest members communed with their aquatic companions while Dwayne kept an eye on them from the inclined bleachers a few yards away. Victory and Jason gathered rocks and lined them up along the base of the Reptile House in preparation for handing them up to Mateo and Kyle. Mia and Sinnamon gathered and organized more firewood and kindling, stashing the supply inside the Reptile House.

Between trips to gather wood, Dante, who was resting his painful leg, waived his hand to summon Sinnamon. She reluctantly honored his gesture and slowly approached the large rock formation upon which he sat. He extended his right hand and opened his palm. Sinnamon sneered in reaction... and held her ground.

"What?" she smugly asked. "You expect me to just hand it back to you? The pistol is zoo ordinance; not your personal property, anyway. Am I right?"

Dante bristled, "You really *are* a crazy bitch. Are we gonna have a problem, you and me? As if we don't have enough shit to deal with."

"Oh, I was just thinking I might hang on to it a little longer," she coldly answered.

Dante was in no mood to play games. He snapped his fingers and glared at her menacingly. For a moment, Sinnamon considered walking away and hiding the pistol somewhere he would never find it. She was concerned about his emotional state, but also worried her actions could push him over the edge. He might try something while she had her back turned. Rather than risk infuriating the frazzled security guard, she thought it more prudent to stay on his good side, at least for the time being. She placed the pistol in his open palm and displayed her sexiest smile. Dante stashed it back in its holster and asked, "What's the verdict on us getting out of here?"

When You're Homesick and Need a Change

In reaction to his nonchalant acceptance of the gun, she breathed a sigh of relief before responding. "It sure as shit isn't a pretty picture," she began. "There's just no friggin' way we can climb that northern wall. I mean, you know better than anyone here that it would be a ridiculous long shot to head in that direction anyway, hoping that by some miracle we'll discover a route out of here. We checked it out, just because we have to, but you and I know there wasn't much point to it. The others checked out the south and it isn't any better as far as being climbable. I hate to be the bearer of crappy news, but my guess is we're stuck here until someone comes looking, so we're probably gonna have to come up with a Plan B."

Dante winced as he shifted his weight to get more comfortable, "Yeah... yeah, I figured as much. I know the layout of the place as well as anyone, and there's no way heading north makes any sense, even if we could climb that ridiculously huge mountain of mud. To the south or southeast – that's the only way, but what'd the other group tell you they found?"

Sinnamon arched her back and shook her head like a dog that had just splashed through a pond, before answering. "They weren't exactly high-fiving anyone when we met up, y'know? We have to compare notes, but there are things that have to get done before that storm hits. I mean, look at those clouds. We're gonna be stuck inside for a while, yet again, and we'll have plenty of time to kick stuff around then, but at the moment I've gotta finish collecting wood, so we can make another fire when the rain passes. We may be forced to make a move during the night, if that's the only time the weather cooperates, so I'm prepping torches."

Before turning her attention to completing her chores, Sinnamon inquired, "How's that knee? I don't imagine it's any better, is it?" As an athlete, she had experienced her fair complement of injuries, ranging from occasional strains and sprains to a torn Achilles tendon that took over a year to fully heal. During that year, Sinnamon had initiated a romantic relationship with her voice coach, Amber Bourke.

Possessing the face of a top model and the physique of a goddess, she and Sinnamon shared a passion for long-distance running. They had met just prior to the start of the San Diego Marathon and were instantly infatuated with one another. Before long, they were spending a lot of time together; training, singing and competing in triathlon competitions up and down the California coast. Amber was of African-French descent. Her unusual moss green eyes were sprinkled with accents of gold. A creamy coating of mocha-colored skin covered her beautifully toned frame. She was slightly taller than her younger protégé and possessed a uniquely charismatic personality.

Rebecca Sinclair had grown up a mildly eccentric small town girl who developed typically unrealistic dreams of becoming a recording star. What separated her from so many of her peers was her relentless determination. In high school, she participated in nearly every theatrical production, as an actress, singer, or both. She flashed potential as a visual artist too, intrigued by photography and digital art. She was the product of a dysfunctional home, ravaged by alcoholism. As her parent's marriage fell apart, 16-year-old Sinnamon dropped out of school and fled to Los Angeles with her boyfriend. She was full of dreams but by no means prepared to cope with the harsh realities of life. Ultimately, she returned home and toughed it out until she completed high school.

Somewhere along the line, the disenchanted young girl discovered the will to survive and the self-discipline to not only earn High Honors but to carve out a reputation as the school's top creative talent. She toyed with the notion of attending college to major in digital art or photography, but instead decided to embark on a career as a freelance photographer and musician. For years, she waited tables in the San Diego area until she managed to build a portfolio of work, which in time led to the gradual building of a solid regional reputation. At the same time, she was working to explore her potential as a singer/songwriter, so whenever she could find time, she performed at Open Mic nights. After being scouted for several months, she joined an established rock band as their lead singer.

For several years, she was simply "Becca", lead singer and guitarist for the punk/funk band, *Fingers O'Riley*. After they dissolved, she joined another band… and then another. None of them ever resulted in great monetary success or fame, but she never regretted one moment as she continued to grow as an artist. Years later, she decided to test the waters as a solo performer and started billing herself as "Sinnamon" – her old high school nickname. She built a playlist of cover tunes and originals, and decided that voice lessons could help enhance her performance. That led to meeting Amber, who was five years her senior and ten times more worldly; a globe-trotter who exuded confidence.

Amber was more than just Rebecca's first same-sex lover; she was the most influential force in her young life. Her hard-edged cynicism seeped into the younger woman's psyche, as did her aggressive, sometimes ruthless approach to going after what she wanted. They not only became intimate, but Amber served as Rebecca's manager and mentor, helping her with promotions as well as suggesting refinements to her act. In many ways it was an ideal relationship, save for one factor: Rebecca was inherently heterosexual.

After a few years of playing house in Amber's posh Burbank condo, and despite her budding career, Rebecca finally decided she had no choice but to break away from her alluring Svengali and return to San Diego. Despite her decision to relocate, the record company never wavered from their intent to sign her. However, Amber spitefully delayed the process by filing a lawsuit against her former student and lover, claiming she had subsidized Rebecca's lifestyle for years and was entitled to reimbursement as well as a percentage of the profits realized from any recording contract she signed.

Rebecca was disenchanted and angry at her former partner, amazed she would put her recording career in limbo by her litigious action. She resolved instead to put more emphasis on freelance photography and digital illustration as her primary sources of income. In time, her versatility as a performer and visual artist generated sufficient income to allow for a comfortable lifestyle in her cozy San Diego suburb. And, in time, she put aside her anger and focused on building a future of her own design.

She had come to the zoo on the 27th of December for two reasons: to take photos for her web site and to acquire the unique peacock tail feather. She had very efficiently realized both goals, but in the wake of the destructive events, neither accomplishment meant anything. The full impact of being caught in the middle of a life-and-death situation was sinking in. Sinnamon realized that the extent of the damage was most likely much greater than any of the survivors initially believed. She looked Dante over one last time before walking away, and felt a tinge of genuine sympathy for the man, who suddenly seemed so depressed and defeated.

Dante watched the plucky redhead walk away to gather up broken tree branches and wood from demolished structures, and could not help but take note of the strange-looking sky along the mountain top beyond her. The region had recently been transformed into a surreal landscape of broken ground, twisted metal, and dark, confining walls; and now the sky had changed, to add to the palpable sense of impending doom. An expanding cluster of clouds approached from the west. They were carried by the intensifying breeze, which was infused with the acid-laced stench that saturated the atmosphere. Within seconds, the wind kicked up, spraying dirt and debris across the shattered basin.

Dwayne and Violet efficiently ushered the children out of the dolphin tank and toward the Reptile House, where Mateo and the others finished the patch job on the roof. As they all spilled through the doors a powerful wind gust knocked Dante off balance, betrayed by the painfully swollen leg that buckled beneath him.

When Jason reached out to grab his hand to help stabilize him, the physical contact triggered a remarkable reaction. The instant their hands met a jolt of what could only be described as electrical energy shot throughout Jason's body, and in the space of a micro-second an image exploded within his subconscious mind. He fleetingly "saw" Dante grimace as he squeezed the pistol's resistant trigger, producing a loud *Bang!* amidst a blinding burst of light. There was a strangely ominous feeling accompanying the imagery and although hazy, it left an indelible impression and inspired new concerns surrounding the conflicted security guard.

In the not-so-distant rancid sky, flashes of heat lightning served as subtle precursors to prolonged baritone rumbles of thunder. The rain had arrived in sheets of fine mist, the droplets illuminated by the waning sunlight. When he entered the building, Jason's mind was still reeling from the disturbing imagery that invaded it moments earlier. Slumped over the tabletop display, he was upset that his vivid dreams were coming more frequently and that he was beginning to experience waking visions, too. Besides that, he felt a genuine sense of trepidation surrounding Dante.

Sinnamon was last to enter the muggy confines of their only sanctuary. White lightning filled the darkening afternoon sky, followed by a prolonged pregnant pause… and then a deafening crash of thunder signified the advent of yet another period of violent weather. She left the doors propped open to allow the refreshing, cooler air to circulate within the building.

'Trapped inside again… and we're running out of time.'

Mateo looked around the room and felt a deepening concern regarding their chances for survival. Dante's emotional state was steadily deteriorating, along with the condition of his knee. Dwayne's knee was not in much better condition. Although his leg was less swollen than Dante's, the knee was locking up, making walking increasingly painful. Mateo asked Violet to round up some painkillers or anti-inflammatory drugs. She promptly scavenged a handful of capsules from the collection of personal effects on the tabletop.

She delivered a bottle of water and the painkillers to Dwayne and asked whether he would like her to say a healing prayer along with Leanna and Hanna, who hovered nearby. He thought for a second and then quickly shook his head and answered, "No, but thanks just the same." He had caught the attention of his wife, who was clearly indicating with her eyes that she did not approve of such things. She was raised in a Bible-fearing home and preferred to put her faith in the God she knew.

Violet assured Dwayne no disrespect was intended. She then motioned to the other girls to stay where they were for a moment. Meanwhile, she slowly walked over to Dante, who was seated on the hard concrete floor with his back against the wall. His injury was more severe than anyone could have known and he was fighting to tolerate the searing pain emanating from the shredded ligaments in his right knee. Making matters worse, he was both physically and emotionally spent. He felt no particular aversion to the notion of psychic or spiritual healing, but simply was unreceptive to being approached in his present state of mind.

In reaction to every tentative step in his direction, Dante's feelings of resistance swelled. He refused to lift his head to look at her. As thoughts of despair percolated in his tormented mind, he sat with his head bowed – motionless and despondent. Violet was acutely aware of his precarious state, evident in his body language as well as the wave of negative energy he involuntarily projected. Nevertheless, she risked almost certain rejection in an effort to ease his suffering. She gingerly sidled next to the sweaty, depressed man; hoping she could win his confidence.

'I'm sure I can help him.'

"I'd like to offer my help," Violet timidly offered, despite obvious disinterest from the crumpled figure at her feet.

"Not interested," he grimly replied. "We're gonna have to wait this out and hope someone drops in from the sky to pull us out of here. They'll be able to tend to our injuries then. We have to tough it out for now."

Violet slowly dropped to one knee to put herself on his level in an attempt to help ease the tension she could literally taste. She attempted to assess Dante's aura, but multiple conditions were interfering with a clear reading. The energy field enveloping him was a convoluted mash-up of tones and gradations. She saw a mass of pulsing ambiguity, ranging from subdued greens and blues closest to his body to an outer shell of grey, interlaced with fluctuating bands of black. Violet had never seen anything like the conflicted energy field surrounding the defeated and obviously disturbed man seated next to her.

I Miss Your Purple Hair

For a moment, she was unsure how to react to Dante, yet still felt compelled to do what was in her power to ease his discomfort. She knew, instinctively and through experience that the best chance of achieving an effective emotional connection hinged on enticing him to willingly make visual contact with her. She was wary of saying or doing anything that might elicit an angry or even possibly violent reaction. From the opposite side of the room, both Kyle and her father were tuned into the exchange and discreetly observing their interaction. A surge of adrenaline involuntarily pumped through Mateo as his paternal instincts were on high alert, but he willed himself to relax and have faith that his daughter would make wise decisions.

'This man is afraid and in pain – we need to respect that, but we can do something to help heal him.'

Violet thought it odd that she could virtually hear a voice inside her head, clearly speaking these thoughts. And then she heard additional voices: those of her father and both of the Armstrong sisters, who had been busy reorganizing some of the unused supplies. Their thoughts spoke to her quite distinctly, sounding off with, *'I'm with you,'...* *'With you,'* ... and, *'Ready to help.'*

She understood that her father, Leanna and Hanna were connected with her on a psychic level. Furthermore, they were conveying, through their thoughts within *The Web*, their readiness to combine their healing energies with hers. This powerful linkage with the other sympathetic spirits in the room was a new development for the gifted child, and the revelation surprised her a bit. Before she could fully grasp the meaning of it, she was confronted with Dante's reaction.

As loud, low rumbles of thunder growled ever closer, Dante finally cocked his head to look into her eager eyes and said, "Look, you might mean well, but I'm not into that kind of thing. I just don't believe in whatever it is that you and those others seem to think you can do." Violet immediately realized she had reached him on some very intimate psychological level. Her resoundingly sincere intention to heal him, combined with the shared conviction of the three other kindred spirits somehow communicated to Dante. Violet recognized it as a watershed moment – an important breakthrough in her evolving enlightenment.

She experienced a sudden and distinct diminishment of intensity in the blossoming force created by the harmonic resonance of their four souls. It felt as if the supportive individuals within *The Web* went into stand-by mode in direct reaction to resistance by the intended subject. While they remained poised and ready to resume focus, they were all well aware that such resistance would render their efforts completely ineffective. In Violet's mind, the feeling was similar to shifting a vehicle from Drive into Neutral, in that the gathered energy – a mere moment from being summoned into action – was temporarily relegated to dormancy.

Dante's aura remained turbulent, an obvious indicator of inner turmoil caused by physical and emotional stress. In assessing the brooding man, Violet picked up a specific thread of an emotional disturbance that raged beneath the surface. She detected severe emotional discord at the root of the angst he was displaying. In trying to focus her undivided attention on his energy, Violet discovered an innate ability to meld with her subject on a surprisingly intimate level.

Not that she could read his thoughts, but was able to discern the composition of the unique energies at the depths of his psyche. For the first time in her young life, she intentionally tapped into another person's true energy core in such an in-depth manner she experienced what the other person was feeling. In this, her first-ever "soul merge", she truly felt the sense of profound guilt at the foundation of Dante's vibrant, living energy. She was able to stand within the undulating waterfall of emotional signals and become one with it, yet had no way of comprehending the root causes of his intense personal conflict. It only told her that whatever he was withholding from the group was adversely affecting the normally jovial man.

'Whatever it is that's bothering him comes from the fact that he means to be good and to do the right thing. He failed himself in some way...'

Just then, she heard her father calling out to her from some distant place within her subconscious. Was he invading Dante's thoughts, too? She finally realized that he was calling to her from the physical realm, trying to pull her out of her self-induced meditative state and back to reality. When she opened her eyes, she found her father standing directly next to her, softly repeating her name, "Veronica. Veronica."

"What is it?" she asked, a trifle annoyed at his persistence. "Was I asleep?"

Her question initially perplexed Mateo, but then he surmised she must have entered *The Zone*. He placed his calloused and scraped right hand behind her neck and said, "You weren't asleep, Vi. You were somewhere 'out there' again, honey. Where did you go this time?" While father and daughter shared an intimate moment, their fellow survivors were trying to grasp what had transpired.

All of the other adults hovered nearby, a handful on either side of where Dante, Mateo and Violet remained. To a person, they seemed clearly dumbfounded by yet another episode involving unfamiliar behavior of a psychic nature. Suspicious eyes locked onto Violet and Mateo as they spoke in hushed tones about the most recent of several profoundly revealing episodes.

Violet assured her father that she felt fine and would explain everything to him later. He understood by her body language that she felt uncomfortable under the scrutiny of everyone else, so he nodded and planted a soft kiss on the warm, soft skin of her forehead. "We all need to try to relax and band together," he said to no one in particular. "We have no choice but to wait this storm out, so why don't we make this place a little more comfortable." Victory, Mia, and Kyle finally began to putter about; organizing the remaining supplies and the firewood they dropped off.

Mia suggested they pool their information and draw a map of all the areas they had investigated on their separate excursions. She joined Dwayne and Sinnamon in sketching out a rudimentary map, using a black marking pen and a blank page torn from Violet's journal. They compared notes and collaborated to create a simple map complete with labels and directions. It was obvious that depicting the identifiable landmarks helped make it easier to communicate going forward.

To the sardonic delight of her fellow amateur cartographers, Sinnamon initiated the nicknaming by scrawling a bold label across the craggy wall representing the site of Aaron's futile escape attempt: *Kemper's Folly*. Labeling *Wormhole Wall, Mudslide Mountain, White Wolf Peak* and *Sunrise Summit* only took minutes. Hanna aptly labeled the super steep, sheer-faced barrier lining the southern perimeter behind the dolphin exhibit, *The Cliffs of Insanity*. She offered the all-too appropriate nickname in partial tribute to her favorite movie, *The Princess Bride*. "As you wish," Dwayne cleverly declared as he added the term to the hand-drawn map.

Computer geek DeAngelo took another black marker in hand and scrawled *Fire Wall* to label the barrier that shielded them, if only temporarily, from the smoke and flames moving toward them from the northeast.

Jason had found a stack of flattened cardboard boxes tucked next to a storage shelf in the half-destroyed back room, and distributed them. "They aren't much, but these will make decent substitute mattresses if we have to spend another night here. It's better than nothing, anyway." When he handed one to Mateo, he whispered into his ear, "I want to talk to you about something a little later on, okay?" Mateo nonchalantly grunted in acknowledgement, respectful of Jason's apparent desire for discreetness.

Over the next hour or so, while the storm intensified, a renewed sense of calm came over the disparate souls trapped within the half-building. While most of the group sat in an informal conversation circle in the open area of the main display room, DeAngelo and Ravi used the charred end of one of the torches to draw something in the middle of the floor. "What's that for?" Dwayne asked his young son.

"It's the Sun, Dad. It makes rays of hope and we can all sit around it so each person can have a ray of hope for themselves."

"Where did you get that idea?" his perplexed father asked.

"Ravi told me that his grandfather taught him to pray and he would think about the rays of hope the Sun sent down every day, whenever he said his prayers in the mornings. So, I thought we should draw our own Sun to remind us that it's always up there, even when it's raining."

"Wow," Violet enthusiastically offered. "I really like that idea. Isn't that cool, Papa?"

Mateo looked across the circle from where he sat cross-legged on the floor, and savored the moment. *'This is how we're going to survive this,'* he thought. *'We just have to keep hope alive.'*

He smiled at the very pleased-with-themselves DeAngelo and Ravi as he replied, "Yeah, I do like it. It's important to remind ourselves we have many things to be grateful for."

The words had barely escaped his lips when Dante, still sitting propped up against the wall in self-imposed solitude, muttered almost involuntarily, "Like what?" His guttural response cast a gloomy pall over the light mood that had begun to develop.

Victory felt compelled to nip Dante's negative attitude in the bud and honor DeAngelo's faith-based contribution. She had just retrieved a bottle of water for her husband, and as she sat down on her makeshift bedding, she responded to the cynical remark. "Well, we have our lives. That's the main thing we can give thanks for. We're still breathin', which is a miracle in itself... an' we have each other. Imagine how it would feel to be cut off from all others, completely alone and lost out there. We found each other by the grace of the Lord, because He knew we would need each other. That's a pretty significant blessin' and I've been givin' thanks for it since we all came together."

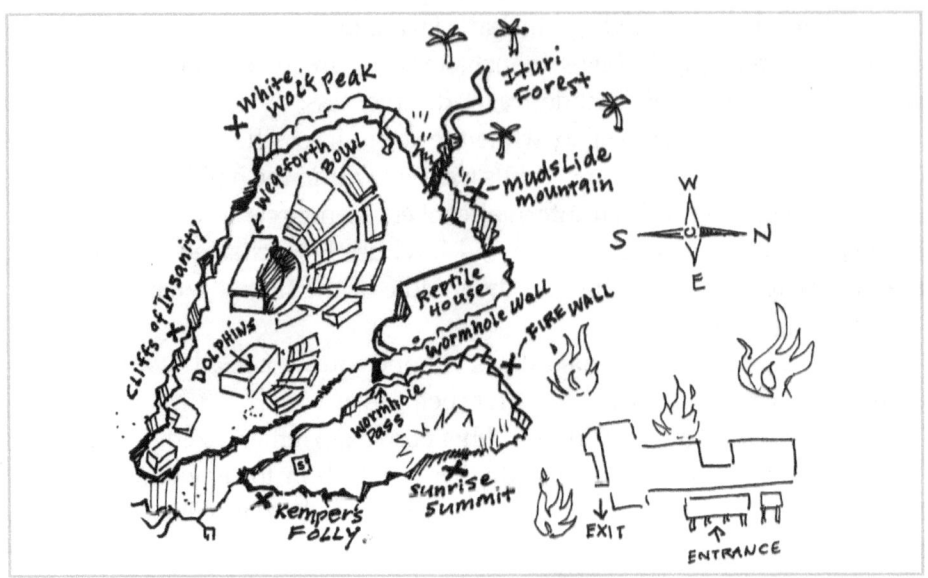

Violet elected to observe rather than interject her own thoughts, but fully appreciated the conviction in Victory's sincere affirmation of faith. She watched the corners of her father's mouth curl up in reaction to Victory's statement. Mateo had taught her the art of listening, and she had always been a very apt pupil. He encouraged her to identify the profound messages within the dialogue. She knew her father was adept at maintaining hope, even in the most challenging circumstances, reflected in how he adjusted to the role of single parent after her mother's abrupt departure.

Mateo demonstrated his typical attitude by adding, "It may not be the song I requested... but I'm going to dance just the same."

Jason meekly added, "I'm grateful we didn't get injured when we dropped from that cliff in the mud slide the other day. That we both walked away from that fall unscathed was just amazing." Sinnamon seconded the sentiment, telling the rest of the group she crashed down atop Jason's prone body during that episode, but added she wished he would've gotten out of her way when they were running through the bramble. She shot a verbal barb his way, sneering, "Dude, you run like you've got a load in your pants. Hell, you were so spooked back there... maybe that really *was* what slowed you down!" The wisecrack drew laughter from everybody, except Dante, who was still silently brooding.

Around 3:13 p.m., a drawn-out rumble of thunder, apparently much closer than before, heralded yet another period of steady rain. Kyle examined the patch covering the hole in the roof before ambling over to speak with Mateo and Violet. He had been itching for a conversation with them, and the storm provided an ideal opportunity. As he walked by, Sinnamon lifted her cell phone to her ear again only to discover the dead silence she dreaded. She suspended her evaluation just long enough to savor the sight of Kyle's well-toned backside as he brushed past. A wry smile graced her Sun-scorched face as Kyle approached Violet and Mateo in front of the display of poisonous frogs.

The absence of functioning air conditioning and ventilation had caused all of the glass on the displays to fog up. Thick condensation made it nearly impossible to see, but Mateo and Violet peered through the few clear patches to glimpse several brightly colored frogs moving about. The air in the Reptile House was stale, even with the doors propped open.

Violet stood alongside her father, wondering what fate had in store. Her instincts told her there was a great purpose behind all that was transpiring; that this nightmarish circumstance was part of a plan that would reveal itself in time. She instinctively knew there would be more suffering, more deaths, and much more uncertainty before answers were revealed, but she somehow felt at peace nonetheless.

Violet wondered, *'How strange... I should be much more frightened than I feel. Am I losing touch with reality?'*

When Kyle approached, Mateo sensed a surprisingly powerful kinship between the three of them. Before Kyle could pose the question he intended to ask, Mateo asked one of his own. "So, you're a teacher?" he inquired of the slightly taller man. Kyle was taken aback by the unexpected question.

"Where'd you get that idea?" the somewhat reserved young man asked with a smile.

Mateo clarified, "I'm sorry if I misunderstood, but your sister mentioned something about the kids you work with and I gathered she was referring to students in a classroom. She only told me you work with children, but I didn't get the details. So, what exactly is your job, if not teaching?"

Kyle removed his round glasses to wipe them on his dingy shirt before answering the question. "I work with some very gifted children in a foundation we're developing back in Pittsburgh. Mia and I were born back there. I never left but she moved here a few years ago. There are educational elements to the Foundation, but I'm a Child Psychologist rather than a traditional teacher."

"These are super-intelligent children?" Mateo inquired. "What ages do you work with? I'm not sure I understand."

Kyle returned his glasses to their rightful place and happily shared more information about his passion-driven work. "These kids are not necessarily superior in intellect, although many of them are gifted in that sense, too. These children are what we call "Quantum Qids"; at least that's become our catch-all term for them."

Violet remained silent, content with listening intently to every word. Intrigued by Kyle, several questions popped into Mateo's mind, foremost of which related to his mention of "psychic abilities". "What types of psychic talents do these children exhibit?" he asked.

Kyle enthusiastically answered, "Most of the kids we work with are highly-evolved on multiple levels: not only intellectually advanced, but displaying highly-developed senses of intuition and perception. We work with plenty of young people who are quite advanced in the area of psychic healing, too. Some of it, our staff doesn't fully understand… but we've seen an amazing array of skills demonstrated by all ages in clients as young as three years old, and in our residents who range in age from around twelve to twenty-one."

Mateo was a bit confused. "Clients? Residents? What, exactly, do you do there?" he probed. Violet was absorbing all the energies exchanged between her father and the gentle man with whom he was speaking. She felt a pleasant sense of harmony between them. The more she listened, the greater affinity she felt with Kyle – and with Mia, who had quietly joined the intimate clique.

Mia suggested that Kyle share his observations regarding the Armstrong sisters, something he had expressed to her earlier in the day. After checking to make sure the girls weren't within earshot, he expressed some thoughts that had been running through his mind. "Those two girls; they're obviously highly evolved. We've all seen the evidence. However, most impressive to me, in the short time I've observed their behavior, is their affinity for healing and the way they so naturally combine energies. They're psychically connected to one another on an exceptionally deep level; a phenomenon sometimes inherent in twins, especially identical twins – only these girls are a year apart in age. At The Foundation we've worked with three other sets of siblings in the past two years, who demonstrate a very similar connection. We've coined the term 'telepathic tether' to describe the invisible link they share."

Mia directed her reaction toward her brother. "I can literally *feel* their energy, unlike anything I've ever experienced. It's like basking in the warmth of the Sun, just being near them. Is that something you've seen or felt before?"

"Yeah, actually… it is. I've worked with a handful of young children and teenagers that generated similar energy residue, but probably none quite as palpable. These girls represent something even more evolved in that regard. And, like I said; their healing powers seem exceptional... remarkable, actually." Kyle then turned his attention to Violet and surprised her by asking, "*You* have the same type of ability, don't you?" Caught off guard, she hesitated while nervously considering the question. After shuffling her feet a bit, she sheepishly replied.

"Yes... I do," she simply stated. "It's normal for me to do it, but I realize it's not understood by most of the world, so I keep it hidden."

Kyle smiled reassuringly. "Well, we're working to change that, Violet. Our mission is to advance awareness and research while we help young people like you and those two girls in the other room feel less alienated. We're making inroads every day. It's going to take time, but we're seeing results and I believe the work we're involved with is important. We have a growing number of clients and have just finished construction of a residence hall for those who can benefit from more structured support."

Mateo asked, "What do you mean by 'more structured support?'"

Kyle sighed noticeably before replying, "Mateo, there are many young people who are completely at odds with their own families – some have been ostracized by their parents or their entire families, just for openly demonstrating their abilities. We decided to devote the lion's share of our funding, mostly from the private sector, to build dorms to protect young people who've either run away or been kicked out of their homes or schools. It's absolutely tragic what happens to some innocent kids who are merely naively displaying their natural abilities. We can't allow them to fall through the cracks any longer, because in many ways they represent humanity's best hope for the future."

Violet asked, "Why do you say that?"

Kyle answered, "There's a quantum leap in human evolution occurring right under our noses, and yet the world's societies have done a terrible disservice to the one minority for which no one has adequately advocated. When an individual displays any sort of psychic talents or tendencies, they're typically ridiculed or labeled. That's barely changed throughout history, and countless gifted individuals have had to hide their true abilities or suppress them until they're rendered dormant. Just like many natural abilities – what we don't nurture often withers and dies. To think that we've historically applied such a negative stigma to what is truly a critically important advancement within our own species is nothing short of insanity. Our Foundation is going to change that over time."

Mateo innocently asked, "Do you refer to your clients as 'Indigo Children'? My mother used that term in relation to children with psychic abilities, long before I ever read about it."

Kyle's eyes lit up as he eagerly shared a bit of what he knew about the term and its history. "We no longer use that term exclusively, but I see you have some understanding of it as it applies to those who personify the evolution. We prefer the term 'Quantum Qids' or simply 'Quantums', because we've learned there are too many complexities to lump them into categories like 'Indigo Children' or 'Crystal Children'. Those labels worked for a time, but we've learned through our research that our clients are displaying a multitude of innate abilities that blossom as they grow. In many cases, their abilities continuously evolve, in ways we've never previously been aware of."

He continued, aware that he had struck a chord with Mateo and Violet. "We have a growing staff of psychiatrists, psychologists, and researchers working with our clients, either during in-house visits or while they're residents. We work with other social agencies to reunite families when possible, and also get involved with vocational placement when appropriate. There's a lot more we hope to achieve as funding enables future growth, but I'm proud we're helping keep families together and educating people in the process."

Mateo looked into his daughter's sparkling eyes, well aware that she fit the description of a Quantum Qid as much as anyone. He asked Kyle whether he and Violet could visit his foundation when things returned to normal. Kyle enthusiastically extended an open invitation, adding, "Maybe one day you might consider working with us, Violet. We need young, dynamic mentors and I can't imagine anyone having more potential for such a leadership role. Our scholarship programs with Carnegie-Mellon and the University of Pittsburgh enable members of our staff to pursue degrees while working as Mentor/Advisors. When you visit, I hope you'll be inclined to investigate some of those options for yourself... with our assistance, of course."

Mateo thanked Kyle for his comments and assured Violet they would plan a visit to Pittsburgh once a semblance of normalcy returned to their lives. Having no prior awareness of its existence, she was invigorated just listening to Kyle's description about the Quantum Qids Foundation.

Violet thought, *'It's about time someone did something like that. Maybe there's some way I can help.'*

The brief respite from the harsh realities outside came to a screeching halt when the first wave of major aftershocks struck at 3:33 p.m.

△△△

Chapter Eighteen
Waiting for a Sign

"Your vision will become clear only when you look into your heart.
Who looks outside, dreams. Who looks inside, awakens."
~ Carl Gustav Jung

T he tremors arrived unannounced, and like a band of oafish trespassers, rudely left chaos in their wake. Obscured behind the sound of rolling thunder, they caught the huddled survivors off guard, sending them reeling across the concrete floor. While they were flung about the room, the tremors did what they were designed to do. Succinct and purposeful, the seismic waves reshaped the geography, continuing the work initiated by the earlier quakes.

Just outside the open doors of the Reptile House, the ground violently shifted and split apart. As powerful underground vibrations coursed through the region, every structure and every living creature felt the effects. The intensity of the storm had escalated in eerie synchronization with the arrival of the tremors. A long, jagged crack menacingly crept across the concrete floor, while the sounds of nature in crisis were sickening echoes of the nightmare they had all so recently lived through.

'Is this the one that ends it all?' Violet wondered, as she rolled across the floor and into the cinder block wall.

The terrifying thuds of debris crashing down upon the roof only served as accents to the gruesome roar from underground. Sinnamon fell awkwardly against the corner of the large display case, striking her right forearm on its metal frame. She then spun and tumbled to the floor in a crumpled heap, not far from where Dante was propped against the wall. Dwayne Cooper clutched his wife and son close to him, to save them from being banged around.

Kyle and Mia both reached out for Ravi the moment they realized what was happening. Mia grabbed his shirt sleeve and clutched him to her bosom before they toppled to the floor in a tangled heap. She contorted her body in an effort to protect him, straining her lower back in the process. Though he maintained his footing, Kyle slammed his shoulder into the front of the poisonous frog display behind him, fracturing its thick glass.

I Miss Your Purple Hair

Having sensed the impending tremors seconds before they struck, Hanna and Leanna had instinctively wedged themselves inside the door frame in the back of the main room. The latest storm cloaked the region in darkness. Their lone sanctuary was under siege and there were no guarantees it would withstand the onslaught. Violet closed her eyes and prayed. She consciously focused on calming her nerves by slowing her breathing and embracing the moment. She gracefully accepted what was happening around her and, rather than panicking, consciously marveled at the power of Nature's resonating voice.

She thought: *'We'll survive... we knew this was coming. We just didn't know when.'*

Mateo reacted similarly, rolling *with* the furious undulations. By relaxing his muscles and allowing the tremors to take him where they intended, he rolled across the concrete floor like a rag doll. He finally wound up alongside Mia, still clutching the frightened eight-year-old in her arms. From the back of the room came sounds of shattering glass. The violent shaking and twisting had caused the glass front of one of the snake exhibits to explode, raining countless glass fragments over Jason and Sinnamon.

At the height of the turmoil, the disjointed sounds of destruction played like one of Mephistopheles' twisted symphonies. Dante had been lingering near the outer doors, mesmerized by the lightning, when the tremors knocked him off his feet. His battered body ended up sprawled across the threshold, besieged by the storm. Angry bolts of electricity came crashing down less than 50 yards from where he lay motionless.

Then, more suddenly than it had begun... the tremors stopped.

The group held their collective breath, awaiting the next onslaught... but the storm provided the only noise, pummeling the surface of the disfigured terrain with an onslaught of heavy, acidic raindrops. Dante lay prone across the steel threshold, stunned and barely conscious, the cold raindrops pecking at the back of his neck like a flock of voracious birds. He struggled to raise his head, and then extended his tired arms to lift his upper body off the rain-spattered asphalt. Bolts of purple lightning flashed nearby, followed almost immediately by menacing crashes of thunder. Every concussive pulse resonated in his sternum.

As he finally got to his feet, Dante stood in the doorway and gazed out upon a world further dismembered. The pain in his knee had transformed into numbness. He blinked his weary eyes and tried to comprehend the latest chapter of the tragedy. He had to remind himself to begin breathing again, as did his companions, scattered about the floor like abandoned toys. One by one, his beleaguered comrades began taking full breaths again, assessing the damage and regaining their bearings following Mother Earth's chaotic display. Dante pulled the heavy entrance doors shut again to shut out the storm.

Mateo gathered his wits and reached out to touch the exposed skin of Mia's arm, to offer gentle reassurance. The instant the palm of his hand contacted the lightly sunburned flesh of her upper arm, both of them sensed profound kinship. After he helped her and Ravi to their feet, he rejoined Violet and hugged her for a very long time, drawing her sweet essence into his soul. He squeezed his only child tight to his chest and made a declaration to himself.

'I refuse to let her die here. She has so much more to do; so much more to live for. There is an answer... somewhere out there... and I'll find it.'

Violet allowed herself to melt into her father, as she had done so many times. She recalled the times when she had scraped a knee or was stung by a bee, and he swallowed her up in his strong, sinewy arms and hugged her pain away. Although her fears were now much greater and the stakes infinitely higher, the effect was largely the same. As her inner voice repeated, 'It'll be okay,' she consciously connected with the rhythm of her father's pulse. Gradually, Violet began to feel her confidence returning.

The rest of the group slowly regained their bearings as they checked for injuries and dusted themselves off. While the others slowly gravitated toward the middle of the large exhibit area, Sinnamon split off to shake countless glass particles from her thick hair. She nonchalantly removed her green tank top to reveal a black sports bra and shook the glass from her shirt. Wispy surface lacerations further adorned her already-sliced-up shoulders and arms, but she had not suffered any significant injuries.

Jason ambled over to the same spot and brushed most of the bits of glass from his clothing and matted hair. Sinnamon assisted by picking broken glass from the collar of his shirt, smartly commenting, "Dude, you need a shower something bad. You okay? You're lookin' kinda shaky." Surprised at her uncharacteristic expression of compassion, Jason smiled as best he could under the circumstances.

He replied, "I'm okay – just a bit light-headed, but it's no big deal. You?" Sinnamon returned a reticent smile and shook her head to indicate she was not significantly injured. For a moment, she felt genuine concern for Jason, who seemed to have lost hope.

Once they'd both gathered their composure, they remembered that the now-shattered glass had provided the only barrier between them and what resided within the display. Quickly, Sinnamon located the nearby plaque on the wall depicting the occupants of the large display case. A sigh of relief accompanied the realization that the residents were...

"Iguanas," Sinnamon announced to the concerned onlookers. "Thank God it's only iguanas. I used to have a couple as pets."

Mateo was curious to note the time the tremors subsided, but could not understand why the hands on his watch's analog display had stopped moving. There was no visible damage, yet the digital display was frozen at 8:12 p.m., which he knew was obviously far from correct. He checked with Dwayne, who wore a rather rugged looking sports watch, and was informed the actual time was 4:31 p.m.

Mateo muttered, "Strange, isn't it, that the readout is frozen at 8:12. When I checked the time a couple of hours ago it seemed to be working fine, but that was around 2:30. It makes no sense." He held his watch to his ear and was surprised to hear it ticking normally. *'Probably got messed up when I fell,'* he speculated. Mateo promptly reset the watch to the proper time and took a sip of lukewarm bottled water. The hands were moving normally, and he was satisfied it was functioning again.

While Victory and Dwayne helped tend to DeAngelo and the three other children, Mia and Kyle sought out Mateo and Violet on the opposite end of the great room. The tremors had ceased and the sounds of thunder and rain were subdued now that the doors had been closed. Feeling emotionally connected with Mateo and Violet, Mia was interested in becoming better acquainted. She asked Violet whether she could give her a hug and was pleased with her warm response.

Sensing from her body language that Violet wanted to talk, Kyle slowly approached and patiently waited for her to speak. Mateo was stunned when Violet somewhat hesitantly asked, "You're from the same place where Nathan, Prajna, and Corinne go to school, aren't you?" While her father was completely caught off guard by her question, Kyle seemed to have expected it.

The handsome Psychologist calmly responded, "Y... yes I am, Violet. I guess you've been in communication with them again, huh?"

"What's *this* about?" Mateo asked.

Violet started to explain, "Papa, I'm friends with a few of the kids at the Foundation. They live in the dormitory at Dr. Nordstrom's place in Pittsburgh. I finally added everything together and figured out he's the one they sometimes talk about."

Mateo was confused by the revelation and asked, "What do you mean, you're 'friends with a few of the kids?' Have you communicated with them through your web site?"

"Well... sometimes, but mostly in *The Web*," she answered. "We've been communicating for almost a year but I didn't make the connection until now. They've told me about Dr. Nordstrom and other people who work for him at the Foundation, but I never imagined meeting him in person... not here anyway."

"How strange," Mia chirped. "So many coincidences happening around us; it's uncanny."

Mateo asked Kyle, "Are *you* part of this 'Web', too? Did *you* know Violet before we all wound up here together?"

Kyle struggled to answer accurately. "I can't say I knew her, but I've been made aware by others. Her name has been mentioned before by a few of our students but we've never had any direct contact. I have been reading her blog and some of her posts on other sites but didn't make the connection until now, partly because she uses the name Veronica in her online discussions." Turning toward Violet, he asked, "You also go by the screen name 'IndigoLight', don't you?"

The question took her by surprise, but Violet confirmed he was correct before posing a question of her own. She used the alternate screen name to make anonymous posts on occasion, seeking to protect her true identity. "But... how do you know that?" she asked.

Mateo and Mia felt a bit lost and listened intently. Kyle smiled before responding, "We're fortunate to mentor a bunch of very clever young people at Foundation headquarters. Some of them know more about you than you may realize. They've been following your blog and reading your pseudonym's posts on other web sites for quite some time now. You have a growing nucleus of disciples in Pittsburgh, you know. The kids, primarily Nathan and Prajna, quote you quite often... and have recommended your blog to their peers. These children have been energized by your teachings and are understandably anxious to meet you."

Violet excitedly replied, "I feel like I already *have* met some of them: Prajna, Nathan, and Corinne. We understand each other and, even though

I Miss Your Purple Hair

Nathan's so *young* – I think only 10 – he understands where we have to take things now. He and I are like brother and sister in some ways. We finish each other's thoughts and have similar ideas about how people like us can make a difference in the world. I'm impressed that he figured out one of my other screen names. He must've read some of my posts on other sites and recognized my style. Pretty clever!"

"Veron… I mean, Violet… can you see what's happening here?" Kyle asked somewhat ominously.

She pursed her lips and pondered his question for a moment, before answering thoughtfully, "I'm beginning to, I think. Some things are becoming clearer now."

Mateo was perplexed with the course of the conversation. "I wish you'd get the rest of us caught up. I'm not sure I understand what you're talking about. You said the children have been energized by Violet's *'teachings'*? Your choice of words is very curious."

Kyle grinned and shifted his focus to Mateo. "My friend, your daughter is what we call a 'galvanizer.' You're obviously aware of her heightened sensory abilities and healing skills as well as her unique communication talents. She has been blessed with great intellect and intuition, and also with the rarest human trait of all – a gift for visionary leadership. In our Foundation, we prize that ability above all others, because we believe it's the key to solving many of the ills plaguing humanity. Leadership, of the right kind, has the potential to lift us out of the seemingly hopeless plight we find ourselves in at this moment in history. Violet is one of many key individuals who are already playing their roles in the next great shift... propelling us one step closer to our ultimate destiny."

"What are you talking about?" Mateo incredulously inquired. "She's just a teenage girl who happens to be wiser than her years. You seem to know more about her than you let on over the past two days. What's this really all about?"

Kyle tried to reassure Mateo, while remaining completely candid. "Truth is… I failed to make the connection until just now. Through her online persona, Violet's consistently demonstrated her innate leadership abilities. You saw how well received she was when she made that television appearance not long ago. The groundswell of excitement she generated was remarkable, her age notwithstanding. When some of the kids we work with saw the broadcast or the online video, they immediately identified her as a person they wanted to emulate. That's when more than a few of them began following her blog posts, sometimes reading them aloud to one another. That's when I realized what she might very well be."

"And... what's that?" Mateo pressed.

"I'm convinced she's one of the 'non-Messiahs'," Kyle flatly stated.

"*Non-Messiah*? What is that supposed to mean; an anti-Christ?"

"No, no, no!" Kyle quickly clarified, "A non-Messiah can be defined as a human being who, despite exhibiting abilities that could be construed as supernatural or divine, rejects all such notions while serving the greater good – by utilizing their charisma to lead others toward salvation. Violet possesses all of the key traits and seems to be precisely what I alluded to earlier – a natural *galvanizer*."

"I detect awe in your voice when you say that word," Mateo observed.

Kyle calmly explained, "They only come along rarely – these individuals with such advanced levels of intelligence and intuition, coupled with a profound sense of purpose. With such traits in perfect balance, they are irrepressible forces – catalysts who can help turn the tide for an entire civilization."

Mateo looked into his daughter's eyes and searched his soul... and his memories... in reaction to all that Kyle said. As he reflected upon her life, he was humbled by the realization she had indeed been just what he described. It had often been Violet who helped him cope in times of stress. She had been enormously influential in helping him shape his own outlook and attitude. Wise beyond her years from the beginning, it was Violet who taught him about aura reading, healing prayers and mind-over-matter techniques.

While he formerly believed Violet had learned all of her amazing techniques through reading and researching, he finally realized he had been rationalizing all along. The time had come to face the facts and he was trying his best to see her in a new light. Mateo asked his wide-eyed daughter, "Does all of this seem right to you, baby?"

She suddenly felt like a very young girl again, awash in fear and trepidation as she fought back tears. Conflicting emotions swirled in her mind, and she just wanted to be a little girl in her daddy's arms more than anything else. She ran to him and allowed herself to be enveloped by her father's protective embrace. A solitary tear escaped her eye and rolled down her cheek before being absorbed into the fabric of her father's shirt.

With her thoughts clouded by a maelstrom of emotional conflict, she tried to ground herself and reflect upon Kyle's observations. The crushing weight of responsibility bore down upon her as she reluctantly accepted his statements as truths. She had understood, yet not fully accepted, her calling. She had suspected, but not previously embraced her destiny. That was now changing; she could no longer hide behind the façade of denial. Now that another had enunciated her life's purpose with such clarity, there were no options left but to acknowledge what she had suspected her entire life. She finally accepted as her new reality that she was one of the *non-Messiahs* and had been preparing for this day for fifteen years. With her nose buried in the folds of her father's soft, familiar shirt, she ceased her crying and psychologically crossed the invisible barrier between childhood and adulthood.

Mateo squeezed her tightly, not wanting to let go. Throughout her lifetime, she had been everything to him: playmate, pupil, motivator, teacher, counselor, inspiration, and muse. First and foremost though, she was always simply "daughter" – a term carrying reverential meaning for him since the day she was born. They locked minds with one another, as they had done many times, and shared a moment of timeless intimacy as father and daughter... as protector and vulnerable child... one last time. Then, she gently pushed away from him to look him in the eyes again. In each other's gaze, they both recognized acceptance of the truths brought to light by Kyle.

The thunderstorm raged outside as the cluster of tired, disheartened people remained trapped inside their sanctuary. Dante had not heard any of the conversation between Kyle, Mateo, and Violet, his attention split between the pain in his knee and the lightning and thunder outside. Sitting on the floor, he leaned against the set of external doors. With his grimy right index finger, he lazily traced the contour of a long, irregular crack the tremors created in the thick glass. Sullen and plagued by some mysterious angst, he had separated emotionally from the rest of the group. To no one in particular he muttered, "We have to get out of here. We have to get out of here..."

Sinnamon and Jason encouraged Dante to join the rest of the people in the main room, but he ignored their suggestions. They soon gave up and regrouped with the others. Once gathered around the large display case covered with their collected supplies, they reviewed what they discovered that morning in an effort to plan their course of action. Dwayne expressed that he felt feverish, and his wife and son remained at his side off to themselves. Victory wiped her husband's forehead with a damp cloth, while silently praying for his well-being.

Mia opened the conversation by asking if anyone had seen any possible pathways over or through any of the obstructions. Expressions of dejection came to all of their faces. None of them had seen any conceivable spot that might lead them out. Following a long silence, Sinnamon said, "There doesn't seem to be any way we could even attempt to climb out, especially with two of us injured. We didn't see any way to get a foothold on *Mudslide Mountain*. Not only is that the wrong direction to go, that wall of mud can only be a bigger mess now, after all this rain."

Hanna brought up a good point, meekly suggesting, "We don't know if the tremors we just had did anything. Maybe they created a way out, if the mountains were changed at all."

"Good point," Kyle replied. "When the storm breaks, a small group of us can go investigate any changes to the terrain that may have occurred. It's possible that a new opening was created." Immediately, Mateo, Sinnamon, Mia, and Jason volunteered to form two groups to search the perimeter once the weather cleared.

Victory commented that she and anyone willing could build a huge bonfire in the pit while the others explored, suggesting that the smoke would attract any rescuers in the vicinity. "We have to do everything we can now. I don't see how we could ever hope to climb out of here – not the way it looked to me today. There ain't no way I'm leavin' my man behind. If he can't climb, we're gonna have to find another way."

"Yeah, well...," Sinnamon piped in, "time's come to try anything we can think of, so I say let's cover all the bases. We'll collect all the firewood we can and once we light it we can start searching the place for any changes. If we take all the dry wood we brought in here and scrounge up anything else we can find, we ought to be able to make a pretty huge fire. The wet wood will create a lot of smoke and that can only help our cause."

Violet felt compelled to speak up, recommending, "I have to say this, and I apologize if it sounds negative, but... there's no sense in looking for a new way out. There isn't one. We should focus all our energy on building the biggest fire possible, and then wait for help to come. I know there are people out there searching, but they aren't in much better shape than us. There's no way to climb up and over. We have to be patient..."

Mia seemed puzzled by Violet's comments. "Why are you so sure? Isn't there a chance the landscape got shifted around again by the tremors?"

Jason spoke up from behind Mia. "I believe she's right. There's no way out over one of these walls. Nothing changed enough to make that possible. The fire's our best hope now."

From across the room, Victory asked, "How do you know that? We haven't even been able to see out there yet, with all this rain."

I Miss Your Purple Hair

"Trust what Violet said. I know it's true. The mountains weren't changed by the tremors – not enough to make a difference, anyway," Jason stated with conviction.

Kyle suspected Jason of failing to be completely forthcoming with information but had no way of knowing why. He detected some behaviors in Jason that seemed akin to those in some of his Quantums, but was not familiar enough to draw any conclusions. In an effort to serve as peacekeeper he suggested they build the fire and still send out a party to investigate the perimeter, just in case the seismic activity had opened up a way out. The ensuing silence of the tired and hungry survivors indicated their approval.

They took inventory of the remaining provisions and realized how precious little remained. They were left with only a half-dozen bottles of water and a pathetic collection of snack foods. DeAngelo suddenly scrambled to his feet and dropped two sealed bags of salted peanuts on the table before retreating to his father's side again without saying a word. His mother pulled his head close enough to plant a kiss on his cheek to acknowledge his act of responsibility.

The rain was coming down harder and the blustery wind was blowing foliage and other debris across the ground. The tarp patching the roof flapped in the wind, creating a rhythmic tick-tick-tickety-tick sound, but was holding fast for the time being. A bolt of lightning struck nearby, shaking the building's foundation. Everyone twitched in reaction to the harsh noise and both Ravi and DeAngelo clung to Victory, sitting on the floor – clutching her red Bible.

Mateo glanced at his watch and saw that it had malfunctioned again. He asked if anyone could tell him the correct time, and Kyle informed him it was actually 6:18 p.m. "Now my watch is frozen at 8:21," he explained. "I reset it to 4:30 earlier, so how could it get stuck at 8:21 if only a couple of hours passed? Well, I guess after all that shaking and..."

Victory, flanked by the two boys clutching her arms, politely asked him to repeat the time displayed on his watch.

"8:21," Mateo answered.

"And what time was it showin' the other time it was stuck?" she inquired.

Mateo thought again carefully and replied, "I think... it was frozen at 8:12 the first time. Yes, it was 8:12 the other time. What does it matter though? It's shot."

She thought for a moment before answering, "I don't know. It reminds me of something else, I guess... not sure, really. It *is* strange that the time would jump around like that and then stop. You must have banged it on the floor during the tremors."

"Well, yeah..." Mateo responded. "No doubt I slammed it pretty hard. I guess they don't make 'em earthquake-proof just yet." He removed the watch from his wrist and tossed it among the supplies clustered atop the display case. He walked over toward the window that looked out on the open courtyard, gently patting Violet on the head as he brushed past. Dante stood staring through the rivulets of water streaming down the window at the torrential downpour.

In the distance to the west, jagged lightning bolts danced along the summit of the towering ridge they had labeled *White Wolf Peak*. The foreboding barrier appeared even more intimidating against the darkening backdrop. Dante felt hopeless and had intentionally disconnected from the rest of the group. When Mateo arrived at his side, Dante's face was coated in perspiration and his breathing was nearly imperceptible.

"Quite a scene," Mateo half-whispered, hoping to draw a response.

Dante failed to react in any discernible manner. His gaze remained fixed upon the top of *White Wolf Peak*, watching the display in the sky orchestrated by a seemingly furious Mother Earth. Mateo realized Dante's energy was at low ebb. Although it was clear he was not very receptive, Mateo attempted to ease the younger man out of his semi-catatonic state. "Breathe," he whispered near Dante's right ear. "All you need to do is breathe, my friend."

Many thoughts collided within the mind of the security officer: worry for his girlfriend, who was finishing her undergraduate education in Salt Lake City; fear for his parents and younger brother back on the East Coast; deep concern for his zoo co-workers; and guilt surrounding Aaron Kemper and all that had transpired on the other side of *Wormhole Pass*. His right knee sent pain signals up his spine and into his head, clouding his reason and exacerbating his fears.

Through his quagmire of subconscious thoughts, he heard Mateo's measured words and slowly regained awareness of his surroundings. Everything slowly came back into focus and he finally was able to process the words being spoken for his benefit. "Breathe... oh, right... sorry, I was lost in thought, I guess," he mumbled dejectedly. "Okay, okay... I'll be fine."

Mateo calmly restated, "Breathe in deeply and slowly let it out. Close your eyes and breathe in and out slowly a few more times. In your mind, hear the words, 'Everything will be alright'. Repeat the thought while you continue to breathe. Dante trusted Mateo's intentions, so he followed his advice and repeated the thought while keeping his weary eyes closed. A tangible wave of rejuvenating energy poured from Mateo into Dante, resurrecting his determination and reassuring him that he could go on. Within a few minutes' time, he felt clearheaded once again.

Dante declared, "I feel better now, thanks," as he reopened his brown eyes and looked directly at Mateo. "It's been one hell of a ride, huh? I need to stop thinking about everything at the same time. That's my problem: I've been worrying about my family, my co-workers, my dog, myself, and everyone else all at once. It's too much to process and I need to stop letting it snowball on me."

"That's absolutely right," Mateo concurred. "We all need to stay in the present and not project. We have to stick together... and *think* together. There's always a way out of any situation and we'll find it. Trust me."

Having been rescued from the quicksand of hopelessness, Dante felt he could go forward with some semblance of hope. "Thanks, man," he said in a raspy voice, his throat dry and sore from lack of water. "I'll try to do better." Mateo realized that escape seemed implausible, but also knew that the answer could come from any one of his fellow survivors. In his estimation, it was in everyone's best interest to help one another maintain their spirit.

For a moment, Mateo and Dante stood at the large picture window, humbled by Nature. The fury of the storm rivaled that of the last. Ferocious winds carried tree branches and fragments of shattered structures while sporadic flashes lit the entire sky. The thick glass vibrated from shock waves sent out by the bursts of thunder.

Suddenly interrupting the sounds of the storm was a woman's voice. At the back of the large exhibit room, Victory projected her voice so all could hear. "... *Again, Jesus spoke to them, saying, 'I am the light of the world. Whoever follows me will never walk in darkness but will have the light of life.'*"

She then paused for a moment before exclaiming in much the same forceful manner, "*Again He said to them, 'I am going away, and you will search for me, but you will die in your sin. Where I am going, you cannot come.'*"

Dante and Mateo joined everyone else, close to where Victory sat with her husband and the two youngest children at her side. She was reading aloud from her small red Bible. No one knew what to make of her sudden outburst, nor did they seem willing to break the pregnant pause hanging in the air. Victory slowly and clearly enunciated the first lines again, after flipping back to where she had dog-eared the page in her Bible.

"'Again Jesus spoke to them, saying, 'I am the light of the world. Whoever follows me will never walk in darkness, but will have the light of life.'"

With a child at each side, the graceful, brown-skinned woman epitomized the proverbial Mother-Nurturer. Her attention remained fixed upon the pages of her prized possession, never once looking up at the transfixed souls surrounding her. She then repeated the second passage, as if to stress its significance. *"'Again He said to them, 'I am going away, and you will search for me, but you will die in your sin. Where I am going, you cannot come.'"*

Victory then simultaneously closed the Book and her eyes, and drew in a deep breath while she reflected upon the words. Violet felt an icy chill wriggle down her spine from behind her heart to her solar plexus. She knew the answer before Victory provided it for the rest of the confused listeners.

She calmly explained, to no one in particular, "The first verse is *John 8:12*. And the second... is *John 8:21*. They're both very familiar to me, but I hadn't made the connection... until now."

Mateo felt humbled as he understood the "connection" she was referencing. "The times on my watch," he stated flatly. "The times my watch froze on earlier today... 8:12 and then 8:21... but, what does it mean?" He rescued his watch from the collection of supplies on the tabletop and drew it to his face in the dim light. He read the time aloud so everyone could hear. "7:13," was all he said... and the room fell silent again.

A barrage of thoughts ran through Mateo's mind.

'Why is the watch working properly now – and how did the display skip to the correct point again? Is there significance in the Bible verses or is it just coincidental? Maybe Victory's reading something into this and it's just her way of making sense of another curious development.'

△ △ △

I Miss Your Purple Hair

CHAPTER NINETEEN
I Watched You Float Away

"With synchronicity, all the resources we need are made available to us at the precise moment that is appropriate. The people who come into our lives are the ones we need at that moment in time. Everything is perfect.
We only need to recognize this to tune into the flow."
~ Alex Chua

After a stormy night of restless sleep, the sweat-soaked, disheveled band of survivors reluctantly awakened. They had spent the evening deliberating on many topics: the Bible verses and what, if anything, they signified; the weather and how it might delay the building of the fire; their hunger and thoughts of scavenging for more food or climbing trees in search of edible fruit. Kyle scratched his head and tried to get his eyes to open fully, grumbling, "What I would give for a pot of hot coffee right now." Sinnamon and Jason volunteered to search the grounds for anything edible and Mia, Kyle, Mateo, and Violet all offered to get to work on building the fire.

After trying his cell phone and walkie-talkie to no avail, Dante offered to join Sinnamon and Jason, in part, to protect them from any animals that might have been released as a result of the latest tremors. With Dwayne still hobbled by the swelling in his leg, he and Victory planned on keeping watch over the younger children near the dolphin tank and doing what they could to clean up the mess the storm undoubtedly left behind. By the time they had all awoken it was 7:25 a.m. and still raining.

Violet hugged her father to say "good morning" and he squeezed the back of her neck to express his love, just as he had done hundreds of times before. "We'll find our way home, baby; don't worry," he whispered. She gave him a quick hug and then moved to the large picture window, fogged up from their collective breath. Using her sleeve, she cleared an ever-widening circle in the steamy glass and pressed her nose against it. The rain was still coming down in fat little droplets, but the wind of the previous evening had all but spent itself. Judging from the temperature inside the building, it was decidedly warmer this morning than the previous two.

Violet noticed the storm had further eroded the nearby mountainsides, coating much of the broken asphalt in a veneer of rust-colored mud. Filled with water, their fire pit resembled a muddy fishing hole you might find on a neglected old farm. She looked to the sky to discover a dense canopy of clouds, still relieving themselves of their pent-up accumulation. Violet suddenly realized that water pouring off the steep-pitched roof had created the illusion it was raining harder than it actually was.

Mateo helped Violet prop open the two doors using the thick, wet sticks they had left just inside the threshold. They were greeted with warm, yet refreshing air blowing gently from the southwest. Mateo thought, *'Everything feels so alive out here. Nature certainly wears many different faces.'* He was not at all surprised when Violet bolted from his side and into the rain, splashing her bare feet along the mud-coated pavement just outside the doorway. She giggled and held her hands high above her head, spinning around like a whirling dervish. "I'm takin' a shower, Papa! This feels awesome!" For a moment, he just laughed and enjoyed his child's irrepressible spirit. Her enormous smile seemed to light up the gloomy environment and within seconds, he found himself dancing in the rain alongside her.

They found themselves celebrating the moment together, eerily different yet in many ways similar to countless others before. Almost always able to enjoy the simplest wonders life offered up, it was not their first dance in the rain together. Mateo lifted his 15-year-old daughter onto the nearby broken bench and then hopped up to join her so the rain could wash the red mud coating off his bare feet. The combination of the warmer-than-usual air and the slightly cooler raindrops made for a delightfully comfortable romp, and the rest of the survivors had a good laugh observing the pair from the front window.

"They're a matched set, those two," Victory affectionately commented.

"Yeah… they're both *nuts*!" Sinnamon snickered. Then she burst through the doorway to join them, spinning around in the mud just as they had done moments ago. She pitched her head back and fully exposed her freckled face to the refreshing rain while she twirled as if performing a ceremonial dance. For the first time in a long while, Sinnamon laughed heartily and allowed herself to stop worrying about the lives of those she loved most. She stomped her feet in the oozing mud, and then ran and jumped into the water-filled fire pit. Violet and Mateo hopped down from the bench to join Sinnamon, and soon all three were holding hands and twirling in a circle.

Suddenly, Sinnamon bumped into Violet, who had come to an abrupt halt for some reason. When she followed Violet's eyes to learn what had demanded her attention, she understood immediately. There, only 20 feet away, was a peacock cowering beneath the vegetation that bordered the muddy walkway.

"Is that *our* bird?" Sinnamon wondered aloud.

"Yeah… maybe. It sure *looks* like our bird," Violet replied. Father, daughter and mercenary all watched in stunned disbelief as the peacock willingly abandoned its sanctuary and purposefully approached them. All they could hear was their own breathing, echoes of distant thunder and the incessant hiss of the rain. It was like a surreal dream – the three of them standing in the muddy water, rain cascading around them and this fragile creature approaching as if to greet them.

"How do you know it's *our* bird?" Sinnamon asked Violet.

"I can *feel* it," was all she replied.

Sinnamon knew not to question that, after all she had witnessed of Violet's abilities. Ever so slowly, the peacock strutted toward the fire pit, the rain obviously an annoyance that forced it to maintain a lower than normal profile. "There… see?" Violet whispered. "A tail feather is missing."

Mateo squinted to focus through the water falling from the sky and dripping down his forehead. "Oh yes," he replied. "I see what you mean. That's the same one, alright." The frail bird stopped at the edge of the pit and lifted its head, then nervously looked side-to-side before taking a drink. The rest of the survivors watched the proceedings from the dry interior of the Reptile House, marveling at the bizarre scene. It was a peculiar reunion; the young girl who had merely wanted to see if the bird was real, the father who granted her wish, and the opportunist who only sought another payday. The seeker, the supporter and the cynic – all together for one more encounter with the innocent creature.

Startling everyone, Violet suddenly stomped her feet, spraying mud-tinged water everywhere. She flapped her arms and shouted "Shoo! Shoo! Go!" at the frightened bird, which immediately made a beeline away from the pit.

Sinnamon jumped back, jarred by Violet's loud outburst. "What the hell are you doing?" she asked rather angrily. "Why'd you do that?"

Back in the doorway to the Reptile House, Dante eased his grip on the pistol and allowed it to slide back into its leather cradle. No one had seen him reach for the weapon, yet Violet intuitively sensed what he was thinking. She understood how hungry he and the others were, but was not about to let any more pain befall the innocent bird. She scared it away, despite wanting to spend more time in its presence. Mateo completely understood Violet's actions, as he too, felt an ominous ripple of energy from the nearby building.

I Miss Your Purple Hair

The rain began to lighten, gradually reduced to fine droplets. The rest of the group emerged from the stuffy building to allow the rain to wash them clean of their grime. For a short time, they all surrounded Violet and Mateo, who remained in the middle of the fire pit; arms at their sides, content to bask in the refreshing shower. Violet thought about the peacock and the incredible feather stashed in her pocket.

'Was I supposed to come here for some specific reason? Is it possible all of us were brought together for some unknown purpose?'

Mia surveyed the landscape through the misty veil of rain and fog. Water cascaded down the sides of the foreboding formations of earth, pooling along the ground and transforming puddles into small ponds. "If only we had some way of collecting and storing this rain water," she thought aloud. "Our supply won't last beyond this afternoon." Dante, who had been standing nearby, limped back inside the Reptile House, only to return a few minutes later.

"Here," he said, as he handed something to Mia. "One of these might open the door at the back of the dolphin tank. I just remembered that one of my keys opens the Office in there and found these in the file cabinet. It's a backup set of keys to miscellaneous locks. Almost all of those buildings are gone now, but maybe we'll be lucky for once."

Mia accepted the ring bearing ten keys of various shapes and sizes. She asked Dante, "What's in that room... anything that'll be of use?"

"I honestly don't know. It might be empty for all I know. That's a recent addition and I rarely work this section of the zoo. Hell, the right key might not even be on this ring. It's worth a shot, though."

Mateo interrupted with, "What else is in the Office? Is there anything in there we can use?" Dante shot back a somewhat irritated reply.

"There's a computer in there – for what that's worth now. There's also a bunch of rolled-up blueprints from the building's recent expansion... some pens and pads of paper... and a nice office chair. Other than that, I think there's a bunch of file folders and an old coffee mug with *'World's Best Dad'* printed on it. Why don't you go check it out to make sure I didn't miss something?"

Mateo calmly replied, "No need to do that right now. It's more important that we see if those keys are good for anything." Mia and Violet offered to accompany Mateo to investigate the locked door at the back of the dolphin exhibit's base, while Sinnamon and Jason headed back into the Reptile House to investigate thoroughly the now opened Office. While Dante limped back to his perch on the bench outside the building, everyone else scrambled to move the larger pieces of wood out of the rain and into the Reptile House to dry.

With Mia leading the way, the trio soon found themselves in the narrow channel between the dolphin tank and the foot of *The Cliffs of Insanity,* as Hanna had dubbed them. The tremors of the previous night dislodged debris from the mountainside, leaving the area littered with large and small chunks of rock and thick mud. The footing was treacherous, and they moved cautiously across the muddy, uneven terrain; Mia followed by Violet, and Mateo in back. Finally, they arrived at the nondescript white metal door bearing a heavy steel padlock.

Mia tried the keys and needed four attempts to identify the correct little round-headed gold key. With fervent anticipation, she turned it to open the thick padlock. The door was stuck shut due to the mud accumulated at its base, but Mateo and Mia threw their shoulders into it and it reluctantly opened. Though the rains persisted, the grey sky leaked just enough light into the expansive crawlspace beneath the dolphin tank. Forced to crouch to fit the cramped quarters, Mia entered while Mateo and Violet hovered just outside the threshold.

Mia quickly discovered that the area was primarily dedicated to the tank's filtration system. A cluster of large cylinders and a network of PVC pipes connected to the saltwater habitat above. The disruption of electrical power had rendered the pumps silent, and it was obvious the dolphins could be in peril. With all the acid rain entering their habitat, they would not survive long without a functioning filtration system. Continuing to poke around in the poorly-lit quarters, Mia discovered a few useful items: a pair of spades; three aluminum pails; two five-gallon molded plastic gasoline containers, one of which was full; and a coil of yellow nylon rope.

Behind one of the thick, steel support columns, she discovered what looked like some type of motor. Mateo crouched and entered the space to investigate. "This looks like an emergency generator for the pumps," he declared upon wiping a coating of dust from a cluster of gauges mounted to the dark grey metal. "Yeah, it's connected to the pumps here." Mia pointed out the fuel cap and Mateo opened it to check the levels. He reported, "It's empty. Once we fill it with gas we'll just have to figure out how to start it up." He filled the reservoir with the contents of the container they had found, while Mia continued to search.

Mia cleared dust from the surface of a flat panel on one side of the column and discovered a printed "guide." "Here!" she exclaimed. "This is a description of the generator. It says it's equipped with an 'Automatic Transfer Switch', whatever that means. There's a diagram depicting 'Manual Restart Procedure', too. We just have to toggle a switch to the manual setting and press the 'Restart' button. They should be in the panel on your side."

Mateo pulled on the handle recessed into the flat panel and opened the tall door to find the generator controls. He announced, "This is the switch, but it's already set to 'manual'. Wonder why they wouldn't have had it set to automatic all along…"

"Maybe the quakes jarred it loose?" Mia speculated. "Whatever; let's get it started if we can."

Mateo toggled the switch to the 'auto' setting and discovered that it was indeed loose in its mounting assembly. "Hey, the housing's loose and the whole panel's split!" he exclaimed. "There's a long crack down the middle and the lenses covering two of the meters are shattered, too. The toggle ought to hold steady, but I don't know if the internals are messed up or not. The generator won't work if the connections are seriously damaged. The battery compartment is dented and cracked and I can't open the panel they're stored behind, so there's no way to check them out."

Mia declared, "Well, we have no choice but to give it a shot. Is there any danger in trying to start the motor?"

Mateo pondered her question and then recommended that Mia join Violet outside before he pressed the button to start the generator. "Take the pails and the rope. I'll bring out the shovels and one of the gas cans when I'm done." Mia agreed and shuffled outside with the supplies. Mateo looked around the crawlspace one last time and noted a slow trickle of water riding down the wall and pooling in the nearby corner.

'There must be a crack in the tank or in one of the fittings'

There was insufficient time to investigate properly, and no way to repair it if the tank's integrity had been compromised, so he took a deep breath and pressed the red "Restart" button with his grimy left index finger. As the generator whirred to life, Mateo was surprised at how pleasantly it hummed. He breathed a sigh of relief as he listened to its soft purring sound and then the telltale sounds of the pumps springing to life.

After a brief uncomfortable moment when air was noisily forced through the pipes, only the gentle *whooshing* sound of water coursing through the PVC network accompanied the soft hum of the generator. From outside he heard Mia and Violet cheering and high-fiving each other in reaction to the sound of water circulating through the tank again. Mateo performed a final visual check of the dark crawlspace and gathered the remaining supplies. He identified no broken fittings or cracked pipes, yet was still concerned about the water accumulating in the corner.

He carried one of the gasoline containers of and the two spades to the doorway and rejoined Violet and Mia in the muddy area behind the building. Violet took the shovels and they moved to the front of the tank as the rain continued. As they rounded the side of the tank, Violet detected a sense of renewed energy in Tidus and Yuna, clearly in reaction to the restoration of the pumps. She smiled at the two young dolphins and their animated behavior.

'I'm glad you guys are happy. Just hang in there until we figure some things out.'

When they arrived at the front of the tank, near the broken bleachers, they saw that Leanna and Hanna had climbed onto the surrounding platform and were walking around the back. Kyle, barefoot and stripped to his white T-shirt and shorts, was in close pursuit. The bond between the dolphins and the children, especially the Armstrong sisters, was undeniable. Kyle gestured to the girls to join him at the back, where the tank containing the feeder fish was embedded into the platform.

The water circulated through the tank for the first time in days, yet the dolphins still seemed a bit listless. Kyle turned the latch and lifted the door to take inventory of the remaining food supply. Leanna announced, "Only sixteen left... wait... I mean fifteen. I think I counted one twice." Kyle flipped the lid all the way open and reached into the tank to grab the small bucket used to extract the fish.

From behind her sister, Hanna commented, "They're starving. We have to give them enough to live on or they'll just keep getting weaker. Look at them." She pointed to the pair of dolphins, who had positioned themselves as close to the feeding tank as possible, obviously desperate for nourishment.

Without wasting any more time, Kyle scooped six little silver fish into the pail. Hanna and Leanna walked to the edge of the platform, taking turns tossing them into the waiting mouths of the hungry dolphins. "They're still starving," Hanna told her older sister.

It pained Leanna to reply, "I know, but we have to save the rest for later. Maybe we can give them more at the end of the day, but we can't use them up now. They're strong. They'll be alright." She felt a slight surge in the dolphins' collective energy, but was aware they were wilting with each passing hour.

Kyle agreed with Leanna's assessment and praised the girls for their sincere concern. "Getting the pumps working again can only help and they'll be alright for a while, now that they've eaten something. We can't do much more than what we're doing." Despite the rain, the temperature started to ramp up again. Kyle remarked that he would stay with them if the girls wanted to swim with the dolphins for a while. "At this point, there isn't much else we can do until the conditions change and we start building the fire," he explained as he closed the feeding tank.

"No," Hanna surprisingly replied. "Let them save their strength for a while. If we go in there, they'll feel they have to play, and that could tire them out. Let's let them rest for now." Leanna echoed her opinion and they both walked to the ladder and started down the side of the tank. Kyle shook his head in amazement at their maturity, as well as their obviously profound connection with the dolphins.

Leanna paused before following Kyle and her sister toward the camp, and suggested that they move all of the remaining water bottles into the dolphins' feeding tank, where the water temperature would keep them much cooler. Kyle praised her for coming to such a conclusion, confessing, "I wish I'd have thought of that a while ago. We've been drinking warm water when we didn't have to!"

When they finally rejoined the others, everyone was busy with a chore of their own. Mateo, Mia, and Violet were examining the newly recovered equipment with Sinnamon and Jason. DeAngelo and Ravi were rummaging through nearby heaps of debris, collecting large pieces of plastic and metal under the watchful eyes of Victory, who was gathering wood. Despite his exhaustion, Dante used one of the aluminum pails to rid the fire pit of water. There had been little sense in starting the process until the rainfall had diminished. He stood inside the pit, laboriously removing water one bucketful at a time. Violet and Dwayne each grabbed a pail and joined him.

After checking in with Violet, Mateo asked Mia to accompany him on another investigative tour of the area's perimeter. She readily agreed after Kyle promised to help supervise the children. He went to assist Victory in gathering wood and watching over the boys. Leanna and Hanna followed him to the area just northwest of the Reptile House, where Ravi and DeAngelo had begun to amass a collection of plastic and metal from scattered piles of debris.

Mia grabbed her waterlogged walking stick from where she left it the previous night and caught up to Mateo, who was carrying the nylon rope and a long metal pole he had found in the mud. He held the pole at his side and declared to Mia, "This will have to do as a deterrent if we run into any wildlife out there." Mia smiled and said, "I just love your accent… especially the way you say 'dee-TAIR-ent'." She blushed and apologized for blurting out what she was thinking, but he quickly put her at ease in his typical self-deprecating style.

In an exaggerated Latin accent Mateo asked, "Are you prepared to embark upon our *leetle ex-ped-EE-shun*?" For the first time in days, Mia laughed and felt like herself again, if only for a moment.

She searched her soul and admitted to herself that she felt attracted to Mateo and fleetingly imagined a time in the future when they could reunite under much better circumstances. She could not help but wonder whether he felt a similar attraction. Once again though, the harshness of their situation brought her back to reality. A fine mist continued to fall and rolling thunder echoed in the distance. The Sun eventually penetrated and burned away the dark grey clouds. As they headed southwest, Mia fanned the flame of lingering hope within her heart – hope for her family and friends... and for all humankind.

Back at their "home base", Sinnamon and Jason prepared to head out to investigate the other end of the region again. They took one bottle of water to share, before letting the others know they were leaving. "We should be back within an hour," Sinnamon matter-of-factly announced, her back already turned to the group. Jason looked back and admired the way they all seemed to be working independently, yet toward the same goal. The ominous dark wall dominating the background reminded him of how steep the odds were against reuniting with their loved ones anytime soon.

After Sinnamon and Jason headed off to the northwest, Kyle sought out Leanna and Hanna, who had already deposited the remaining water bottles in the feeding tank, and were stacking kindling against the exterior wall of the Reptile House. "Mind if I give you girls a hand?" he asked. Leanna indicated her acceptance by shoving a bundle of loose sticks against his midsection without losing stride. "Oomph! Th... thanks, Leanna... I think," he mumbled sarcastically. Hanna chuckled as she walked by to fetch another bundle of wood, while Kyle collected himself and added his wood to the rest of the supply.

The Sun had burned away the remaining clouds and dominated the mid-day sky. Dwayne and Victory helped the two young boys construct a fort from miscellaneous scraps. DeAngelo and Ravi had cleverly assembled a little A-frame structure, and the group was covering the exterior with vegetation they had collected. Kyle and the girls had collected an impressive amount of sticks, twigs, and broken two-by-fours and agreed to take a much-needed break, so they grabbed some water and sat down in a shady nook behind the Reptile House. Dante had exhausted himself bailing water, and had fallen asleep in the shade of *Wormhole Pass*, flat on his back.

Leanna sat upon the wet grass across from Kyle and drank a couple of gulps of water before offering it to him. He took it and immediately handed it to Hanna who was sitting cross-legged next to him. When she returned it to him, Kyle screwed the cap back on and set it behind him, saying, "I think I'll save mine for later." He wiped his brow with the back of his hand and then leaned back on his outstretched arms. After a brief silence, he asked, "Would it be alright if I ask you girls a few questions?"

Both sisters remained silent; still a bit uneasy, surrounded by so many unfamiliar people in the bizarre setting. Kyle reassured them that he would not ask anything "weird", but just wanted to get to know them better. "So much has happened to us all, and it's happened so fast. You've both been very brave throughout this whole... uh... adventure. I've really been impressed with how well you've handled everything, especially as young as you are." The girls listened intently but remained tight-lipped. Kyle tread carefully as he probed for a little background information.

"I'm actually visiting from Pittsburgh. Mia and I grew up there, but she moved away a while ago. I'll probably live there for a long time to come. There's something special about that city that's hard to put into words. Do you live here in San Diego?" Kyle inquired.

Generally more talkative than her sister, Leanna finally felt compelled to open up. "We aren't from around here, but our grandparents live in San Diego. We live with our mother in Reno, Nevada. Do you know where that is?"

"Sure," Kyle replied. "Well, sure. I've seen it on maps and in movies, but have never been there myself. Were you here visiting your grandparents with your Mom?"

Hanna answered this time. "No, Mom had to go to Texas for her job, so we're staying with our grandparents while she's gone. She's supposed to come back on January 2nd and then we're all flying back home together."

"And who did you come to the zoo with the other day?" Kyle gently asked.

Leanna started to sob and Hanna immediately got up, ran to her side, and knelt next to her. She wrapped her arms around Leanna in an attempt to console her. Kyle apologized for upsetting them, explaining that he simply did not know what their situation was. While Leanna gradually composed herself, Hanna spoke for them both. She said, "Our Grandma stayed home that morning because her arthritis was acting up, so Grandpa brought us here. Since his stroke, he uses a cane and needs to rest a lot. He told us to meet him at the entrance but when the storm came we got separated and..."

"It's okay... it's okay," Kyle stated in his most reassuring voice. "I know what happened after that. If your grandfather was at the entrance, he probably got out because they evacuated everyone right before the earthquake hit."

"We don't know for sure if he made it out or not, so we're really worried about him... *and* our mother," Leanna said in a weak voice.

"You mean you're worried for him and your grandmother, right? You said your mom's in Texas, didn't you?"

With a sense of resignation, Leanna replied, "No, we're worried about our mother, too. The earthquakes are happening *everywhere*... you didn't know that?

Kyle felt like someone had just kicked him in the stomach. He knew these girls were psychically tapped into some indescribably rich network. Her tone told him it was most likely fact rather than a figment of their collective imagination. He had worked with enough children possessing similar intuitive abilities to know he would be foolish not to respect what they said. Leanna's comment had him feeling sick with concern; not only for his family, friends and the children with whom he worked so closely, but also for the fate of the world.

He almost did not want to pose the question, but felt he had to. "Girls... exactly how widespread *are* these earthquakes?"

Leanna resisted eye contact with Kyle and instead silently stared at the glistening blades of grass at her side, the droplets of moisture sparkling in the sunlight. Following an uncomfortable silence, Hanna answered for the two of them: "Australia, Russia, China, Japan, and across Europe... they're happening everywhere."

A chill enveloped his entire body before the last syllable registered with Kyle. "*Everywhere...*" He repeated the word, perhaps hoping that in doing so it would not sound as bad. It only seemed more horrible, however, as he considered what it could mean if it proved to be true. It led him to ask another question of the two mysterious girls.

"Did you both know Violet before all this happened?" He was not quite sure what prompted him to ask the question, but as soon as he saw Leanna's expression, he understood.

I Miss Your Purple Hair

"In a way… we kind of did," she replied. "We knew she was part of *The Web*, but didn't really know her by name. It's hard to explain."

Kyle thought about what she said. "You mean you didn't make the connection right away when you met her here? Is that because your relationship in *The Web* is purely on a psychic level and it's very different when you're together physically? Does that come close to what it's like?"

"Well, sort of," Hanna said. "We know so many in *The Web*, and it's a way different feeling than when you meet someone in this world. Here, it's all about things like hair color and physical size and stuff like that. In *The Web*, it's about ideas and a different kind of communication – you know... without words."

"Now you're losing me a bit," Kyle admitted. "When you say 'without words'… that confuses me. Don't you still need words to communicate telepathically?"

Leanna fielded his question, responding thoughtfully, "It's hard to describe. We communicate in thoughts, but not in words the same way we do when we speak. It's kind of like looking at a whole paragraph and knowing what it says without having to read one word at a time, if that makes sense to you."

Hanna chipped in with, "Yeah, that's pretty good. It's a lot like that, I guess." In hope of clarifying a bit more for Kyle, she added, "We probably walk right by hundreds of people we know from *The Web*, but unless you're projecting at the time, you might never have any idea who you're walking past."

"Projecting?" Kyle asked. "You mean, sending out communications? Is that the idea?"

"Yeah," Hanna replied. "If you're just walking around, talking with your friends or something, you can walk right by people you might know in *The Web*, but you don't make the connection because neither one of you is projecting at the time. Makes sense, right?"

Kyle hesitantly agreed. "Yeah, I guess I follow what you're saying. So, you and Violet didn't have any idea you'd wind up here together the other day. It just happened, by some strange coincidence."

"Yep," Leanna succinctly answered, as a light breeze played with her hair and helped dry her wet clothing.

Kyle felt strangely satisfied with their answers and knew he had just received a valuable lesson in the use of *The Web*. His thoughts turned to the natural disasters that, according to the Armstrong sisters, were sweeping the planet. He feared for his family and considered what the outside world might look like if and when they ever got out of their forced confinement. He looked at the eerily identical sisters and felt impressed by their intelligence, maturity and above all else – their connectivity to the universe. They seemed to absorb *everything*, connected to the energy within every living thing. Kyle recognized that the dynamic combination of their superior intellect and heightened psychic awareness opened up endless possibilities for them.

"So, you're both connected with hundreds of other young people in *The Web* you've described, right?" Kyle asked both girls.

"Yeah… maybe thousands, actually," Leanna mused.

Kyle felt intrigued to probe further. "What's the point of it all, besides the social interaction? I mean, is there some shared purpose or common thread that ties you together?"

His question struck a nerve with Hanna, who quickly replied, "We've kind of known this was coming for a long time now. We knew we would see it happen, but didn't know exactly *when*."

"You mean… the earthquakes? You *knew* they were coming?" Kyle asked incredulously.

"Uh huh," Hanna answered. "We spread the word around *The Web* and have been talking about it for about a year, I guess. We've been talking about what we might have to do afterwards, too."

"And what is that?" Kyle asked somewhat apprehensively.

Hanna looked him directly in the eyes and rather somberly replied, "Rebuild."

Leanna offered her opinion on the notion of rebuilding. "There are thousands of people in *The Web*… maybe a lot more than we realize and just like any large group, there are lots of different attitudes and opinions. Not everyone agrees on what to do. We need to have strong leadership or else we'll fail – and we can't let that happen."

"Are the two of you part of this leadership you're referring to?"

"No, not really," Hanna said. "We aren't that type."

"Is Violet one of those people?"

"All signs point to yes," Leanna shot back wryly.

Hanna's tentative smile reflected her approval of her sister's playful remark. Leanna added, "Violet can say things in a certain way that gets people to care. A lot of people already seem to listen to what she says."

More thunder off to the west heralded the return of the first of the two exploration parties, dragging themselves back from their latest fact-finding tour. The temperature had steadily risen into the high 80s, and Sinnamon and Jason returned exhausted and dehydrated. The two girls and Kyle all jumped to their feet to find out what they had discovered.

Slamming her spear to the ground, Sinnamon exclaimed, "Fucking hell! We're wasting our time with all this useless searching. It's hopeless! There's just no damn way… why keep kidding ourselves?"

Mateo and Mia returned just at that moment, and reconvened with the rest of the survivors, who had intercepted Sinnamon and Jason. Violet ran across the muddy ground to her father's side and asked what he and Mia had discovered. Mateo shook his head dejectedly, wearing an apologetic expression, while Mia fought back tears of disappointment.

Bathed in sunlight, Mia's beautiful blue-white aura was once again obvious to Violet, who had begun to regard her as beneficent. She looked into the angular woman's aquamarine eyes and felt more closely connected than before.

'I wonder if she was brought here to be Papa's angel.'

After disappointing reports by the two fact-finding teams, it was clear to everyone that there was simply no hope of successfully scaling any of the walls along the borders. The recent rainfall had rendered *Mudslide Mountain* a completely impassable mass of muck, providing no way to get a foothold. With *White Wolf Peak*, over to the west, the main obstacle was its sheer height. Its fragile, crumbling face dispelled any notion of scaling it. Due to its makeup of asphalt and jagged rock, *The Cliffs of Insanity* to the south were simply too steep. The wall was angled in such a way that, without proper climbing equipment, there was no way to ascend more than halfway to the summit.

Adding to the frustration of the survivors, there was no evidence that the recent tremors had created any new opportunities to exploit. Though dejected, Mateo was relieved to be reunited with Violet. He looked at his watch, which seemed to be functioning normally again, to learn that it was 2:22 p.m. Upon making eye contact with his daughter, he recalled carrying her limp, unconscious body in his arms, only a short time ago. He also reflected upon the fruitless search he and Mia had just conducted.

While he and Mia stopped to take a brief water break during their exploration, he was presented with a beautiful, yet disturbing vision. When the growing heat and humidity compelled them to take a five-minute respite, they sat upon an enormous boulder half-buried in the ground behind the Wegeforth Bowl. Mia closed her weary eyes and urged Mateo to do the same in an effort to gather strength through meditation. After pouring a small amount of their bottled water onto his forehead and irritated eyes, he shut them and tried to envision a better day – filled with the peace of mind he so craved.

He quickly scanned his memories and selected the time he and Violet had paid their very first visit to Martin Luther King Park. In the image restored in his mind, Violet had just returned to where he sat upon a red blanket sprawled out beneath a towering palm tree...

The cloudless sky was a brilliant blue, and the gentle breeze was laced with a pleasant floral scent. Over the crest of a subtle hill, Violet approached, returning from her latest curiosity-driven romp; this one, to check out a cluster of yellow and orange butterflies hovering over a patch of lavender and purple flowers.

As she slowly appeared over the crest of the green mound, her two arms were fully outstretched. With her palms held open to the Sun, in each hand a butterfly fluttered its gossamer wings. In her right palm lit a large, yellow swallowtail and in the other, a magnificent orange Monarch. The two delicate creatures appeared content to remain in her hands while the barefoot teenager walked toward her father. Mateo relished the awe-inspiring sight of his daughter communing with Nature on such an intimate level. Much like him, she was someone animals always gravitated to; most likely because they sensed they were completely safe in her presence.

Mateo basked in the soothing memory and a sense of tranquility gradually replaced helplessness and dread. The cherished memory had been faithfully accurate to the moment when Violet and her fluttering adornments approached from the top of the little emerald-green hill. Then, quite unexpectedly, the mental image shimmered and transformed. At first, the memory seemed only slightly altered and he imagined that he had subconsciously embellished it – as we often do with fond recollections. But then, it became obvious something altogether different was happening and that the fundamental imagery had somehow become distorted...

As Violet approached, he saw that a milky white-blue glow enveloped her entire body, from head to feet. The pulsating aura was not only sparkling as if sprinkled with tiny reflective crystals, but she was no longer walking. Instead, Violet levitated a foot or two above the lush grass at the top of the hill, just twenty feet in front of him.

I Miss Your Purple Hair

She ceased moving at the hill's apex; arms still fully extended to each side, when suddenly, more butterflies gravitated to her from the open field behind her. There were dozens, of many sizes and colors, and some flitted about one hand while the rest danced over the other. Suspended above ground, the glowing aura surrounded Violet and the fragile living wonders. The multicolored creatures were content to flutter over her palms in a cheerful celebration of life. Mateo was awestruck as he basked in the intensely beautiful, albeit mysteriously altered memory... until it unexpectedly changed once again.

Violet remained fixed in the same pose while her entire body slowly ascended in stunning fashion. She rose more than six feet off the ground, still accompanied by the fluttering, colorful congregation. Immersed in the vision, Mateo savored the surreal image of his only child suspended in front of the blue backdrop with the butterflies dancing at her fingertips. And then... an unsettling feeling replaced the sense of wonderment as he felt he was losing connection and thereby his ability to protect his daughter.

'How can I protect you if you're out of reach? What if I can't get to you when you need me?'

Mateo felt overwhelmed by fear. He realized he knew no way to get her back down to Earth. He had lost touch with reality and was adrift in an illusion created by his subconscious fears... or perhaps by some external force. He had no way of knowing where the memory left off and something altogether different took over. All he knew was the gut-wrenching angst of being powerless to protect his daughter... and that was intolerable.

'You belong with me, Violet. Come back to me. Come back!'

He partially emerged from the dreamlike memory, literally shouting, "Come back ... Come back!", before a warm hand on his wrist finally brought him all the way back. Mia had forced his return by vigorously shaking him.

"You're okay. You just had a bad dream or something," she speculated.

"I know," Mateo sighed. "We're all stuck in the bad dream together... but it's time we wake up."

△△△

CHAPTER TWENTY
Strung Out and Feeling Brave

"The entire universe is a great theater of mirrors, a set of hieroglyphs to decipher; everything is a sign, everything harbors and manifests mystery. The principles of contradiction, of excluded middle, and of linear causality are supplanted by those of resolution, of included middle, and of synchronicity."
~ Alice A. Bailey, Esoteric Psychology II

By 4:15 p.m., frustration was running high in camp. With the cloud cover burned away, the sky sported a scorching yellow Sun that drove the temperature beyond 85 degrees. The water supply was as dangerously low as everyone's spirits, yet the ground was so saturated, any pieces of wood left outdoors were waterlogged.

Ravi and DeAngelo holed up inside their homemade "fort", which turned out to be an impressive structure: a sturdy little A-frame complete with a thatched roof of palm fronds and other organic materials. They had used anything they could find to lash the pieces together and had managed to secure the building to a pair of tree trunks, a broken metal fence post, and a protruding pillar of rock jutting up from below the Earth's surface. Now that the heat had transformed their humble sanctuary into a convection oven, they asked if they could cool themselves in the dolphin tank again.

"Let's hold off on that," Victory told them. "After we organize the wood and get the fire started, we can all go in the water to stay cool." Dwayne seconded her sentiments and suggested that the boys drink a few sips of water and then help carry some of the smaller pieces of wood over to the fire pit. DeAngelo spoke for both of them and agreed to help build the fire. He felt very grown up, taking charge and trying to inspire his younger comrade to contribute just like the adults.

He proudly declared, "We can find more kindling wood, too! I saw a bunch near the place where we saw those hummingbirds. Let's take a drink and then start collecting wood, okay?" Ravi fed off DeAngelo's enthusiasm and pledged to help him gather all the wood they could find. They each took a gulp from their dirt-coated water bottle before scampering off.

Dante ended his brief break and started bailing water from the pit again. Without so much as a word, Sinnamon grabbed one of the other silver pails and joined him in the middle of the steamy quagmire. They stood back-to-back, evicting the remaining water from the ten-foot-wide indentation in the soil. The Sun beat down mercilessly while, in the distant northwest, a heavy rumble sounded like more thunder, yet was somehow different. Within mere seconds, a wave of tremors vibrated beneath them, creating concentric rings on the surface of the water surrounding Dante and Sinnamon's legs.

"Another quake on the way?" Sinnamon nervously asked. "Felt really weird..."

Dante sighed heavily and hung his head. "Jesus... this just keeps gettin' better, doesn't it? This isn't good. We'll probably get more tremors, and I wouldn't be surprised if another big quake comes through here. That's how it usually goes anyway."

Mia checked on the third silver pail set next to the Reptile House, to see how much rainwater had been collected. It was full to overflowing when she picked it up and the underground vibrations almost knocked her off her feet. Mateo had just exited the building, and arrived just in time to steady her and prevent the water from spilling. "Whoa," Mia exclaimed. "What the heck was that?"

Mateo replied, "Don't know for sure. It sounded like thunder off in the distance, and then the wave of tremors came through. It seems to have calmed down already, though."

Mia steadied herself and said, "I figure we can keep a reserve of rain water inside the building and use it to fill our bottles. Do we have to boil it? I'm not much of a camper, I guess."

Mateo smiled and considered what a pleasant woman she was. She projected intelligence, humility, and gentle humor despite the dire circumstances. He felt a boost to his own energy whenever in close proximity to her. In answer to her question, he replied, "Yeah, we have to boil it. The sky smells of acid and sulfur, and these pails were stored under the tank with God knows what else. Once we get a fire going, we can start boiling and bottling water. It was a good idea to collect the rain when we had the chance. I'll get the other pails when they finish bailing out the pit, so we can clean them out and fill them too."

Leanna and Hanna started bringing wood to the area behind the pit while Dante and Sinnamon finished ridding it of muddy water. Finally cleared, they tossed the pails aside and staggered over to a patch of thinned-out grass to collapse from exhaustion. They both flopped on their backs and tried to catch their breath. The constant pain in Dante's knee was somewhat masked by numbness. Sinnamon looked at his heaving chest, impressed at his willingness to fight through his discomfort.

"You did good, getting that shit out of there almost single-handedly," she eked out, between heavy breaths.

Dante's head ached as much as his knee, a direct result of toiling under the blazing Sun while already dehydrated. "I'm... done," he rasped. "The fire's our best hope ... our only hope..."

Sinnamon agreed, "Totally. There's gotta be some rescue operation going on out there. If we can generate enough smoke, they're bound to spot it – from the ground or the air. Weird... there hasn't been even one plane or helicopter since this all started. The airport must've been hit hard, too... and maybe the Naval Base..."

Although Dante hoped to catch a second wind, he was completely spent, due to lack of nourishment and water. He shut his eyes tightly in reaction to the Sun's intensity, and tried his best to think clearly. His thoughts, though, were scattered and unrelated to what Sinnamon was saying. His mind wanted to shut down and he drifted into semi-consciousness, thinking about loved ones and wondering how he ever wound up in the mess he was in.

Dante's thoughts leapt from childhood memories of sitting on his mother's lap to the ordeal with Aaron Kemper just two days earlier. As he drifted in and out of consciousness, he inadvertently spoke. "... They'll blame me ... can't let you do that ...," he mumbled. Sinnamon could barely make out the words but her curiosity was piqued. She surmised he was reliving the episode with Aaron; the topic everyone else had been avoiding. She had wanted to ask him about it several times, but the urgency of their situation always served to distract. She suspected there had to be more to the story, and curiosity had always gotten the best of Rebecca Sinclair.

She rose on one elbow and listened intently to Dante, only a couple of feet away. He mumbled, "... fool... we're all gonna die here..."

Sinnamon demanded, "What was that? Who are you talking too?"

Though semiconscious, he perceived her question and eventually managed a one-word response: "Kemper..." His eyelids fluttered wildly and a scowl came over his sunburned, swollen face as he repeated himself, "Kemper..."

Sinnamon sensed his anguish, and gathered he had been agonizing over what had happened on the other side of *Wormhole Pass*. Another low, drawn-out rumble from the northwest startled both of them. "What'd you say?" Dante asked in delayed reaction to her prior question. He was so exhausted, he could barely force his eyes open. She girded herself for his reaction, uncertain whether he would take offense to the question.

"Who were you talking to? Was it Kemper?" she timidly inquired. Dante's brow furrowed and his jaw clenched, leading Sinnamon to regret posing the question. He breathed in deeply and tried to relax his facial muscles. Finally, he began to speak, still lying flat on his back, his face fully exposed to the Sun's searing heat.

"The bastard... was ... losin' it. I mean, really losin' his mind," he slowly divulged in a monotone growl. His throat was dry and parched, causing his voice to sound deeper and that much more ominous as he related details never before shared. He continued, "He had a gun... his own gun, hidden inside his jacket. When I said I was leaving him to join you and the others, he freaked out."

Dante rolled onto his side and reluctantly opened his eyes so he could be sure no one else was listening, for reasons only he knew. Something about Sinnamon's demeanor appealed to him. He trusted her for reasons he did not fully understand, so he continued with his story. Sinnamon sensed his pain and sympathized that he had been transformed from a gregarious young man into a broken and beaten shell.

"It was when I threw the money back in his face that he really got pissed. That was a huge insult, I guess. I was just sure we were killing ourselves for nothing, trying to climb that ridiculous wall. Way too steep and high... there was no way in hell anyone could scale that thing, but he was too pigheaded... or desperate... to admit it. I think he felt he could buy his way out of any shit he fell into. Well, I wasn't in the mood to risk my ass trying anymore. So, I told him I was done and started to climb down when he pulled his little silver pistol on me. That's when I threw the cash in his face... and he deliberately kicked my injured knee – the bastard."

Though she listened intently, Sinnamon maintained a stoic countenance. Dante swallowed hard and then continued. "I fell onto my back and hit the ground like a ton of bricks. I think I might've blacked out for a minute, and when I looked up he was straddling me and pointing the gun in my face. The money was blowing in the breeze all around us. It was quite a scene to wake to. He told me to get up and said we were climbing if it killed us... and I felt that's what would've happened if we kept pushing it. He was in no shape for that, and my knee was ... well, you know."

Dante grimaced just thinking about the agony in his knee, and reliving the incident only brought the pain to the surface once again. Sinnamon finally asked, "What'd you do then?" While she could see it was difficult for him to finally divulge the truth, she could also tell he needed to get it off his chest.

"You were all out of range by then. He told me to get to my feet, and I tell you it hurt like hell – but when someone has a gun in your face, you'll do some amazing shit. I couldn't believe what was happening, to tell the truth. I knew there was no way I was gonna be able to climb on this leg. I pretended to go along with it for a few minutes, dragging my lame ass in front of him while he pressed the gun into my back. There just weren't any footholds, though. We barely made any progress when the distraction I was hoping for happened."

"What was that?" Sinnamon asked.

"That … wolf. Remember that white wolf we spotted? It must have been curious about the commotion and showed up at the base of the wall. When it flashed into view, it spooked us and Kemper turned to see what it was. As soon as I felt him turn, I reached around and grabbed the gun out of his hand. He never knew what hit him, and fell backwards... all the way down. That's really what killed him. I lied before... when I said he shot himself. I guess I didn't want to be held responsible for what happened."

Sinnamon was not sure what to believe, after the conflicting stories involving Aaron Kemper. "So, he's really dead, right?"

"Yeah," Dante answered brusquely.

"But he accidentally fell when the wolf scared him, so it wasn't your fault. If anything, it was totally his doing, since he forced you to climb after you told him the deal was off. You shouldn't feel any guilt over it," Sinnamon added, as if to provide some sense of closure for Dante.

"Yeah well...," he added. "It's not that easy. You kind of had to be there."

Sinnamon was concerned not to upset him with too much probing, but felt the urge to ask more questions. "So, the wolf is still roaming around over there? And you're sure there's no sense in us going back and trying to get to the parking lot that way, right?"

"Uh, yeah... the wolf ran off when Kemper fell, but it's definitely still over there and it's a huge animal. Trust me; I kept my gun drawn the whole time I was trying to catch up to you, even when I was in the passage. And there's no way in Hell anyone could climb that *Kemper's Folly*... no way. Believe me; no one wants out of here more than me. If I thought there was a remote chance we could get out that way, I'd have suggested it long ago.

The fires were all to the east and north, too. They're eventually going to reach that area, unless the rain completely kills them off."

"One more thing," Sinnamon added. "Where's Kemper's gun?"

Dante hesitated for a second before succinctly replying, "I dropped it somewhere in that wormhole tunnel. It fell into a deep gap near the entrance." Satisfied that she had helped him purge some guilt, Sinnamon offered to fetch drinking water from the nearby building. As she walked away, she felt he was still emotionally distraught, but since it was impossible to know what was going on within his troubled mind, her focus shifted to moving ahead with the plan to construct a massive fire.

Sinnamon brushed past Victory and Leanna as they carried bundles of kindling to the edge of the pit where Mia, Mateo, Kyle, and Violet were preparing the fire. They had been scrounging for every scrap of dry kindling and managed to scrape together a meager amount. Little by little, they strategically arranged the larger pieces of wood around the kindling. Kyle splashed a small amount of the remaining gasoline over the wood and then stashed the container behind the Reptile House. Finally, at 5:20 p.m., Mateo used his lighter to ignite the fire.

Jason had just finished digging a trench around the entire pit, using one of the spades recovered from the storage room. The air temperature was over 90 degrees and the breeze had withered to the point where it provided no relief. While transporting a bundle of wood, Violet suddenly felt unsteady on her feet and dropped to one knee near the towering fire. Her faltering movement caught Mateo's eye and he immediately ran to her.

As he knelt beside her and wrapped his arm around her shoulder, she seemed especially frail. "Are you okay?" he asked.

Downplaying her weakened condition, she replied, "Yeah, I'm fine. Maybe I breathed in some smoke from the fire... that's all. It made my head feel funny."

Mateo lovingly lifted her chin to peer into her brown eyes and, despite her forced smile, could tell something was wrong. The usual sparkle was absent and she was having trouble keeping her eyelids open. Lack of sleep and nourishment obviously played a part, but she was showing signs of after-effects from what was most likely a concussion. He recalled the dream in which Violet seemed to be floating, her entire body shrouded in a corona of glowing white energy. Suddenly, a new level of concern for his child formed.

'I can't fail her. There has to be something I can do.'

Strung Out and Feeling Brave

He helped her to her feet and they slowly moved toward the dolphin tank, away from the burgeoning heat of the fire. Mateo glanced over his shoulder to see everyone else was following their lead, eager to cool themselves in the soothing water. DeAngelo and Ravi sprinted past the others, both coated in a fine layer of red dirt and mud. They had been so focused on building their makeshift fort; they had not realized that the Sun turned it into a kiln.

Ravi stopped abruptly when something on the ground commanded his attention. He picked up a shiny object from the patch of grass and mud and then caught up to DeAngelo, who had joined Mateo and Violet near the now-familiar tank. He displayed the object in his outstretched hand and proudly exclaimed, "I found something! Look!" DeAngelo shrugged his shoulders to indicate how unimpressed he was. Violet felt sorry for Ravi, dejected by his friend's lack of enthusiasm, but was genuinely curious to see what he was holding in the palm of his dirty little hand. She leaned in closer to see for herself and the little boy with the red dust sprinkled over his jet-black hair eagerly showed her.

The object was a simple ring of some kind, and the Sun glinted off its silver exterior. Upon closer inspection, it clearly was a utilitarian band of unpolished metal and not a piece of jewelry, as Violet first thought. She softly asked, "Can I hold it?" and without any hesitation, Ravi dropped the object into her open palm. Holding it closer, she surmised it was one of the zoo animals' identification bands. The small strip of metal, open on one end; bore a short numerical sequence of numbers followed by some letters, all etched into its outer surface.

Violet realized her vision was blurred when she tried in vain to read the various characters and numbers inscribed into the metal. She held it up to her father's face so he could read it. "It says… '0812-PFM-AADESH'," Mateo said. "This must have fallen off one of the animals. It's so small – that would be the only thing I can think of that would make sense, right?"

Violet blinked her eyes repeatedly, but still could not focus her vision. She said, "It must've fallen off our peacock! He was in that same area when I scared him off earlier. Do you think that's his name: Aadesh?... sounds like it could be."

Ravi laughed in response to her comment and Violet asked what he thought was so funny. He giggled, "Aadesh is my cousin's name. That's funny… the peacock has the same name as him!"

When Violet attempted to return the little metal band to him, Ravi said, "You can keep it. I'm going in the water with the dolphins again! It's too hot out here and I want to wash this dirt off." She looked at the inscription again, but simply could not focus enough to read the tiny words.

"Papa, why can't I read this?" she innocently asked.

Mateo guessed she was unable to focus due to dehydration or some residual damage from her concussion. "Do you feel sick to your stomach, baby?" he hesitantly asked.

"A little... but, why...?"

"Just drink this and we'll get you in the water to cool down," he firmly stated. "I want you to finish the entire bottle. We need to get your body temperature down. I don't want you near the fire, but in the water, okay? And I'll stay with you until you get your strength back."

Violet insisted, "I'm fine... *really*. I just got a little woozy in the Sun 'cause I haven't really had enough to drink today. Once I have some water I'm sure I'll feel fine." He knew it was her style to downplay illnesses or injuries, so he could not blindly accept that she was alright. Mateo pulled the plastic bottle from his back pocket and was ready to hand it to her when Leanna called out from atop the platform surrounding the dolphin tank.

"Here! Give her this water instead; it's a lot cooler!" she exclaimed as she tossed a wet bottle their way. Mateo caught it and immediately thanked Leanna for her thoughtfulness. The bottle felt considerably cooler in his warm hand and he quickly gave it to Violet. She eagerly removed the cap and began to drink; slow sips at first, quickly followed by large gulps. She drank her fill and then handed the half-empty bottle to her father, who refused it.

"Vi, you need to finish it. We still have more and can ration it. You're showing signs of dehydration and I want you to finish this... for my sake, please?" She knew not to argue when he spoke in that tone, so she nodded and smiled before downing the remaining water. Mateo kissed her forehead as he took the empty bottle from her. "We'll save all the empties, and when we boil the rain water we can pour it into bottles so it's more comfortable to drink."

Slightly rejuvenated, Violet remarked, "That's my Pops... always thinkin'!" Mateo and Violet shared a laugh over her comment and then climbed up onto the platform surrounding the tank. Tidus and Yuna swam in tandem, lazily patrolling the perimeter. They seemed to be conserving their energy while enjoying the fact that the familiar hum of the filtration system had returned and the water was circulating in the customary manner.

Before long, the raging fire became a towering mass of swirling orange and red reaching into the angry sky. The prevailing winds mercifully carried the billowing light-grey smoke away from the dolphin tank and toward the northeast. The band of survivors prayed it would quickly draw the attention of rescuers. Most everyone was soon submerged in the cool, swirling water – either frolicking with the dolphins, or contentedly soaking away accumulated dirt. Most importantly, the water restored some of the precious energy sapped by the heat. Only Violet and Mateo remained on the platform, stripping down to minimal clothing in preparation for joining the others.

Mateo was still concerned that Violet had not yet shaken the cobwebs from her mind so he asked if she would prefer to just dangle her feet in the water rather than go all the way in. In typical style, she immediately answered, "I'm fine. I want to swim with the dolphins again. It might be my last chance." Before her father could question her decision, she dropped into the water and disappeared below the surface. At first, the cool water provided a shocking, yet welcome contrast to the searing heat of the late afternoon. Violet's waif like body slowly sank until the sore soles of her feet touched down on the bottom of the pool's shallow end.

The filter's engines hummed below her and the mechanism sent tingling vibrations into her toes and through her entire body. Air bubbles rose and enveloped her amidst the dark liquid depths. She opened her eyes and looked up through the water at the shimmering form of her father, still frozen in place atop the deck. A rush of movement in her peripheral vision compelled Violet to turn toward the tank's deep end. Tidus and Yuna approached rapidly, and were suddenly within arm's length.

A momentary sense of fear was quickly replaced by awe and then by the irrepressible urge to touch them. Floating inches from Tidus' nose, she reached out and gently stroked the top of his head. Yuna circled around behind Violet and softly brushed her back with a flipper as she glided by, to extend a gentle greeting. As the pair of dolphins hovered nearby, a unique connection began to form. Violet's first thought was that their psychic rapport felt very similar to what she shared with Leanna and Hanna. She felt a sense of trust and acceptance, so it seemed completely natural when she grasped Tidus' dorsal fin with her right hand.

As though connected by an invisible mind tether, Tidus took Violet on an exhilarating tour of their watery domain. Cool water rushed through her hair while a dazzling array of bubbles tickled her cheeks and neck. She marveled at the physical power of the young dolphin, and was even more amazed by his obvious mental capacity. They became psychically intertwined – so much so, that the inability to verbalize thoughts proved no barrier whatsoever. In fact, there would have been no benefit to spoken words.

I Miss Your Purple Hair

As they glided around the far end of the pool and headed back toward the shallow area, Violet noted how the Sun's rays pierced the water's surface and created glimmering shafts of gold for them to swim through. She perceived Tidus' exhilaration as he wove between the beams of diffused sunlight. Soaring through the watery realm on the back of the playful creature, Violet felt a sense of unity that extended well beyond the immediate experience – she felt connected to the entire Universe. Her thoughts turned to her father, who had jumped into the water just ahead, ready to intercept her.

'Papa, we have to survive this... and do what we can to help the world recover.'

She clearly heard his reply in her mind: *'We will survive, baby. We'll do whatever it takes to get home safe.'*

As Tidus delivered Violet to Mateo's waiting arms, she realized this was the first time she and her father's thoughts wove together so distinctly. It was a breakthrough; a moment she would cherish forever – even beyond her lifetime on Earth.

Violet had never before held her breath for such an extended period, and was gasping for air when Mateo lifted her from the water. He held her in his strong arms, pressing her close to his bare chest, and then eased her onto the platform tethered to the framework at the tank's shallow end, where she continued to recover.

"Whoa, what an awesome ride!" she finally gushed, as soon as she was capable of speaking again.

Mateo pulled himself up onto the platform alongside her as Tidus and Yuna splashed them both with little bursts of water. "Hey, knock it off!" Violet jokingly admonished. The dolphins clearly felt more comfortable and connected with Violet than with anyone else, and they were extending another invitation to play. Her eyes sparkled and her smile broadened as she waved them off, still trying to catch her breath after her exhilarating underwater romp. "Maybe later, guys. I need to rest for a while," she reluctantly admitted.

Mateo rubbed her shoulders and asked if she was warm enough. She quickly reassured him that she was comfortable, but was feeling very tired and light-headed. He wanted to say he did not approve of her exerting herself, but knew she was smart enough to gauge her own limitations. He did suggest she relax for a while on the platform while they observed the younger children splashing about with the dolphins. She readily agreed, realizing she was not strong enough to press the issue. The lingering after-effects of her concussion contributed to her overall light-headedness, and she understood the need to conserve her strength.

Mia had been treading water in the middle of the tank, enjoying Violet's excursion with the male dolphin. She swam over and hoisted herself onto the platform next to Mateo. He noticed how beautiful her light-blonde hair looked, coated in droplets of water. Mia touched Violet on the wrist and gushed, "I've never seen anything quite like that."

Violet was puzzled. "Like what?" she asked.

"The thing you did with the dolphins," Mia explained. "I've never seen such a magical moment as that. It was as if you've known them forever and done that a thousand times before. Do you always have such a magical way with animals?"

Violet pondered the question briefly before answering, "I don't think of them as animals."

Confused, Mia asked, "The dolphins?"

"Yeah, but I mean *all* animals. I don't think of them as animals, really. It helps to forget the differences between us, just like I try to do with people."

While Mia tried to understand, she was not sure she fully comprehended Violet's approach. She asked, "So, you really don't think of animals as being much different than us?"

"Well... *we're* animals, after all... and I believe we all have souls. So, no... I don't see much of a barrier between us. The only thing that separates us is fear and prejudice, and that goes both ways."

"What do you mean?"

"I mean, if I approach a dog and it starts to snarl or growl at me, I understand that fear and mistrust are what's making it hostile. Obviously, animals tend to lash out when they feel threatened or are starving."

Mia was puzzled. "What's that got to do with what we're talking about?"

Violet explained further, "I guess I've learned to look beyond the surface with people *and* with animals. I always assume we can connect on a deeper level, and that makes it much easier to form some type of bond. We speak in a special language."

Mia was fascinated. "And what type of language is that?"

Without hesitation Violet answered, "A language without words."

I Miss Your Purple Hair

"I wish I could learn how to speak that language," Mia mused.

Violet smiled and said, "You already know it, but just need to learn to rely on it more. I'm sure I can help you, if you want. Maybe after we get out of here and things settle down, we can hang out and I'll explain it better."

Mia felt an unwelcome chill and a lump in her throat, reminded of how badly she missed her normal life. What's more, she truly feared they might never find a way out. "I'd really like that," was all she said in response.

Just then, Leanna called to Violet and asked if she would join her at the opposite end of the tank to play with the dolphins. All of the younger children were gathered there, along with Dwayne, Victory, and Sinnamon, who was snapping photographs. Realizing her father was concerned about her stamina and overall well-being, Violet asked, "Papa... if I stay on the deck, can I go over where they are?" She flashed a subdued smile and admitted, "I promise to stay out of the water. I just want to play with the dolphins and everyone else for a few more minutes. Then I'll come back to you." Mateo agreed, reminding her to keep a healthy distance from the water as she walked around the far side of the deck. Mia slid a few inches closer to Mateo as they watched Violet walk away.

By now, it was obvious to everyone there was a growing attraction between Mia and Mateo. Mateo splashed a little water from the tank on his head so that it dripped down his back and chest. Mia admired his strong jaw and piercing eyes while they sat side-by-side with their legs in the water. Mateo pulled his attention away from his daughter and the others and turned his focus to the charming woman at his side. Their rapport had swiftly developed and he felt a growing urge to confide in her.

Mateo asked in total sincerity, "How are you holding up?"

Mia reflected on their bizarre ordeal and realized how strange it was to be sitting pool side with Mateo amid the ongoing threat of more tremors. She felt she should be more worried, but Mateo's quiet confidence helped keep her fears in check. She blurted out, "I wish I could be more like you."

"In what way?" Mateo asked with a smirk. "Do you mean... intriguing and sexy... or sunburned and sore?"

Mia laughed and then playfully punched him in the upper arm. "Well, maybe you're *all* those things, but I meant something else." She paused for a moment and looked wistfully across the tank, where Kyle had just jumped into the water. She continued, "The way you are with Veronica. I've never seen anyone more dedicated to their child. I know how concerned you are for her, especially after she got hurt."

Mateo sat up a little straighter when reminded of his daughter's injury. "What are you getting at?" he asked, as Mia slowly kicked her legs beneath the water's surface.

She continued her thought, "With all that's going on around us and as concerned as you are for Veronica, how do you stay so cool and calm? I mean, I've seen little flare-ups by almost everyone else, but you've managed to keep your wits and have been a quiet leader. You've given most of your water to your daughter... and others... and have never lost your temper or shown fear. How do you do that?"

Mateo replied, "I don't see why you think I stand out. I mean, you've been calm and collected... and Kyle has, too. All of the children have been really amazing."

Mia confessed, "I've broken down and cried a few times, but not when anyone could see. As for my brother – he was born with ice water in his veins. He never shows much in the way of outward emotion, but he's different than you in that way. You seem to be completely in touch with your feelings, and it's apparent that you put on a brave face for the rest of us. It's just an observation, but I think it must take a lot of inner strength to do that. I admire you, is what I'm trying to say."

Her statement made Mateo blush and squirm a bit. He politely replied, "Thank you. I know you're sincere so I have to appreciate your words. But the thing is... I know Violet is tuned in to pretty much whatever I feel, so it's even harder than you realize for me to display what I want her to see. She can see into my mind if I let down my guard, so it's trickier than it appears."

"What do you mean?" Mia asked.

Mateo thoughtfully replied, "Well, you've seen a *little* of Violet's abilities. I remind you though... she's still growing and learning about herself every day. It's getting more and more difficult for me to keep anything from her, because of her ability to connect to my thoughts. Right now, I'm still able to deflect her somewhat. It isn't easy anymore; not like it was a few years back. And, I need to prevent her from knowing everything I'm planning on doing."

Mia was concerned by the suddenly ominous tone in Mateo's voice. She put her soft hand on his forearm and asked, "What are you talking about? I mean... I kind of understand what you mean about Veronica because I've felt it myself. But, what do you mean by 'planning on doing?'"

Mateo sighed and explained, "Mia, the smoke may very well draw some attention, but there are *lots* of fires around this area. It's worth doing, and we had to try it, but the hope that our fire will bring help is a long shot – a pipe dream. I can't stomach waiting any longer, so I'm going to try something else. Please, don't say anything to anyone, especially Violet."

Mia was baffled. "I won't say anything if that's what you want, but what exactly are you thinking of doing?"

Mateo's expression remained very serious as he watched the children splash water on the dolphins. He confessed the rudiments of his plan, confident he could trust Mia to keep it to herself. "I'm a good climber – having climbed many mountains growing up in Costa Rica. There's no way I could drag everyone with me. Alone, I can move very quickly. When everyone's asleep tonight I'm going to go through... uh, what did we call it?... *Wormhole Pass* and find a way out."

Mia protested, "But you don't understand how steep *Kemper's Folly* is! Dante said it's impossible to climb above twenty feet. Besides, that wolf is over there, too... remember? And, it's another day hungrier now. I think we should wait here and see if the smoke brings anyone..."

Mateo interrupted, "Mia; all my instincts tell me this is right. I have to trust those feelings and make at least one more attempt to find out if there's any way out of here. Besides, I think Dante is hiding something and I need to investigate for myself. The latest tremors might have shaken things up on the other side, too. I need to find out... and with us out of food, it might be now or never."

In her heart, Mia knew Mateo was right. She was unaware she had tightened her grip on his wrist while he explained his plan. Mateo playfully said, "You have sharp fingernails... *like a wolf?*" He glanced down at the image on her left thigh, peeking out from beneath her cargo shorts. She released her grip on his arm and raised the material to display the entire tattoo: a white wolf standing proud, and in the background... a full Moon.

Mateo asked the obvious question, "Why a wolf?"

Mia replied, "I've always admired wolves. They're strong... intelligent... and fiercely loyal."

△△△

CHAPTER TWENTY~ONE
Gone to Save Your Tired Soul

*"The whole course of human history may depend on a change of heart in one solitary
and even humble individual - for it is in the solitary mind and soul of the individual
that the battle between good and evil is waged and ultimately won or lost."*
~ M. Scott Peck

Much of the evening of December 30th was spent stoking the fire and replenishing the wood supply. Although a large quantity was exhausted, an adequate amount remained for the next day. Having made it their personal challenge to forage for food and water, DeAngelo and Ravi discovered a few edibles by scouring through previously unexamined debris. After almost two hours of searching, they had managed to find three boxes of animal-shaped crackers, two bottles of water and two small bags of pretzels. They had also uncovered a pair of broken eyeglasses with shattered lenses, three mud-coated children's sneakers (two of which matched), a grimy Los Angeles Dodgers baseball cap and a flattened baby stroller.

Everyone understood the need for rationing, so most of the newly-collected items remained unopened when they prepared to retire to the Reptile House for the evening. Mia and Victory had poured the boiled water into more than a dozen plastic bottles, and placed the supply in the dolphin tank's feeding compartment to keep them cool. At one point in the early evening, Sinnamon combed through the building's tiny office. In addition to the useless computer and desk drawers filled with files, she found several pads of ruled paper, an assortment of pens, a nearly-empty bag of beef jerky, a stained coffee mug and a large, red-and-white First Aid Kit bolted to the wall.

The kit contained the usual gauze, bandages, ointments, anti-inflammatory medication, and an array of anti venom serums in pre-packaged syringes. Once darkness fell, the fire kept the area illuminated, allowing everyone to feel safe – until disturbing sounds emanated from two different directions. Around 9:40 p.m., a prolonged howl came from an elevated point to the northwest. Clearly the baying of a mature wolf, the sound startled everyone. DeAngelo and Ravi burst from their fort and clung to Dwayne and Victory, realizing that a predator was in close proximity. Only minutes later, another wolf answered, this time from the east. The response clearly originated on the other side of *Wormhole Pass.*

The howling sporadically continued; it was obvious the wolves were communicating. Though relatively secure in the glow of the nearby bonfire, the proximity of the animals became unnerving to everyone. Around 10:00 p.m., they agreed to retire to the Reptile House for peace of mind and much-needed sleep. Mateo and Mia used the pails to pour water into the narrow moat they had dug around the fire pit, as a precaution against the fire spreading to nearby vegetation, should the tower of wood topple over.

Physically exhausted, Mateo unintentionally drifted to sleep when he merely intended to rest his eyes. Violet slept soundly, curled up a few feet away. Physically exhausted from swimming and maintaining the fire, everyone in the party was asleep by midnight; everyone, that is... save for one restless soul. Sitting alone in the front room by the fogged-up window, Dante's mind raced a mile a minute, his thoughts a jumbled quagmire. His hunger pangs, coupled with the persistent pain in his leg made it impossible for him to sleep. Even so, his emotional anguish easily trumped his physical exhaustion.

Ravaged by fatigue and injuries, Dante's faith had been put to the ultimate test. He felt isolated, confused and resentful. Amidst feelings of desperation, and despite his determination to forget, his thoughts kept turning to Aaron Kemper. He had lied to the others about what had actually happened two days before, and concerns about the desperate man he left behind plagued him ever since. Shortly after everyone else had fallen asleep in the humid darkness, his guilt drove him to a decision.

In truth, his encounter with Aaron had ended differently than the various versions he told the others. After the two of them had tried in vain to scale the towering obstruction they now referred to as *Kemper's Folly,* Dante had indeed thrown the five thousand dollars back in Aaron's face. That infuriated the arrogant snob and he reacted by kicking Dante's injured knee, resulting in the ejection of his unsecured gun from its holster when he fell on his back. Brandishing the pistol, Aaron forced Dante to get to his feet. The story, as he had told it to Sinnamon, was *nearly* accurate, except for one important detail... Aaron was still alive.

While Dante and Aaron painfully struggled to climb the face of the rock wall, the white wolf made a startling appearance at its base, and its unnerving growl forced Aaron to turn his head. He had been climbing directly behind Dante, with the nose of the pistol pressed into his back for motivation. The moment Aaron was distracted, Dante reacted and regained possession of his weapon.

Contrary to the various stories he told the others, he then punched Aaron squarely in the face, knocking him onto his back on the jagged ridge, nearly 20 feet above ground. The truth was; he left him lying there, unconscious and unprotected against the elements and any other potential threats. At that point, anger and resentment got the best of Dante and all he could think was, "To Hell with Aaron Kemper. The wolf can have him for all I care."

Wedged between uneven rock outcroppings, Aaron remained unconscious for hours and woke to rain pelting his prone body. By that time, Dante had caught up with the others and found shelter off to the west. Ever since, Dante had expected Aaron to emerge through the wormhole... but he never did. He could only imagine that Aaron had either met a tragic fate or succeeded in escaping. In actuality, the fall left him with multiple fractures in his left leg, and he had been struggling for survival ever since.

Despite his bitterness over the entire episode and concern for his own safety, his own unresolved questions surrounding Aaron Kemper finally compelled Dante to take action. At 2:02 a.m. on the morning of December 31st, he stealthily departed the Reptile House and began the arduous ascent back to *Wormhole Pass*. With torch in hand, he willed his pain-riddled body up the uneven face of the massive barrier, and entered the dark passage.

The air was unreasonably hot and humid for the pre-dawn hours, and the stench of sulfur had grown thick like paste. Dante's knee had swollen badly, but the pain was masked by numbness and that allowed him to maneuver, albeit slowly. He carried only a bottle of water, a torch, and his sidearm. Knowing full well he was likely to encounter the wolf or other wildlife, he still felt he had no choice but to set his fears aside in his quest to know what actually happened to Aaron Kemper. Never an ideal motivator, guilt can nonetheless be extremely compelling.

The flickering torchlight danced along the jagged interior walls of the wormhole. The most recent aftershocks had jostled the mountain and slightly shifted aspects of the passageway. Dante feared there might be a false floor that would give way or loose rocks that might come crashing down at any moment. Portions of the twisting passageway had indeed collapsed further, yet Dante managed to make his way through by contorting himself to work over, under and around an assortment of obstacles created by Nature.

The toughest part of his journey came when he had to leap across a chasm separating him from the exit point. With his right leg numb and nearly useless, he feared he might fall short and drop into the dark pit, to his death. He also considered that he would need to twist his body in mid-air to make sure his weight came down on his good leg. Beads of sweat coated his forehead and upper lip as he rehearsed each step in his mind. After a prolonged moment of reflection, he decided he was ready. He adroitly tossed his torch across the divide, where it bounced before flipping and coming to rest on the hard foundation, still providing critically necessary illumination.

Dante felt the surge of adrenaline just before he took four painful, yet determined strides... and launched his exhausted body toward the opposite side of the fissure. With a loud thud, he came crashing down, just barely clearing the divide. The air was loudly expelled from his lungs as he rolled across the hard-packed surface before coming to a rest just inside the point of exit. "Thank you, Jesus," he winced, as he realized how fortunate he was to have cleared the obstacle without further damaging his knee. After he struggled to his feet and retrieved his torch, he vowed that he would never return to the other side. "I'm done," he said aloud to the darkness. "No more Indiana Jones crap for me."

At 3:15 a.m., Mateo woke to an odd feeling that something important had changed. At first, he thought it might have been a fragment of a bad dream when he opened his eyes to the notion that someone was missing. Fearing something had happened to Violet; he instantly broke out in a cold sweat and reached beside himself in the pitch-black surroundings. He was infinitely relieved when his hand made contact with her shoulder. She was comfortably curled up just a foot or two away and the sound of her shallow breathing soothed his worried mind. "Then... who else might've gone outside?" he wondered.

While his eyes slowly adjusted to the darkness inside the building, he took inventory of those he could tell were in the room, sleeping in various poses around the perimeter. In his mind, he ran through the checklist and performed a quick head count. "Violet... Leanna... Hanna... DeAngelo...," he rattled off names in his head as he recognized either their silhouettes or their snoring. "Mia... Kyle... Victory and Dwayne...," he ran through each one as he verified their presence. "Ravi... Jason... "

He realized he had scanned the room completely and was unable to account for anyone else. That meant two people were unaccounted for: Dante and Sinnamon.

'They must be sleeping in another room.'

Able to see just barely enough to move very cautiously, he quietly got to his feet and tiptoed into the hallway to check the Office. No one was there. He slowly stepped between sleeping people and gradually made his way into the foyer, where he spotted a dark mass alone in one corner. Mateo could still barely see, yet his eyes had adjusted as much as possible. He listened to their breathing, but was still unable to identify who was curled up in the corner; that is until he closed his eyes and relaxed. Finally, an image became clear in his mind – it was Sinnamon, in a fetal position on the floor, her back pressed against the concrete wall. She slept with her walking stick clutched to her chest, prepared for the unexpected.

He ran through the impromptu roll call in his mind again and realized that the only missing member of the party was Dante. All of the children were present, which relieved his primary concern. Not knowing most of them very well, he understood that it could have been possible for any of them to be a sleepwalker.

Mateo tried to imagine where Dante might have gone and guessed that he must have had trouble sleeping and gone outside to clear his head. His instincts were screaming there was more to the situation and since he had long ago learned to honor such feelings, he tried to tap into them more completely. Standing at the doorway, he peered out onto the moonlit terrain and allowed his senses to simply absorb the messages embedded in the invisible energy of his surroundings. It took less than thirty seconds for him to understand where Dante had gone.

'He went back to where he left Kemper.'

Mateo had been planning to investigate the place where the ordeal with Aaron had occurred. The story Dante told rang false and he was curious to know what really happened. Aside from that, he wanted to make absolutely certain there was no escape route through that region. He held out some hope, albeit faint, that the tremors had created a new pathway or a means of finally climbing the insurmountable mountain they referred to as *Kemper's Folly.* Convinced that Violet was experiencing ongoing issues related to her concussion; he knew he had to leave her in the safety of the building, determined to return with his findings later in the morning. Suspecting that Dante had already headed through *Wormhole Pass* only bolstered his determination.

'Why would Dante head back there if there was no reason to go?'

Mateo crept back to where his daughter lay sleeping, and crouched on one knee to gently wake her. She groaned softly as he squeezed her shoulder.

"What's going on?" she mumbled in a raspy, half-asleep voice. Her father was accustomed to her clinging to sleep and smiled at her familiar little groan when he kissed her forehead. "Is it really morning already?" she growled under her breath.

Mateo laid his calloused and sore right hand on the middle of her back and leaned in close to avoid waking the others. He felt he had to explain himself to Violet in case something happened to him during his expedition. He would never forgive himself if he left her to wonder and worry. He leaned in close and explained, "It's still night, so you sleep now. I'm going through *Wormhole Pass* to see if Dante needs any help. He went that way a while ago, and I'm worried because of his condition. I was planning on checking things out over there, anyway; so, now at least I'll have company. Okay, Vi?"

The gravity of what her father said forced Violet to wake up a bit, but she struggled to focus due to the residual effects of her concussion. Regardless, she understood what he was proposing. "Papa, why do you have to go now? Let's wait until the Sun comes up. I want to go with you..."

Mateo shushed her and quickly put the thought out of her head. "No, no, no," he whispered. "I won't hear of that. You're in no shape for it and need your sleep. I can go much faster alone. I have to go now because Dante's already halfway there and he might need help. We'll come back together and let everyone know whether anything changed on that side. Promise me you'll rest and keep drinking water while I'm gone," he requested, as he set a bottle of water next to her on the floor. "Besides, I need you to keep an eye on things here until I get back, alright?"

Violet felt uneasy with him leaving in the middle of the night, but her post-concussion cobwebs were clouding her thoughts. She was drained of energy and had a pounding headache, but never mentioned that to her father, wanting to spare him from further worry. As she started to drift back out of consciousness, she offered a weak, "Okay, Papa... be careful. And ... come home safe."

Mateo started for the door when he remembered the paper and pens that had been gathered and piled up on the corner of the large display table behind him. His eyes had adjusted just well enough that he could make out their shapes. He fumbled for a pen and took one of the pads of paper from the stack. Despite being barely able to see what he was writing he scrawled something on the top sheet, quietly flipped it and wrote something else on the next one, too. He set the pad down on the corner of the table and silently worked his way to the front door, where he exited as discreetly as possible. Once out in the open area they referred to as "camp", the air's poisonous content stung his eyes and reminded him that their time was running out.

While curious about Aaron's demise and Dante's condition, he also wanted to make one last ditch effort to find a way out. In his imagination, he foresaw himself standing at the foot of *Kemper's Folly* and discovering something they had missed – a way of escape. Standing near the smoldering ash in the fire pit, Mateo looked at his own hands and was struck by their odd coloration. When he looked to the sky, the cause was obvious. The pregnant Moon now appeared blue-violet and its reflected light draped everything in a rich indigo hue. The irony was not lost on Mateo, who managed a smile as he thought about his daughter and her magical ways.

'It's the beginning of a new day, baby. We're getting out of here; don't worry.'

Whether or not he was imagining it, the determined father "heard" his daughter's reply in his mind, as clearly as if she had been next to him.

'I know we will, Papa. I won't worry anymore.'

Imbued with newfound energy, Mateo quickly prepared for the journey. He was grateful that the Moon's ample illumination made it easier to gather the necessary supplies. He grabbed one of the torches, a coil of yellow nylon rope, and a shovel from near the fire pit. He had the presence of mind to take one of the metal pails and made a spontaneous decision to take a half-empty can of gasoline, thinking there could be vegetation blocking a potential escape route. He slung the rope over his left shoulder and slipped the gas can and the torch into the pail. With a bottle of water in his back pocket and the shovel in his right hand, he began the treacherous climb up the steep face of the mountain.

He wondered how Dante had the strength and determination to climb it in his physical condition, but staggered footprints told him his assumptions were correct. Mateo imagined that Dante was carrying some guilt or feelings of obligation; or perhaps he was simply sick and tired of fruitlessly searching the same region. Whatever his motivation, Mateo was certain Dante had come this way earlier and he felt a growing sense of his presence with every step he took. Thirty minutes of climbing finally brought Mateo to the mouth of the passageway, slightly reshaped by the most recent tremors.

I Miss Your Purple Hair

Mateo paused to light the torch and catch his breath, already exhausted from the first leg of the climb. He realized how empty his stomach felt and how much his beard had grown. He steadied himself along the narrow ledge adjacent to the crack in the stone monolith, gazed down upon the Reptile House and thought of his daughter and the now-familiar companions in her company.

He reflected on all that had happened since he and Violet first set foot in the zoo several days prior, and shook his head in amazement over their resilience. He realized however, that the food was gone, the power was not coming back on line, and that there had been no signs of human life outside their microcosm. It was time for desperate measures.

Mateo disappeared into the dark chamber and assessed the challenge before him. He noticed a few partial footprints along the floor of the rocky passageway, heading in the same direction. Obviously, Dante had recently passed the same way. The equipment he was toting slowed his progress, but Mateo used his guile and resourcefulness to find the means to navigate the treacherous passage without losing any of the items. At one point, he tied the rope to the pail's handle and swung it across a deep pit before he made the leap himself. At times, the torch was tossed and then relit. He refused to allow anything to impede his progress for long. By 5:45 a.m., Mateo was approaching the other side of the mountain and on the verge of unveiling the answers to some nagging questions.

The early morning Sun was doing its best to illuminate the indigo darkness, but a strange looking mass of clouds had moved in from the northwest. Mateo stood at the threshold of the opening on the eastern face of *Wormhole Wall* and looked upon the claustrophobic region below for the first time since the quakes occurred. Due to the clouds muting the tiny amount of available sunlight, it was difficult to make out many details. Mateo was struck by how similar the region was to the one he left behind; a triangular area, surrounded by three towering barriers. This area, marked by the demolished entrance pavilion and the remains of the demolished *Skyfari®* trams, was only slightly smaller in scale than the region in which they made camp.

The descent would be arduous but Mateo clenched his teeth and kept focused on the mounting urgency to get his daughter and the rest of the survivors to safety. As he prepared to climb down the eastern face, he flashed back to his childhood in Costa Rica, where he and his classmates would often climb one particular formation of rock overlooking a beautiful spring fed by a high waterfall.

Mateo was seven years old and accompanied by his cousin, Carlos, the first time he made it to the summit. A few other children were splashing and swimming in the cool spring water on that sunny June day, and Mateo had begged his 10- year-old cousin to show him how to jump off, just like the older boys.

Mateo was a good swimmer, but had never taken the leap before. His parents had forbidden it, but he could not tolerate the other kids calling him a "baby" any longer. Carlos swore to keep it secret, but Mateo felt a little nervous as he stood next to him at the summit. Looking down, it was scarier than it appeared from the ground level. They stood side-by-side and Carlos offered his hand. Young Mateo pushed it away, stubbornly stating, "I'm not a little baby. I'm jumping by myself!" As if to challenge his younger cousin, Carlos shrugged his tanned shoulders and jumped feet-first into the water, nearly fifteen feet below. He plunged into the cold water and submerged to a depth of ten feet before he made his way to the surface. As soon as he emerged, Carlos shook his head and looked up... to where he expected to see Mateo hesitating to jump.

Most younger children either lingered at the precipice for what seemed like an eternity, or they turned back and climbed down the first time they tried to muster the necessary courage. When he looked to the spot where he had left Mateo, Carlos realized he was not there. The thought went through his mind that there must have been very little conviction behind his cousin's bravado... just before he was startled by a loud splash, only a couple of feet away.

A moment later, Mateo's head popped up, a huge smile pasted on his tanned face. He laughed excitedly as he shook water droplets from his coal-black hair. "Let's go again!" he blared, energized by his first experience and proud that he pushed through his fears. Carlos was amazed at how quickly his little cousin had mustered the courage to jump. Then again, he realized it was not out of character at all for Mateo.

After organizing his equipment, Mateo began his descent, anxious to locate Dante. While climbing, he looked at the mass of grey clouds and noted the strange way they were swelling and moving like an enormous living organism. There was only the slightest breeze, yet the billowing blanket was moving in rapidly from the north and northwest. While he thought it odd, he had more pressing concerns – specifically, trying to reach ground level without any disastrous mishaps. He proceeded with great care, intensely focused on making sure of his footing with every step. Once within ten feet, Mateo used the nylon rope to lower the pail and gasoline canister to the ground. He then tossed the shovel so it landed where he could easily retrieve it.

Back in the Reptile House, Mia was the first to wake. She was surprised to learn it was already 7:00 a.m., when she looked at her wristwatch.

I Miss Your Purple Hair

Muted daylight was seeping in through the makeshift patch in the roof and she could see all the sleeping bodies around her. She savored the silence for a few moments before rubbing her eyes and trying to gather her wits. She thought, *'What I would give for a hot bubble bath!'*

Mia still felt drowsy but realized that this would be a critically important day. The food supply was gone, and soon they would be out of available firewood. Without fire, they would be unable to boil water and the risk of infection would increase dramatically. If the fire failed to attract rescuers, she felt they all might very well starve to death, trapped behind the great barricades. She wondered, "And what happens if more earthquakes occur? Would any of us survive?"

She realized that starvation would force them to abandon reason, and they would have no choice but to attempt to scale one of the walls in a desperate attempt while they still had strength left. Would only one of them go? Maybe she and Kyle, still physically strong, should pair up and make the effort to get out and find help. Many scenarios ran through her mind, none of them appealing. The temperature was still tolerable in the early morning, but she knew it was going to be another oppressively hot and humid day. That meant they would deplete the water supply that much quicker. Mia made up her mind the first order of business would be to make another fire, and then boil and bottle as much water as possible.

Her thoughts turned to her family: Mom and Dad back in Pittsburgh, sister Anna, and niece Emmi just north of San Diego... and Kyle – softly snoring about six feet from her. In a silent prayer she asked God to protect them from harm. As her attention shifted to Violet, who was beginning to rustle nearby, she asked God, "Please watch over this girl and her father... and the rest of these innocent people." She removed the cap from a plastic water bottle and drank a small sip of lukewarm water. She could not help but think, "A toothbrush would sure be nice. Never knew how much I take for granted every day..."

Violet sat up slowly on crossed legs and stretched her arms overhead. "Too bad we don't have any coffee," she lamented, drawing a smile from Mia. She shifted closer to the teenager, so they could talk quietly without rousing anyone else from their slumber. Mia recognized the comforting bond that had formed between them, and wondered whether Violet felt the same way. She looked into the soulful eyes of the charismatic teenager and immediately found her answer. The level of trust and familiarity established between them belied the fact that they had only known each other for a handful of days. When Mia looked into Violet's eyes, she felt as if she was "home."

"'Morning," Violet whispered. She appeared so fragile; so young and vulnerable all of a sudden. Mia felt a profound desire to protect her from any more pain or harm, a growing instinct that had been steadily building the past several days. She smiled and patted the back of Violet's hand. At that moment, a soft breeze blew through the front door, left slightly ajar when Mateo snuck away. It felt good to have any air movement inside the stuffy interior. The gentle disruption barely moved the blonde hair atop Mia's pretty face, but it caught the edge of the notes atop the display case, and the two leaves of paper came drifting down until they came to rest on Violet's lap. The first thought that popped into Violet's mind was, *'Papa!'*

Just enough light spilled into the room to permit reading the scribbled messages on the sheets of ruled yellow paper. Barely legible, the first note read like a cryptic poem.

"Veronica – faith, patience and courage… trust instincts… be open to signs… stay put and stay strong. Help Mia and the others… went to find Dante… will return soon… love you! – Papa"

Mia's name was scrawled in all capital letters at the top of the other sheet of paper, so Violet handed it to her. Her note, hastily scribbled by Mateo, was quite succinct.

"Mia – trusting you to watch over Violet… we'll find a way… stay strong – Mateo"

Mia was touched that Mateo had left a message specifically for her, but she would have kept watch over Violet without being asked. Still, the fact that he trusted her brought her that much closer to him… and his daughter. She understood that Mateo was convinced time was running out and had decided to make an attempt to find a way out on the opposite side of *Wormhole Wall*. What confused her was the fact that he mentioned he was 'helping Dante' in his other note.

Mia whispered to Violet, "What do you think Dante's up to?"

"Probably the same thing," Violet mused. "They must have been curious to see if the last tremors shifted things around over that way. Maybe they'll find a pathway after all. I'm sure my dad will make sure he's safe with that injured knee and everything."

"Yeah," Mia agreed. "They must have woken up early and made plans to go before any of the rest of us insisted on tagging along. Your father would never have let you take the risk before he checked it out himself. Dante must have wanted to go pretty badly to have talked your dad into taking him along."

Violet suppressed her concerns and was relieved that her father was not alone. She tried to remain confident that they would find some new path out of the zoo or at least return with more food. "My dad's awesome at climbing, so he'll be fine. It's hard to imagine how Dante can do it, the way he's been limping... but Papa will help him, I'm sure. At least they have the gun with them, in case they run into any dangerous animals over that way."

She imagined her father getting into an argument with Dante or encountering a desperate creature, and began to worry. Then she quickly recalled what her father had said to her a hundred times: "Relax. Don't project. Deal only with what's in front of you – the now." Just imagining the sound of his voice brought her a sense of peace and she controlled her fears just as she had done many times throughout her childhood. The sunlight was creeping into the room more noticeably and others began waking.

Jason had slept soundly in the chair behind the desk in the cramped office. By the time he finally woke up it was 7:55 a.m., and he headed outside to join the others. Although the cloud cover diffused its intensity, the Sun hurt his eyes when he staggered out the building's front doors. "What's up?" was all he could muster, still drowsy from the best night's sleep he'd had in four days. He emerged to a scene of bustling activity. Dwayne, Victory, and Sinnamon were stacking more wood in the center of the fire pit. Kyle and the two young boys were scouring the area for any remaining scraps of viable kindling.

Mia and Violet checked the status of Tidus and Yuna. A discussion ensued over whether or not to feed them the few remaining fish in the feeding tank. Violet suggested, "We have to eat the fish ourselves, don't you think? I mean, it seems we have no choice at this point." Mia was initially surprised the suggestion came from her.

"Well... I understand your point, but I'm not sure what we should do," Mia sighed. "There are only five fish left. I don't know how long these two can last with absolutely nothing to eat – and they're helpless, trapped here for who knows how much longer. The same thought occurred to me last night too, but I figured we would find more food somewhere... or be out of here by now."

Sinnamon eventually made her way over to see what they were discussing. She scampered up the ladder and knelt at the edge of the water, then submerged her entire head and retracted it just as quickly. She threw her head back, letting her wet, twisted tresses cascade about her shoulders. She remained at end of the tank, simply observing the dolphins as they swam back and forth beneath the surface. "I have an idea," she said to Mia and Violet. "We can eat them."

Violet innocently commented, "Yeah, we were saying the same thing."

Mia corrected her. "I don't think we're talking about the same thing. She means we should eat *them*," she emphasized while pointing toward the dolphins.

Violet gasped. "You... don't mean *that*, I hope!"

Sinnamon let it be known she was more than ready to do precisely that if need be. "Look, I'm as fond of them as anyone and not really thrilled at the prospect, but if it comes down to us or them, well... that's an easy choice as far as I'm concerned. For now, let's just be happy we're having fish for lunch." She yelled to Kyle to toss her one of the pails so she could transport the last silver fish to prepare them for cooking, but he did not hear her. Relieved that the dolphins weren't on the menu just yet, Violet offered to get the pail. As she started to run off to fetch it, she suddenly stopped in her tracks and dropped to one knee.

"What is it? What's wrong?" Mia asked.

"I...I'm okay. It's just my head... everything's spinning a little. I'll be fine," Violet reassured.

Mia felt concerned and remembered that Mateo asked her to watch over his daughter. "Why don't you sit down in the shade over here," she instructed. "I'll get the pail and some drinking water for you. Just sit still for a few minutes."

Violet felt utterly drained of energy. She had silently suffered with frequent headaches over the past few days and had periodically taken aspirin she found among their stash of supplies. The pills took away the worst of the pain, but she continued to experience episodes of dizziness and disorientation. "Stupid concussion," she muttered to herself, while she waited for Mia to return. Sinnamon had moved next to the feeding tank and popped open the lid to extract the "catch of the day."

While Sinnamon and Kyle used the silver pail to collect the fish, Violet attempted to collect herself. After she performed her breathing exercises and meditated for a moment, she began to feel less woozy. When Mia returned with some water and a half-full bag of pretzels, she saw that Violet had taken the peacock feather out of her pocket and was examining it closely. "It's really beautiful, isn't it?" Mia asked with a smile. Violet held it up where the sunlight could dance across its beveled surface, slowly twirling it in her slender fingers to inspect both sides.

I Miss Your Purple Hair

"It's a miracle of some kind, I think. The more I look at it, the harder it is to believe it's real," Violet gushed. "What's weird is that I keep thinking it's more than just a coincidence that this same feather brought Sinnamon here on the same day it caused me and my father to come. I was really angry when she cut it off, but I forgive her now that I understand her better. And I can't help but feel like we were meant to meet for some reason. Maybe we were *all* supposed to be here on the same day, for reasons we don't understand."

Mia considered Violet's notion and tried to consider the possibility objectively. After some thought she offered, "I'm not sure why you feel that way. I mean, yeah… Sinnamon and you both happened to come to look for the peacock you read about, but the rest of us were just here at the same time for random reasons."

Violet had given it considerable thought and already made up her mind to some degree. "What I'm saying," Violet replied, "is that the peacock was the main reason for some of us to be here, but maybe all of us were destined to meet and go through this together. Maybe there were multiple lures designed to bring us together at this particular time."

Puzzled at Violet's contention, Mia urged her to explain. Violet decided to be more direct, confessing some things she had been keeping under wraps. "Look at it this way. Doesn't it seem a bit amazing that Leanna and Hanna were here at this particular time? We actually already knew each other from *The Web*. They happen to be two of the most highly evolved people I've ever heard of. Jason appears to be clairvoyant or something and is just starting to understand his gift. Kyle 'just happens' to be one of the leading experts working with psychic children… and he 'just happens' to be at the zoo on the same day. Too many coincidences to just be coincidental! These are all examples of synchronicity, as my father would say."

Dwayne and Victory approached in time to hear some of the conversation. Dwayne's complexion appeared ashen as a result of the building heat and humidity. "I… I heard some of what you were talkin' about," he stammered. "Something's been buggin' me these last few days, too."

"An' what is that?" his wife asked in a concerned tone.

"Well, I been feelin' guilty… like getting' into this mess was all my fault. Remember how you and Dee wanted to go see The Grand Canyon so bad, and then I talked you into the San Diego trip?"

"Yeah, of course I do. But that's old news now. What is it that's troublin' you?" Victory asked sympathetically.

"Well, Vic... I never explained the dreams I was havin' that made me want to see the dolphins so badly. For weeks, I had these repeating dreams that I couldn't shake outta my head when I woke up. I'd be out on my morning run and wouldn't be able to get the images out of my head. It just went on for so long I felt like I wouldn't be able to live with myself if I didn't come see these dolphins right away."

Victory wore a look of great concern as she asked, "Now, why didn't you ever think to mention these dreams to me?"

"Well, I did... but, then I didn't know how you'd react. I mean, every day I figured that would be the end of it, but then I'd have another dream and then another the next night. All of 'em were pretty much the same thing. It was always me and two dolphins swimming in the big, blue ocean... but, it was like I was one of them, not the man I am. Isn't that strange? I was worried you would think I was possessed or somethin'."

"Well, that's just plain silly now," Victory reassured. "You should have more faith in your wife than that!"

Dwayne went on to finish, with tears in his eyes – from fatigue and in reaction to Victory. "When I read a news story online – about these dolphins and the new exhibit, I just felt I had to come see them right away. My imagination was filled with images of you and me and Dee holdin' hands and walkin' these same sidewalks... well, the ones buried underneath all this. I don't know if you can forgive me for getting you and Dee into this mess, but I just had no way of knowing..."

Victory laid two fingers across Dwayne's lips to stop him from continuing. "No more. You did nothin' wrong, my dear. We're gonna be fine. An' maybe it was fate, after all, that brought us here for some greater purpose. It might just be somethin' bigger than any of us understand. The Lord works in wondrous ways and protects us through our struggles. We're alive, ain't we? An' we're together... as a family. We have to hold onto our faith in each other and in God, and he'll show us the way home when the time is right. There's no reason to apologize."

DeAngelo and Ravi ran over out of curiosity. Dwayne tried to wipe away any telltale tears but could not fool his alert child. "What's wrong, Dad?" Dwayne was generally very open and honest with his son, but had never cried in front of him. To protect his child's sense of security, he had always tried to display strength and stability. Especially under such dire circumstances, he wanted to project reassurance that everything would eventually work out.

I Miss Your Purple Hair

Dwayne released his wife and bent over to clasp DeAngelo's shoulders and look him in the eye. "Everything's alright, son. We just had a little talk about our plan of action for this afternoon."

"But why are your eyes all red? Were you crying?"

Dwayne smiled and rubbed the top of DeAngelo's head. "You're right, I was cryin'... but just a little. It was because I realize how lucky I am to have you an' your Momma with me during this time. This has been one crazy adventure, hasn't it?"

"Yeah, Dad... it's been pretty cool. But next vacation... can we go to The Grand Canyon?"

Dwayne and the other adults all laughed and young Ravi joined in, despite not understanding why they were laughing. Sinnamon pulled her digital camera from her back pocket and took a few candid shots of the Coopers and the others milling about in front of the dolphin exhibit. She caught a poignant shot of DeAngelo embracing his father, with a backdrop that included the ominous dark wall of rock and a magnificent tangerine sky. Sinnamon thought, *'They'll probably want that shot for their living room wall when we get out of this fuckin' nightmare.'*

Sinnamon had stealthily taken a handful of photographs and was already heading back to the Reptile House to prepare the fish. Jason intercepted her and asked if he could lend a hand, which she graciously accepted. Violet's thoughts were on her father, filled with questions that had no ready answers. She was frustrated and concerned because her headaches persisted and affected her ability to concentrate. She was unaware that her concussion was largely responsible for her inability to make a psychic connection with her father. She took a sip of her already-warm water and once again attempted to meditate. A hazy image briefly flashed within her subconscious: that of a young boy, apparently running from something. The look of desperation in his eyes told her he was acting out of fear, but she had no way of knowing what it all meant.

Suddenly, a surprising sound broke the relative calm and pulled Violet out of her daydream. She heard the sound of distant sirens... ambulances! Her eyes flew open and she started to run to catch up with the others, who had returned to tending the fire in the pit. She advanced only three steps before nearly passing out from the debilitating effects of stress, dehydration, and brain trauma. Mia spotted Violet in her peripheral vision and quickly caught her by the arm and prevented her from falling on her face. "Veronica!" she exclaimed. "What's the matter?"

Violet's head hung low and she was suffering migraine-severe pain. When she attempted to lift her head the pounding agony intensified. She wanted so badly to have her father by her side to comfort her and tell her it would all be fine. In his stead, it was Mia who consoled her and helped her to walk slowly past the already raging fire. They found a shaded area beneath an overhang formed of rock along the base of *Wormhole Wall* and sat down on a small grassy patch. Violet could not open her eyes without experiencing searing pain behind them. In spite of the agony, she put up a brave front for her new friend. "I'm... uh.... I'll be fine. Just need a few minutes to rest my eyes," she bravely said.

Mia insisted, "You have to rest until you get a little stronger. In a little while, we'll have some cooked fish. That'll help. You also have to keep drinking water all day long. We're gonna boil more so there will be plenty." Violet nodded timidly, afraid to set off the booming drums inside her head. She wondered how much damage was done when she fell and struck her head that first day. She was having a difficult time putting thoughts together, so she asked Mia to help her lie down. Mia removed her own short-sleeved cotton shirt, rolled it up, and gently slid it underneath Violet's head and neck.

Lying there in the Sun-dried grass, Violet asked a question before drifting off to sleep. "What about the sirens?" she asked. "What happened? Why don't I hear them anymore?"

Mia felt a deep sense of concern. She whispered, "There *aren't* any sirens, sweetie. You were just having a dream or something." Violet scowled and wanted to protest. She knew she heard ambulance sirens just minutes earlier, but the fatigue and debilitating pain forced her to fall asleep. That argument would have to wait.

On the other side of *Wormhole Wall*, Mateo had finally made it to the base and already set foot upon the floor of the tiny canyon. As he visually scanned *the Fire Wall* to the north, he spotted something stirring among the rocks, approximately 12 feet above ground level.

△ △ △

I Miss Your Purple Hair

CHAPTER TWENTY~TWO
Gone to Save Our Lives

"I believe that man will not merely endure. He will prevail. He is immortal,
not because he alone among creatures has an inexhaustible voice, but because he has a soul,
a spirit capable of compassion and sacrifice and endurance."
~ William Faulkner

After dropping his supplies, Mateo climbed to where he had spotted the flash of movement among the jagged rocks. The air was thick, and a light fog had settled in over the area. The caustic chemicals in the atmosphere singed his eyelids and tongue. As he approached, he realized he had found both Dante and his nemesis sprawled along a deep ridge in the side of *the Fire Wall*. Elements of the terrain obstructed his vision, but as Mateo reached their position, he recognized the gravity of the situation. Dante crouched alongside the prone body of Aaron Kemper, who appeared to be either unconscious... or dead.

Mateo found a place to perch a few yards away from them, and once he caught his breath he finally spoke. Dante had not even noticed him until that moment. "What's the story?" Mateo asked between gasps. The frazzled security officer appeared completely exhausted, his face and arms turned crimson by the unforgiving rays of the Sun. Having removed his torn white shirt, he was now clad only in his dark blue tank-top undershirt and torn trousers. Mateo noticed that one of the sleeves Dante had torn off his dress shirt covered Aaron's face, prompting him to inquire, "Is he... dead?"

Dante, who had yet to acknowledge his presence, finally turned toward Mateo and grimly stated, "No... well, not yet anyway. He's in bad shape, though. Shock, I think... "

"Has he been laying here for long?" Mateo asked.

"Don't know how long, but it's been a while. I think he must've been afraid of the wolf so he wedged himself between these rocks. He probably passed out from dehydration. No water for three days? Not good... not good at all." Dante was the personification of a beaten man; not just physically exhausted, but emotionally spent as well. The back of his neck was badly sunburned and blistering. His thick brown hair was matted and messy and his voice raspy and weak. Mateo saw that Dante had apparently wrapped what remained of his shirt around Aaron's right calf, as a makeshift tourniquet.

"What happened to his leg?" Mateo asked, pointing at the blood-soaked wrap.

Dante sighed and shook his head as if he could not believe he was finally about to tell the truth. "That... that's where the bullet went clean through. It must have hit the bone. Even if he regains consciousness, he can't walk on it; that's obvious... lost a good amount of blood too, but I got it stopped for now."

Mateo was confused, having heard conflicting stories regarding the altercation between Aaron Kemper and Dante. He felt the truth had still never really come out. "What really happened between you two? Why did you come back all this way?" he gently asked.

Dante choked back tears and bowed his head. The time had come to finally admit the truth. "I lied before," he began. "Kemper never had his own gun. When I threw the cash in his face, he flipped out on me. For some reason he lost it when I told him I was gonna join the rest of you. That's when he kicked me in the knee and tried to take my pistol. I shoved him away when he went for my holster. He fell, got back up, and came right back at me again with this crazed look in his eyes. I just reacted..."

Mateo's expression reflected heightened concern. "Wh... what do you mean?"

"Damn it... I fuckin' shot him, *that's* what it means... in the leg. I know; it was the wrong thing to do. If I had just stuck the gun in his face, maybe he would've backed off. But things were gettin' squirrelly enough and I wasn't in my right mind either, y'know? Now I regret it, but at the time I just wanted to get the hell outta here and this guy had just busted up my knee. I lost it, I guess." Dante sighed and looked at Kemper's motionless form. "I had to come back to see what became of him. I was hoping he somehow made it out of here, but I guess I knew all along that wasn't likely... sure as hell not on one leg."

Mateo reassured the weakened security guard, "You were afraid for your own safety – your own life. Perhaps you overreacted but you have to forgive yourself. It says something, that you decided to come all the way back here, which couldn't have been easy in your condition." He looked at the pasty complexion of Aaron's hands and asked, "Do you think he'll make it?"

Dante shook his head again. "He's not likely to come out of this until he gets some nutrients into his body. Unless we get him to a hospital soon, I don't see how he can hold on. He's been without water longer than the rest of us."

Mateo knew Dante was right. Aaron Kemper was on the verge of death, having lost blood in addition to being gravely undernourished. The fact that he was suffering from diabetic acidosis severely complicated matters. He asked Dante if he felt strong enough to help carry Aaron down to the base of the mountain. "Yeah," he replied. "I was actually going to try to move him myself. It's a damn good thing you came this way. Maybe together we can at least get him out of the direct sunlight... and buy him another day."

Before making another move, Mateo asked, "Hold on. You mentioned the wolf, but where is it? I haven't seen any sign, but it must still be in the area."

Dante swallowed hard when reminded of the predator still at large, and informed Mateo, "Haven't seen it in a long while, not since I came back through the Pass, for sure. Maybe it climbed out of here during the night."

For inexplicable reasons, Mateo felt little fear regarding the wolf. He shrugged and lifted the unconscious man by the armpits, and waited for Dante to follow his lead and grab the unconscious man's ankles. Moving Kemper's limp body turned out to be a titanic struggle, due to their weariness, assorted injuries and the treacherous footing. After some precarious moments, they finally reached an ideal spot closer to ground level. They deposited the injured real estate baron in a secluded nook in the shade of a young palm tree. Both men desperately gasped for air afterwards. Mateo wrestled the water bottle from his pocket and handed it to Dante. He waved his hand as if to reject the offer, but Mateo insisted. "Take it," he told Dante. "You two need it much more than I do." He lied, adding, "I drank an entire bottle just before I headed into the passageway."

Reluctantly, Dante took the bottle from the iron-willed man. He noted Mateo's sunburned skin and the obvious weariness reflected in his eyes. He tried to understand what had motivated this soft-spoken man to leave his comrades – not to mention his daughter – to crawl back through *Wormhole Pass*. "So... what the hell are we gonna do next?" he asked with a tone of resignation.

Mateo's expression reflected his growing concern surrounding Violet's deteriorating condition. She was his first priority and always would be. He did not hesitate long before answering, "We have to get out of here, now. And we have to do it while we still have some strength left... or we may never get out. I don't believe there is anyone *able* to come help us in time."

The look on Dante's face expressed fear and acceptance all at once. He knew Mateo was probably right to assume there would be no rescuers to save them. He imagined the entire world in flames, and worried for those he loved. Mateo surveyed the immediate surroundings and asked, "Tell me what else you found over here." While Dante updated Mateo on the few resources at their disposal, the rest of the survivors were considering their dwindling options.

Leanna and Hanna each held one of Violet's hands while they quietly recited a prayer for health and strength. While everyone else had worked on keeping the enormous bonfire going, Violet had slipped in and out of consciousness, suffering from debilitating headaches. Nearby, Mia and Kyle debated what action to take next. Less than five yards away, the fire sent a thick column of grey smoke into the orange-raspberry sky. The temperature had reached the high 80s and the crackling fire only added to the oppressive heat. Her cadre of attendants kept Violet's brow cool while she slept, but she was finally beginning to stir. The Armstrong sisters stopped chanting and helped her sit up once she was awake. Mia moved closer and helped support her back as they all gently helped her to a seated position.

As Violet sipped a bit of water, Mia inquired, "How are you feeling?" The weakened teenager was disoriented, nauseous and light-headed. Mia handed her three Ibuprofen tablets and waited while she downed them before asking, "You were talking in your sleep. Did you realize that?"

Violet replied in a tired, raspy voice, "Uh, I guess I'm not surprised. I had a pretty weird dream... or three." Mia felt relieved to hear Violet eke out a weak little giggle. "So... what did I say? Did it make any sense to you?"

Mia tried to remember the exact words she mumbled in her sleep. "At one point, I think you said, 'Thank God you're alive... I was worried.' Do you remember who you were dreaming about? Did it have anything to do with your father?"

"It may have, but I'm not sure, to tell the truth," Violet answered. "Part of the dream was about some of the kids in *The Web*... I think I mentioned them to you before. Nathan, Prajna, Corinne... they were all in it. They told me that the other kids in The Foundation dorms are alright, even though they had earthquakes there, too."

Hearing this, Kyle snapped to attention. "Those are three of *my* kids! Are you sure it was a dream... or was it possibly something else?" Kyle probed, suspicious that Violet may have received telepathic messages specifically directed to her.

As honestly as she could, Violet answered, "It's funny... I was wondering the same thing. It *felt* like a dream, but it felt very real, too. The three of them were definitely in the dream. Even though I never met them in person, I still recognized them, somehow. They were sitting on the floor in a dark room, surrounded by all these other people – kids, mostly. A couple of people had candles and there was just a small amount of flickering light... "

Kyle anticipated her description, but wanted to establish the facts as clearly as possible while the memory was still fresh in her mind. He gently asked, "You say you recognized Nathan, Corinne, and Prajna... yet you never met any of them in person? How can that be?"

Violet was equally perplexed. "I have received a photo or two, but it has nothing to do with physical appearance. When they spoke, I recognized them from our conversations in *The Web*... although now that I think about it I've never actually heard any of their voices, other than in my own imagination. I guess I'm a little confused. My head really hurts."

After a few deep breaths, Violet recounted more from her dream. "They said they were safe and sound in Pittsburgh, somewhere not far from The Foundation. Corinne told me the quakes were bad there, but that she and the other kids were on a field trip when they struck. That was lucky timing because even though The Foundation was nearly destroyed, the place they were visiting was safe."

"The Foundation was damaged? Please tell me no one was injured!" Kyle exclaimed.

"They didn't say if anyone was hurt," Violet answered. "But they did say all of the kids from the dorms went on the trip Sunday."

Kyle's mind was racing. *'How is it possible the quakes reached that far away? How many other places have been damaged?'* He then searched his memory and said, "Wait, that's right... we had scheduled a visit to The Aviary for Sunday... that makes sense now. I forgot about it, with what's been happening. Thank God, if they were really spared because of that trip. I know all of them were going to be accompanied by their families, too... thank God..."

"Weird..." Violet muttered under her breath.

"What's weird?" Kyle asked, still a bit on edge.

Violet looked at him through squinted eyes, the drum in her head still pounding. "That peacock Sinnamon and I came here to find originally came from The National Aviary in Pittsburgh. You *just happen* to live and work in the same city. On top of that, some of my best friends from *The Web* are students at *your* Foundation. It's all very strange, isn't it? I mean, there's got to be more to all of this than *coincidence*, don't you think?"

Kyle felt tingling energy course through his entire body. He realized that the coincidences *were* astonishing, but had no idea what to make of it all. He felt a sense of awe regarding the teenage girl in front of him; for her peaceful nature, her courage and for the way she seemed to trust him wholeheartedly. After a moment of reflection, he finally mustered a reply. "Violet, there are a lot of things going on that I don't understand. It feels like the whole world changed overnight." His words shook Violet at the very core of her soul.

'Maybe everything has changed. That just might be true.'

In a flash, Violet received a mental image of her father walking alone across a barren, Sun-scorched landscape, surrounded by flames and smoke. Only one thought went through her mind...

'Come home safe, Papa.'

On the other side of *Wormhole Wall*, Mateo was thinking of Violet and praying, as he dragged himself to the spot Dante had identified. Farther east, multiple plumes of grey smoke spiraled into the sky, evidence that the once-distant fires had crept much closer over the past several days. The air was sickly sweet and the temperature had soared to 90 degrees. Along the string of demolished structures close to where the Zoo Entrance once stood, a partially exposed storage shed was sandwiched between a mass of twisted metal and the thick trunk of a towering palm tree. Its roof and one side had been crushed by heavy debris, making it impossible to discern what the building originally looked like. Its door was torn off the hinges and jammed within its misshapen metal frame.

He yelled to Dante, "Why didn't anyone see this before... when you were on this side the other day?"

Dante replied, "The latest tremors must have shaken stuff loose again. It was probably uncovered when those aftershocks came through yesterday." Unfamiliar with the building's purpose, he began to get excited at the prospect of its contents. He yelled, "I hope it's a food storage shed. Let's hope it's where they keep all the good stuff!" Dante salivated at the very thought of discovering a cache of edibles.

Mateo had similar hopes as he forced the steel door of the lopsided building to one side, providing the first glimpse of its interior. The sunlight spilled across the ruined terrain and through the doorway of the structure embedded in the rock. Grateful that the tremors had not only revealed the building but allowed entry, Mateo cautiously stuck his head inside. He was dismayed by the condition of the mangled building's interior once he entered. The roof was crushed and supplanted by a ceiling of rock. Similarly destroyed, the floor still contained remnants of the concrete foundation. Most everything had been severely damaged by the quakes. A pungent chemical odor of indiscernible origin permeated the cramped quarters, forcing Mateo to hold his breath while he poked around.

The odd-shaped structure's interior was sufficiently illuminated and Mateo was able to push a few steel shelves out of the way to investigate fully. To his disappointment, it was readily apparent that this was not a storage facility for foodstuffs or beverages of any kind. Instead, it was a moderate-sized building used by Maintenance staff to store fertilizer, cleaning products, crushed gravel, and similar items. He poked around in the limited light to make sure he did not miss anything useful. Bags of cement and crushed stone were strewn about, some ripped open and contents spilling out. More fertilizer and mulch mixed with the other supplies, but it was becoming apparent that there was nothing of use. The only other object was a dented metal drum, lidless and empty, except for a family of spiders crawling around inside.

Finally, while digging through all the similar-looking heavy bags along the ground he discovered two wooden crates stacked in the front corner of the building – the area least affected by the crushing weight of the rocks that caved in the roof. The word "DANGER" jumped out at Mateo, despite the dim lighting. Investigating closer, he made out the words printed in red along the longer sides of the crates: "Explosives: Handle with Extreme Caution."

'What on Earth is this?'

Mateo returned to the doorway and summoned Dante to join him, calling out, "I need your help. Quickly... come over here!"

Dante sarcastically responded, "Uh, it isn't gonna be very quick, but hang on." He covered Aaron's forehead and eyes again with his damp shirt, and then limped toward the bizarre-looking shed. Mateo had already dragged one of the crates toward the door, where the box hung up on a jagged rock jutting out through the fragmented concrete floor. He waited until Dante arrived to help lift the crate before sliding it through the doorway and into the open.

"Oh yeah...," Dante finally acknowledged. "These are the fireworks inventory they stored here. They were brought in for a New Year's Eve celebration."

Mateo was puzzled. "You mean the Zoo sets off fireworks in the midst of all the animals? Doesn't it frighten them?"

"No, no," Dante quickly explained. "Fireworks aren't allowed anywhere near here. The celebration is sponsored by the city, not the Zoo, and the actual site is quite a ways away, right on the coast. The only reason the supply was stored here was due to the delivery truck breaking down right out front on the day after Christmas. The Zoo has had a relationship with the company for years, so when they asked to store the stuff here overnight, it was never an issue. We had the space, and it saved them some hassle."

Mateo asked, "If the Zoo doesn't allow fireworks, how is it they have a business relationship with the company?"

"The same company does excavation and construction. They helped build and install the dolphin exhibit," Dante explained.

Mateo could not help but string together the mounting litany of coincidences. He shook his head, pondering the circumstances, as he understood them.

Dante winced in pain before adding, "Shit, I'd completely forgotten today was New Year's Eve, until just now. What else did you find?"

Mateo urged Dante to sit down and rest his knee while he reentered the building. After poking around again he discovered little else besides the other box of fireworks, a pair of heavy gardening spades, a coiled hose and a green wheelbarrow firmly embedded in the ground, its wheel broken off. He rejoined Dante in front of the building, with the shovels in hand.

"Do you have the strength to dig?" he asked the sore-legged security guard. Dante barely grunted a response indicating he was willing, so Mateo stuck one of the shovels out for him to grab.

"What're you thinking?" Dante asked.

Mateo, who obviously had formed some type of plan, gestured toward the corner where he had discovered the water percolating beneath the surface.

"Over *there*," he explained, "... let's find out what's happening below ground." Dante nodded, following Mateo's logic and eager to replace the hopelessness he had been feeling.

Where *Wormhole Wall* and *Kemper's Folly* converged, Dante had identified a spot where a small pool of water had collected. In the shadowy corner, at the foot of the earthen barricades, he had discovered a spongy patch of grass, clearly saturated with water. By pressing his fist into the emerald patch, Mateo got his first impression that something other than surface moisture was responsible. The wet soil beneath the grass offered only moderate resistance, further indication that a water source existed just beneath the surface.

Mateo grabbed the shovel and began digging, determined to uncover the origin. With the very first scoop of soil, it was obvious there was more to the odd discovery than he originally imagined. Water immediately flooded the hole he created, rushing in with surprising force. Mateo immediately understood. Beneath the rock formation, separating the isolated region from the outside world, was a source of flowing water. Whether it indicated a natural spring or perhaps, a broken water main was unknown. It was, however, the first real exciting discovery since becoming stranded within the confines of the disfigured Zoo.

Mateo quickly dug out a few more shovelfuls and the water once again rushed to fill the void. He tasted it – only to be surprised by its salt content.

'It's saltwater! We're miles from the Pacific... so where's this coming from?'

"There's saltwater beneath the soil here... saltwater!" Mateo excitedly announced. "You know this place much better than I do. Any thoughts on how that could be? I mean, where might it be coming from?"

Dante pondered the bizarre discovery and scrunched up his forehead before speculating, "In this location, it can't be anything except a broken main from one of the habitats. Sea water is pumped into attractions like the Wegeforth Bowl and the dolphin tank. It *has* to be coming from something like that beneath the surface. With all the quakes, that makes sense."

Mateo agreed that the water had to be the product of a man-made source damaged by either the initial quakes or subsequent tremors. Still, it intrigued him due to its proximity to the base of the barrier which had stymied the group from the beginning. He asked Dante, "You know the layout of this place better than I do. The most efficient escape route is beyond this mountain and then toward the south, isn't it?" he asked.

Dante scratched the sunburned skin on the side of his neck with his finger. "Well... yeah, I still think we'd have our best shot that way, because the parking lot is that way. If the quakes didn't completely reshape everything, I'm guessing we'd be more likely to find wide-open spaces... and hopefully, functioning vehicles, over the mountain to that side. But, you've got to accept that it's just impossible to climb over this... "

Mateo extended his hand to prevent Dante from completing his comment, and calmly interjected, "Not *over* it... what if there's a way to go *under* it?"

"Under it? Under *what*?" Dante asked, concerned that extended exposure and breathing in the toxic atmosphere had warped Mateo's thinking. Then he watched as Mateo directed the point of his heavy shovel at the spot where the water seeped to the surface. With as much strength as he could muster, he thrust the pointed tip into the wet earth. As the spongy soil gave way, water immediately rushed in to fill the hole. Mateo immediately understood...

'It's coming from beneath the mountain!'

He excitedly informed Dante, "There's a significant source of underground water here, for certain. Maybe the water table was affected during the earthquakes. I don't know why or how it happened, but you can feel the force behind it. We've got to dig and see just how much water there is. It's obvious there's more to this than meets the eye."

Still confused, Dante asked, "How do you mean? What good will it do us if there's water collecting down there?"

"Don't you see?" Mateo replied. "If water is getting in, then it stands to reason it could also get out the same way. We might be able to figure a way out if we trace it to its source. It's possible the water could lead us out of here, or at least to someplace we haven't yet been able to reach. And, there's another possibility I just thought of."

"What's that?" Dante anxiously asked.

Mateo speculated, "With even the slightest force behind it, water erodes dirt, rock... and just about anything else in its path. For all we know, when the initial quakes hit, they caused major changes to underground water tables or the facilities' filtration systems, or both. What if there's a river flowing underneath this mountain?" His eyes suddenly lit up, and he enthusiastically speculated, "This might be our best chance to get out of here – the only chance, really, since this all started."

Dante suddenly felt reinvigorated by Mateo's hopeful tone. "Yeah; you might be on to something here. Let's dig and see what we can find out. I may only have one good leg, but since I've been hittin' the gym the last two years, my arms are twice as strong as they used to be!" He and Mateo high-fived each other and Dante picked up the other shovel. "Hey, before we start, I feel I need to thank you."

"For what?" Mateo innocently asked.

"For coming back this way. I had my own reasons to catch up with Kemper again. It was gnawin' at me all this time. But you risked everything and left your daughter behind to check things out over here. You never gave me a hard time for lying or for how I left him here in the first…"

Mateo interrupted, "Look, my friend; I have my own motives, too. I crawled through that passageway because I felt there had to be a way out on this side. That feeling was nagging at me, just as your guilt was driving you. I figured you came back for your own reasons, and was curious to see what happened. But, I'm determined to do whatever it takes to get us out of here and if I have to… I'll find a way to climb this thing myself. We're running out of time and there's no rescue coming – at least not soon enough. My little girl's not doing well and all those other people are at risk. I was concerned for you and curious about Kemper, but my mission is to get my daughter out of here… sooner, rather than later!"

"I understand," Dante uttered with resignation. "Well, what're we waiting for? Let's get going."

With that declaration, the two men attacked the soil at their feet with fervor, finding that water rapidly displaced dirt. Before long, they had excavated so much mud and rock at the foot of the obstruction that they found themselves standing thigh-deep in saltwater. The air burned the tender tissue of their lungs, but they continued to dig, stopping only momentarily to wipe sweat out of their eyes or to take a swig of water. With very few words exchanged, they chipped away in the isolated corner of the region, now cloaked in shadow.

Exhausted and sore, they finally stopped digging to rebuild their strength. The humidity level was torturously high and with every passing minute, it seemed the temperature rose another degree. Dante asked, "So, do you think this is worth it? I mean, are we just killing ourselves out here for nothing?" Mateo merely smiled in reaction to the question. Incredulous, Dante asked between gasps for air, "Wh… what's the smile for?"

Rather than speak, Mateo demonstrated the reason behind his expression. He lifted his shovel high and drove it into the face of the mountain, about a foot above the hole they created. A wide chunk of rock broke off and plunged into the water, creating a breach in the formerly impenetrable-looking barrier. Dante's jaw dropped at first, before he finally declared, "I'll be damned. You were right! There's probably water under this entire thing! Maybe it's not what we assumed it was..."

Mateo had closed his eyes and was employing deep breathing techniques in an effort to clear his mind. The Sun was obscured behind a hazy gauze of clouds and smoke from nearby regions, but the heat was no less draining. Coupled with the exertion required to dig out the soil, the extreme heat had sapped almost every ounce of their energy. Mateo opened his eyes and suggested, "We'd better check on our friend over there. We need to see if we can wake him. Going without water much longer could have devastating consequences."

Dante nodded and they tossed their shovels onto a flat expanse of rocks before trudging to Aaron's side. Mateo was surprised to see it was 8:12 p.m., when he glanced at his watch. He tapped its face with his dirty index finger, to no effect. Once again, the watch's readout was frozen at the wrong time. He raised his arm to his ear, and heard the watch ticking. He shrugged it off and asked Dante, "What time you got?" Dante cleared mud from the face of his rugged wristwatch and held it close to his eyes, so he could make out the digital reading through the grime-coated fob.

"Uh, it's closing in on 3:30," he replied as he cast his gaze skyward, noting that the dark grey smoke had begun to dominate the horizon to the east and northeast. Before the two men could reach Aaron's limp body along the craggy face of *Sunrise Summit*, the unexpected happened. From the west, came the sound of a powerful explosion, immediately followed by a wave of tremors that nearly knocked both of them to the ground. Their line of sight blocked by the towering walls, all they could see was an enormous plume of grey smoke spiraling toward the heavens.

Debris tumbled down the intimidating walls on every side, some larger chunks narrowly missing the two men. Mateo quickly barked, "Hurry! Let's get back to Kemper. We've got to shield him – and we'll be safer over there until this settles down." Mateo led the way as they climbed to the spot where Aaron lay behind a protective half-wall of rock. What had just transpired still had not fully registered with either man. They were operating purely on survival instinct. Once safely alongside Aaron's prone body, they were relieved to find him still breathing normally. Mateo kept vigil over the vulnerable man's body, and wondered what the latest incident meant.

Back at their camp near the Reptile House, the rest of the survivors moved away from the walls to avoid the avalanche of debris. Kyle's arms were still wrapped around both Ravi and Hanna, who had fallen to the ground when the tremors triggered by the explosion occurred. Jason and Sinnamon, who had been dangling their legs in the dolphin tank, were knocked into the water by the jolt. As they climbed onto the deck, Jason cast a wary glance to the west. "Volcano," he muttered, almost inaudibly.

Sinnamon demanded clarification. "What'd you say? I thought you said 'volcano'."

"I did," he sheepishly replied. "That has to be what happened: an eruption. Look there!"

Sinnamon turned her attention to the west and immediately saw he was right. An enormous volume of thick grey smoke poured skyward and combined with the already heavy blanket of clouds moving in. Aftershocks sent vibrations up through the tank and into their bodies via the deck's metal structure. Sinnamon's expression turned decidedly somber. "How can all these things be happening at once? It's like the end of the World or something. We better get back to the others," she dryly commented, weary of the endless litany of disastrous events.

Moments later, after everyone regained their bearings, the survivors regrouped around the fire. Sinnamon and Jason had gutted the five silvery fish and handed the tiny fillets to the volunteer cooks, Victory and Kyle. The smell was intoxicating to everyone – except DeAngelo, who refused to eat fish. They did not take long to cook, and the group came together for their final meal. DeAngelo had stashed away one last chocolate chip cookie and retrieved it from the fort he and Ravi had built. Mia and Victory refused any of the fish, both claiming they felt strong enough to give their portion to the hungriest. Violet took only one small piece and claimed she knew how to eat in such a way that even such a small portion would fill her senses and stomach. Leanna and Hanna followed suit, without so much as a word between them. Kyle observed the three girls and their selfless act, and he too, only took one small cube of baked fish for himself.

Under her breath, Sinnamon commented, "Who *are* these people... really?"

Jason smiled before responding quietly to Sinnamon, "They aren't so weird, actually... just a bit more enlightened than most."

Just then, Hanna pointed to the sky and exclaimed, "Hey, it looks like snow!" Her older sister whipped her head around, still chewing her modest portion of food. Looking skyward, she immediately understood what was going on. Large white flakes cascaded lazily through the stagnant air. Beautiful to behold, the scene was like something from a science-fiction movie. Enraptured by the surreal beauty of the fluffy white particles against the red-orange backdrop, no one spoke for what seemed like minutes. Although undeniably breathtaking to behold, the ash introduced yet another concern.

"If that volcano creates a big enough cloud, it could be extremely hazardous," Jason flatly suggested.

Sinnamon could not resist another chance to jab him and sneered, "Oh, is that so? What... did you make a pretend volcano for the 5th Grade Science Fair? What do you mean by 'hazardous'?"

Jason managed a smirk, having learned to roll with Sinnamon's verbal slaps. "If anyone has allergies or any sort of breathing problems, then it might not be healthy to be sitting out here in this fallout."

"Big whoop!" Sinnamon sneered. "We've got dehydration, poison air and lack of toilet paper to deal with. A few flakes isn't really gonna put a cramp in our party."

Jason laughed aloud, soliciting an icy glare from Sinnamon, who folded her arms and leaned toward him as if to dare him to say something. Defiantly, he shot back, "Hahaha... it's 'crimp', not *cramp*... seems to me *you're* the only cramp in this party, anyway!" He relished the opportunity to return a little dose of sarcasm, but Sinnamon was not amused. She just turned and stomped back toward the dolphin tank.

Mia turned her attention to Jason, who was still beaming over one-upping the feisty redhead. She told him, "I believe you're right about the ash cloud. I read that somewhere online. The other concern for us, though, is if this worsens... it'll be nearly impossible for anyone to spot us from the air. Aircraft will have to steer clear, because of lack of visibility... or fear of engine failure. And, the smoke from our fire is just going to get lost in the ash cloud – as if we don't have enough working against us."

Jason agreed. "We have to keep thinking of other ways out of here. This is our last fire, too. Hopefully, someone will spot it before the ash gets any thicker. I wonder what Mateo found across the way. Maybe a couple of us who still have the strength should follow and see what's going on. I know he said he'd hurry back, but it's been a long time already. What do you think?"

Mia knew Mateo would do just about anything to save the rest of them, especially his daughter. In her heart, she knew he would not stop trying until he found a way out. In her mind, she pictured his face and felt as if he was calling out to her. Not willing to wait any longer, Mia bravely told Jason, "I'm willing to go with you, to see if Mateo and Dante need help. We're two of the healthiest people here and ought to be able to handle the climb. Let me talk to my brother and see what he thinks. Meanwhile, you'd better get a few bites of fish for yourself." Jason nodded and went over to take one of the last remaining pieces of fish, fully aware it might be the last morsel of food he would have for the foreseeable future.

When Mia approached Kyle, he was just finishing his own miniscule portion. "Funny how, when you're starving anything tastes like fine cuisine." He asked, "Did you have any?" Intentionally misleading, Mia nodded as if to indicate she had eaten some. Her older brother stretched his arms out as wide as possible and leaned his head back for a moment. He twisted at the waist a few times, trying to work out the kinks in his back.

"Sleeping on concrete is really getting old," he grunted. "We've done pretty well though, huh Sis? I mean, this group of people has been amazingly tough. I have to say I'm impressed – but enough is enough. This volcanic eruption was the last thing we needed on the day we're burning the last of our firewood."

"Yeah, I know," Mia replied. "We haven't caught a break yet, but I agree with you that everyone's done a remarkable job of holding it together. We're lucky in that way."

"So, what're you thinking?" he asked. "I know that expression. You want to ask me something?"

Mia wore an expression of resignation. "I have to go after Mateo. Maybe just take a couple of the strongest people and catch up to him. I'm prepared to go alone if I have to, but I just can't wait any longer."

Her protective brother was not keen on the proposal, turning more serious in tone. "I don't know if I see the point, Mia. We've been over there and saw there was no way out. Fires were moving in on the area from two directions… and then there's that wolf lurking about. It might be best to wait for Mateo to return. If he discovers some miraculous escape route, we can always gather up our supplies and go back over with him. You don't think he'd leave without us, do you?"

"I never thought *that*. He would never consider leaving Violet behind for long. No, I'm just worried about him." Mia's plea was impassioned, but Kyle still struggled with the lack of logic in taking the associated risks when they knew it would only lead to a dead-end.

Violet piped up from where she was sitting, having overheard the end of their conversation. "I've had a hard time connecting with my father, but I sense he's alright. It's hard to get a clear sense, but I think they discovered something new when he caught up with Dante; something to do with water... at least I think that's what it is. I'm sorry I can't be more sure about it." Intrigued, those within earshot moved closer. Victory finished bottling more water and then approached to hear Violet elaborate on what she had detected.

Violet continued, "I'm getting a hazy image of where they are and it looks like they might have found some body of water... in a dark place. I wish I knew more, but messages are coming at me from many different people. Thoughts get scrambled and sometimes it's hard to unscramble the signals... especially with this headache."

Kyle urged her to elaborate. "Other than your father, who else are you connecting with?"

Violet tried to make sense of it for the others. "My father and I have a constant connection; meaning, I sense some of his thoughts and emotions without him consciously projecting to me. When he *does* intentionally reach out, I usually hear him in my head, loud and clear. When I'm sick or real tired, it gets fuzzy; and when someone else is trying to connect, I have a hard time filtering... so I get confused... and frustrated. Does that make sense?"

Eager to demonstrate his unique understanding, Kyle responded to Violet. "Someday in the near future, I'd like to get you to Pittsburgh... to The Foundation. We can help you with things like what you just described. We're working on just those types of skills and have begun to make some amazing progress. I'd really enjoy hosting you and your father, as soon as our lives get settled again."

Violet could no longer hold back her tears. Kyle's kind words came at a particularly difficult moment. Her headaches had been coming with more frequency, she was trying to maintain a brave demeanor in spite of being worried for her father, and she was fatigued in every way imaginable. His sympathetic understanding reminded her of a hundred memories of her father. The fact that someone else understood her, even a little, made her feel like less of a misfit. She wiped her eyes and tried to compose herself as both Kyle and Mia knelt next to her.

"I have to come to Pittsburgh... alone," she resolutely stated in a soft voice. The fair-haired siblings were somewhat perplexed by her comment, but chose to wait before reacting. Violet drew in a deep breath and then exhaled slowly, before adding, "A vision came to me... just a minute ago. In it, my father wasn't with me... I was surrounded by many people, and both of you were there, too. We were surrounded by water and there was a fountain shooting high into the air. It had to be Pittsburgh, near the three rivers I've read about." She looked down, as if embarrassed to share an intimate secret. "And... there was a word suspended in the air, above my head. It looked like it was... glowing; like white, sparkling light was coming from behind each of the letters in the word."

Mia gasped, "What was the word?"

"Synchronicity," whispered Violet.

Kyle's eyes opened wide. He felt she was right in assuming the images represented the city he called home and was compelled to probe further. "Violet, why do you think that word made such a profound impact?" While aware it would be inappropriate to carelessly interpret her vision, he felt it essential that she consider every detail. She breathed slowly and deeply again, her body rising and falling subtly with each breath.

"It's beginning to add up," she began. "My father taught me some stuff about synchronicity... or synchrodestiny... whatever you want to call it. The signs have been everywhere, since we got here and all this stuff started happening. The peacock, the birthdays, the connections with Pittsburgh... it's impossible to ignore the signs when there are so many. I mean, how can it just be 'dumb luck' that you work with the kids I became friends with through *The Web*? Some other things are beginning to come clear to me, now that the end is closer."

Alarmed, Mia asked somewhat frantically, "The end? What...?"

Quick to reply, Violet elaborated. "*Something* is definitely coming to an end. I feel it very strongly now. I don't know yet what it is, though. It isn't clear, but I do feel that we're close. I see us walking beneath the stars, in a setting much different than this." She gestured toward the angry, smoke-filled sky and added, "This part of the nightmare will be over soon. The next part will look very different, and then... even more changes are coming. I just feel it's going to be very different... soon."

Still concerned and confused, Mia asked, "Veronica, *what's* going to be different?"

"*Everything*," was Violet's simple response. She then turned to Kyle and asked, "I need to know something. Does Pittsburgh have a nickname like some other cities do?"

"Yeah, of course," he replied. "People like to call it the 'Steel City' ... or 'Iron City.' There's a local beer called *Iron City*, in fact. The city has many nicknames, actually: 'City of Bridges', 'The Burgh'... Why?"

Violet picked up a small stick and frantically etched letters in the packed dirt. "My father and I play our *Anagram Game* all the time, remember?" Violet rhetorically asked. "See what I realized just now?" Mia and Kyle eagerly waited while she etched large block letters into the soil, spelling out the word: "S Y N C H R O N I C I T Y." She then began to print, in capital letters, several more words directly below it. She looked up at Mia and Kyle and said, "Look what its letters spell when unscrambled."

In the red-tinged dirt, she had scrawled three words made from all the letters in "S Y N C H R O N I C I T Y."
Beneath it, she had written... "S Y N C H   I R O N   C I T Y."

Kyle looked at Mia, who had reached the same conclusion he did. He turned his focus to the ballet of white flakes floating to the ground. "Synch Iron City... Synchronicity... the same letters, only scrambled. I can't believe I never saw it! Maybe we were always supposed to meet here... or maybe *there*. I've been getting a sense that we were all destined to meet for some reason... but, why?"

Mia locked eyes with Violet. She could feel her heart pounding as she finally began to consider the inevitability of everything they were experiencing. She turned and assured her weary brother, "I think we'll find out soon enough."

The good-natured siblings turned away just as Violet discreetly scribbled over another anagram she had etched in the dirt. She wanted to hide the fact that she had also unscrambled the Deepak Chopra-coined term, "Synchrodestiny" to spell out a much more ominous message...

... "D E S T R O Y   I N   S Y N C H ."

△ △ △

CHAPTER TWENTY~THREE

On a Bed of Nails I'll Wait

"A man who was completely innocent, offered himself as a sacrifice for the good of others, including his enemies, and became the ransom of the world. It was a perfect act."
~ Mahatma Gandhi

Mateo Lima was tired and weak – from lack of nourishment, the relentless heat, and the emotional stress of the past several days. Nevertheless, he resolved to make a desperate attempt to alter destiny. He had managed to chip away a portion of the brittle outer shell of *Kemper's Folly* to reveal a hollow gap flooded with water. He lit his makeshift torch and stuck it through the aperture to discover, to his amazement, a cave-like interior. The mass of rock everyone had presumed impenetrable was actually a hollow shell. The discovery reminded Mateo of one of the basic tenets he tried to live by: "Always look beyond the surface."

Having convinced Dante to rest his aching knee and tend to Aaron Kemper along the face of *Sunrise Summit*, Mateo gathered up all of the equipment and laid the items along the ground, not far from the gap he had carved into the base of the wall. As he took inventory of his limited resources, a clear course of action revealed itself and thereby, replenished his energy. His faith restored by the epiphany, Mateo felt prepared to take action. After prying open the two wooden crates with a flat metal rod, he thought, *'There's a lot of explosive power here, but I need to focus it somehow.'*

Dante surprised Mateo by suddenly calling out, "Hey! He's awake! Come over here... and bring the water!" Aaron had regained consciousness and began to move his arms and head. Dante had very little water remaining in his bottle, but he lifted Aaron's head and encouraged him to take a sip. His Sun-scorched eyelids still shut; Aaron tentatively sipped the warm water. Once Mateo arrived, he handed his bottle to Dante, who in turn helped Aaron take a few substantial gulps. Passing over his blistered lips, the lukewarm water felt incredibly soothing. Aaron's crusted eyelids eventually creaked open and he managed his first words in more than two days.

"... Unh... tell me we've been rescued...," he growled in a barely recognizable voice.

I Miss Your Purple Hair

Neither of the men tending to him was interested in delivering the bad news. Mateo put his hand on Aaron's shoulder and said, "Try to drink all the water in this bottle. Don't worry about anything else right now."

Aaron, a man who always preferred to get straight answers, responded, "... Son of a bitch... I *knew* it... how long was I out?" He winced as he lifted his scraped and bloodied right arm to take the plastic bottle from Dante's hand. Slowly, he struggled to drink a few more sips. The two men teamed once more to turn his body so he could lean back against the rocks and finally sit upright again. They helped remove Aaron's blazer and necktie, and then unbuttoned the top three buttons of his sweat-soaked dress shirt.

"The heat and humidity has drained every ounce of energy from your body," Mateo observed. Aaron was bathed in sweat and limp as a rag doll. He could not keep his eyes open, but managed to ask, "How long have I been laying here?"

In reply to Aaron's question, Dante finally came clean, "It's been a couple of days. I left you here, and should never have done that... but don't know what happened after that point."

"Neither do I, "Aaron grunted. "All I know is, I smacked my head and... I think my damn leg is broken... at least, it feels broken. I can't... move it."

Mateo cautiously examined him and could see that his right leg was moving but that there was obviously something wrong with the other. He gently felt the leg from the hip to the ankle and was relieved when he did not identify any compound fractures. "It's probably fractured somewhere. You need to rest and drink all of this water. Dante will stay with you."

Aaron winced and nodded. Pain and fear had stripped away his arrogance and bravado. He inquired of Mateo, who had abruptly stood, "... Where... the hell... are *you* going?"

Mateo directed his response to both men, "I'm going... to get us out of here. Just stay alive and in one piece until the time is right."

Unsure of Mateo's intentions, Dante was concerned. "What are you talking about? How the hell will we know the time is right?"

Mateo started to walk away while responding, "You'll know. Trust me... you'll know." He carefully navigated the rocky terrain to the valley floor, and returned to the collapsed shed they had discovered earlier. The air temperature was 95 degrees, and the wind had died down to nothing. Large flakes of volcanic ash fell Earthward in slow motion, painting an eerie scene. Mateo's watch still read 8:12, but he had glanced at Dante's timepiece to learn it was actually close to 4:25 p.m. He knew the light would soon be gone.

On a Bed of Nails I'll Wait

Despite the growing sense of urgency, Mateo felt he should search the shed one last time, in hope of finding anything useful. He lifted every scrap of wood and turned every fractured rock. Amidst the rubble, he discovered a small, nondescript object bound in thick brown paper. He unwrapped it to discover a packet of fuses bound together; likely originally packed inside one of the fireworks crates. Next to the doorway, he found what appeared to be the lid for the metal barrel he previously extracted from the building, and he rolled it outside. He then stuck the fuses, enclosed in a small plastic pouch, into his shirt pocket along with his disposable lighter, and headed to the entrance of the cave.

Standing in the pool of waist-deep water at the mouth of the aperture, Mateo realized he had no choice but to enter by submerging himself. The thought of groping through the cavernous, pitch-black interior was unappealing and somewhat intimidating, but his mind was already set. He carefully tossed the torch into the cave, making sure it landed upon a large rock just inside the entrance. After tucking the plastic lighter and packet of fuses inside his mouth, he ducked as low as possible and then eased himself into the water. Initially an affront to his warm flesh, the cooler saltwater actually brought relief to his overheated body.

When Mateo popped up inside the cave, he removed the objects from his mouth and began to breathe again. Despite the fact that part of the torch was submerged when he retrieved it, he was still able to ignite its dry end. To his relief, the foundation was composed of solid rock, albeit predictably uneven. Even though the torch provided only minimal illumination, Mateo was grateful for the first glimmer of hope since their ordeal had begun. Only a trickle of light leaked through the cave opening behind him but he could see well enough to understand that he had discovered a great cavern behind the thick façade. The enormous barrier that separated the survivors from salvation turned out to be nothing more than a mirage. Perhaps the latest wave of tremors had helped open up the previously undetected discovery, or maybe it had been accessible all along. While Mateo wondered if they could have possibly followed the same path days earlier, he refused to dwell on what he was powerless to change.

He cautiously slogged through the water, wary of any drop-offs or gaps that could spell disaster. Mateo estimated a ceiling height of 12 - 15 feet at the apex. Some powerful force was obviously propelling the water toward him from the south or southwest. He imagined a water main or network of pipes must have ruptured during the quakes. Multiple sites within the zoo required saltwater – among them, the Wegeforth Bowl and dolphin tank, and Mateo fully understood that any critical damage to the pipes could jeopardize the well being of Tidus and Yuna.

The moment he recognized that the water provided a critical element of his plan, Mateo understood exactly what had to be done. He retraced his steps and emerged from the water where he had left the other supplies. The Sun was setting, which added to the sense of urgency. In the waning light, he saw the shadowy silhouettes of Dante and Aaron propped up among the rocks to the east. They had both apparently fallen asleep from exhaustion. *'It's just as well… they'll be safe there,'* Mateo thought, as he tied the nylon rope around the empty steel drum.

As the Sun set, he completed the transfer of the explosives from the wooden crates to the steel canister. He threw the torch in with them and pounded the lid shut with the heel of his clenched hand. In the dying sunlight, he stood at the mouth of the subterranean realm and gathered his courage. Propelled by desperation, he tucked the fuse packet and lighter into his mouth once again, grabbed the shovel in his left hand and submerged himself. Once he reemerged in the darkness and transferred the fuses and lighter to his shirt pocket, he tugged the nylon rope to drag the drum into the water. Using the weight of his body, he submerged it just enough to clear the constricted opening.

Mateo felt a great sense of satisfaction when the barrel finally popped up and floated in the cold water at his side. He took a few deep breaths and composed himself, knowing he would need all his remaining strength and courage to complete his plan. Unable to pry the lid off the steel drum, he had to strike it repeatedly with a softball-sized rock before it finally released and splashed into the water. After replacing the lid on the drum, he ignited the torch he had previously soaked in gasoline. Suddenly, the dark and foreboding world inside the mountain came alive.

The first thing that struck Mateo was the enormity of the cavern. The area expanded at the midpoint to a width of close to 30 feet. As he slowly dragged the unwieldy barrel deeper into the cave, he discovered that the water's depth remained fairly consistent at a little more than three feet. The cave interior was composed of rock and dirt, but anomalous reminders of a world that no longer existed protruded from the walls and ceiling. An electric utility vehicle was suspended in rock, directly above Mateo's head. Only part of its mangled frame was visible while the rest was embedded beneath the surface. The corner of a colorful building jutted out from the water to his right.

On a Bed of Nails I'll Wait

The torchlight revealed a whimsical embossed graphic that identified it as part of the obliterated Children's Zoo.

A bright, pulsing glow commanded his attention just as he maneuvered around a thick panel of green corrugated plastic that had been jammed into the surface of rock. In the distance, glowing rivulets of molten lava slowly slithered down the wall to the east. Mateo watched in disbelief as three thick, serpentine columns worked their way down the jagged surface. As white-hot magma contacted cool water, a plume of steam was born, quickly followed by another, and then another. Within seconds, the mist-like residue crawled along the water's surface in Mateo's direction. Only a few steps later, an even more ominous sight froze him in place.

A few yards to the west, a collection of nondescript objects floated in the shallow water, buffeted by the ebbing current. Mateo felt powerfully compelled to investigate, despite the sense of urgency to get on with his plan. His sense of dread grew as he hesitantly approached. To shed more light on the surroundings, he raised his torch. As feared, floating among the inanimate objects that littered the surface were several human corpses. He first identified an elderly woman, floating face-up, with a clear plastic rain bonnet still secured atop her head of grey hair. He found it peculiar that her narrow-framed eyeglasses were also still in place, resting squarely on the bridge of her nose. Her dress, dark blue with a pattern of tiny white flowers, billowed around her lifeless form. Mateo finally diverted his attention when he realized he was staring into her permanently opened blue eyes.

He forced himself to press onward, dragging the steel drum in his wake. Out of respect and revulsion, he did his best to avoid contact with the other bodies suspended in the frigid water. A few steps further, Mateo encountered one of Dante's fellow security officers, his blue cap bobbing in the water a couple of feet from his head. The tall young man appeared no more than 25 years old. His right arm was broken and twisted at an impossible angle and all Mateo could think was that the unfortunate soul may have been one of Dante's close friends. His light blonde hair floated around his head, resembling a halo around the innocent face turned a haunting alabaster by the saltwater.

He brushed past the carcasses of two small grey goats, likely once popular residents of the Children's Zoo. Next to one of the goats were the remains of another Zoo employee, her name tag visible at the surface. Through the liquid veneer, he was able to read the letters etched into the plastic base. Mateo was sure he would never be able to forget her name: "Marie Beecham."

I Miss Your Purple Hair

Many more bodies surrounded the solitary figure, who hung his head in abject resignation.

Mateo waded through the gruesome reminders that he and his daughter were immersed in a tragedy of epic proportions. That grim realization motivated him to move with alacrity to the far side of the nightmarish cavern. A patchwork of irregular-shaped apertures in the southern wall allowed only a whisper of air to pass through, while water forced its way through gaps below the surface. Mateo listened intently and surmised that the wall through which the water flowed was not significantly thicker than the one on the opposite side of the cave. He maneuvered the steel barrel onto a mound of rock, and then took shovel in hand to test the integrity of the surface. He repeatedly smashed the shovel into the wall at various points above and below the water's surface, to negligible effect.

After numerous attempts, covering a wide area, he had only managed to pierce one narrow band of brittle material – at waist level. He poked at it and then repeatedly thrust the shovel into it with all his might... until the head broke off, embedded between the rocks. The wood handle had been cracked long before he discovered it in the ruins of the storage shed. Frustrated and drained of energy, Mateo collapsed to his knees in the flowing water. His plan all along was to use the fireworks to try to blast through the rock, but he knew the odds were against him if the wall was too thick.

Mateo surveyed the morbid scene, a dark realm littered with dozens of innocent souls suspended in the frigid water. As tempting as it was to give up and return to his daughter, he decided there was no way he could turn back. He turned away from the grim landscape to survey the situation before him once again, more determined than ever. He stood again and slowly swept the torch over the area to survey the situation.

The southern wall was pocked with several more narrow slits that penetrated to the outside world, but there was no evidence of any substantial weak points. Once his eyes returned to the sight of the shovel head stuck halfway through the cavern wall, an idea was born. Using a pointed rock to smash open the steel container once more, Mateo retrieved a pair of sizable rockets from the assortment of fireworks. He recalled, as a young boy in Costa Rica, observing a pair of unruly carnival workers...

A carnival had just set up on the outskirts of town. The strong man was showing off to his much skinnier comrade. Both were very drunk and unstable on their feet. The slightly-built fellow – one of Mateo's fellow villagers – was goading the larger man to set off one of the rockets before the actual display was scheduled to begin. Largely due to the level of alcohol in his system, he defied his boss' policy and grabbed a large rocket from the supply truck. He staggered over to a nearby partial brick wall, the surviving remnant of a long-ago demolished building, while young Mateo watched from his hiding place in a nearby tree.

He gestured, 'watch this!' and wedged the rocket sideways in a gap between two columns of brick. After lighting the fuse, both men scampered behind the truck parked several yards away. Blaaaam!! The resulting explosion was not only deafening to both men and the few witnesses lurking in the vicinity, but by virtue of its strategic placement, the blast had obliterated the top portion of the wall. The annoying ringing in Mateo's ears persisted for several hours...

Mateo set his torch atop a nearby slab of limestone. He then tucked the two rockets under his arm and hoisted himself onto the shovel head embedded in the wall. It was wedged tight, but he was concerned it would fail to support his weight. He grabbed onto a protruding rock for added support and was pleasantly surprised to spot a wide, narrow notch in the surface of the wall, within easy reach. After embedding a fuse in each of the two rockets, he carefully wedged them into the shallow gap. Aware of the inherent dangers in handling explosives, he had rehearsed the next steps in his mind before lighting the intertwined fuses.

Once lit, he jumped off the shovel head, grabbed the torch and moved away as quickly as possible. The shallower water along the cave's western side enabled Mateo to move only slightly faster, and his heart pounded as tucked himself behind a large rock formation. He plugged his ears a second before the resounding blast rattled him from the bottom of his feet to the crowns of his teeth. Once the resulting debris fallout diminished, he went back to assess the damage.

To his utter dismay, the explosion had not produced the hoped-for result. It did knock a large chunk out of the wall, from shoulder level to just above the water, but an unknown depth of rock still prevented access to the other side. Try as he might, the embedded shovel head could not be pried from the wall's resolute clutches, so he was forced to use his hands to clear away loose material.

Despite his initial disappointment, Mateo understood that there was reason to believe his original idea could work – provided conditions were just right. The newly created recess afforded him an ideal opportunity to execute his original plan. He rolled the explosives-filled metal drum into position against the base of the wall. In his weakened state, Mateo worried he would never be able to lift the heavy object. He tried bending at the knees and using one leg to help support it, but the wet drum proved unwieldy. A second attempt was even less successful, sending Mateo splashing into the frigid water on his backside. When they popped out of his shirt pocket, he nervously snatched the pack of fuses out of the air before they reached the water. His heart beat wildly when he realized just how close he had come to losing them.

Mateo regained his footing and paused to catch his breath. Light-headed and disoriented, he told himself to "get it together." Understandably, he wondered if he truly had enough strength left to overcome the fatigue ravaging his mind and body. He supported himself by placing one outstretched hand against the rim of the metal barrel. The determined man then closed his eyes and began his breathing exercises, as he had done hundreds of times before.

Slowly drawing in and exhaling the stale air, he attempted to enter a state of tranquility. He ceased focusing on his doubts and discomfort, and simultaneously willed his pulse rate to decline and his adrenal glands to increase production. Within a few minutes, he could feel renewed strength in every muscle of his body... and a growing restoration of his faith.

Inevitably, Mateo's thoughts turned to Violet, and with minimal effort, he received an impression. In his mind's eye, he saw her splashing cool water over her face while faint music played in the background. He smiled as he sensed she was engaged in friendly conversation. A thousand memories flashed through his sub conscience: Veronica as angelic infant, joyful toddler, curious little girl, remarkable teenager... he so enjoyed every stage, and the innumerable precious moments packed within those 15 years.

Veronica. Mateo so loved the name he had given her. Even after he became accustomed to calling her Violet, every handwritten note packed into her school lunches was addressed to "Veronica."

'Veronica... the future is ours to create, remember? What do I always tell you before you get on the bus for school?'

For some reason, those words popped into Mateo's head once again, and he projected them to his only child. Though mired in surreal solitude, entombed in rock and earth, when her mental response infiltrated his mind, he felt he was... home again.

On a Bed of Nails I'll Wait

'Come home safe. That's what you always tell me, Papa. Come home safe.'

Mateo chuckled at how connected he and his only child had become, and his laughter echoed throughout the stone sanctum. It triggered a memory of Violet – from the weekend they moved into their new home in San Diego...

Violet ran to show him a little green lizard she had caught in the side yard of their new condo. "Papa!" she gleefully exclaimed. "Look! We're going to have lots of good luck living here!"

Acknowledging her discovery, he asked, "He seems like a friendly little guy, but why do you say we'll have good luck?"

Little lights sparkled wildly in her chocolate brown eyes as Violet explained, "We learned in school that some of our ancestors felt lizards were good luck, especially if you catch one during the daytime. They believed they protect us from unseen dangers. Do you think that's true?"

Having been nervous about leaving all that was familiar behind and starting over across the country, Violet was clearly seeking some reassurance. Mateo gave it a moment's thought before replying, "Sure, I think that could be true, but then again... we've been pretty lucky all along. If your new friend there brings us even a little more good luck, you've got to believe we'll do just fine living here."

Back in the present, Mateo realized he could ill afford to reminisce any longer. Following one more deep breath, he knelt down and firmly grasped both ends of the explosives-packed barrel. Focusing every ounce of energy, he hoisted it onto one knee, and in one smooth motion drove it into the indentation in the wall. By propelling it with the weight of his body, he succeeded in firmly embedding the barrel in the open niche the previous blast had created. He thrust his fists overhead in exultation. "Damn right!" he exclaimed, reveling in the cascading echoes.

Mateo took the fuses from his shirt pocket and began twisting the ends together to fashion them into one. The combined fuse needed to be long enough to buy sufficient time for him to get away. During the process, a new concern suddenly dawned on him. *The water!* He had not fully considered the cave's flooded foundation. In order to prevent the fuse from getting wet, he realized he would have to string it along the wall.

I Miss Your Purple Hair

After twining the shorter fuses into one, Mateo connected it to those he had already implanted in several of the largest rockets. He then strung the fuse along the wall, careful to secure it so it would not fall into the water. It only stretched a few yards, however, and he realized he would still be uncomfortably close to the barrel when he ignited the fuse. As disconcerting as it was, Mateo knew he had no choice.

He thought to himself, *'I've always believed actions speak louder than words.'*

As he glanced at the blurry silhouettes of the deceased floating in the water, he resolved to deliver Violet to safety at any cost. With that thought in mind, Mateo said a silent prayer... and lit the fuse. Relieved to see it ignite and start to burn down, he quickly turned and lunged toward the cave opening to the north. The water level had risen while he made his preparations, and Mateo found it more difficult to move through all of the dead bodies and debris.

He stumbled on some unidentified object beneath the surface and fell into the cold water with a loud splash. Though he managed to break his fall, he nervously looked back to check the progress of the spark burning its way along the fuse. His heart sunk when he saw it had already burned to within four feet of the barrel. Calculating the time elapsed and the length of fuse remaining, he realized he would never reach the exit in time. Mateo instinctively closed his eyes, dove beneath the murky water... and visited Veronica once more.

'Be brave, baby. Have faith, and remember... I'll never let you fall.'

'Papa?...'

Violet had been sitting on the deck, dangling her legs in the soothing water while watching Leanna and the other children play with Tidus and Yuna. Seated nearby on the other side of the deck, Victory and Dwayne talked quietly and tried to stay cool in the oppressive heat. Her red Bible in hand, Victory had just finished reading a section aloud to her husband. Mia, approaching from the direction of the fire pit, noticed the expression of concern on Violet's face. "What's wrong, honey?" she asked in all sincerity. Violet just stared straight ahead, not really seeing who was in front of her.

"… my father... I feel something... something's... happened..."

At that moment, the tank's filtration system ceased functioning. Without warning, the pumps completely shut down, leaving an eerie silence. Sinnamon had just finished splashing water over her face and chest. She cocked her head and matter-of-factly said, "Out of gasoline. The generator stopped 'cause we burned through all the gas last..."

Before she could finish, a shocking explosion rocked the entire region. Violet and all the others whipped their heads around to the southeast, to witness a dazzling rainbow of light rip through twilight's gossamer fabric. The vivid rocket trails contrasted sharply with a sky that had just turned a deep cerulean blue. The weary survivors watched in stunned silence as bursts of color illuminated the entire region. While the fireworks shot skyward, a mushrooming field of white mist crawled over the top of *Wormhole Wall* and spilled over them.

As quickly as it began, the display ended... leaving the shocked observers nervous and confused. Violet felt her father must have been responsible, but had no explanation for the pyrotechnics display. The blast had obviously been powerful enough to pose danger to anyone in close proximity, and the last telepathic message she received bore an ominous tone. With no way of ascertaining her father's involvement, her concern grew. She swiftly stuck her wet feet into her sneakers and announced, "I have to go."

Violet climbed down from the deck and walked purposefully toward the fire that was burning down to nothingness. Mia ran after her, calling out, "Wait!", but the determined girl just kept walking. Mia turned to Kyle, who was still staring at the colors dissolving into the sky, mouth agape. She implored, "Kyle, we've got to go, too. We have to help her…" Her stunned brother required a moment to gather his wits. The quick-hitting blast and subsequent display were unnerving, and he was as stunned as anyone. He recognized something momentous had occurred, and several scenarios ran through his mind as he and Mia pursued the teenage girl they barely understood.

Despite the fear in her heart, Violet remained composed as she entered the Reptile House to fetch her weathered denim backpack. She efficiently stuffed two bottles of water and a butane lighter inside, before slinging it over her shoulder. Upon exiting the familiar sanctuary, she grabbed a torch and brushed past Mia and Kyle on her way to the fire. In a trancelike state, the determined teenager lit the torch in the dying flames and then began climbing *Wormhole Wall*.

Dumbfounded by the explosion and ensuing pyrotechnics, just about everyone else was immobilized by confusion. Violet sensed their collective state of disarray and paused to look down upon the now-familiar home base illuminated by the dwindling fire. All of the others had scooped up their meager supplies and caught up with Mia and Kyle. Addressing the gathering, Violet succinctly stated, "It's time to go."

Sinnamon had already loaded a few essential supplies into the bag slung over her shoulder. With clear purpose she literally followed in Violet's footsteps and announced in mid-stride, "You heard her. It's time to go." Neither Violet nor her one-time nemesis looked back as they began the slow ascent toward the obscured gap between the rocks. The rest of the group suddenly snapped into action; corralling children, throwing together gear, and swarming toward the base of the mountain in Violet's wake. Their figures disappeared into the eerie white mist as the faltering bonfire sent hundreds of red cinders twisting skyward.

By the time they reached the passageway's opening, it was 5:10 p.m. and the last traces of sunlight had relented. The congregation stood together on the wide ledge at the mouth of *Wormhole Pass* and looked down upon what had been their home for the past four days. DeAngelo clung to his father's weathered shirt and summed up his feelings with, "Let's not come back here again, okay? I'm tired of it… except I'll miss Tidus and Yuna." With that, each individual briefly reflected upon their long ordeal before they entered the narrow gap.

From behind them to the west, they heard a prolonged howl – the unmistakable call of an adult wolf. The haunting sound momentarily stopped them in their tracks. "Yeah, yeah, yeah," Sinnamon sarcastically retorted. "We'll miss you too, pal. You're just lucky we didn't run into you or you'd have ended up on the menu." On that note, the group pressed onward, each of them determined to make it a one-way journey back through the dark, foreboding tunnel.

Surprised by the fireworks explosion, Dante and Aaron remained hunkered down between the jagged rocks. Dante had suspected Mateo's plan, and although he felt it was worth trying, was convinced it was doomed to fail. He expressed his thoughts out loud: "That rock is too thick. Punching a hole in it would take one hell of a blast... and a lot of luck, but I'll hope for a miracle anyway. What else is there to do?"

He expected Mateo to emerge from the thick fog to share the results, but there was no sign of him. Dante's pain was a growing distraction and he felt more desperate than ever when he admitted, "Damn knee. It's completely locked up on me. I guess... now we're a matched pair." Aaron was drifting in and out of consciousness, suffering from lack of insulin and dehydration. His eyelids fluttered in reaction to the sound of Dante's deep voice.

He woke up, if only temporarily, to ask, "Did you hear it... is that a helicopter?"

Dante had not heard anything since the blast from the far side of *Kemper's Folly*. He watched Aaron's eyelids shut again and then answered, "Uhh... I don't think so, buddy. But I'll let you know if I hear something. We can't move on our own, so Mateo had better come out of that hole soon." He had no way of estimating the damage caused by the explosion, nor did he have any clue as to Mateo's proximity to the blast. He was concerned for his safety, for selfish reasons as much as anything. Dante and his strange bedfellow were crippled by their injuries and, therefore, at the mercy of the elements... and the wolf. While praying Mateo would emerge from the mist, Dante cursed the day he applied for his position at the Zoo. Before long, he surrendered to fatigue and drifted to sleep.

Along the horizon, the sky had become an unearthly blend of violet and orange. Creeping closer from the north and east, the raging fires cast menacing flames into the swollen underbelly of the clouds. Those same fires provided just a hint of light; enough to tease, yet inadequate for navigating the unpredictable terrain. Although well after sundown, it was an unsavory 96 degrees when the band of beleaguered survivors emerged from *Wormhole Pass*.

Sinnamon poked her head out from the odd-shaped gap along the eastern face of *Wormhole Wall*, into a thick white mist. Torch raised high, she helped usher the rest of the party out of the passageway, one by one, until all were gathered on the ledge. The milky fog presented yet another obstacle, rendering their torches nearly worthless.

"Give me a break!" Sinnamon angrily exclaimed. "If it's not one thing, it's another friggin' problem. We'll break our necks trying to climb down in this soup. The Moon will be full tonight, and if we had clear skies we'd have more than enough light. But with this stuff hanging around, we can't see our stinkin' hands in front of our faces! What are we supposed to do now?"

Violet had been suffering with yet another severe headache during the arduous trek through the dark passageway. When she fumbled to pull a bottle of water from her dirt-covered backpack, Dwayne instinctively knelt to help her, and his right knee buckled. Despite nearly falling off the edge of the narrow ledge, he unsnapped the backpack, retrieved a bottle and handed it to

I Miss Your Purple Hair

Violet. She managed a barely audible "Thank you," and slowly unscrewed the cap.

Victory stepped in to help stabilize her husband and admonish him at the same time. "Darlin', I'm not about to lose ya now! Stay still and take a drink yourself. After all we been through, this is no time to be careless." After a few gulps, Violet handed her bottle to Dwayne. He thanked her and drank half of what remained before offering it to the others. Once reassured there was enough to go around, he finished the contents.

The flat area of rock upon which the survivors clustered seemed quite stable. It was narrow, yet broad enough to comfortably support everyone. Violet tried to get a sense of her father's whereabouts, but her throbbing headache made that impossible. Kyle consulted with Mia and then suggested, "We have no choice but to wait here until daybreak. The fog's only getting worse. I'll stay awake and keep an eye on things. Everyone okay with that?"

While Jason eagerly agreed with waiting for morning, he volunteered to be the one to keep watch throughout the night. He was nervous and fidgety, and afraid of having yet another prophetic dream. Denial had always been a crutch learned from his mother, and he had worn it like a comfortable bathrobe for most of his life. He was afraid he might dream a tragic end, so he had fought sleep for the past two nights, unbeknownst to the others. It would take a Herculean effort for him to stave off sleep yet again, but he was determined to do just that.

Sinnamon spoke up, demonstrating a new take-charge stance. "Okay, we'll camp right here. Anyone needing a bathroom break – go squat in the cave we came from. I don't intend to sleep in a litter box. We'll take shifts staying awake, in case any wild things pick up our scent. Jason, you look like crap warmed over, so why don't you be first to take point until Midnight – so you can sleep after that. Kyle – you can take it from there until 3:00 a.m., and then I'll do the late shift until dawn. Hell, I wake up around 4:00 a.m. most days, even when I'm not in the middle of Armageddon." Turning toward Kyle, she purred, "Just whisper somethin' sweet in my ear if I fall asleep; okay Doc?"

Ravi, who had been yawning repeatedly, tugged on Kyle's elbow and asked, "What does Arm-a-giddin mean?"

DeAngelo pounced on the chance to illustrate his superior knowledge, and quickly corrected the younger boy. "It's not 'Arm-a-giddin', Ravi. It's 'Armor-geddon.' It means you have to get your shield and armor so you're ready for battle; right, Dad?"

Dwayne had to struggle to see the innocent humor in the moment, given the circumstances. Wanting to play down the gravity implied by the actual term, he decided to play along. "You' right, Dee," he told his son. "An' the best offense... is always a strong defense. So, let's try to get some sleep here and we'll talk about it in the morning, okay?"

"Yeah," DeAngelo agreed. "We can't even see our faces in front of our noses!"

In the time-honored spirit of prepubescent one-upmanship, Ravi laughed loudly at the older boy's faux pas. "Dude! Your *face* is in front of your *nose*? That's what *she* said! Hahahaha!!" His nonsensical retort drew laughter from everyone... except Violet, who was lost in physical pain and awash in concern for her father.

Time crawled as the evening wore on and everyone made use of backpacks, tote bags, and clothing to get as comfortable as possible in preparation for sleeping. While the volunteer sentries adhered to their schedule, both Kyle and Victory stayed awake all night. Despite taking more Ibuprofen, Violet felt almost no relief from her headache. Exhausted in every way, she finally fell asleep around midnight with her head in Mia's lap. Mia gently stroked her forehead and hair for hours, while she drifted in and out of sleep herself. Leanna and Hanna sat nearby and prayed for Violet's health, until they too, drowsed off.

Jason was unable to stay awake despite his best effort. At some point during the middle of the night, his fears proved as prophetic as his dreams and a nightmare once again invaded his sub conscience...

Jason found himself crawling on all fours through a field of green grass. The wispy vegetation had grown tall, similar to sawgrass or a primordial variety one might find in the Amazon. Naked, Jason crawled across the soft, fertile field on all fours. When he forced himself to stand, he found the adjustment inexplicably painful... as if he was not meant to do so. Suddenly, directly in front of him, a white wolf stuck its large head though the curtain of overgrowth.

In his waking life, he would have fled in terror. In the bizarre dream realm, however, he felt compelled to approach the large predator. He was powerless to resist and soon found himself within range of its breath. Right in front of his eyes, the animal suddenly vanished into thin air and Jason heard it moving through the tall grasses. Still unable to stand, Jason blindly crawled through an endless maze of waving emerald blades. Just as he was convinced it was gone forever, the wolf's head poked through the curtain of grass again. Once again, he pursued the creature... and once again, when he drew close the strange beast ran off in another direction.

Their game of cat and mouse continued until the wolf failed to return. Jason found himself alone and abandoned – clueless as to where to go next. Inexplicably, he was finally able to stand again. Without warning, he was startled by the wolf's haunting howl. Jason was certain it had finally returned to lead him out of the maze, until he realized the call was not coming from the grassy plain, but from overhead. Standing amidst the sea of grass, he also realized it had become nighttime. He slowly turned in place to survey the environment, but as far as he could see, there was nothing but more grass.

Just as Jason felt like he was drowning in an endless sea of nothingness, the howling returned, louder and clearer than before – still coming from above. He snapped his head back to see millions of twinkling stars, widely varied in size, color, and intensity. The heavenly bodies were so sharply-defined he felt he could reach up and pluck any of them from the sky.

Suspended directly overhead was the full Moon, ripe like it was ready to burst. The pallid sphere was larger than he had ever seen it, with all of its familiar craters and beautiful imperfections in ultra-sharp focus. He stood alone at the apex of a subtle crest in the middle of the field, gawking in wonder. The howling continued while Jason basked in the sensations of the soft bed beneath his feet, the soulful cry of his lupine companion, and the awesomeness of the Universe.

Then he woke up.

△ △ △

Chapter Twenty Four

A Star That I Can See

*"Knowing our personal mission further enhances the flow of mysterious coincidences
as we are guided toward our destinies. First we have a question, then dreams,
daydreams, and intuitions lead us toward the answers, which usually are
synchronistically provided by the wisdom of another human being."*
~ James Redfield

J ust before dawn on the first day of the New Year, Jason slipped out of his dream world. As his eyes slowly opened to the darkness, he struggled to sort dream from reality. Neither made much sense to his anguished mind. His parched throat motivated him to grope for the nearly empty water bottle stashed between two rocks. After drinking the remaining contents, he drifted off to sleep again.

His rustling woke Violet, who had just experienced her own unusual dream. Though her headache had lessened overnight, she still felt tired and disoriented. As she slowly rejoined consciousness, she recalled some of the memorable scene in her dream, involving a young, brown-haired boy...

Running and spinning playfully, the boy was surrounded by a candy-colored cloud of hummingbirds. The curious little creatures hovered and darted about in all directions, forming a living halo that moved wherever he did. He giddily frolicked through a beautiful flower garden, giggling with delight at the vibrant beauty orbiting his head.

Violet's thoughts turned to the young friends her father fondly referred to as "The Pittsburgh Triad" – Nathan, Corinne, and Prajna. There had been others she connected with psychically, but these three had become especially close to her in recent months. She had received a few photos via the Internet, and the boy in her hummingbird dream reminded her of Nathan in age and appearance. The persistent theme of birds, coupled with the garbled telepathic message she received the day before, suggested a correlation. Despite the absence of natural light, she quietly rummaged for her small note pad and pen at the bottom of her backpack.

Violet switched on her scarred iPod®, sacrificing its waning energy for much-needed illumination. The display upon its screen informed her it was

I Miss Your Purple Hair

5:33 a.m.; still nearly an hour before sunrise. Due to the darkness as well as the persistent mist-like fog blanketing the lower level of the canyon, she could barely make out the obscure silhouettes surrounding her. Although anxious to locate her father, she understood the danger in attempting a descent without adequate light. She decided to turn her attention to the rumpled note pad in her left hand and began to write down some details that had been nagging at her for days.

The Quantum Qids' field trip took them away from The Foundation on the fateful day the quakes tore through Western Pennsylvania. Their destination that day, The National Aviary, had donated to the San Diego Zoo, the peacock that bore the miraculous tail feather. The fortuitous timing of the excursion most likely saved their lives, in light of the extensive damage to the dorms at Kyle Nordstrom's facility. Since reestablishing her unique connection with "The Pittsburgh Triad", Violet had received some garbled messages, wherein Nathan kept repeating the words: "National Aviary." The message initially made little sense to her. Then, the possibility dawned on her that perhaps he was simply obeying a compulsion to transmit its name to her – a compulsion *he* did not fully understand.

Her father was fond of suggesting, "When in doubt… sound it out," and Violet often heeded that advice to analyze unfamiliar words. She sometimes went a step further, writing a word out in an effort to identify its origins. She had become adept at their "Anagram Game" by routinely taking words or phrases and reassembling the individual letters to create different words. She fumbled for her felt-tip pen and wrote NATIONAL AVIARY in the note pad. She began reorganizing the individual letters, writing each letter in random order along the same ruled line. She scrutinized the 14 letters, searching for words within the words.

It was easy to identify a handful of short words, and she jotted them down… ON; NO; YIN; OAT; NAIL; TAIL; ANT; AIRY; LAY; ROT; YARN; TIARA; TINY; TONY; ANVIL; VIAL; VAIN; TOY. During the process, she quickly stumbled upon several interesting words by switching some of the letters around. She wrote them down: NAVAL; RAYON; NOTARY; AVATAR; VITAL; ANVIL; OVARIAN; and VALIANT. Some discoveries brought a smile to her face: RAVI was hidden within the letters, as were ironic discoveries such as RAIN; LAVA; NIRVANA; and TALON… the bird theme persisted.

She continued to rearrange and cross out letters, as she had done many times before to pass the time. In developing their game, Mateo and Violet's rule had always been that one had to use *all* of the letters to form a new phrase or singular word. Her persistence led to the discovery of the two-word term: TRAIL AVIAN. Was this yet another strange message related to birds?

'Was I destined to follow that peacock? What does it all mean?'

Violet wondered if there might be some hidden message buried within the words at which she kept staring. Perhaps Nathan, the young friend she had never met in person, was merely respecting an inner urge to transmit the term, assuming it would make sense to her. After a few more minutes of trial and error, her persistence was rewarded. She finally identified a four-word phrase hidden within NATIONAL AVIARY, utilizing every one of the letters, configured in a new order.

'RAY... ON... AVIAN... TAIL... the peacock feather!'

Violet felt an enormous weight lifted the moment she wrote the last letter on her ruled paper. She reached into the pocket of her shorts and pulled out the feather. With her right hand, she held it close to her face. Focused on admiring the wondrous details woven into the eye, she had never attempted to interpret the meaning behind the symbols. She finally understood that the three elements represented more than just some freak accident of Nature.

Even in the diffused light, the feather's iridescent surface sparkled. Violet gently held it by the quill and slowly rotated it to perform a careful examination. In the early morning silence, she reviewed the three golden symbols fused into the rich copper background: the dominant sphere; the small, five-pointed star; and the elongated triangle positioned in between. She examined them and tried to relate the objects to the anagram she had just discovered.

'Ray on avian tail... Ray on avian tail...'

Obviously, the object in her hand qualified as the "avian tail." The golden, elongated triangle could be described as a "ray" of light. Violet deemed that term appropriate, since its position and shape suggested it emanated from the sphere and fanned out slightly as it approached the tiny five-pointed star.

'But, how do they all relate? And what does it mean?'

I Miss Your Purple Hair

Violet stood up slowly, her head throbbing worse than the previous night. She held the feather at eye level and closed her eyes to meditate. She silently prayed for a definitive answer to her questions. Seated a few yards behind her, Hanna and Leanna silently observed. They understood that their angst-ridden friend was struggling to piece together the elements of a mystery. They clasped hands and joined with Violet in *The Web*, praying for enlightenment and contributing their combined energy in support.

The thick cloud canopy had drifted eastward, gently ushered by a developing breeze. At 6:26 a.m. on this strange New Year's morning, the temperature was already 86 degrees and rising. Mia, Kyle, and Sinnamon – curled up and huddled together – also began to rise, following a night of uneasy sleep.

Within a few minutes, everyone was awake except DeAngelo and Ravi, who seemed able to sleep through any disturbance. Violet had been praying, bathed in the light of the full Moon that had gradually been unveiled as the clouds dispersed. As if in answer to her prayers, a now-familiar sound stirred her from her peaceful meditative state. The unmistakably chilling howl of the wolf pierced the early morning silence. Its distinctive call clearly came from the south, in the direction of the gargantuan monstrosity Aaron and Dante had attempted to scale on that first fateful day... the wall they had dubbed *Kemper's Folly*.

In the limited light, Violet struggled to spot any movement among the rocks. She cautiously leaned over the precipice and narrowed her eyelids in an attempt to locate the wolf. Again it howled, enabling her to finally pinpoint its position. Barely more than a hundred yards to the south, she spotted the white wolf along the summit of *Kemper's Folly*. The creature's large blue eyes glowed in the moonlight, seemingly fixed upon Violet. The enormous Moon dominated the deep indigo backdrop and for a moment she basked in the beauty and imposing scale of the celestial body. While staring at its remarkable surface details, she detected a milky trail of light in her peripheral vision – a moonbeam – stretching across the sky from the Moon to a solitary, twinkling star on the horizon ... directly above the white wolf.

'That's it! It all finally makes sense. Papa, wait for me there. We'll get home safe... together.'

Mia approached Violet, gently placed a hand upon her shoulder, and eased her away from the edge of the precarious perch overlooking the canyon.

"What is it?" she softly asked, as Violet turned to face her.

She pointed to a specific area of the southern sky and explained, "See? That ray of light points to the super-bright star... directly above the wolf. My father... went *that* way," Violet stated flatly. She then laid out the remarkable truth for Mia and everyone else. "An anagram for 'National Aviary' is 'Ray on Avian Tail.' It's not just a coincidence. It's something more. The diagram on the peacock feather points out the path we have to follow. The three symbols represent a ray of light between a Moon and a single star."

The sky had gradually become lighter with each passing minute, and the ray to which Violet referred was no longer visible.

Kyle commented, "I... I don't see it. Where is this ray of light?"

From behind them, Dwayne chimed in, "You say there's another wolf over there? Can you pinpoint it for us?"

Violet pointed to the spot where she had seen the mature white wolf. "Yeah, there... it's right..." But, the wolf was gone; as if it had suddenly vanished into the sky. "Well, it *was* right there... at the top of *Kemper's Folly*. Maybe it climbed down the other side, but it was right there – where the two walls meet. Didn't you hear it howling?"

Mia and Kyle were puzzled by Violet's contention. They had not heard the howling, nor had anyone else besides her. A minute of awkward silence ensued, until Sinnamon finally changed the tone. "Maybe there *was* a wolf, and the rest of us were asleep and missed it. Who cares? It's light enough now to climb down and find the others. Let's get our asses in gear and see if we can't get the hell out of this place, once and for all." The burgeoning breeze escorted more clouds to obscure the enormous Moon, and none of the clues Violet had witnessed were any longer visible.

'I know the wolf is there... and so is Papa. I need to lead everyone that way.'

None of her companions heard the wolf or saw the critical elements she had seen, yet Violet was certain they existed. In her heart, she knew the message was expressly meant for her. Perhaps it was a sign sent by her father. All she knew was that she had no doubt about the direction they needed to take. "Alright," Violet sighed. "Let's get to the bottom and find the others." She then pointed to the spot revealed by the strange symbols and emphatically announced, "But after we find them, we have to explore *that* area." The group acknowledged her, quickly collected their gear, and started their descent.

I Miss Your Purple Hair

By 7:13 a.m., they had finally reached the valley floor. It took very little time for the ultra-observant Armstrong sisters to sense Aaron and Dante, obscured among the rocks along the western face of *Sunrise Summit*. Without hesitation, Leanna and Hanna took several confident strides in that direction, leading Kyle to demand an explanation. "Girls! Where are you going? Hold up!" he barked. They paused for a moment but then continued walking very deliberately through the mist, toward a destination only they had identified.

DeAngelo left his parents' side and ran ahead to join the girls. Just as abruptly, Ravi pulled away from Mia, who'd been firmly grasping his hand, to join his new friends. "I see something up there!" he shouted, excited to have been among the first to visually spot movement among the rocks. Sure enough, Leanna and Hanna had psychically pinpointed the life forces nestled among the rocks. When Dante lifted his head in reaction to the unexpected voices, DeAngelo pointed him out to the others. The group of children then stopped, deferring to the adults for guidance.

Sinnamon called out to Dante, "What the hell are you doing up there?" She thought for a second before adding, "Are you hurt?"

Dante was both relieved and excited. The condition of his damaged knee had worsened considerably overnight and he was no longer able to put any weight on it. He cleared his dry throat before weakly shouting in reply, "I have Kemper up here with me. Neither of us can walk! Can someone come help us down?"

"How badly hurt is Kemper?" Kyle yelled to Dante.

Dante wearily answered, "Pretty bad shape, man. Someone will need to carry him."

Jason instantly volunteered. Sinnamon suggested, "At least three of us need to go, if we're gonna bring two grown men down safely. I'll go with you." Jason smiled, and flashed back to the first hours spent with Sinnamon, in the Ituri Forest. It felt like years had passed, since that first encounter. He had begun to see more depth of character in the woman he originally felt was little more than a cold-hearted mercenary. In multiple little moments, he had observed glimmers of sincere compassion.

Dwayne threw his name into the mix, but his protective wife quickly vetoed the notion. "You're in no shape for more climbin' my dear," Victory insisted. "You sure can't be supportin' someone else's weight on that leg. Besides, I need you to stay right here an' keep an eye on these young ones. I'm feelin' strong ... so I'll go." Dwayne was inclined to protest her decision, but relented, recognizing his physical limitations as well as the futility of arguing with his headstrong spouse. Ultimately, he agreed to gather and protect the children at the base of the mountain, while concerns about the wolf lurked ominously within everyone's minds.

Violet yelled to Dante, "Where's my father? Did you see him come this way?"

While Victory, Jason and Sinnamon began their ascent, Dante responded, "He was here... but he went through an opening in the southwest corner. You must've heard the explosion when he set off the fireworks we found, but I don't know if it accomplished what we hoped." He pointed in the general direction of the cave opening in the opposite corner of the region. "You might be able to catch up to him that way, unless the blast sealed the entrance."

Without replying, Violet grabbed her walking stick, pivoted and walked off in the direction she had already planned on heading. "Wait! Veronica!" Mia called out. "It could be very dangerous!" Kyle had just instructed Ravi, DeAngelo, Leanna, and Hanna to stay close to Dwayne. He stood up from his kneeling position and whipped his head around to watch Violet disappear into the milky mist. As she crossed the uneven terrain, glass shards and splintered pieces of wood crunched beneath every step.

Kyle exclaimed, "Hold on, Violet! Don't go off alone!" He looked at Mia, who already was gesturing her intention to follow her new friend. He then turned to Dwayne and asked, "Are you feeling up to watching the kids alone? I have to go with her." Dwayne assured him that he was alert and physically capable of ensuring the well-being of the four children. Kyle patted him on the shoulder as a gesture of confidence and urged the young ones, "All of you have to stick together and listen to what Mr. Cooper tells you. I promise we'll be back soon." He and Mia then quickly vanished into the mist.

Dwayne ushered the four children into a well-protected nook at the base of *the Fire Wall*, directing them not to wander out of his reach. They found a small patch of grass to sit on while they awaited the return of Victory and the others. No sooner had they sat down when the unexpected occurred. Suddenly and without exchanging so much as a word, Hanna and Leanna stood back up and began walking away, obviously in hot pursuit of Violet, Mia, and Kyle. Dwayne called out to them, "Hey! Come back! You need to stay here with us, girls! It could be dangerous..." He quickly recognized that the sisters had completely tuned him out; hell-bent on catching up to Violet's party.

DeAngelo eagerly offered, "Dad... you want me to go get them?" Dwayne rubbed the stubble growing atop his shaved head. "No, son. You stay right here with me. Those girls may be young, but they aren't your average teenagers. They'll be alright once they catch up to the others. I don't think they would obey, anyway." Ravi and DeAngelo crept closer to Dwayne, seeking some semblance of security amidst the developing uncertainty of the quickly evolving events. Dwayne switched on his MP3 player, and the Coldplay song "Viva La Vida" began to play through the device's built-in speakers.

In pursuit of her father, Violet set her jaw and strode with great purpose, closely pursued by Mia, Kyle, Leanna, and Hanna. They walked past the site of the damaged tool shed, jumped across jagged fissures in the ground, and sidestepped plumes of steam laced with toxic chemicals. Along the way, they encountered various insects, including a pair of blue dragonflies – the first they had seen in days. A trio of seagulls circled overhead, their pristine white feathers sharply contrasting the grey canvas of the morning sky.

Rumbles of thunder once again sounded, signaling the advent of yet another storm. By the time Hanna and Leanna caught up to the others near the entrance to the cave, rain had returned to the region. Tiny droplets began to fall, decorating both the inanimate and the living with miniscule specks. Tipped off by the pool of water at their feet, Violet realized that her father must have made the bold decision to submerge himself to enter the darkness beyond. She could hear debris splashing into the water from above, which informed her that there had to be an open cave beyond the cramped threshold.

Kyle instructed Mia, "Hold your torch over this way," and used his lighter to ignite it as well as the one he carried. "There's enough of a gap above the water," he added, looking into the knee-level breach in the mountainside. "We can pass the torches to whoever goes in first."

Violet announced, "I have to do this... but the rest of you can stay here if you want. It's up to you. But I don't have a choice... my father went this way."

Without further deliberation, Violet plunged into the cold saltwater and popped up inside the dark cavern. She immediately discovered how treacherously uneven and slippery the foundation was. The water, flowing steadily toward her from the south, was easily three feet deep near the point of entry. Kyle quickly extended his long arm through the opening, delivering a lit torch into Violet's waiting hand. She was then surprised to see Hanna pop up alongside her in the chilly water, followed immediately by Leanna. They stood to either side of her and each placed a hand on Violet's back.

A Star That I Can See

Mia emerged next and Kyle handed her the second torch once she got to her feet. Kyle had a slightly more difficult time squeezing through the constricted opening, but finally joined them inside. They were all stunned at the discovery, never having envisioned that the foreboding barrier contained an open interior. Violet and Mia raised their torches high to better illuminate the dank, gloomy area. The ubiquitous mist crawled along the surface of the slow-moving water. Hanna pointed to the jagged ceiling and warned, "Look out!" as several chunks of rock plummeted from above and splashed into the water a few yards from where they stood. In the wake of the explosion Mateo orchestrated, the interior was still unstable, resulting in debris periodically splashing into the water.

The light produced by the torches bathed the expansive interior in a surreal orange hue. As they moved further from the entry point, they began to comprehend what had happened. Telltale signs were all around them. The damaged terra cotta roof of one of the quaint little shops in the Children's Zoo protruded from the water, half-embedded in the rock below. They were shocked by the sight of a twisted and dented automobile, embedded upside-down in the cavern ceiling.

As they slogged through the cold water, they discovered that the irregular foundation crested in the middle. With each tenuous step, the water became shallower around their legs until they found themselves standing upon a crude walkway of rock leading through the heart of the cave. Eventually, they were relieved to find themselves completely clear of the water.

The fireworks explosion succeeded in creating a massive rupture in the cave's outer wall, but it also triggered a partial collapse of its fragile ceiling, raining debris over Mateo. The collapse created the raised walkway upon which the party now stood – while tragically burying him in the process.

Unaware of her father's fate, Violet led the band of survivors onward through the relentless mist, with torches held high. To their left, they spotted the glowing amber lava snaking down the wall from some unknown source. They could feel the intense heat generated by the molten mass, which was less than twenty yards away.

Though humbled by the succession of disturbing sights and infused with a growing sense of dread, the nervous party moved ahead with single-minded purpose. Violet desperately tried to get a reading on her father, but was frustrated by a barrage of confusing signals. At the very moment she felt the first strong impression of his presence, something out of the corner of her eye shattered her concentration.

I Miss Your Purple Hair

The tiny, pale hand of a young child projected from the water, no more than five feet from the walkway. Mia gasped in horror when she spotted the object of Violet's focus. She quickly urged Leanna and Hanna, who were walking between her and Kyle, to avert their eyes... but it was too late. They had already noticed the child's body, as well as others, floating beneath the veil of mist.

Littering the water on either side of their bridge of rock were countless human bodies; some old, some very young. Hanna and Leanna showed little outward expression, but felt sick to their stomachs. They had developed such intrinsic powers of self-control that they instinctively went into a state of emotional detachment as a defense mechanism. Mia asked, "Are you alright? Please… avoid looking at the water. Try to look ahead and help us find a way to the other side."

Leanna nodded and Hanna replied, "We… we're okay," sounding less than convincing. The sights only got more gruesome as they eased their way over the irregular rubble. Kyle noted that the molten lava seeping through the eastern wall was creating voluminous steam when it contacted the cold saltwater. The mist dominating the cavern was primarily a by-product of that interaction. The cloak of fine mist served as a blessing in that it obscured some of the horrific details of the mass graveyard at their feet. "Let's keep moving," Kyle suggested as they tried to pick up the pace as best they could. The sounds of more debris plunging into the water all around them served as ample motivation.

Violet had been silently praying along the journey, pleading with the Collective Soul to protect her father and lead her to him. She clung to her belief they were on the right path and would soon reunite. She tried to locate him psychically, still to no avail.

'Where have you gone, Papa? Why can't we connect?'

She surmised that he must have created or discovered a passageway to the outside, and was likely summoning help. In her imagination, he was somewhere out there, rallying a rescue operation. That would be his first priority.

Visibility was severely limited, due to the thick fog and the torches' limited effect. The group slowly pressed onward, shivering from the cold water enveloping their legs. Finally, Violet's ears picked up a subtle sound that restored some of her waning hope. It was the breeze; soft and nearly indiscernible, but unmistakable nonetheless. As they moved beyond the dozens of bloated corpses, she detected the slightest sense of air blowing toward her. Violet's nostrils flared as she took in the first hint of fresh air she had smelled in days. Unlike the acid-laden stench that dominated their cloistered environment the past four days, this air smelled fresher – like the air along the coast. Invigorated, she called out, "Come on! We're almost there!"

Within her next few steps, Violet finally saw what she had been anticipating: the muted morning sunlight seeping through an opening in the wall. The others caught up to her and saw the same soft, glimmering light between the haphazard arrangement of rocks.

Leanna exclaimed, "There's a breeze blowing in!" and she and Hanna felt reenergized by the discovery. In contrast to the cave's gloomy interior, the sunlight forced Violet to shield her eyes. She doused her torch in the nearby water. The bridge of rock had conveniently led them to the opening, providing dry footing all the way through to the other side. Water flowed in along either side of the narrow aperture through which Violet passed.

While Violet and the two younger girls were able to slip through the irregular opening with little trouble, Kyle and Mia had to pry away chunks of rock before they could breach the same portal. The five bedraggled friends emerged to a steady rainfall and rapidly escalating temperatures, already oppressively hot and humid at 7:45 a.m.

A strange landscape awaited, dominated by incongruous rock formations, demolished buildings and further evidence of death. The remains of animals and humans alike littered a landscape of broken asphalt, dirt and debris, surrounded by towering pillars of rock. A narrow valley between the strange earthen monoliths provided a serpentine pathway.

Violet looked at her companions in confusion, trying to get her bearings after the unnerving trek through the cavern's hellish interior. Mia broke the silence by speculating, "This has to be more of what's left of the Children's section of the zoo. That means we're close to where the main parking lot should be… only it looks like there's nothing left of it. These poor people must have been trying to get to their vehicles or waiting for buses here." She felt deeply pained by the sight of so many innocent victims strewn about the otherworldly landscape. Mia proposed, "If we follow along this valley, maybe we'll find some of the parking area still intact. That must be where your father went, too."

While Violet agreed, she was immobilized by a sense of dread. Leanna and Hanna gravitated to her side in a gesture of support and understanding.

I Miss Your Purple Hair

Their actions brought to mind something her father had recently said...

'Summoning the courage necessary to push through fear is one of the most telling traits of a true leader. When you feel afraid you must try to understand what's governing the emotion. Only understanding can lead to overcoming... and overcoming fear often leads to enlightenment.'

Violet could literally hear her father's voice speaking the words, as clear as if he were standing next to her. She considered what was causing her immobility. It was not only the horror of so much death surrounding her; it was the fear of learning what fate had befallen her father. She was not sure she wanted to know. Then again, she realized she had no choice but to know the truth – good or bad. Although she reserved hope he had survived the blast and was somewhere up ahead of them, it greatly concerned her that she was unable to get any "read" on his whereabouts. It felt as though his spirit had been completely extricated. Her hope still rested on the possibility that he had gone ahead to seek help.

"One of us should go back for the others," Kyle suggested. So focused on the thrilling discovery of the pathway leading out, they nearly forgot that their fellow survivors were still waiting for word. He added, "If the four of you feel secure here, I'll go bring the rest of them through. Can you hold this position until we rejoin you?" Mia nodded and expressed her willingness to protect the teenagers, but Violet protested.

She disagreed and firmly announced, "I'm going on ahead." I'll go alone if I have to, but I've got to find my father. This has to be the path he followed, so I have to go where it leads. I'm sorry, but I can't wait. I have to go now." Leanna and Hanna immediately declared their intention to stay with Violet, too. Mia shook her head and managed a half-smile, amused but not surprised by Violet's resolve and the Armstrong sisters' loyalty.

Mia turned to Kyle and told him, "I agree with them... and I need to do what I can to help find Mateo, too. He could be in trouble, so we should keep moving. You go back to get the others, and I'll keep an eye on the girls. We'll stick to this path and find out where it leads. If we hit a dead end, we'll return to this spot, okay?" Kyle accepted her proposal, in part because he knew there was no point in trying to change her mind, but also because he had faith in the character of the four amazing women. He asked Violet for her torch and then headed back through the cave, leaving them to face the unknown.

They quickly searched the immediate vicinity for walking sticks and then moved ahead along the pathway so conveniently carved into the desolate landscape. Violet took the lead and Mia purposely kept to the rear of the pack, keeping all three girls in sight at all times. They followed the winding path and noted that the surrounding walls of dirt and rock were gradually diminishing in scale as they progressed.

The path twisted in snakelike fashion around great mounds of earth and between increasingly large pools of water. The sky had become a strange hue of red and purple, and the familiar sounds of thunder continued in the distance. Amazed that the serpentine path seemed endless, they kept moving – sidestepping the occasional uprooted tree and climbing over small obstructions protruding from the ground.

Violet was the first to see it. Alongside a large flowering bush covered in white flowers was the white wolf, no more than twenty yards ahead. When she first spotted it, Violet immediately froze and held out her arm to alert the others. Mia and the other girls quickly understood and they all reacted by taking a couple of backward steps. Violet, however, experienced a surprising emotional reaction the moment she locked eyes with the magnificent beast.

A long-time animal enthusiast, familiar with some aspects and behaviors of wolves, identified the animal as a variety of arctic wolf – with two outstanding features: a coat of pure-white fur and blue eyes. At birth, wolf pups generally have blue irises that eventually change to a yellow-gold or orange. She had read that it is highly unusual for an adult wolf to retain its blue-colored irises. She was convinced it was the very same creature they had repeatedly encountered, but wondered why it had remained, when it was finally free.

Leanna had already taken several steps back toward the cave. "L... Let's go back," she whispered. Careful not to agitate the imposing animal, Mia held a finger to her mouth to urge Leanna to be silent. With her other arm, she tried to reach out to grab Violet's shoulder, but surprisingly – she had already taken a handful of steps *toward* the white-furred creature. Mia was aghast. Both of the Armstrong sisters clung to her side and tugged at her shirt to suggest they all run while the possibility of escape existed. Ultimately, she could hold no longer her tongue.

In a stern whisper, Mia insisted, "Veronica! Come back here! You don't know anything about that animal! What are you doing?!" Violet waved her off as if to suggest there was no need for concern. Mia, Leanna, and Hanna remained stuck in place, wanting to run away but unwilling to abandon

Violet. They could not quite muster the courage to join her either, leaving them in limbo for what seemed like hours, although only seconds had transpired. An awestruck Mia simply could not believe her eyes as she watched Violet approach the wolf in what felt like ultra-slow motion. She tightly clutched the end of her long wooden walking stick and leaned forward, thinking she might have to spring to Violet's defense if the wolf became aggressive.

The tension escalated as Violet moved to within a few feet of the snow-white creature, which stood beneath a lush overhang of emerald leaves decorated with tiny white blossoms. The rain continued to fall and the wind gently swept the region, while the omnipresent thunder growled in the distance. Just as a bolt of lightning flashed about a mile to the southwest, the wolf abruptly turned and then vanished into the thick overgrowth.

Relieved that the animal exhibited no intention of harming Violet, Mia breathed a sigh of relief. However, that momentary sensation was incredibly short-lived when, to her horror and amazement, she watched Violet dart into the same thicket in pursuit. Leanna and Hanna were equally shocked, and they cried out in unison, "Violet!" The three of them ran to the spot where they last saw her.

Dense overgrowth obscured what sounded like a flowing stream that split the lush region of wild grasses. It was nearly impossible to see anything through the thick network of gnarled, thorny branches. While the rain continued, Mia led the two girls in pursuit of Violet by following her footprints in the wet soil. She had expected to see the wolf's paw prints too; but oddly, there were none to be found.

The three pursuers fought their way through the overgrowth, struggling to push aside bramble as they followed the sporadic impressions. Scarlet scratches covered their exposed flesh as they maneuvered through the area with alacrity. Mia kept calling out to Violet all the while, praying she was not in imminent danger. For what felt like an eternity, there had been no response, and her concern escalated.

Finally, as the edge of a clearing loomed directly ahead, a familiar voice called out. "Over this way! Just keep going in the same direction and you'll find me." Within a few minutes, Mia and the two girls emerged in the clearing where Violet waited. Before Mia could interrogate Violet, the scene in the background rendered her speechless. They found themselves in a clearing that opened up onto a scene for which none of them could have been prepared. Ringed by lush foliage and flat terrain, they had finally stumbled upon the way out, only to face a horrible realization.

A Star That I Can See

The clearing spilled into a great expanse devoid of trees or the strange rock formations which had dominated their existence the past four days. The scene provided the first real hint as to the untold story of the destructive event that forever changed their lives. Their worst nightmares had truly become reality.

On the horizon, The Pacific Ocean lapped at a shoreline that only days earlier consisted of paved streets and suburban dwellings. Completely destroyed were many magnificent examples of mankind's technological prowess, and lost along with them were millions of lives. Power was obviously out everywhere, and the only lights they spotted through the layers of mist and smoke belonged to the few functioning ambulances and police vehicles.

The coastline had been dramatically redesigned, bringing the crashing waves of the mighty ocean much further inland. Their sight was severely limited due to the pervasive mist and obstructions within the surrounding terrain, but what they saw was frightening enough. Although only able to glimpse a small portion of the new West Coast, they suspected the damage extended far beyond their little corner of the world.

The rain continued to fall, but they no longer felt any concern for the weather. The white wolf was nowhere to be seen, nor did they detect any evidence of its presence. It seemed apparent to Violet that the noble animal had purposely led them to this spot, one they otherwise might have been unable to find for a very long time. There was no way they could have known that the only route to this particular inlet was through the mass of tangled bramble which obscured it.

The white wolf had led them to their first glimpse of the New Earth and to their ultimate salvation. Now, it had disappeared. A strange notion spun through Violet's sub conscience. Was there possibly a direct connection between her father and the wolf? They inexplicably found no footprints left behind by either of them... as if neither had ever existed.

'Papa... did you lead us here? Is this your way of saying... goodbye?'

Violet recalled the passages that Victory read from her Bible...
'Again Jesus spoke to them, saying, 'I am the light of the world. Whoever follows me will never walk in darkness, but will have the light of life.'

'Again He said to them, 'I am going away, and you will search for me, but you will die in your sin. Where I am going, you cannot come.'

I Miss Your Purple Hair

As tears filled her eyes, Violet felt a profound emptiness at the core of her being. She looked at the somber faces of her three companions and resigned herself to the truth. They all began to understand what her father had done and the price he paid to ensure their survival. All of them were drowning in a deluge of emotions: sorrow, exhaustion, sympathy, relief... and had to come to grips with their harsh new reality. There had been much pain, suffering, and death amidst the devastation across the angry planet. They could only wonder how far-reaching the destruction extended, but suspected the worst as they looked out upon the smoldering, surreal landscape.

Violet stood at the edge of the clearing overlooking the new coastline while Mia, Leanna, and Hanna stayed back and allowed her a moment to reflect. As tears streamed down her sunburned cheeks, dozens of memories swirled through her anguished mind. She recalled one of the earliest memories of her father, when she was a First Grade student in Miami...

Mateo worked two jobs at that time. While utilizing his web design skills during the day, he also worked part-time in construction to make ends meet. Injured when he took a tumble on a project site, he came home one Saturday afternoon with a cast covering his fractured right wrist. Young Violet had never before seen her father injured and the sight of his strange-looking arm frightened her to tears. She sobbed uncontrollably, afraid that he would always have the scary white wrap on his arm. He picked her up, despite his injury, and sat her down upon the kitchen counter. Violet asked, "Why did this happen to my Papa?"

Trying to make light of the injury in an effort to console her, he laughed and said, "Oh, it was my own fault for being so clumsy, my angel. I zigged when I should have zagged, and then fell down and went boom!" Her tears persisted. Violet could not accept that any harm could befall her indestructible father. She subconsciously refused to consider his mortality because he provided such a vital sense of security – in sharp contrast to her irresponsible mother.

"You have to stop doing that job! I don't want you to go back ever again, okay!?" she demanded through her sniffles.

Mateo recognized a perfect opportunity to deliver a lesson to his pride and joy. He quizzed, "What does Papa do at his job? Do you remember?"

"Uh-huh. You... build things," she replied.

"That's right, baby. We build things."

"So?" she obstinately pouted.

"Well, my charming daughter; you need to remember that there's always

a little bit of pain involved whenever we build something. Building things is important, but it takes hard work. It's a lot easier to break something apart than it is to build something new, right? Remember when I installed your swing set? I strained my back building it, but now you have a beautiful swing set to play on with your friends. Wasn't that worth a little trouble?"

Violet's tears had eased and she looked a bit less concerned once he helped put things in perspective. She answered, "I guess so. I love my swing set!"

"Alright then," he said through a toothy smile. "Papa was good as new soon after that... and now you have a beautiful swing set to play on every day. Soon this silly cast will be gone, and we'll go visit the new library we're building! We'll visit that library many times so this little boo-boo is going to be worth it one day. Anything worth building takes hard work and a little pain. But, we should be happy any time we have the chance to build new things. That's called... progress."

As a pair of red crabs nimbly skittered across the flowing stream, Violet recalled not only her father's words, but also every nuance of his voice. His reassuring tone had always supplanted her fears with a sense of hope. He always felt it was one of his primary responsibilities to prepare his only child to gracefully manage difficult times, and he had frequently reminded her that life was certain to present unexpected challenges. Over the years, he helped her develop and refine her coping skills as a means of protecting her. As always, his motivation was to equip her to be courageous, self-reliant, and resilient.

She understood that she had lost him and allowed the rain to wash her tears into the soil at her feet. Violet realized that throughout his life, he had always built things and worked to enhance communications; always building and communicating, building and communicating. As she gazed upon the new coastline, she pledged to her father that she would keep evolving and moving forward... and never stop building... until the day they would reunite.

'Papa, I swear I'll work hard to make you proud.'

'You can't help but make me proud, Veronica. I have faith in you.'

I Miss Your Purple Hair

I Miss Your Purple Hair

Epilogue:
Hope You Remember Me

"In the name of the best within you, do not sacrifice this world to those who are its worst. In the name of the values that keep you alive, do not let your vision of man be distorted by the ugly, the cowardly, the mindless in those who have never achieved his title. Do not lose your knowledge that man's proper estate is an upright posture, an intransigent mind and a step that travels unlimited roads. Do not let your fire go out, spark by irreplaceable spark, in the hopeless swamps of the approximate, the not-quite, the not-yet, the not-at-all. Do not let the hero in your soul perish, in lonely frustration for the life you deserved, but have never been able to reach. Check your road and the nature of your battle. The world you desired can be won, it exists, it is real, it is possible, it's yours."
~ Ayn Rand

Twenty months after the Great Destruction ~

Kyle Nordstrom motored through the congested streets of downtown Pittsburgh and mistakenly turned the wrong way down a one-way street. Typically running late for an important appointment, he wheeled his silver Audi onto the nearest side street and sped toward his destination with little time to spare. It was a beautiful Saturday morning in early September, with no clouds in sight. The Lenny Kravitz song, "Are You Gonna Go My Way," played through the car's speakers. Kyle smiled as he listened to the lyrics, *"… I don't know why we always cry; This we must leave and get undone; We must engage and rearrange; And turn this planet back to one…"*

Kyle drove through a city that had seen massive damage during the quakes that left no corner of the world unscathed. The rebuilding continued and he drove by countless new and ongoing construction projects. The bright red-orange sky heralded a new day and welcomed thousands of visitors to the confluence of the three rivers. Upon arriving at Point State Park he noticed, in the background, a partially destroyed Heinz Field still filled with tarpaulin-covered construction scaffolding. In the distance to the north, not far from the stadium, The National Aviary stood undamaged. The park itself had been equipped with rows of temporary seating – full to capacity.

Security personnel intercepted Kyle and Mia and escorted them behind the stage that had been constructed in front of the landmark fountain. Television cameras were set in strategic positions, and news reporters and public officials filled the large section of seats closest to the stage. From behind an indigo curtain, Violet emerged to great cheering and walked confidently toward a clear acrylic podium that rose from the stage. She spotted Hanna and Leanna Armstrong among a sea of enthusiastic young people. They waved at her from a section filled with clients and staff from Kyle's Quantum Qids organization, most of them fidgeting and chattering in restless anticipation.

Jason Connor-Sable and his parents had made the trip from San Diego to witness the event first-hand. To Jason's surprise, he spotted Rebecca Sinclair milling around, taking snapshots of the crowd. She was wearing an official "Media Access" tag around her freckled neck, indicating to him that she was on assignment to cover the event. They had stayed in touch and he was aware she was considering accepting Kyle's offer of a permanent position with the Foundation. When he finally caught her eye, she walked over and smothered him in a vice-like embrace.

"You sneaky bastard... stalked me all the way from San Diego, didn't you?" Jason laughed and simultaneously shed a tear as her scent reminded him of their shared experiences and of the affection he harbored. Sinnamon turned to make her way to the front of the stage, but quickly added, "I've gotta run, but meet me at the Press Tent later and I'll take you to dinner. I know this awesome Sushi joint that just reopened downtown." Jason nodded and wiped away another tear as he watched her run to get into position to document Violet's address.

One of the Foundation's long-time Assistant Directors hurriedly escorted Kyle to the stage. He located his seat alongside Mia, who had become one of the Quantum Qids' favorite Mentors over the past year. Shortly after the incident in San Diego, she relocated to Pittsburgh at Kyle's urging. While living with him for six months, he convinced her to help him develop new curriculum and establish the future direction of the Foundation as they embarked upon the rebuilding process. From their nearby seats, they waved to Violet, who was approaching her 17th birthday. Mia had helped pick out the simple, white dress she wore, and gave her friend a little 'thumbs-up' gesture and a wink. Violet returned a smile and then waved a playfully admonishing finger at Kyle for once again arriving at the last possible second.

Violet, wearing a tasteful crown of fresh flowers atop her head of long dark hair, waved excitedly to the people in the surrounding stands and then paused to compose herself. She closed her eyes and took in some long, deep breaths. While she absorbed soothing waves of positive energy from the audience, she thought of all she had learned in her young life: the many lessons from her father and the spiritual leaders she admired; the harsh lessons

Epilogue: Hope You Remember Me

delivered during the Great Destruction; and the enlightenment she garnered from her mentors within the Nordstrom Foundation. As the applause waned, Violet addressed the enthusiastic, yet respectful crowd.

"Good morning, friends – and welcome to this weekend's festivities. My name is Veronica Lima... although many of you have come to know me as 'Violet.' I feel truly humbled and privileged to be with you at the start of what promises to be a glorious inaugural event. My appearance here today... actually, my utter existence... must be credited to the tremendous sacrifice of my late father, Mateo Perez Lima. His selfless act enabled me to be here with all of you... and millions worldwide... to celebrate our first crucial steps in this journey known as 'The New Renaissance.' In his honor, I state my personal dedication to its construction."

Violet paused in reaction to an eruption of cheers and applause from the audience, many of whom were aboard boats surrounding the Park. Once the noise subsided, she continued her speech.

"I am the first of several speakers you will hear during this morning's program. Those of us privileged to have the opportunity to make presentations today and tomorrow are humbled by your gracious hospitality and are here to pledge our continuing commitment to our shared mission. That mission begins with empowering every citizen of the World... to take action.

We are here to demonstrate our faith and to extol the virtues of developing and maintaining a sense of self-worth – one of the most vitally important tools required to build the New Earth. We are here today to restate our commitment and to encourage every citizen of the planet to work together in peace and in the spirit of community to construct the next iteration of the world."

A prolonged outburst of applause and enthusiastic cheers pulled Violet's focus from her prepared speech and allowed memories of her father to infiltrate her thoughts.

She remembered an early morning walk along the coast just a few days after they had relocated to Southern California...

Violet held Mateo's hand as they explored the beach near Seaport Village for the very first time. They both carried their sandals since they preferred going barefoot in the sand. Violet was feeling lonely and out of place but the ocean breeze and warm sand reminded her of Miami.

It was just after daybreak and the early morning light was a beautiful blend of pink and light purple. She had brought along her camera and asked her father to pose with his back to the Ocean. He obliged and struck an exaggerated pose, flexing his arms overhead like a bodybuilder. Violet giggled and snapped a few pictures while he switched poses. "Papa, you won't be mad if I post these on my blog, will you?" Mateo laughed and just shook his head as he retrieved his sandals from where he had tossed them.

Just then, Violet saw a dolphin breach the ocean's surface in the background. She pointed to the spot but when Mateo turned to look, there was nothing to see. Violet informed him, "You just missed it. Wait... keep looking there!" The moment he turned his head to look out to sea again, a pair of bottlenose dolphins breached the surface and did a forward flip together, before splashing back into the water. Violet squealed with delight and applauded. "Good timing, huh?" she asked her father.

Mateo smiled and walked to where Violet stood. "I think you'll get used to this place in no time. Look how happy those two are!" He understood how difficult it was for her to leave her childhood friends behind and start anew. He also understood that she was struggling with her mother's erratic behavior. "You know what I think? Those dolphins are trying to tell us something."

"What do you mean?" she asked.

"Well, look how carefree and happy they are. They could just as easily be nervous and afraid," he suggested. "If you think about it, they have a lot of things they could worry about. The ocean is so vast. They have no walls or fences to protect them from the elements or from other creatures. And so much is temporary in their world – the environment is constantly in turmoil."

Violet was not sure what he was getting at, but quietly listened to his comforting voice while she kept her eyes fixed on the area where she had last seen the dolphins.

Mateo continued to make his point. "Despite all their challenges: the storms; the changing temperatures; the ships and the fishermen... they choose to be happy. In some ways, maybe they're smarter than people. They go with the flow and, at some deep level; they must realize that there isn't much they can do to change the fact that they live in an uncompromising environment. But rather than allow reality to dominate them they have chosen to dominate their environment, and as we just witnessed, they thrive and celebrate each new day as if to give thanks for the gift of life."

Epilogue: Hope You Remember Me

"So," Violet surmised, "you're saying that we should be more like them and be grateful for each new day – instead of worrying about the things we can't change?"

Mateo smiled, knelt down in front of her and gave her an enormous hug. His only reply was, "Something like that."

Holding onto the image of her father enveloping her small hand with his as they walked along the shoreline, reality set in again and Violet continued her speech.

"Together, we must draw upon all the wisdom we have acquired through the hard lessons of the recent past, in order to draw up new plans. We are rebuilding our planet and the task in front of us appears monumental. Before we pick up one more hammer or pour another concrete foundation, we must renovate our souls. We must clarify our true mission and infuse its purpose and vision into the blueprints for everything we set out to build, for everything we choose to do and for everything we aspire to be.

When the storms arrived almost two years ago, they not only delivered rain and lightning – they announced a period of great cleansing. When the world was torn asunder, it was more than just a time of destruction and upheaval. It harkened an era brimming with new opportunities. Regretfully, far too many innocent lives were lost during the agonizing transition, but there is always pain associated with birth... and much greater pain associated with rebirth.

We have been granted a glorious gift; a chance to create. One era has ended and many things have changed forever. Corporations once dominating the economic landscape were brought to their knees. The politicians and cumbersome bureaucracies in which we foolishly placed too much faith were exposed as flawed conveniences. We now understand that we have to redefine our notion of government, just as we have had to revise our notion of humanity. It is our good fortune to have been witness to the Great Destruction, because we survived it and learned the most valuable lessons in the process.

We have been spared for a reason – all of us – to learn from our mistakes and seize this opportunity to move forward with newfound awareness. We survived the economic collapse. We survived the retribution of an angry planet. And we are going to survive the extinction of many of our old, flawed concepts about humanity. We must leave behind the unenlightened and destructive prejudices built upon fear, ignorance, and insecurity.

I Miss Your Purple Hair

We are now positioned to finally realize our potential and must do so together; hand in hand, and with faith – faith in ourselves and our limitless potential as individual souls… and faith in one another. By excluding no one, we will craft a future set upon a foundation of lasting stability.

When we learn to honor and develop all of the innate abilities dormant within each of us, the unlimited potential of the human race will be unlocked. Rather than ridiculing notions we never honestly attempted to comprehend, while blindly accepting limitations imposed by others, we must open our minds and learn to develop our inherent abilities for the common good. As we set out to reconstruct our cities and our technological infrastructure, we must simultaneously demolish the limits we have imposed upon our potential as wondrously gifted beings – and then revise our concept of the human soul.

Our past mistakes are irrelevant now. What matters is how we move forward and how we help one another to realize the potential of the human race. Our destiny obviously led us to the painful chapter we just endured, but our destiny has also led those of us who survived that terrible time to the advent of a new day... and a new chapter we get to write together. We carry with us the memories of those we loved and lost as we embrace the endless opportunities before us.

We have a regrettable record of allowing ourselves to be handcuffed by fear – manifested in the forms of racism, sexism, and nationalism… not to mention superstition, corruption and destruction. We can and must do better – and are now poised to write a much different *new* chapter. Within that same history, we can find countless inspirations that provide ample reason for optimism. Our ancestors often demonstrated indomitable faith by sacrificing, suffering and scrounging – through war after war, economic recessions and depressions, and far too many shameful instances of man's inhumanity toward his fellow man. We ravaged the Earth out of ignorance and greed, but then employed our ingenuity and imagination to create alternatives designed to respect and preserve the planet. It is not too late.

Technological advances over the last several decades have connected humanity in unprecedented ways, enabling us to share information and ideas on a level never before realized. Inspired by The Nordstrom Foundation's Quantum Qids Academy, *The Renaissance Web* will connect every city, every town, every village, and every household – *at no cost* – because there is no technology involved.

This previously untapped communications network is an example of the potential we have simply squandered in the past. Construction of worldwide training centers has already begun. Within the next five years, there will be over 100 such facilities in operation in more than 50 cities. At this time, Dr. Nordstrom's Foundation is developing thousands of Quantum Coaches, who are preparing for assignment in over twenty nations by the beginning of next year.

So much was lost in the turmoil of nearly two years ago – more than 40 percent of the land was either destroyed or rendered uninhabitable. Nearly six billion human lives were lost and countless more displaced, crippled, orphaned, widowed, or left to mourn precious children taken far too soon. We experienced this *together* and we all have had to dig deep to comprehend, to accept and to find the will to continue.

The most important fact is … we are still here. We are still standing. We have a destiny to fulfill, and we *will* get there – all of us… *together."*

A delicate breeze carrying an unmistakable scent of Vanilla Chai from a nearby refreshment stand suddenly lifted Violet's plain, silver-wire necklace. She calmed its motion by clutching the laminated eye of the peacock feather against her heart. Mateo was making his presence felt, which brought a smile to Violet's face and a tear to her eye. Still clutching her memento, she pressed on with her address.

"When I was invited to speak today I gladly accepted because of an important commitment, a sincere pledge I gave my father. I promised him that I would always strive to reach my potential; that I would not allow myself to be cynical, lazy, or passive. I assured him that I would not waste my talents and would never stop learning. He asked me to consider my personal mission and decide for myself what I could and could not do. He knew my likely conclusion, after searching my soul, would be to realize that I simply have no interest in assessing my *limitations*. He knew I would, instead, be more likely to focus my attention on the blank slate before us that is the very definition of the word 'future' – *a book yet unwritten* – and that I would diligently serve as one of its many authors.

I'm proud to be representing the Quantum Qids Research Center today, and am humbled to have this opportunity to pay tribute to my father before introducing the other speakers on our agenda. I'm truly grateful to be alive and feel truly *privileged* to be part of an organization designed to help all of us achieve our true destiny. That destiny undoubtedly involves more than we may realize today, but I fully believe it is a destiny of limitless greatness, prosperity and spiritual fulfillment. We are more than adequately equipped for the journey, provided we maintain unwavering faith in ourselves and love for one another.

I ask your indulgence as I close by once more expressing my gratitude to my father – for giving me the guidance, the opportunity and most of all, the inspiration to move forward in the wake of his sacrifice. He taught me many things; most important, to maintain faith in myself and to never stop working toward my goals. He will always be with me and his spirit will play a significant role in everything I do in the future.

My father demonstrated what true faith looks like. He reminded me, every day, what love really feels like, and not only did he give me my first opportunity at life... he gave me my second chance, as well. The way I see it, all of us have been granted a second chance and the only way to demonstrate our appreciation is by making the most of the opportunity."

Violet gently stroked the delicate gold chain around her neck, until her fingertips found the tiny red crystal heart at the end.

"My father is somewhere out there, looking after me... as always; and I intend to make the most of the lessons he taught me. Thank you all for your participation – not as members of an audience, but as fellow leaders, teachers and agents of change – because the days of sitting idle must end. The time has come to embrace the next chapter in our evolution and to do so with courage, conviction, tolerance, and genuine compassion for all life in the universe. In closing, I would like to invoke the enduring advice of Saint Augustine: *'Love, and do what you will.'*

Now... let's get to work."

I Miss Your Purple Hair

"Never Let Me Fall"

by Alyssa Coco (Coco)

Now, I hear myself calling to you,
Once more, you help me as you usually do.
My time to realize is here,
but no, I will never fear.

'cause you give me hope,
And never, ever let me fall
You never let me fall

Today, I'm giving you this thank you
And never, ever will it stop
You don't even know how much you mean to me
Each night I pray and I thank God

'cause you give me hope
And never, ever let me fall
And I want to give you all you've given to me
That's a lot I can say, but I'll give it back eventually
'cause you never let me fall

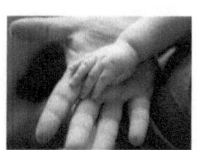

Never Let Me Fall
Original song lyrics by Alyssa Coco
© 2007 Alyssa Coco
www.alyssacocomusic.com

About the Author

Robert R. Chandler is a native and current resident of Rochester, New York. He has always enjoyed writing and created his own comic books as a child. During his years at McQuaid Jesuit High School in Rochester, he focused on writing short stories, often in the realm of Gothic horror and fantasy. Early writing influences included J.D. Salinger, Harlan Ellison, H.P. Lovecraft and Stephen King. A visual artist since birth, he developed his painting and drawing skills during his formative years, and had his heart set on a career in art and design. After attending Rochester Institute of Technology, he embarked upon a career in advertising. Over the next several decades, he served in many capacities, including Art Director, Graphic Designer, Commercial Illustrator and Marketing Specialist. Throughout those years, he applied his creative writing skills to advertising and promotional efforts. Creative writing remained a passion and in 2005, he decided to pursue novel writing. In May 2008, he published his first novel, *Minus the Imple*, which he labeled "a fictionalized true story." A personal memoir, the book has been well received and the author was encouraged to write his next novel, *I Miss Your Purple Hair*, a work of fiction. The story is a reflection of the author's philosophy, inspired by his own real-life visions and synchronicities.

Contact:
Robert R. Chandler
c/o *Privileged Publishing*
web: www.robertrchandler.com
e-mail: robertrchandler@gmail.com

For more information on the novel:
www.imissyourpurplehair.com

Minus the Imple and *I Miss Your Purple Hair* **are available at Lulu.com:**
Minus the Imple: http://www.lulu.com/content/2035657
I Miss Your Purple Hair: http://www.lulu.com/content/6194009

Download the Official Soundtrack on iTunes:
http://tinyurl.com/ybjk7v9

www.ingramcontent.com/pod-product-compliance
Lightning Source LLC
Chambersburg PA
CBHW031057260626
47172CB00001B/108